ALSO BY ALEX SMITH

JAW BREAKER

A DCI ROBERT KETT NOVEL

ALEX SMITH

RELENTLESS
MEDIA

This one's for Dave, and Grimm.

PROLOGUE

Friday

IF SEBASTIAN REILLY HADN'T KNOWN ANY BETTER, HE would have thought the world was ending.

It was like the ground had opened and all the legions of hell had spilled out of the wet dirt, a carnival of sound and screams and lunatic laughter. Toltham village was mobbed, a hundred people or more joining the procession that made its way down the main street.

The Greenies formed the head of the snake, the crazy fuckers who worshipped trees and probably spent most of their time having orgies down at the pub they called their church. They were all wearing heavy robes and masks sculpted from leaves and twigs, banging their drums and chanting their nonsense as they pranced along like idiots.

The rest of the village wasn't dressed up, but they all seemed just as eager to make fools of themselves—adults and kids and old folks alike. Bunting flapped along the sides of the shops, chattering in the wind. Somebody let loose a firework with a dud pop overhead. Everyone laughed.

Everyone except Seb.

He pulled his hood over his wet hair, hunkering into the warmth of his camouflage-patterned North Face puffer. His mood was all over the place because he was still coming down from last night, the drugs clinging on inside him like they had hooks in his veins. His head throbbed, and even his teeth felt sore like they were too big for his mouth. He'd had a couple of hits today, of course, just to soften the blow, but if anything, it had made him feel worse.

Somebody thumped into him, a fat prat who was dancing along behind the crowd with a baby in his arms. Seb didn't recognise him from the village, but then talk of Toltham's February Parade had become legend recently and half of Norfolk seemed to have turned up this year to take part.

"Prick," Seb called out, his voice lost to the music, to the rising wind that rattled the roofs of the shops.

He waited for a break in the procession before crossing the street, stepping into the porch of the butcher's to pull out his silver snuffbox. It had been his granddad's, but there was no snuff in here. He took a pinch of cocaine and sniffed hard, the darkness of the night peeling back, the pain in his head dulling. His heart pounded wetly, too hard, too fast. This new shit they were dealing kicked like a mule, seemed to make reality shiver. He felt like if he looked too hard at the sky he'd see something else right behind it.

He'd see hell.

Come on, mate, he told himself. *Pull yourself together.*

He took another pinch, just to be sure.

"Seb?"

A voice in the crowd, his name unwelcome. He pulled

the hood down over his face, wading into the swirling currents of people. There were more of them than ever, he couldn't really tell which grinning faces were masks and which weren't anymore.

Still, it was good. It meant he was less likely to be noticed.

"Seb? I can see you. Turn around!"

He glanced over his shoulder, seeing a flash of purple hair right behind him, a slim, worried face.

"Fuck off, *Niamh*," he yelled. "I told you, I don't talk to fucking dead girls."

She reached him, grabbed hold of his arm so hard that her nails raked against his skin. He pushed her face away and heard her jaw clack, her teeth like a mouse trap. Then he started running again.

"I'm not the one who's going to die," she screamed at him. "He's too dangerous, Seb. You can't trust him. Please! I love you, don't go!"

He pushed past an older couple then cut to his left, running through the crowd. He heard his name screamed two more times before it was swallowed by the beating drums. When he looked back, he couldn't see any sign of her purple hair. Maybe that was because *everything* looked purple, the colour rising from the crowd, hanging in the air. He blinked and the parade of people seemed to swell like a wave, ready to drown him.

"Fuck."

He was nearing the end of the main street, but his business wasn't here. He left the procession, passing a couple of girls who were making out in the bus shelter, before jumping over the verge onto the back road out of town.

Here, away from the music, away from that horde of demonic laughter, things seemed easier. So easy, in fact, that he wasn't even aware of the fact he was walking until he passed the last house and the woods seemed to swallow the world whole—their darkness and stillness somehow *alive*.

He could feel eyes crawling over him and he switched on his Samsung's feeble torch to see nothing except the swaying trees, their branches clacking like old bones. Were *they* watching him? They were laughing, he was sure of it.

"I'm not scared," he said, stopping to snort another pinch of cocaine. The rush of it was electric and he whooped into the starless sky. "Fuck yeah!"

His voice felt too soft in his throat, like old cloth. He wondered if he'd spoken at all. A sudden sickness gripped him, one that didn't seem to stay in his stomach. It travelled outwards to his limbs, to his face, and he grabbed his cheeks and groaned.

"Focus," he said, hearing himself this time.

It was a short walk to the broad and he'd done it a thousand times before. This time felt brand new, though, because this time was going to change everything. This time was going to make him rich. He'd been dealing for the London gang for over a year now, selling the cocaine and heroin that came in off the boats in Yarmouth. He'd done well, he'd kept his head down, he hadn't stolen—well, no more than he could snort, anyway, and nobody would miss that.

And now the top boys wanted to meet him face to face.

It was a promotion. He knew it. More drugs, more money. He had the note in his pocket to prove it, the one that had been pushed through his letterbox just an hour ago.

Seb, your willingness has been noted. Meet me in the woods north of Toltham Broad, the range, 9.30, and accept your reward.

He was already minted, thanks to the gang. And it

looked like he was going to get a lot richer. The rush of adrenaline washed out some of the confusion, dulled the raging song of the cocaine. He thought he might have been smiling but his face was too numb to be sure.

A gust of wind whipped past him, triggering a wave of dizziness that stopped him in his tracks. He pinched his nose, his blood on fire from the coke, his head roaring so loud that he didn't hear the engine until it was almost too late. He looked back, seeing headlights, throwing himself into the trees and ducking down as low as he could without messing up his coat.

The police car purred slowly up the road, a shimmer of blue and yellow. A familiar miserable face sat behind the wheel, a monstrous silhouette in the passenger seat. Seb waited until they'd rolled past before standing up—immediately sitting down again when his legs started shaking. He took a breath of wet, cold air then tried again, rising to his feet in slow motion.

"Where are you two wankers off to?" he asked quietly, and he almost had second thoughts before shaking them off. He was untouchable in this place. He'd proven it time and time again, the police couldn't hurt him.

Nobody could hurt him.

He realised his feet had stopped walking without his permission, his shoulder leaning against a tree. He breathed, feeling the tree take a breath with him, its trunk groaning with the relief of it.

"What the—" he started, then stopped because for a second it wasn't a tree there, it was a person, a giant man with needles for fingers. One slid into the meat of his arm, another into his cheek, dozens more punching through his skin.

He screamed, staggering back to see that the shape was

a tree once again, its twig fingers flailing blindly as they reached for him.

He opened his snuffbox, taking a pinch only for his fingers to spasm painfully. He swore, trying again. He didn't hop back onto the road, he cut through the woods instead, taking his time to avoid tripping on the thick roots, to avoid being scalped by the branches.

It wasn't long before he spotted the first of the lights from the lodge reflected in the calm water of the lake. Another couple of minutes and he found the archery range, the equipment sheds locked up tight.

There was nobody in sight, and only now did he start to wonder why he'd been asked to meet here. He rubbed his numb hands together, turning in a circle to locate any sign of life. The trees trembled and he thought for a moment he could hear them singing, a chant as loud as the earth, one that rattled up the bones of his feet and shins. Another surge of adrenaline threatened to burst the walls of his heart and he put a hand to his chest, staring into the blur of branches to see faces, dozens of them, *hundreds*, as if the procession had followed him here.

"What?"

And the word chased them away like scattered birds, the woods empty again.

He opened his snuffbox and snorted another pinch of cocaine, and this time his entire head jerked back without his permission, hard enough that he could hear his tendons crack. His hand went numb, the snuffbox tumbling to the ground, its contents lost.

"Fuck!" he said, his jaw strangely stiff.

Maybe he'd been overdoing it. He'd been hitting the coke pretty hard these last few weeks, even though he'd promised himself he'd stop. But it was difficult when the others were doing it too. Pete had a bigger habit than him, and Neil was worse than both of them.

He felt a sudden chill worm itself into his spine. Maybe they'd been skimming off more than they'd thought.

Maybe the gang *did* know about it.

"Fuck," he said, or tried to say, because his jaw was still doing something weird. It felt almost like it had been wired. His arm spasmed again, the pain unbearable. Then his head twisted to the side as if wrenched by invisible hands and he cried out.

Something was approaching through the twisted trunks. Something that seemed too big to be a person. Seb watched it for a moment then turned to go, the world spinning with him and refusing to stop. Vertigo stripped his legs from under him and he found himself facedown in the dirt. Was he *sinking* into it? It felt that way, his hands disappearing up to the wrists like he'd landed in quicksand, his legs unresponsive.

He tried to push himself back to his feet but his body wasn't doing what it was supposed to, his head snapping forward into the mud, jerking to the right like he was a puppet. His back arched like a giant was folding him in two. This time there was no pain, but that was worse. The numbness was *so much worse*.

"Help," he tried and failed to say. "Please."

Footsteps, and his head twisted itself around of its own accord. Once again there were shapes in the trees that might have been people. The tremors were too fierce now for him to make any sense of who was out there, but were those robes they were wearing? Masks? One of them threw something at him and it landed in the mud by his face.

A doll, its eyes made of buttons and its grinning smile stitched on.

Fuck this, he said, screaming as he fought to get to his hands and knees. His body was a broken machine, every part of him seeming to snap and twitch. His mouth was the worst, he couldn't close it and it was getting wider every second, like somebody had a crowbar wedged between his teeth. He felt something tear, a splash of blood on his tongue, but when he tried to put a finger to his lips he couldn't even feel enough to know if his hand had responded.

He crawled past more phantom shapes, more grinning faces, onto what might have been the road. The air seemed to flash and shimmer with blue light. Could he hear music? Drums? Fireworks? Maybe sirens? Or was that silence in his mind, deafening him? Nothing made sense anymore, the world turning cartwheels around his head, the trees howling their laughter at him.

I didn't steal, he screamed wordlessly. *I swear, I didn't steal anything.*

And the night screamed back, loud enough to shatter his skull into fragments.

Yes. You. Did.

Terror drove him up, even though his legs danced like they didn't belong to him, even though his arms whipped like the ribbons around the maypole, even though he heard the skin of his face tear and the bones of his jaw uncouple themselves. Terror drove him up and he was running, running away from this place, away from the monsters who chased him, deep into the woods, into the trees who did their best to arrest him, cracking their fists against his head, scratching the skin from his face.

The world still turned, spinning fast, faster still, and Seb realised he was falling. And in the madness of that moment, in the endless quiet, he thought about his mum and dad. He was five years old again, running to them, waiting for them to catch him.

But they weren't here. There was only the end of the world, only hell, the ground opening up to swallow him.

And just like that, the jaws snapped shut.

CHAPTER ONE

Saturday

"Robbie, are you *sure* you'll be okay with them all?" asked Billie, the weak signal making her voice sound faint and too far away.

DCI Robert Kett pinned the phone between his ear and his shoulder as he manoeuvred the buggy off the pavement into the car park. Inside it, three-year-old Moira was wrestling with the safety bar and bouncing in her seat hard enough to rock the entire contraption from side to side, the wheels squeaking. This, in turn, was earning a round of protests from Evie, who was perched on the buggy board and doing her best to cling on.

Alice was in a world of her own and hadn't even noticed that they'd turned off the main street. Kett looked back to see the nine-year-old wandering down the wide pavement all by herself.

"We'll be absolutely fine," he said to Billie. Then, a little louder, "Alice, we're over here."

"Absolutely fine," Billie echoed, with more than a little sarcasm.

"Earth to Alice," Kett called out. Then he barked her name so loud that every single person in the car park turned to look at him. Alice finally heard, whirling around with wide eyes. She clattered over the road without looking, her arms spinning like cartwheels as she rejoined them.

"Stop it!" Evie said as Moira continued to bounce.

Alice put her hands over her ears, screwing her face up.

"I want to go home," she said.

"We're absolutely fine," Kett said into the phone. "They're going to be brilliantly behaved, aren't you girls?"

Moira jiggled, Evie wailed, Alice was hunched over and gurning. Kett took that as a yes.

"Get something sensible," Billie said. "But fun."

"Sensible but fun," Kett said, taking the phone in one hand and pushing the buggy with the other. "I have no idea what that means."

They reached the showroom door and Kett put his back to it, pushing it open.

"I'll get something good," he said. "Trust me."

"I do," said Billie. "But I know what our girls are like, and I know what *you're* like, you big softie. Don't let them pressure you into anything."

Kett almost choked.

"Soft? Me? I'm hard as nails."

"You're really sure you'll be okay with them?"

"They're fine," said Kett. "They're..."

He looked down to see that the buggy was empty, the buggy board too. All three of his daughters were tearing hell-for-leather across the showroom floor, darting in between the gleaming used cars.

"I'd better go," he said. "I love you."

He hung up, chasing the girls into the enormous space. Alice was doing her best to open the door of a second-hand Porsche 911, tugging on the handle like she was trying to snap it off. Thankfully, Evie and Moira had spotted a coin-operated *Peppa Pig* ride in the corner and they were both clambering inside it, Moira's legs up in the air and wiggling.

Alice was using both hands on the Porsche now and Kett called her name before she could set the alarm off.

"Can we get this one, Dad?" she shouted back, loud enough surely to shatter every single windscreen in the showroom.

"It might make things hard, seeing how it's only got two seats," he replied as he walked to her. "Look at those ones over there."

He pointed to a little line of family estates sitting at the back of the room like the unpopular kids at the school dance. Alice frowned. She muttered something he didn't catch because a salesman was walking this way, his polished shoes clacking like he was about to start tap dancing. He was young, fit, immaculately manicured, and the smile he wore was as sharp as a knife. Kett immediately didn't like him.

"Looking for something special?" the man asked, stretching out a hand that Kett took reluctantly, then doing his best to pump the life out of it.

"No," Kett said.

"I'm Josh," the man said.

"I'm very happy for you."

Josh watched Alice as she tugged on the door of the Porsche again.

"Are these yours?"

It was tempting to say no, but Kett nodded.

"She probably shouldn't be doing that," said Josh.

"Can you show me what you've got in the way of family cars?" Kett asked, the tone of the man's voice making him feel instantly defensive. "The harder wearing, the better. Something sensible."

There was a growing duet of rage from the ride in the corner but Kett pretended not to hear it. The salesman rubbed his hands together and led the way towards the estates. Alice finally left the Porsche alone and ran between the cars, squeaking her fingers along the paint and whooping with excitement.

"This one!" she yelled. "No, this one!"

"So..." Josh said. "This is the best of what we've got. There are some cheaper ones outside that might be better suited to your budget. What's your time frame?"

"I could do with driving it out this morning," Kett said. "I need it for a work trip."

"What kind of trip?"

"It's an Extreme Crime thing," Kett said, distracted by Alice as she tried the doors of a Peugeot.

"Um... What?"

"Crime," barked Kett. "Alice, leave them alone please."

"Are you replacing another car?" asked the salesman.

"Yeah," said Kett. "We had an XC90."

"Nice. Pretty indestructible. What happened to it?"

"Destroyed," said Kett. "It was shot up."

The man swallowed hard.

"Shot up?"

"Human traffickers," Kett said. "They had a shotgun."

"Uh..."

There was a clatter of little feet and Evie appeared, red-faced and frowning. She huffed, stamping her foot with no real force.

"I know karate, mister," she said, her favourite phrase at the moment. "I'm going to use it on *her*."

She pointed at Moira, who sat in the *Peppa Pig* car with a look of smug victory.

"Which one do you like, Evie?" Kett asked before she could start demonstrating her martial prowess. She huffed again then turned her big eyes to the cars.

"None of them," she said. "I like our old car."

"Can we have this one?" Alice yelled.

Kett turned to see her standing next to an angular Skoda with faded red paint. She had draped herself over the bonnet like she was giving it a hug.

"I don't think so," he said. "It's pink. How about the BMW there?"

"3 Series," said Josh. "Great car. Only has 47,000 miles on the clock. One owner."

"It's gross," said Evie. "It looks like a radiator. That one."

She pointed at her big sister.

"I'm not getting a pink car, Evie," said Kett.

"It's red," she said.

"It's definitely red," said Josh with what looked like a smirk. "Octavia, just over 60,000 miles. Great value for money. Skoda doesn't have the reputation it used to when your generation was at school. The police use this car, you know?"

"I know," said Kett. "But they're not pink."

"Red," said Evie.

"Red," confirmed Josh.

"It's pink."

"It's the light in here, makes it look pinker. Trust me, this is pillar box red. Girls, you want this car?"

"Yes!" said Evie, beaming.

"I want it," Alice added. "Please, Dad?"

"All your friends will be jealous," Josh said to Alice.

Kett glared at him, which only seemed to make him grin harder.

"Go on, *Dad*," Josh said, which almost earned him a slap.

"I don't think—"

"Please!" said Alice and Evie together. Kett glanced at the *Peppa Pig* ride again to see Moira halfway out of it, hanging upside down with her leg caught inside.

"Bloody hell, hang on."

He ran to her, scooping her out. She squirmed in his arms until he put her down again, by which time Josh had opened the Octavia and ushered the other two inside. He looked back at Kett and winked.

"That one!" Moira said, seeing her sisters inside the Skoda. She ran over and scrambled into the driver's seat, sitting on Alice's lap. All three of them wrestled with the steering wheel. The salesman was halfway through the door, showing them something that made them all giggle.

"What about this one?" Kett called out, gesturing hopelessly at a smart black Audi.

"I think they've made their minds up," said Josh. "You want to hear the horn?"

"No!" Kett yelled, answered by a feeble honking that dribbled from the Octavia. Alice threw herself on the steering wheel again, then again, all while the salesman turned his grinning face to Kett.

"This one," Alice yelled, each word punctuated by the horn. "This one. This one."

"Enough!" Kett roared, pointing his angry finger at the windscreen. "Alice, no more."

She looked like she was about to ignore him, then decided not to. Evie and Alice were doing their best to push the horn but fortunately they weren't strong enough. Their laughter was almost as loud.

"You want to try it?" the salesman asked Kett. "I think it suits you."

Kett was sorely tempted to point his angry finger at the man too, but Moira was sliding out of the door and preparing to make a run for it.

"I'll have a think about it," said Kett as he chased her.

"You can drive it away right now," said the salesman.

"I've got to take the girls home first. No car seats. I'll come back."

Kett lunged for Moira and missed. She must have thought they were playing because she crawled underneath a Jaguar, laughing hysterically.

"Moo-moo, please come out," Kett said, his heart beating in his throat, his cheeks blazing. "It's not safe."

"Please, Dad," Alice yelled out of the open door.

"I'll get the paperwork," said the salesman.

"Wait," said Kett. He eased himself onto his knees, everything aching, and peered under the car.

"If you come here, I'll get you some Smarties."

Moira nodded, letting him fish her out. He heaved her up, holding her to his chest. The room seemed to fizzle like it was coming to the boil, and he rested his hip against the Jag while he tried to get his breath back. Alice and Evie were in the back seat now, the Skoda rocking as they danced around.

"It's been serviced, it's got a fresh MOT, it's ready to go," said Josh as he walked back across the room, a sheaf of papers in his hand. "You need finance?"

Kett shook his head. He watched his girls inside the car,

heard their laughter. It was a good sound, the *best* sound, and it made him remember their old tank of a car. He and Billie already had the Volvo when the girls were born. They'd bought it when Billie first found out she was pregnant, purely because the man in the showroom had told them it was the safest car on the road. They'd travelled for mile after mile in it, crisscrossing the county. It had been an honest to God member of the family. Kett felt a shredding sense of remorse that they were here to replace it—*guilt*, even.

Then he heard their laughter again and knew that not all changes were bad.

"You're sure it's red?" he asked the young man.

"Sure," he replied. "Happens to all the red cars in here, they turn pink in the light."

Kett raised an eyebrow in doubt as he scanned the room, looking at all the telephone-box-bright sports cars.

"You sure you want this one?" he asked the girls. They cheered together, and he felt a smile land on his lips.

"Okay. You've got yourself a deal."

He offered his hand and the salesman shook it just as eagerly as before.

"Come this way," he said, studying the paperwork. "One 2018 Skoda Octavia in... oh, would you look at that, dusky pink."

"You utter bast—"

And Kett was cut off by the cheers of his girls as they piled into the sales office.

CHAPTER TWO

"WHAT IN THE NAME OF TOSS IS *THAT*?"

Kett yanked up the Skoda's handbrake and switched off the engine, heaving a sigh. Through the windscreen he saw Superintendent Colin Clare, his face creased with apparent disgust. The Super locked his ancient Mercedes and walked over, peering at Kett's new car like he'd just watched it crawl out of an elephant's backside. He rapped on the window and stood back as Kett opened the door.

"Please tell me that toss-mobile isn't yours," he said. "It's *pink*."

"It's red," grumbled Kett.

"Right. And I'm a supermodel. It's pink, Kett, and if you can't see that then you can hand over your warrant card right now."

Out here, there was no denying that the car was obnoxiously pink. Kett wasn't sure how he ever could have mistaken it for red in the showroom. Billie was right, he shouldn't have taken the girls, it was hard to have a straight thought of any kind when they were there. He'd walked them home after he'd bought the car, then walked back to collect it. Plenty of time to change his mind, but Billie was right about that, too. When it came to his daughters, he was soft.

He closed the door and patted it gently on the roof, as if to reassure it.

"The girls were with me."

"Say no more," said Clare. "I took the triplets with me to buy a car once and we ended up with a VW Camper."

"Doesn't sound so bad," said Kett.

"Didn't have an engine."

"That's—"

"Or wheels."

"Right."

Clare sighed.

"Good times, though." He patted the car too. "Got a name for her?"

"Yeah, Mac."

"I like it. Manly. Means son in Scottish, as you probably—"

"It's short for the Mermaid Adventure Castle."

Clare nodded, and they stood there for an awkward moment before heading towards HQ.

"Still quiet out there after the Sweet Briar Rose case," the Super said as they walked through the main doors.

"It's only been a few weeks."

It had been just under three months since they'd caught the serial killer who had kidnapped five women and killed one. Three months of reviews and tribunals and interviews, several of which Kett thought would lead once again to his dismissal. He'd crossed a line in his last case, he knew. A line that he wasn't sure he'd ever forgive himself for. Every time he closed his eyes he was right back in that barn, driving his boot into the gunshot wound in Bert's leg. He could still hear Bert screaming for mercy, and the shame of it made him feel like he had hot coals stitched beneath the skin of his face.

But he was still here. He was still working.

The job wasn't going to let him go that easily.

"A few weeks is nothing," Clare said. "But it's a good sign. The Sweet Briar Rose case was all over the news. People saw what happened to Bert. Not his death, obviously, because that was out of our hands. But they saw how hard we went after him, they saw what we did, what we're capable of. It will give the bad guys second thoughts."

Clare pushed through the double doors into the Major Investigation Team's bullpen, sighing loudly.

"It won't last, though. You know as well as I do that the harder we push back, the harder they'll come at us. It's in their nature. And we still think the case was personal."

"Any more word on that?" Kett asked.

"On Hollenbeck? No. You'd be the first to hear it. Everything we've found points to the fact that Bert was one of Hollenbeck's ghosts. Or at least he was going to be. We still think bumping you off was a test of sorts. Or an admission fee."

He put his big hand on Kett's shoulder the way he often had in the last few weeks, squeezing gently.

"We're going to get them, Robbie. I swear on my toss-hole, we're going to put them all away. But it's not going to happen quickly. And now's not the time to worry about it."

"Easier said than done, sir," Kett said when Clare had let go. The Super nodded, then strode towards his office.

"Round up the others, meet me in the Incident Room."

"Yes, sir," Kett said. "Is this about the work trip?"

"You'll find out, Detective."

Kett did a sweep of the quiet, open-plan office before

heading towards the kitchen. He heard DI Pete Porter and DC Kate Savage before he saw them, and from the sound of it, they were in the middle of an argument. Sure enough, when he poked his head around the door he saw that they were squared up to each other—well, as square as they could get considering Savage only came up to Porter's chin.

"Pete, don't do it," said Savage, obviously in distress. "I'm telling you, it's a crime."

"*You're* a crime," Porter spat back.

"Nice comeback."

"*You're* a comeback."

"Everything okay in here?" Kett asked, making them both jump.

"No," they said together. Porter started to speak but Savage elbowed him in the ribs. She stood to one side to reveal a steaming mug on the worktop. Kett sniffed the air, seeking the aroma of tea and finding something else instead, something fruity.

"Porter's made raspberry tea," she said.

"*What?*" Kett asked, horrified.

"Raspberry and pomegranate, actually," said Porter. "Green tea."

"*Why?*" Kett added.

Porter cleared his throat, looking uncomfortable.

"It's for the, you know." He looked down at his trousers and Kett shrugged. "You know, for the little soldiers."

"You're losing me, Pete."

"Because Allie and I are trying for a..." He whispered the next word like it was a national secret. "*Baby.*"

"Oh!" said Kett. "Right."

"Way too much information, sir," said Savage.

"You asked!"

"But Pete's making it wrong," said Savage.

"Pete Porter making tea wrong? I don't believe it."

Kett's sarcasm was lost on Porter, who fired a smug smile at Savage.

"See. I'm right. You do add milk."

"To fruit tea?" Kett said, once again horrified.

"Yeah," said Porter, picking up a bottle of milk. "Obviously."

"Criminal," muttered Savage. "But if you're so sure about it then knock yourself out."

Porter nodded sagely as he poured a significant amount of milk into his fruit tea. Kett walked a little closer to see it immediately begin to curdle.

"Is it meant to do that?" Savage asked, leaning over the mug.

"Yes," said Porter. "Obviously."

"Those weird oily floating blobs are normal?"

"Uh..."

"You're going to drink it then, sir?" Savage said, barely able to hide her grin.

Porter took the mug, holding it at arm's length like it might bite him.

"You should definitely drink it," said Kett.

The big DI licked his lips, glared at them both, then took a delicate sip. It was impossible to miss the shudder that passed through him.

"Delicious," he wheezed.

"Better get it all down you," said Savage.

"I will," he said, his voice hoarse. "It's a bit hot."

"Add some more milk," Kett said. "But do it later, Clare wants us in the Incident Room."

Porter seemed supremely relieved at the chance to abandon his tea. He put it down then used his fingertips to push it as far away from himself as he could.

"You know any more about this work trip?" Savage asked.

"Not a clue," said Kett. "And not sure I want to find out. Clare asked me to pack for the weekend, with swimming trunks."

"Me too," said Savage.

Kett took the lead, passing back through the bullpen and along the short stretch of corridor on the other side. The Incident Room door was open and Superintendent Clare was perched on a desk at the front. He looked up at them as they entered, wearing what the team had come to know as his friendly angry face—as opposed to the *angry* angry face he wore most of the time.

"Right, I've kept you in the dark long enough," he said once they'd all taken their seats. "I'm sure you're all wondering what on earth is going on, and why I've dragged you here when you're technically off duty."

"Promotion, sir?" said Porter.

"No, Pete," said Clare. "I'm taking you on a trip. The Sweet Briar Rose case knocked ten bells out of us all. Physically, mentally, emotionally. You've earned a couple of days off."

"And yet here we are, at work," said Kett, earning a scowl.

"I'm taking you on a team-building workshop!" said Clare, lifting his arms in fanfare.

He was met by silence.

"Two days in a corporate resort on Toltham Broad."

More silence.

"Where we'll be engaging in a programme of team-building exercises to help us strengthen our collective engagement, build our leadership skills and enjoy a little rest and relaxation."

Nobody replied, and Clare looked at them in turn with growing impatience.

"Any questions?"

Kett put his hand up.

"Is this optional, sir?"

"No it tossing well isn't," the Super snapped back, pushing himself up from the desk.

Kett kept his hand up.

"Can I let somebody else take my place?"

"You're all going and you're all going to enjoy it. That's an order. You're packed?"

Everybody nodded.

"Swimmers? Tracksuits? You'll be out on the lake."

"In *February*?" said Kett.

"Then let's go."

Clare marched out of the room without so much as a backwards glance.

"Does he think this is a *reward*?" Porter asked. "Because it feels like a punishment."

"I heard that," Clare's voice boomed back from the corridor.

"You never know, it might be fun," said Savage as she stood.

"About as much fun as a rectal examination," grumbled Porter.

"I heard that!" Clare yelled from further away.

They followed the Super into the bullpen. DI Keith Dunst was sitting at his desk and he grinned at them as they walked past.

"Have fun!" he said, wheezing a laugh.

"Anyone need a ride?" Clare asked when they reached the car park.

"I'm driving, sir," Porter said. "Kate's coming with me. Robbie?"

"I'm good," he said. "I've got the Mermaid Adventure Castle."

He nodded across the car park to his Skoda.

"You bought a pink car?" said Porter.

"It's red," said Kett. He sighed. "Okay, it's pink."

"I like it," Savage said. "It's cute."

"Please don't say it's cute."

Clare checked his watch.

"Where is he?"

"Who, sir?" asked Kett.

The Super didn't need to answer. There was a shout from the other side of the car park and they all turned to see an enormous bearded figure lumbering towards them. PC Aaron Duke was wearing a bright yellow shirt that looked like it was about to split, and quite possibly the shortest pair of shorts Kett had ever seen.

"Sir," said Savage. "Why are we bringing a stripper?"

"Sorry!" Duke shouted. "Couldn't find my goggles."

He ran up to them, out of breath.

"Duke," said Kett, studying the PC's shorts. "You do realise it's still winter?"

"You said dress for a holiday," Duke said to Clare, his teeth chattering.

"A holiday in *Norfolk*, in February, you great dolt," Clare replied.

"Oh."

"It's okay, I've got a coat you can wear. Warmest coat you'll ever find."

"Oh no, sir," said Kett. "Not the Big Tossing Jacket?"

"The *what*?" said Duke, terrified.

"He's got some lovely pink trousers you can borrow, too," said Savage.

"I'm fine, honestly, please don't make me wear whatever it is you're talking about."

"Your loss," said Clare, striding towards his Mercedes. "Ride with Kett in his bloody mermaid mobile. You can all follow me. Topiary Lodge, it's thirty minutes away. Don't dally."

They watched him go.

"How bad can it be?" Savage said quietly.

"A weekend with Colin Clare in his trunks?" Kett answered, pulling out his car keys. "I have a feeling this might be the most horrific two days of my career."

Clare climbed into his car and eyeballed them through the rain-speckled windscreen.

"I bloody heard that!"

CHAPTER THREE

THE THOUGHT OF COLIN CLARE IN HIS SPEEDOS MAY
have been frightening, but by the time Kett had followed the
Superintendent's Mercedes out of the city and onto the
dual carriageway he couldn't deny that he was ready for a
break.

Life had been relentless of late. Not just work, although
that had been bad enough, but the girls too. Alice had made
the decision never to go to school again and trying to get her
there every morning was like trying to transport an angry
tiger. Both he and Billie had welts on their arms from their
oldest daughter's tantrums, not to mention the bite marks.
Twice she'd actually bolted out of the school playground
into the road during drop-off, and Kett had lost count of the
times the school had called to tell him she'd needed to be
pulled down from the railings.

It broke his heart, because the older Alice got, the more
he could see the differences between her and her peers. Not
bad differences—not all of them, anyway, and some that
were hugely positive—just the little things that made the
other kids look at her out of the corner of their eyes, that

made them run away when she asked to play; the ones that made other parents cancel playdates and pretend there weren't enough party invites.

At her last parents' evening, her teacher had told them Alice was working two years below her expected levels and Kett had wanted to drag the man to their house and show him the artworks Alice had painted, the bags she stitched with her sewing machine, the incredible Lego contraptions that sat proudly in her room. She wasn't 'behind' anything. She was just Alice.

But the fact that Alice didn't want to go to school meant that her sisters didn't either, which made the weekday mornings a warzone—quite literally, sometimes. It took everything Kett had to hold it together, and his mind felt frayed, ready to tear. It had got so bad that even his mum had moved into a flat a couple of streets over. She'd claimed that she felt like she was getting in the way, but it was painfully obvious she just couldn't handle the noise.

So much noise.

As much as he hated the idea of leaving Billie alone for the weekend, it did feel good to have some space from the kids.

"Are we nearly there yet?" asked Duke.

Well, most of the kids, Kett thought.

"I have no idea," he said. "Toltham Broad. Heard of it?"

"No, sir. I'm not from around here."

Ahead, Clare overtook a slow-moving bus. Kett checked his mirrors as he followed, seeing Porter's Mondeo right behind him. From the look of it, he and Savage were still arguing.

"Where did you grow up?" Kett asked.

"All over the place," Duke said, running a hand through his thick beard. "Started in Scotland and gradually moved south. Dad was a salesman, or so he said. Can't have been much good at it because he never held down a job and we never had any money. My mum was the one who landed us in Norwich when I was fifteen. We never left."

"Yeah?" said Kett, happy to pass the time. "What brought you to the police?"

Duke shrugged.

"You know, cool uniform."

"Right," said Kett. "That's quite a calling."

"What about you?" Duke asked.

"Me?" said Kett. He thought about his own father, he thought about the men who had conned him out of everything he had, who had driven him to take his own life. He thought about how he'd vowed to do everything he could to stop it happening to somebody else.

"Yeah, it was the uniform," he said. "And the big stick."

Duke laughed.

Kett slowed as their convoy approached a roundabout, following Clare as he turned right. They navigated the narrow country roads in silence, the impossibly bright winter sun feeling like it was drilling into the tender flesh of his eyes, even with the visor down.

They passed through village after village, all of them different and yet all of them identical—big greens and white fences and quiet pubs and thatched roofs. Kett was almost convinced that Clare was driving them around in circles until they passed a brand-new estate of half-finished, matchbox-sized houses and entered a bigger village. The sign announced that it was Toltham.

"That must have been some party," said Duke.

The streets were a sea of old bunting, most of it green. Paper plates and plastic cups lined the pavements resembling brightly dressed spectators and balloons floated forlornly between them like lost children. There wasn't a soul in sight, but when they turned a corner Kett saw Clare's brake lights burn bright.

Beyond them were more lights, blue and very familiar.

"Job never lets you go, eh?" Kett said as he pulled the Octavia to the side of the road, parking it behind an enormous silver Rolls Royce Ghost that looked as out of place here as Colin Clare would have looked on a fashion show catwalk.

The Superintendent was already unfolding his lanky frame from his car, calling out to somebody down the road. Kett squinted through the windscreen to see a police IRV blocking the way, an ambulance right behind it. Somebody called out a greeting but Kett couldn't see who.

"Wait here," he told Duke. "Don't touch anything."

He clambered out of the car into the frigid air, the cold making his bones feel as brittle as glass. Bungalows squatted on the side of the road, most of them close to ruin and hiding shamefully behind overgrown hedges and crumbling walls. The IRV was parked outside what had to be the worst of them, a microscopic property with half its tiles missing and one of its windows boarded over. Clare was talking to somebody by the open gate, his brash Northern voice the loudest sound in the village.

"You want us, sir?" came Savage's voice from behind. She was leaning out of her open door but Kett waved her back down.

"We're on holiday," he shouted.

He reached the IRV, stepping past Clare to see another man blocking the bungalow's knee-high iron gate. He had to be in his late sixties but it was hard to tell for sure because he was *enormous*, taller than Clare by a good few inches, his obese body packed into a beige suit that looked about ready to give up on life altogether. His face looked as though it had been padded with foam, so much of it that it had smoothed the wrinkles away. When he turned to Kett, it took his chins a few seconds to catch up, and they swayed back and forth for a moment, almost hypnotic.

Clare glanced over his shoulder.

"Wallace, this is DCI Robert Kett," he said. "Kett, this is Wallace Marshall, formerly Superintendent Marshall."

Marshall's dark eyes narrowed at Kett and he sniffed, wiping the back of his hand over his wet nose. After a second or two he offered the same hand to Kett, who shook it for as brief a period of time as humanly possible.

"No introduction needed," Marshall said, his voice like a bucket of wet gravel. His accent was local but there was a hint of Northern Ireland in there too, from a long time ago. "You're a regular topic of conversation in our house, Detective. And contention. My wife doesn't think we need the violence, but I beg to differ. It's a pleasure to meet you."

"Trouble?" Kett asked, looking at the IRV, then at the bungalow.

"Nothing we can't handle," Marshall said. "We may be rural but we know what we're doing."

"Drug overdose," said Clare.

"We have more than our fair share of them out here," said Marshall, adjusting his position. He was wheezing hard, and it was no wonder. The man really was huge—six-six, maybe even six-eight, and he had to be pushing twenty-five stone. "It's a scourge. A lot of bagheads come down the road from Yarmouth when the supply there gets too scarce, or too expensive."

"It's bad out there at the moment," Clare said. Marshall nodded, his wide face bouncing on that mesmerising assembly of chins.

"And always bad here during the parade."

"Parade?" Kett asked, looking at the bunting that stuck to the wet street, which hung from the bare branches of the trees.

"You haven't heard of the Toltham Imbolc?" Marshall said. "You been living under a rock, son? Biggest pagan festival in the county, a night of music and worship and revelry. The locals live for it, the tourists love it, but for anyone on the job it's a horrendous ballache because people always take it too far."

"Like this guy?" Kett asked, looking at the bungalow.

"Exactly. But don't let us hold you up. Colin here says he's taking you on a weekend away?"

"A team-building programme, yes," said Clare.

"Well, I've known this young man a long time, and I've never once heard of him treating his team to a hotel retreat. You must have done something to impress him. Make the most of it, DCI Kett."

"I plan to," Kett said. "Good luck with this."

Marshall nodded, and they all turned back to the bungalow as they heard the door open. A paramedic stood there, her face creased with worry. She shook her head.

"A scourge," Marshall said again. "Breaks my heart. Jarratt?"

The paramedic stood to one side and a uniformed officer appeared, her hat in her hands. She was tall as well, and she had to duck beneath the low lintel. She looked at Clare, then at Kett—her gaze lingering for longer than it needed to—before speaking to Marshall.

"Sir?"

"Move the car, would you?" Marshall said.

She nodded, replacing her hat on her head as she walked up the cracked path.

"Hurry along now," Marshall said to Clare. He took a couple of steps towards the Superintendent and straightened Clare's tie like a proud father. "Don't keep those avocado and mint smoothies waiting."

Clare shook Marshall's hand again, but he didn't look happy about it.

"Let us know if you need any help," said Kett.

"Thank you, son, but we won't."

They all stood to the side to let PC Jarratt pass, then Clare turned and made his way down the street. Kett hung on a minute more as a second paramedic appeared in the door, but he couldn't see what happened next because Marshall stepped to the gate and blocked his view. The enormous man sniffed again, regarding Kett with a look of cold scrutiny.

"Hurry along," he said.

"Sure."

By the time Kett had walked back, Clare was standing by the open door of his car, Porter and Savage with him. He was wearing his *angry* angry face.

"Interesting guy," said Kett.

"That's one way of describing him," Clare replied. "Marshall's my predecessor. Left the Force a decade ago, and not through his own volition. He retired out here and he's been lording it over the locals ever since."

"If he's retired, why is he giving orders to the wooden-tops?" Porter asked.

"Marshall by name, marshal by nature," said Clare. "He thinks he's a tossing sheriff."

He climbed into the Mercedes.

"I'll handle it. Let's go. The lodge isn't far."

Kett walked to the Octavia, trying the handle to find it locked. He patted his pockets for the keys before noticing them in the ignition. Bending down, he rapped on the window.

"Unlock it," he shouted to Duke.

"It's unlocked," the PC said.

Kett tried the handle again.

"It's locked. I told you not to touch anything."

"I didn't!" said Duke, reaching over and trying the driver's door from inside. "It's—"

The Skoda's alarm started to blare, sounding like an air raid siren on the quiet street.

"Unlock it," Kett yelled.

Duke was wrenching the handle, his face a mask of panic.

"It's stuck, sir."

"The knob, you knob," Kett said, tapping the window. "Pull the little thing up."

Duke did as he was told and Kett heard the crunch of the central locking. He opened the door and started the engine, the alarm cutting out.

"I—" Duke said as Kett climbed in, but Kett's pointed finger shut him up.

He pulled out after Clare, squeezing through the narrow gap that PC Jarratt had left them. As he went, he looked past the rear end of the IRV, past Marshall's obese frame, to the bungalow. The second paramedic still stood in the doorway. He was obviously shaken, his face ashen and his hands in his hair. He stumbled into the garden and doubled over like he was about to throw up.

Then the scene was blocked by the ambulance, and Kett turned to the road and drove.

CHAPTER FOUR

Topiary Lodge had gone out of its way to live up to its name.

Kett drove the Skoda down a long, straight gravel driveway that was lined with immaculately trimmed privet hedges—rabbits, geese, sheep, cars, even one that looked like a giant pair of shears. They were so good that he was convinced they were artificial until he passed a pair of sullen gardeners carefully trimming the tail feathers of a giant green chicken with a small electric hedge trimmer. They stopped what they were doing for long enough to offer a quick wave to the cars, smiling in a way that made Kett certain the welcome had been ordered rather than given voluntarily.

The house itself was almost disappointing compared to its greenery. It emerged from behind a line of tall Cypress trees as they approached the end of the driveway, a drab brick building that had probably been built in the 1970s. Large, dark windows watched with a certain aloofness as Kett pulled the Skoda into an empty space in the busy car park. He cut the engine and turned to Duke.

"You ready for this?" he asked the PC.

"I'm ready for anything."

"Except the weather, apparently," Kett said as he got out.

He grabbed his bag from the boot, waiting for Duke to squeeze his enormous frame out of the car before locking it. It took several attempts before the Octavia stayed locked, the horn beeping every time Kett pressed the button on the fob. Even then, he wasn't sure if it was secure, but to be honest he wouldn't be sobbing if somebody nicked it.

"Those bloody girls," he said to himself.

"Stop dawdling!" shouted Clare from the hotel's front door.

"Sorry, sir," Kett answered.

He jogged over, the gravel crunching beneath his boots. Porter and Savage were on their way as well, Porter holding an expensive leather travel bag and Savage with a bright orange hiking rucksack over one shoulder. Clare looked at Duke as he joined them.

"Where's your bag, Constable?"

"My what?" he replied, shivering in the wind that cut down the face of the building.

"Your bag. Your *things*."

"Uh..."

"Right," growled Clare. "Perfect. Follow me."

He opened the door like he was trying to pull it off its hinges, storming inside. Kett let the others through next, following them into a cosy lobby with an old leather sofa, an empty desk, some large plastic plants and not much else. The chill that met them here was worse than the one outside, and the air was heavy with damp.

"Wow, you really are spoiling us, sir," said Savage.

Clare hammered his hand onto the reception bell so hard Kett thought he might flatten it.

"Hello?" he barked.

"Hello!" came a reply from somewhere behind the panelled wall. "Hang on, give me two seconds."

It was more like two minutes before a concealed door in the wall opened and a woman in her late forties stepped through. She looked flustered, her forehead damp with sweat and her dark hair shaken loose from its ponytail. She looked at them all in turn—her eyes lingering on Duke's tiny shorts for a few seconds—before pointing a finger at the Superintendent.

"Colin Clare?" she asked. "Party of five?"

Clare nodded and she took a seat behind the desk, putting on a pair of gold-rimmed glasses to study her computer screen. There were two crude dolls sitting on the monitor, made of stuffed cotton with button eyes. They both wobbled on their perches as the woman typed.

"My name is Harita and I am very happy to welcome you to the Topiary. I'm so sorry, we're short-staffed today. We always are after the Imbolc."

"The what?" asked Porter.

"Imbolc," she said. "Candlemas, St Brigid's Day, whatever you want to call it. It's an annual parade. Just a bit of fun but the kids love it. So do the teens, if you know what I mean, and half of them are too hungover to come in the next day."

"St Brigid is Irish, isn't she?" asked Savage. "Bit out of her territory around here."

The woman shrugged.

"No idea, sorry. So, four rooms, right?"

"No," said Clare. "Party of five. Five rooms."

The woman typed something and frowned.

"We've got four written here. One super deluxe executive suite, three economy singles."

Clare glanced at the others then cleared his throat.

"As I said, we need five."

"I'm very sorry, we're booked out, we always are this time of year. But we can easily accommodate an extra bed in the executive suite. Would a cabin bed work?"

"A cabin bed works fine," said Clare. He leaned in, whispering something. The woman's frown deepened.

"No, the economy rooms are quite small, I'm not sure it would fit," she said. Clare whispered something else. "Yes, I see. I'm sure we can make it work."

"Great," Clare said, turning to the group. "The bad news is they can't squeeze an extra bed into my room, the good news is two of you get to share."

"Not me," blurted Porter. "Medical reasons."

"Not me," Savage said. "For obvious reasons."

"Looks like it's you and Duke then, Kett," Clare said.

"Wait—" Kett started, but Clare silenced him with a look.

"We have some activities booked in," the Super said to the receptionist. "The team-building programme."

"Indeed you do," the woman replied. "Bear with me, I'll have to check it's all still running. Like I said, not everyone is here. Your first activity was... here, it's basket weaving. Is that right?"

Duke groaned like a cow giving birth. The receptionist looked up at them, one eyebrow hovering near her hairline.

"You don't look like basket weavers."

"Well, they bloody well are," snapped Clare. "Where do we go for that?"

"Down the hall to the right, opposite the breakfast

room," she said. "It starts in half an hour. I'll show you to your rooms first."

She walked around the desk and opened the door for them, ushering them into a wide, sun-drenched corridor with a patterned carpet that seemed designed to give people vertigo. A few people milled around, some of them in white robes with towels wrapped around their heads. Kett shouldered his way past Porter as they walked to the stairs.

"Medical reasons?" he hissed.

Porter grinned. Kett did not.

"You'll have some bloody medical reasons in a minute, Pete, I can promise you that."

"Excuse me," asked Savage as they made their way to the first floor, passing more people in their dressing gowns. "Is there a spa here?"

"There is," the woman said over her shoulder. "It's why most people come to the hotel. It's downstairs on—"

"There will be no time for the spa, Savage," said Clare. "We have a packed schedule."

They reached the landing and the receptionist put a hand to her chest, struggling for breath.

"Phew," she said. "I'm still recovering from last night too. The economy rooms are down there. Numbers 22, 25 and 29."

She dealt out the key cards and handed the fourth to Clare.

"I'll take you up to the executive suite."

"Half an hour," Clare said. "Do *not* be late."

"Those baskets won't weave themselves," muttered Savage when the Super had disappeared.

Kett followed Savage and Porter along the corridor, passing through a fire door then down a half-flight of steps into a much darker part of the building. The doors here were very close together and Kett counted them as they went. They stopped outside Number 22 as if it was a crime scene, not a hotel room. Savage tried her card and the light flashed red. Porter went next and the door unlocked, opening into a small but cosy bedroom.

"Well it's not exactly the Ritz, but it will do," he said. "See you in a bit."

Savage crossed the hall and opened the door to Number 25.

"You guys must be 29," she said as she walked in, shrugging apologetically. "Sorry."

Kett opened his door with the key card, revealing a space that would have been more suitable for a wardrobe.

Or a prison cell.

A single bed sat against the far wall, almost close enough to touch from where he was standing, and an open door to the right revealed a microscopic bathroom.

It was a *glass* door. Opaque, sure, but glass nonetheless

"Nope," said Kett.

"It'll be okay, sir," Duke said, squeezing past. "It's just for a couple of nights."

"That's easy for you to say," Kett replied, following him in. "*I* remembered to bring my pyjamas."

"I never wear them anyway," said Duke. "It's good for your man parts to get a good airing."

"Nope," Kett said again.

He threw his bag onto the bed before Duke could claim it and walked to the window. It was barely bigger than an arrow slit and looked down over what had to be the kitchen roof. An air conditioning vent warbled like a mechanical bird. Behind him he heard the bathroom door close, then a series of noises he knew he would never be able to get out of his head. There might as well not have been a door there at all.

To take his mind off Duke's exertions, he pulled out his phone and fired off a text to Billie:

Help me.

Then, because Duke had started singing the theme tune to *Friends*, he made a call.

"Don't tell me you want to come home already," said DI Dunst when he answered. "It can't be that bad, surely."

"It's worse," Kett said. "Can you do me a favour, Keith? We passed an ongoing incident on the way out here. Police and paramedics, a property in Toltham. Can you find out what it is?"

"You're supposed to be on holiday, sir."

"I am. But there was something weird about it. Can't put my finger on why. There was an ex-copper on-site, Wallace Marshall. You know him?"

Dunst wheezed out a laugh.

"Wally? Sure. He ran the show when I first started here. Good man. Or at least he used to be. I think he got the boot."

"You know what for?"

"Nah," said Dunst. "It was all kept under wraps. I know he's still local, though. Friend of mine goes to the same fishing club, out there on the broad. You said Toltham, didn't you?"

"Yeah," said Kett. "Didn't catch the name of the road."

"Can't see anything on the system," said Dunst. "No 999 calls, nothing on the logs. You sure you didn't imagine it?"

"I'm sure," said Kett. "Thanks, Keith. Hey, you don't fancy two nights away, do you? Gorgeous hotel room, a spa, some great activities. I'll happily swap."

Dunst roared with laughter as he hung up. Kett heard the toilet flush and the sound of the tap.

"Wouldn't go in there for a minute or two, sir," said Duke as he appeared. "Sorry."

"Right," said Kett.

He thought about the paramedic he'd seen leaving the bungalow, the look on his face like he was going to throw up. And he thought about the way Marshall had moved his enormous frame in front of the gate to block the view. Something about it had kicked Kett's Spidey sense right in the bollocks.

But whatever it was, it wasn't his concern.

Like Savage said, the baskets wouldn't weave themselves.

"I'll see you down there," he said to Duke, holding his breath until he'd broken free into the hallway. "I'm going for a walk."

CHAPTER FIVE

KETT TOOK THE QUIET WAY OUT, HEADING DOWN A SET of stairs at the back of the building before pushing through the fire doors. The sun had burned a hole through the clouds but it was brutally cold, and he clapped his hands together as he walked across the crisp grass.

Ahead of him, Toltham Broad lay like a puddle of molten silver, almost too bright to look at. A couple of lonely rowing boats drifted in the middle, their occupants so still they might have been frozen solid, and Kett could hear the roar of a speedboat from somewhere out of sight. It was bigger here than he'd expected, the long, thin broad disappearing in both directions, the far bank lined with a wide swathe of woodland.

He made his way down the shallow hill of the lawn, finding himself on a small strip of beach. Canoes were racked up to his right next to a collection of colourful peda-los. To the other side sat a line of deck chairs and two small wooden huts, both of which looked like they needed a fresh coat of creosote and both of which were padlocked shut. He could smell smoke, and it wasn't cigarette smoke.

He dropped onto the damp sand and walked towards the huts, clearing his throat to give whoever stood there a little fair warning. There was a muttered swear, then a joint arced through the air, landing on the beach.

A young woman peeked out from the narrow gap between the huts, kicking sand over the butt while doing her best not to cough out a lung. Her shoulder-length hair was a remarkably bright shade of purple, so glossy it didn't look real, and she wore a matching shade of eye shadow, curled into points in a way that made Kett think of a cat. There was a black ring through the middle of her nose. She was wearing the same black trousers, white shirt and black cardigan as the woman in reception, and when she looked up there was genuine terror on her face.

She shrank back into the shadows of her hiding place, almost disappearing.

"I didn't mean to scare you," said Kett.

"Oh, shit, sorry," she replied, bending down to pick up an empty coffee cup. "I thought you were the boss. We're not allowed to smoke back here."

"Technically, I don't think you're allowed to smoke *that* stuff anywhere," said Kett. When she started to panic, Kett smiled and lifted a hand, his frozen face managing a smile. "Don't worry, I'm not going to tell anyone."

"Thanks," she said. "Because somebody said there's a bunch of police or something here for the weekend. That's the last thing I need."

Kett laughed, and she looked at his suit and slapped a hand to her forehead.

"You're one of them?" she said, wincing.

"I am, but don't worry. I'm on holiday."

"You won't tell?"

"I won't. But I can't speak for the others, so maybe lay off it for a while."

The woman nodded, staring at her fingers. It was hard to get a good look at her in the darkness between the huts, and the remaining wisps of smoke made her look somehow ghostly, like she might just vanish. But even in the shadows, Kett could see that her brow was creased with worry, and he wasn't sure it had anything to do with him.

"You okay?" he asked.

"Yeah," she said quietly, still looking at her hands.

"You sure?"

"I'm just..." she started, peering out at the lake. The pattern of the water shimmered on her skin, caught in her hair like fairy lights. "I can't..."

She drifted off, lost somewhere in the water. Kett waited, his hands numb from the cold, his jaw locked tight to stop his teeth from chattering. He thought about asking her to step out into the daylight but it wasn't his place.

"I'm just worried about my boyfriend," the woman said eventually. "I was supposed to meet him here this morning and..."

She finally looked at Kett, her eyes darker than the shadows around her. She licked her lips, more there that she wasn't saying.

"Was he out last night?" Kett asked. "The parade?"

The woman nodded, then shrugged.

"We all were. But Seb—"

A door slammed shut in the hotel and the young woman almost shed her skin in fright. She looked back, then started to retreat down the gap between the sheds.

"I'm sorry," she said. "It's nothing. I've got to go."

"If you're worried, call the police," said Kett. "Or talk to one of us."

"It's fine," she said, breaking free and shouting back. "Thanks for not telling on me."

He wondered about asking for her name but she was already out of sight behind the wicker fence panels that separated the beach and the lawns from the service area. He heard a man's voice yelling something, heard the woman apologising, then the crunch of another door.

Kett was about to keep walking when a man walked out from behind the same fence and sparked up a cigarette. He was in his forties, his head almost entirely hairless, and he was wearing chef's trousers and a white top stained with food. He glanced at Kett without so much as a nod or a smile, taking a deep drag of his cigarette.

Kett left him to it, sticking to the beach as he made his way around the hotel. His phone dinged, a message from Billie:

It can't be that bad, surely??? Just enjoy the quiet!

It was too cold to reply and he upped his speed, walking onto a large stone dining terrace that led from the hotel's dilapidated conservatory. Past that was another wide lawn that was empty apart from the crows that rooted in the grass. They hopped out of his way as he passed them, watching him with eyes as dark as the hotel's windows.

A short walk later and he'd reached the far side of the building, making his way down a cobbled path into the car park. As he was passing a window he heard somebody hammer on it and he turned to see Clare gurning at him from inside.

"Where are you going?" the Super yelled.

"I'm making a break for it, sir," Kett replied.

"What?"

"I said I'm on my way."

He checked his watch to see that he still had five

minutes. As he walked through the front door again, the receptionist, Harita, smiled at him.

"Welcome to Topiary... Wait, you've checked in already, haven't you?"

"I have," said Kett. "Just took a walk."

She nodded, evidently flustered as she turned back to her computer.

"Can I just ask, is there a young man off work today? Somebody who maybe didn't call in sick? I think his name might be Seb."

"Uh..." she said, looking at the empty desk for a second, her brow creasing. "May I ask why you need to know?"

"No reason," said Kett. "Copper's instinct. It's hard to switch off from the job."

"I'm honestly not sure," the woman said, flapping her hands. "There's too much going on today. Staff don't call in here, they call in to the main office. Gabriel will know. Do you need me to check?"

Kett popped his lips, then shook his head.

"No. Forget I said anything. Basket weaving is down the hall, right?"

She nodded at her computer screen, pointing a finger through the door without another word.

"Thanks," said Kett.

He turned right at the stairs, heading into another wide, bright corridor. To the left, through a glass partition, was a small café that led into the spa. Past that was a bright breakfast room, and across the hall, outside an uninviting side room, sat a sign.

Basket Weaving, 12:30.

He braced himself, then poked his head through the door to see a dozen people, most of them in their seventies and eighties, look up at him from the tables that were positioned across the room. Three women at a table to the right started giggling as they took a good look at him, whispering something amongst themselves that Kett couldn't quite hear.

Savage sat at the table by the window and she waved sheepishly. Clare stood above her, pacing wildly and checking his watch. When he saw Kett, he pulled out an empty chair and gestured to it.

"Hi," Kett said, waving a hand to the room as he walked to the table. He sat down opposite Savage.

Kill me now, she mouthed, and he almost burst out laughing.

"Where are those tosspots?" Clare growled, loud enough for the entire room to hear. He was answered by a series of tuts and shaking heads.

"Sorry," came a voice from the door as Porter walked in. The three women at the table by the door watched him cross the room, elbowing each other and laughing even harder.

Porter was followed by a young woman whose face was hidden by an armful of craft materials. She staggered to an empty table at the front, grunting as she deposited her things. When she turned to the room, her cheeks were blazing.

"Hello everyone!" she said. "Thanks so much for—"

Duke poked his bearded face around the door, making a man on the next table yelp in fright.

"Baskets?" he said. He caught sight of Clare. "Cool."

"Take a seat," said the young woman. "As I was saying, thank you for picking basket weaving as—"

She was cut off by the sound of scraping chair legs as Duke manoeuvred himself to the empty space between the table and the wall. The three women by the door were almost falling off their chairs as they took in the PC's skin-tight shorts. The young instructor attempted to continue.

"Uh, I'm your activity leader for this afternoon. My name is—"

There wasn't quite enough space for Duke so he used his hip to push the table back, shunting it into Porter's stomach.

"Can you budge up a bit, sir?" Duke said.

"Where?" Porter said, gesturing to the man whose seat backed up against his.

"Just suck it in and sit down you giant tosshole," hissed Clare. "You're embarrassing me."

"My name is Rachel Tur—"

Duke sat down with a noise like a building being demolished. The young woman looked at him in silence for a moment until she was sure he was finished, then she smiled at the room again.

"Rachel Turkentine. And I'll be your instructor for the day. I know some of you already, from life drawing." She pointed at the table with the three women and they all burst out laughing. "And some of you were at this morning's tea brewing relaxation class. Welcome back. And hello to the new faces."

She looked at Kett's table, frowning.

"You do know this is basket weaving, right?"

"It's Duke's favourite thing to do," said Porter, nodding towards the big PC. Duke glowered at him, and Clare glowered at them both.

"Right," said Rachel. "Good! Let's get started. As you've done it before, Mr Duke, would you care to lead your table?"

"Uh..." said Duke, gulping like a landed fish.

"He'd love to," said Porter.

"Great! Then let me hand out the bits and bobs and we'll begin. Oh, and if anyone wants a ticket for the raffle this weekend, I'm the gal to ask."

She turned her back to the room. There was a thud beneath the table and Porter yelped.

"Ow," he said, glaring at Duke.

"Sorry, sir," Duke said. "Just trying to get comfortable."

The entire table lurched as Porter kicked his leg out, the pair of them battling until Clare slammed his fist down.

"Behave!" he roared.

They all sat back as the teacher laid some palm fronds and various decorative beads and ribbons beside Duke.

"If you need any more, just ask," she said.

"He will," said Porter, grinning.

Clare looked like he was about to explode, so Kett did his best to distract him.

"Sir, I called HQ about the incident we passed on the way in. Nobody has logged it."

Clare frowned.

"Why are you calling HQ? We're not on duty, Kett."

"I don't know," he said. "Just something about it felt a little odd. Don't you think? It didn't sit right with me. Something about Marshall."

"Ignore it," Clare said, waving him down. "Marshall's a has-been, a nosy ex-copper who thinks he owns the whole county. But I saw police there, and I saw paramedics. It'll be logged."

"I—"

"Leave it," Clare growled. "And weave this tossing basket."

Kett nodded, turning in his seat as the teacher started to talk.

"So, some of you know what you're doing. For the rest of

you, I'm going to make it as simple as possible. Perhaps Mr Duke here could be my spirit guide?"

"Uh..." said Duke.

"Take a few reeds in your left hand. Maybe three or four."

Duke scanned the table and picked up a handful of wooden beads.

"*Reeds*," said Rachel.

Duke tried again.

"Those are ribbons."

Clare slapped a hand to his forehead with a sound like a firework going off. Savage took a handful of reeds and passed them to Duke, whose nervous grin was so wide Kett could see pretty much every single one of his teeth.

"Then do the same in the other hand and arrange them into a cross."

It was too painful to watch the poor PC trying to figure it out, so Kett turned his attention to the window behind Duke's head. From here he could see his car, looking pinker than ever in the early afternoon light.

The young woman he'd spoken to earlier was out there, her phone to her ear and a cigarette in her free hand. Her hair was incredibly bright, like she was trying to send out a signal. It was hard to tell, but Kett thought she might be crying. She arched her back in frustration before putting the phone in her pocket, grinding the cigarette out on the driveway.

"This is where we need more hands," said Rachel, pulling Kett back to the room. "If somebody on each table could take the horizontal strands, and somebody else could take the vertical ones, we'll start weaving. For this, you'll need to be a real team."

"Ha!" said Clare, looking at them all in turn like he'd just won something. "What did I tell you? Teamwork!"

Luckily, Savage and Porter took over, working like a machine as they folded the reeds into a circular pattern.

Kett turned his attention to the window to see the young woman still pacing. Her eyes scrolled back and forth along the front of the building as if she was looking for something, and she must have found it because her face grew tight, her jawline bulging, her expression as clear as day.

She was terrified.

CHAPTER SIX

"I GUESS IF YOU STAND IN A DARK ROOM AND SQUINT then it might look a *little* bit like a basket?"

Savage held up the unfortunate assembly of reeds, beads and ribbons that they'd cobbled together during the hour-long class, managing a couple of seconds of silence before she broke into a snorting giggle. She put her free hand to her mouth, looking over her shoulder to make sure that Superintendent Clare was nowhere nearby.

They were standing outside the breakfast room, the back doors open into the garden as a couple of staff carried a table outside. The wind cut into the hotel, scalpel-sharp as it sought them out. Kett thrust his hands in his pockets to keep them warm.

"It actually looks a little bit like the Boss," she went on, rustling the basket as though it was a puppet and putting on a pretty decent Clare voice. "Oi, you lot, stop tossing about."

Despite himself, Kett laughed—and it surprised him how good it felt.

"I blame Aaron," said Porter, giving the PC a gentle

elbow. "Claiming to be a basket weaving expert when really he didn't know the first bloody thing."

Duke glared at him, the tendons in his neck bulging.

"Easy, Big Guy," said Porter, his hands up. "I'm joking."

The door to the craft room opened and Rachel, the young teacher, walked out, the last of the materials tucked under her arm.

"Oh," she said when she saw them. "Hello. Well done today, that was a good effort."

Savage held up the basket again, which was already halfway to unravelling. Rachel smiled.

"I said a good effort, *not* a good basket. We're all done in here until three, but if you fancy giving it another go this afternoon then feel free!"

"I think we've had enough baskets for a lifetime," said Kett. "Thank you, though."

"Well, I'm over in the Pavilion Room in the morning if anyone fancies tea and relaxation."

"Tea?" said Kett. She nodded.

"It's a calming exercise. I teach you how to empty your mind while you make a perfect blend."

"Pete, sign yourself up immediately," said Kett.

"I don't need to know how to make tea," said Porter. "I—"

"Sign up, sir," said Savage. "He's got the empty mind already but he definitely needs help with his tea."

"I make a perfectly good—"

"Go," said Kett. "That's an order. What time?"

"Ten," Rachel said, turning her smile up to Porter. "I can't wait."

She walked off, and Savage gave Porter a wink.

"She can't wait."

"Shut up," said Porter without malice. He glanced down

the hall. "Shall we do a runner now before the Boss comes back?"

"Not worth it," Savage said. "He'll track us down."

"And toss on us," said Duke.

Porter shook his head at the PC.

"Disgusting."

Kett laughed again, quieter now. However bad the trip was, it *did* feel good to be on holiday. They'd been to hell and back so many times that being here right now, away from the stresses of a case, away from the horror and heartbreak of the job, felt almost euphoric.

If they really *had* escaped from the job, that was.

"Give me a second," he said, walking away from the group. "Tell Clare I'll be right back."

He made his way to the hotel's reception, passing the empty front desk and exiting into the freezing February air. It was starting to cloud over, the skies darkening on the horizon. He wondered if it would snow, then panicked that he might be stuck here for longer than a weekend.

Pulling up the collar of his jacket, he made his way into the middle of the car park to search for the young woman with purple hair. There was no sign of her, just a handful of guests following him out, their laughter strangely muted as they made for their cars. He moved out of their way as they drove towards the road, then returned to the spot where the young woman had been standing.

From here, he had a prime view of the front of the hotel. The sun was behind him, filling the large windows and obscuring what lay inside. There was no way the woman could have seen him earlier.

The only window that was open was at the far right-hand side of the hotel, in the annex that served as the kitchen. The lights were blazing in there, even though it was the middle of the day, and Kett could see the tops of heads as the staff busied themselves. Had the woman been looking this way when her face fell, when the terror appeared in her eyes? He couldn't be sure, but she'd definitely seen something that had scared her.

You're being ridiculous, he told himself. *You're looking for truths that aren't there.* And he wondered if he was so used to being on a case that he was imagining things.

What did that say about his state of mind?

Nothing good, he thought as he made his way back to the front door. The reception desk was still deserted, even though there was a queue of people trying to check in. He apologised his way past them, back into the relative warmth of the hotel. When his phone rang, his fingers were so numb he dropped it on the carpet trying to pull it out of his pocket.

"DCI Kett," he said when he'd picked it up.

"It's Dunst, sir. Just wanted to let you know that the incident you mentioned before has just been logged. Young lad, overdose by the look of it."

"Was his name Seb?" Kett asked. "Sebastian?"

Dunst clucked his tongue for a moment.

"Uh, no. Neil Enthoven. Twenty-four. History of drug abuse, by the look of it. He's been arrested a handful of times for possession."

"This was in Toltham?" Kett asked.

"Uh-huh. Station Road. Postie called it in this morning when she saw the body through the window, we got there soon after. Paramedics say he probably died sometime in the night. Report was filed by, uh, PC Sophie Jarratt. No sign of foul play."

"Did they say what he overdosed on?" Kett asked.

"Nothing here yet, but he'll be on his way to Franklin."

"Thanks, Keith," said Kett, ready to hang up before Dunst called out to stop him.

"Sir, hold on, I haven't got to the best bit yet. They've just found another one."

"Another body?" Kett said.

"No, another French Fancy. Of course another body."

"Where?"

"Right across the broad from where you're staying. It's just come through. Dog walker found him an hour ago."

"You're kidding. Text me the details."

"Aren't you too busy knitting tea cosies?" Dunst asked. "But in all seriousness, Spalding's across town on the Holmes fraud thing, Pearson's on leave, and you know how much I hate the cold. You'd be doing me a favour."

"I'll bet."

Kett ended the call, making his way down the corridor to the breakfast room. The others were still standing there, Savage doing Clare impressions with her basket and no sign yet of the Superintendent.

"You okay?" Savage asked when he joined them.

"Yeah. Just spoke to Dunst. The house we passed on the way out here, body was a young man, overdose. And they've just found another one."

"Shit," said Porter. "Close?"

Kett's phone dinged, a message from Dunst.

"Very," said Kett, reading the address.

"That's weird," said Porter.

"Not that weird," Savage said, tapping the basket against her knee. "Drugs are rife out here, come in from the sea over Yarmouth way and just spread. We all know where Norfolk sits on the drug death table."

"Yeah," said Kett. "True. Anyway, Dunst asked if we could take a look for him, because it's cold out."

"Lazy sod," said Porter. "We're on holiday. Let him do it."

"Do what?" barked Clare as he marched down the corridor. He had something tucked under his arm, something white and fluffy.

"Another body, sir," said Kett. "Overdose. Just been called in, it's walking distance from here. Dunst and Spalding have their hands full."

"No tossing way, you've got a raft building thing in twenty minutes, out on the broad."

"But it's freezing out there!" Duke whined.

"Then you should have brought a bloody coat," Clare shot back. "And some tossing trousers!"

Duke shivered in his shorts, pouting.

"No way," Clare said. "Dunst can drag his lazy arse out here. You four need to go and do some teamwork."

"Us *four*, sir?" said Porter. "Where are you going?"

"Uh, I need to go and take care of some urgent Superintendent business," said Clare, doing his best to hide what Kett was pretty sure was a dressing gown. "It's important stuff and I don't think I'll make it to the lake. But I want a full report over dinner."

"You're going to the spa, aren't you, sir?" said Savage.

"I tossing well am not!" Clare said with a little too much outrage. "Now piss off or you'll be late."

He gave them all a stare, then turned and walked off.

In the direction of the spa.

"That utter..." Porter started, muttering the rest of the sentence beneath his breath. He sighed, looking through the window at the darkening day. "It is way too cold to be anywhere near that bloody lake."

Kett pulled up the collar of his coat and made his way through the open back door. The hotel's large garden was deserted but a young man in a tracksuit hopped around on the beach, clapping his hands to try to stay warm. He spotted them and waved, calling out words that were too quiet to make out but which appeared as smoke signals over his head. Kett walked onto the beach, taking in the battered plastic barrels and coils of rope that had been laid out beside the water.

"You, uh," the man pulled a piece of paper from his pocket. "Colin Clare and party?"

"Yeah," said Kett. "Minus Colin Clare."

"Great," said the guy, his frozen smile showing far less enthusiasm than he probably hoped it would. "My name is Simon, I'll be your teamworking guru for the afternoon."

He glanced at Duke.

"Might want to put a jacket on, mate. Temperature's dropping."

Duke growled at him through chattering teeth.

"Uh, right. So, who's up for a bit of raft building?"

"Yay?" said Savage.

Kett looked across the water, which was so bright with reflected sun that it left an imprint on his retinas. It almost seemed as if the whole broad was burning.

"Simon," he asked. "Miller's Lane, you know it?"

"Miller's?" the kid said, looking over his shoulder. "Sure. You have to double back around, take the right just after the bridge."

"Much down there?"

"Couple of houses, an old boatyard from what I remember. You can access the north part of the resort from there, the archery range and tree walk, although it's being repaired at the moment. Why?"

"No reason," said Kett. "Can you get to it over the water?"

"Sure," Simon said with a shrug. "It's literally right over there, past them trees."

"Sir?" said Savage, looking at him like she knew exactly what he was planning.

"I mean, *technically* we'll still be working as a team, right?" Kett said to her.

"But who's going to build the raft?" she asked.

As one, they all turned to Duke. The big PC stood there in his shorts, shivering so hard Kett thought he could hear the man's bones rattling.

"What?" he said when he saw them all looking.

"Good luck," said Kett.

He ignored Duke protests, turning once again to Simon.

"We won't be staying to make the boat, but is there any chance we could borrow one?"

CHAPTER SEVEN

DESPITE THE CALM WATER, IT WAS AN UNSETTLED TRIP. The little rowing boat wasn't big enough for the three of them, especially Porter, who sat by himself in the middle seat, the oars grasped in his hands. Kett and Savage huddled together at the stern, Kett grateful for the heat coming off the DC even though it did little to counter the cruel wind that cut across the water. Every time Porter pulled the oars the boat rocked, leaving a rippling wake behind them all the way to the shore they'd just left.

Luckily, it didn't take them long to cross, and after six or seven minutes the boat slid into the tangled vegetation that guarded the far side of Toltham Broad. Trees overhung the water here, their knuckled branches reaching down as if to push them away.

Or push them *under*.

Kett took as deep a breath as he was able, trying not to think about his last case, about the coffin that Bert had left for them in the pond in Wayland Woods. Even after all these weeks, he could still taste the stagnant pond water, he could still feel the insects crawling over his face, clawing into his nostrils and his ears. Toltham might have been bigger, and it was certainly fresher, but he had no intention of ever putting his head below water ever again.

"See a good place to moor?" he asked, staring into the tangled greenery.

"Can't see anything," said Porter. "You sure we're in the right place?"

"Just keep going."

Porter did as he was told, the oars catching in the reeds, the keel grinding along the shallow shore. Kett glanced across the water to see Duke doing his best to tie two buckets together with a length of rope. It didn't seem to be going particularly well, and he almost felt sorry for him.

Almost.

"There," said Savage.

Kett followed her finger to see a small landing area a dozen yards ahead. The trees thinned here, and as they drew closer he realised they'd been cut back, the trunks piled up further inland and the stumps fresh. A gravel path had been laid in the muddy earth, weaving into the darker woodland beyond.

Porter clumsily steered them closer, the boat rocking wildly as he reached out and grabbed the nearest tree stump. He pulled them the rest of the way until they felt solid ground beneath them.

"One at a time," Kett said.

He stood up, holding Savage's hand as he lurched towards dry land. The bank was further away than he'd expected and he almost toppled into the water before somehow managing to keep his balance. He helped Savage out and they each took one of Porter's hands and pulled him free. He, too, almost fell, kicking himself out of the boat so hard that he pushed it back into the lake.

"Nice one, Pete," said Kett as they watched it drift away. Porter scratched his head.

"Probably should have tied it up," he said.

"Doesn't matter, we can walk back." Kett checked his phone, nodding up the path. "Miller's Lane should be right there."

"Did Dunst say much, sir?" Savage asked as they set off.

"No. Just that there was another body. A young man, possible overdose, found by a dog walker."

"Nothing we can't leave to the woodentops?" Porter asked.

"Would you rather be back there building a raft?" Kett said.

"Fair point."

They followed the trail of gravel through the skeletal trees, the sound of their feet like fireworks against the still afternoon. The hotel obviously owned the land on this side of the lake because they passed a small clearing where a huge wooden climbing frame was being built, platforms high up in the trees, the entire area marked off with yellow tape.

Past that was another cleared space dedicated to archery. There were targets here, but that wasn't all people had been shooting. By the fence sat a small doll made of sticks and leaves, swaddled in cotton, its head a ball of silver foil complete with button eyes. It looked like the ones he'd seen in the hotel.

"What is that thing?" he asked, pointing.

"No idea," said Savage. Porter shrugged, looking at the archery range.

"Fingers crossed Clare hasn't booked us in for any of this. I wouldn't trust Duke with a bow and arrow."

"Especially after what we just did to him," added Savage.

They reached a low, wooden fence that was green with age and Kett struggled over it.

"Need a hand, sir?" asked Savage, and he waved her away, dropping down to the road. She vaulted it easily, Porter choosing to duck beneath the top bar instead.

"This way," Kett said, studying his phone again.

They walked in silence. Trees arched overhead like the vaulted roof of a medieval building, cutting the sunlight to ghost-like shreds which wriggled and danced on the asphalt. Despite the fact the hotel was just across the water, Kett couldn't hear a thing here. Even the birds seemed to have frozen.

Until they rounded a corner, that was, and saw the police car up ahead.

The IRV sat on the edge of the road, its passenger-side wheels up on the low bank. Its lights flashed manically, lighting up the trees. It was empty, but Kett could hear voices from deeper in the woods.

"Hello?" he called as he neared the car.

No answer, but when he angled his head he thought he could see movement in the trees. He found a gap between two gnarled, sickly-looking yews and squeezed through, branches snatching at his face, catching on his suit. They were on the other side of the road now to the lake and the woodland here was thicker and darker. The marshy ground was treacherous, opening up beneath Kett's boots like it was trying to eat him.

"I bloody hate the countryside," groaned Porter.

"Hello?" Kett shouted again. "Police."

The voices up ahead grew quiet, then somebody shouted back—a woman's voice.

"Police?"

"Yeah," said Kett. "Where are you?"

"Right up ahead," said the voice. "I can see you. To your left a little."

Kett rounded a clump of trees and saw a flash of yellow, one arm waving. Ducking beneath a low branch he saw a uniformed constable up ahead standing next to another woman, a shaggy Retriever huddled between them.

He had to get a little closer before he recognised PC Jarratt, the same officer who had been at the bungalow they'd passed that morning. She looked at them all in turn as they walked out of the mud onto a narrow dirt path, and to say she didn't look happy to see them was a *huge* understatement.

"Sirs," she said with a curt nod. "Bit early for the Cavalry, isn't it?"

"We were close by," said Kett. "Thought you could do with a hand."

"For an OD?" said Jarratt. "Aren't you a DCI? Thanks, but I think we'll be okay."

Her jaw was set so firmly that Kett thought he could hear her teeth grinding. He turned to the other woman. She was in her fifties and almost mummified in a thick tweed overcoat. A matching hat was pulled so far down her face that she had to lift her head in order to meet Kett's eye. It might have been the cold, but her eyes were full of tears. The dog whined, shaking its mud-matted coat and pawing the ground.

"Good afternoon," said Kett to the woman. "Are you the one who found the body?"

PC Jarratt started to protest, then obviously decided against it. She clamped her mouth shut again, her jaw bulging.

"Yes, dear," said the woman. "I'm so sorry."

Kett wasn't sure what she was apologising for. She used the back of a gloved hand to wipe her face, knocking her hat at an angle. The retriever looked up at her with big, brown eyes then loosed a gunshot bark that startled a handful of quiet birds from the trees. The woman used the same hand to ruffle its head.

"I was just walking Bessie here, like we do every afternoon. I usually go the long way around the broad but she doesn't like the cold, so when the weather's bad we cut through the woods. I only live yonder. I..." She took in a sudden, shuddering breath, as if she had just surfaced from a dive. "I'm used to seeing dead birds, dead foxes sometimes. I thought that's what it was at first, because Bessie was going at it. But it wasn't a fox. It wasn't a fox at all."

"It's okay," said Kett. "I'm sorry you had to see it. But we're grateful to you for calling it in. Can I ask, did you recognise the man?"

"Oh, I didn't look, dear," she said, shaking her head. "I couldn't look at his face. No."

Kett nodded, turning to Jarratt.

"Where is he?"

"There's not much to see," she replied.

Kett looked at her until she sighed, thrusting her thumb over her shoulder as if she was hitchhiking.

"Thank you, Constable," he said. "You've taken a statement from uh...?"

"Mavis Kane," said the woman when she recognised the prompt. "You can call me Mavis. I told Sophie everything I know."

"Sophie?" said Kett. "You two know each other?"

"She's been in the village for years," Mavis said.

"Good," said Kett. "Then maybe she could drive you home?"

Jarratt bristled, and Mavis waved the suggestion away.

"I wouldn't want to put Bessie here in anybody's car, even hers. We're five minutes away, less if we get a wiggle on."

The dog barked again, obviously agreeing with her.

"DC Savage will just take some information from you, if that's okay?" Kett said, and she nodded. He turned to Jarratt. "Lead the way."

Jarratt and Mavis shared a look that Kett couldn't read, then the PC turned and walked into the trees, almost tripping on a monstrous root as she went. Kett took care as he followed, grabbing branches with numb fingers as they dropped down a steep hill. Porter cursed his way after them, the big guy slipping at one point and almost bringing them both down with him. Jarratt stopped at the bottom of the slope, pointing to a fallen tree that was so green it looked almost like a low, mossy wall.

"He's right there."

"Where?" said Kett.

Jarratt kept her finger out, and he almost had to ask her again before he saw it. The tree had been a big one, but not quite big enough to conceal the body that lay behind it. From here, Kett could make out a shock of blond hair, and for a terrible second he wondered if there was no body at all, just a head. He walked closer, spotting the curve of a shoulder.

"He's wearing camouflage," he said when he reached the moss-covered trunk.

"I don't think anyone would have found him if it hadn't been for the dog," said Jarratt. "He's almost invisible."

Kett walked around the base of the tree, past the enormous sculpture of roots that had been unplugged from the earth. The young man was lying on his side, his face twisted into the dirt. His camouflaged jacket was a puffer, and an expensive one at that. His jeans were pricey too, and his trainers—one in place, the other upended beside a bare foot —looked brand new despite the mud. There was blood on the exposed foot, but not much, and when Kett leaned in a little closer he saw the teeth marks there.

"The dog," said Jarratt. "Mavis told me she had to pull her off him."

"You've checked for ID?" Kett asked.

"Of course. Nothing in his pockets."

"Nothing?"

The PC licked her lips, shaking her head as she looked back up the hill.

"I know who it is. Local lad. Sebastian Reilly. He was only twenty-two."

Kett swore beneath his breath, thinking of the young woman at the hotel.

I'm just worried about my boyfriend.

"Seb," he said. Jarratt frowned.

"You knew him?"

"No. How did *you* know him?"

"I've brought him in a couple of times, drug stuff, couple of minor altercations. Boys will be boys stuff, you know?"

"And you know this is an OD?"

"I don't. Not for sure. When Mavis called 999 she told them that's what she thought it was."

"Based on her extensive medical knowledge?" asked Porter. "And the fact she didn't even look at him?"

"Based on pretty much every other death we've had here in the last few months, sir," said Jarratt. "It's a fucking plague. All the kids round here are hopped up, and each new drug is worse than the last. Right now they're using some kind of speedball. It's lethal. We started seeing it a few weeks ago. We get a lot of drugs here. The Yarmouth crews have a network across Norfolk, shipping it to the rest of the country. But the county lines gangs are all over this too."

She sighed.

"That thing this morning was another fatal OD. Something new. I've never seen anything like it. It's worse than the heroin, worse than the speedballs. I don't know if this is the same thing but there's one way of telling. Look at his face."

All three of them turned to the young man, his face hidden in the dirt. The silence of the woods was almost deafening.

"I'll do it," Kett said, more to himself than anyone else.

He moved carefully through the tangled undergrowth, ducking beside the man then instantly reeling back at the smell of faeces. At this angle, he could make out one eye, wide open and bloodshot. A black beetle crawled across its glistening surface, probing the edges as it looked for a new home.

The bottom of the man's face was concealed by damp fingers of vegetation and Kett pulled a pen from his pocket, using it to push them aside.

What he saw there made him want to scream.

The man's mouth was open wide. *Too* wide. Wide enough that the corners of his lips had split, wide enough that his teeth were entirely exposed, all the way down to his pale gums and the stump of his half-chewed tongue, wide enough that something had broken inside the line of his jaw, a jutting ridge of bone pushing against the skin of his cheek. Kett could have fitted his entire fist inside the corpse's mouth with room to spare.

"Fuck," he said quietly. He stood up, his cracking knees the loudest thing in the woods. "What kind of narcotic does this?"

"We're not sure," said Jarratt. "I've never seen anything like this before, not until this morning. Every batch is different, every OD is different. My guess, cocaine and heroin for sure, that's the most common ingredient. But there's been some new stuff in circulation recently. Potassium something."

"Permanganate?" said Savage as she struggled down the hill. Jarratt nodded.

"That's the one."

Savage ran the last few steps, almost falling over before Porter caught her.

"Steeper than it looked," she said when he'd let go. "Potassium permanganate. You find it in chemistry sets for kids. Chemists use it to activate other ingredients. It's a stimulant."

"I don't know," said Jarratt. "Like I say, we've found a dozen different varieties of this shit. But this one is the worst."

She looked at the body and so did Kett. Seb's wet eye stared back at him, almost winking as the beetle finally found its way beneath the lid.

"Jaw Breaker," Jarratt went on. "That's what we're calling it. Jaw Breaker."

CHAPTER EIGHT

"You're telling me you've never heard of this stuff?"

Kett held the phone to his ear, stamping his boots in the mulch to try to warm up. He'd climbed the hill again, partly to get a better signal and partly to escape the sight of Seb Reilly and his ruined jaw, his awful, desperate, unblinking eye. On the other end of the line, DI Tahoor Khan—an old friend from the Met who'd been Kett's go-to guy for narcotics questions—cleared his throat.

"Jaw Breaker? No, sorry, Robbie. We find speedballs everywhere in the east. Cocaine and heroin are the delicacies of choice in this part of the world, especially if you can spend a little more money. It's not unheard of to see it cut with other ingredients, saves the dealers money if they can mix in some baking soda or starch or even crushed painkillers. We've seen batches cut with laundry detergent, even rat poison if you can believe it. Most users are too fucked up to even notice."

"And potassium permanganate?"

"Sure, although that's more of an Eastern European

thing. We call it Jeff. It's nasty stuff. Cut it with over-the-counter meds and it'll give you a high, sure. We're talking maybe fifteen minutes. But after a few months of sticking yourself with Jeff, you'll feel your joints seizing up, you'll find it harder and harder to move, then you won't be able to move at all. The potassium settles on your brain, eats away the protective sheath. You basically give yourself multiple sclerosis."

"Jesus," said Kett.

"It's permanent, too," Khan went on.

Kett looked down the hill. Porter was crouched by Reilly's body, his face gaunt, while Savage spoke to Jarratt. He couldn't hear what they were saying.

"Can Jeff cause your jaw to break?" Kett said. "Dislocate, maybe?"

"I doubt it," said Khan. "Slow paralysis, sure, but what you're describing sounds more like a drug-induced muscular spasm. Acute dystonia, maybe. You'd be looking at something that blocks dopamine receptors, high potency neuroleptics or even anti-emetics. You said it was a young man?"

"Yeah."

"You more often than not find DIMS with young men, something in their pathology, especially if they have a history of cocaine use."

Kett sighed, hearing an engine on the road. He started to make his way back through the trees.

"High potency neuroleptics," he said. "What are they?"

"Antipsychotics, usually. Probably fluphenazine or haloperidol."

"Antipsychotics?" said Kett. "But they're not for recreational use, surely?"

Khan laughed, but there was a sadness to it.

"Robbie, in my experience anything can, has, and will be employed for recreational use by somebody at some point. Some antipsychotics produce feelings of anxiolysis, hypnosis or euphoria."

"Which means?"

"They chill you the fuck out and make you forget the bad stuff."

"Right."

"You can mix them with cocaine as well to amplify their effects. Risky, though. If it goes wrong, it goes very wrong."

"You don't have to tell me," said Kett, thinking of the young man's ruined face. "You need a prescription for this stuff. It's hard to get."

"Yeah," said Khan. "But where there's a will. Have your guys send over their tox report and I'll take a look, see if anything else shows up."

"Will do. Thanks, Tahoor."

"No problem. But get on top of this, Robbie. If this is what we're dealing with then you're going to have a lot more than two dead boys in your back garden."

Kett hung up, dropping onto the road to see another IRV pulling up behind the first. He didn't recognise the officer who climbed out, a balding man in his forties with thick stubble and eyebrows that met in the middle of his frowning face. He was wearing Sergeant's chevrons. He slammed the door of his car and nodded to Kett.

"I know you," he said with a thick Yorkshire accent. "Off the telly. What on earth are you doing out here?"

"DCI Robbie Kett," Kett replied.

"Aye, I said I know, sir. Sergeant Fred Patch. I work out of the Yarmouth nick. How'd you get here so quick? Usually when I ask for a detective I have to wait hours. Now I hear we've got three."

"We were close," said Kett. Patch scratched his stubbled face, looking into the woods.

"Constable Jarratt in there?" he asked.

"She is," said Kett. "She tells me this is the second dead man you've had today."

"These drugs are a nuisance," said Patch. "Got kids ODing left, right and centre. Bad enough when it's the regular shit they use, the cocaine, sometimes the heroin, but this new stuff is on a whole new level."

"You seem pretty certain it's an overdose," said Kett.

"Aye. I am."

"The pathologist is on her way out," Kett said, although he hadn't made the call yet. "I want to be sure."

Patch turned to him, his eyes dull and unfriendly.

"You do, do you?"

The man's tone did a good job of raising Kett's hackles.

"I do," he said. "Unless there's a reason you don't think we should bother?"

"Not up to me, *sir*. But you'd better run it past the Boss."

"Superintendent Clare?" he asked, and Patch sneered.

"Marshall."

"Marshall? I thought he'd retired."

"Never said he hadn't."

Patch hawked up a ball of yellow spit and launched it onto the verge. Then he walked off in the same direction, pushing into the trees. Kett had literally no idea what to say, so he didn't say anything. Besides, his phone was ringing. He looked at the screen to see that it was the Super.

"Sir," he said as he answered.

"Kett," Clare barked. "How's the boat?"

There was soft music playing behind Clare's voice, and the gentle bubbling of water.

"It's, uh, getting there," said Kett. "Duke's doing a great job."

"Well you need to be working together or there's no tossing point. I expect to see *teamwork*, and I expect to see results."

"You will, sir," said Kett. "How's your important strategy planning session going?"

"Oh, it's hard work," said Clare. "Mighty hard."

"Are those panpipes I can hear?"

"No, they're—"

"Another coconut martini, sir?" asked a softer voice.

"No!" Clare growled. The phone scuffed like the receiver had been covered, the Super's voice muffled. "Yes, and make it a big one."

"A big what?" Kett asked.

"A big load of *none of your business*," Clare replied. "Get back to it."

The line went dead and Kett laughed quietly. He called Emily Franklin but it went straight to her voicemail.

"Hey," he said. "It's Kett. Can you come out to Toltham when you get this message? We've got a body. Young man, some kind of overdose. I want to know if it looks suspicious. I'll text you the address."

"You think it looks suspicious?" asked Savage as she ducked beneath a branch and skipped onto the road beside him. Kett slid his phone into his pocket and left his hand there to try to defrost it. His fingers felt ice-cold against his leg even through the fabric of his trousers.

"I don't know," he said. "Probably not, right?"

"Probably," said Savage. "It's hard to keep up with the drug deaths here at the moment. I've never known it to be this bad. There's so much supply and so much demand." She exhaled slowly, shaking her head. "I've had a good look around. No real sign of a struggle. He's covered in scratches and bruises but they seem consistent with running through the woods then falling down that slope. I can't see any secondary prints in the mud, other than what looks like Mavis' boots and some dog prints. Seb has a gold chain around his neck and two expensive rings. If somebody mugged him they would have taken them, I think."

"No phone and no wallet, though," said Kett, remembering what Jarratt had said.

"True. That is weird. They'll know more when they search his house."

"They?" said Kett.

"Yeah, *they*," she replied. "As in *not us*, sir. Because this isn't our case."

Kett popped his lips, pushing out tiny clouds of breath.

"Does something feel weird to you?" he asked after a moment. "Something about this place?"

"You mean Jarratt? And that sergeant who almost knocked me over when I was coming out of the woods?"

"Yeah. Marshall too. I don't know, there's something..."

He stopped, seeing the smile on Savage's face.

"What?"

"You must really hate being on holiday, sir," she said. "Let it go. It's tragic, but this is way below your pay grade."

And he would have let it go, except he could still see the young woman from the hotel, he could still see the fear carved into her expression.

"There's a woman back at the lodge, I spoke to her this morning. She was worried about her boyfriend not answering his phone. Want to take a guess at his name?"

Savage's face fell.

"Oh no," she said. "Sebastian?"

"Yeah. She was... I don't know. She seemed frightened, like something terrible had happened."

"She knows something," said Savage.

Kett nodded.

"She knows something. Go get Porter, will you? I think we need to have a word with her."

IT WAS A LONGER WALK BACK than Kett had anticipated. Toltham Broad wasn't wide but it was long, and the road wove drunkenly back and forth around the various properties that edged it. The water sat to their left, barely visible through the trees. When the road began to curve to the right, heading away from Topiary Lodge, Kett pushed into the woods looking for a shortcut.

"It's getting dark, sir," said Savage as they stumbled across the marshy, root-mined ground. "Not sure I want to be stuck out here."

Kett waved her words away, but she was right. It was past three and the sun had dropped into the outstretched branches, as if the trees had offered to carry it. The wind had picked up, kicking fast-moving clouds across the sky and disturbing the surface of the lake. The water lapped at the shore with some urgency, the sound of it like somebody whispering secrets to them. Topiary Lodge waited quietly on the far shore, its lights blazing.

"Is that Duke?" asked Porter as they broke out of the trees.

Kett followed the DI's finger to see a small, distinctly un-boat-like shape drifting in the water close to the little beach. There was nobody on it, but a shape thrashed and splashed in the general vicinity. A motorboat was approaching from the direction of the hotel, two people in life vests craning over the edge.

"He can swim, can't he?" asked Kett.

"I don't know," said Porter. "He's a big guy, and muscle doesn't float."

They upped their pace, hopping onto a gravel path and following it around the sharp curve of the southwestern edge. From there it was a short and easy walk across the lawned grounds. Kett cut down the side of the lodge, reaching the little beach in time to see Duke being dragged out of the water into the rowing boat. The PC loosed a long, damp groan into the sky.

"He looks like some kind of sick, bearded manatee," said Porter, grinning. "Poor guy."

"Is he okay?" Kett yelled.

One of the men on the boat—it was Simon, Kett saw—looked up and waved.

"He's fine, I think. He just panicked when the boat flipped over."

He was using the word boat in the loosest possible sense. Already the vessel was coming apart, plastic barrels and rope drifting off in every direction.

"He wasn't in any danger," said Simon. "You can actually stand here. The lake isn't very deep."

Porter burst out laughing, the sound of it carrying over the water. Hearing it, Duke sat up. They had given him a wetsuit but he was still shivering uncontrollably, and the look he gave them was even colder. The other man in the boat engaged the engine and steered them in a clumsy circle, powering it for all of three seconds before Simon jumped out and pulled them back onto the beach.

"Sorry, Aaron," said Savage with an expression of genuine guilt.

Duke stood up, lurching out of the boat like Franken-stein. There was the sound of a camera shutter and Kett looked to see Porter taking a photo on his phone.

"Another one for the collection," he said, still grinning.

Duke said something, but his teeth were chattering too much for anyone to catch what it was. Simon clapped the big man on the back.

"It was a good effort, but building a boat on your own is hard work," the young man said. "I won't be able to pass you, sorry."

Porter put his phone away and took out his wallet, glancing over his shoulder before leaning in.

"Are you sure about that, mate?" he said quietly. Simon looked at the wallet with wide eyes.

"Aren't you all cops?" he asked.

"Not today," said Porter, fishing out a couple of twenties and handing them over. "Call it a donation for rescuing this poor, drowning sea creature."

Simon grinned, pocketing the money.

"Congratulations," he said. "You've completed the challenge."

Kett looked at Porter with an expression of disapproval.

"What, sir?" said the DI. "It's teamwork. Duke sinks the boat, Porter saves the day."

"Well, get him inside," Kett said. "Before he catches pneumonia. And lend him one of your suits."

Porter gasped, but another look from Kett kept him quiet.

"Come on, Big Guy," the DI said, taking Duke's elbow and guiding him away from the water. They squelched across the lawn, walking through the back door of the hotel. Savage stamped her feet, her arms folded tightly over her chest. Simon was walking away but Kett called him back.

"Before you go, can I ask if you know a young woman who works here? Bright purple hair, slim. Maybe early twenties. She has a ring in her nose, through the middle bit."

Simon frowned, shaking his head.

"That's... no, you must be mistaken."

"This tall," said Kett, lifting a hand to his shoulder. "She's working today. Smokes a bit of weed. Goes out with a man called Seb."

Simon took a step back like Kett had pulled out a knife, his hands up in front of his chest.

"Seb's girlfriend?"

"Yeah," said Kett. "I spoke to her this afternoon but I need to ask her a couple of questions. You know where she'll be?"

"It's impossible," he said. "That girl, her name was Niamh. Niamh Bradbury."

"*Was?*" said Savage.

"Yeah. That description is spot on. Purple hair, matching eye shadow, and she had piercings, like in her nose and stuff. We always joked it made her look like she was on a farm or something, a bull. But..."

The way the young man looked at Kett made the goose-bumps erupt on his arms, made his scalp shrink so tight he thought it might rip itself clean off his head. Kett knew exactly what the young man was going to say before he'd even opened his mouth.

"But Niamh's dead. She's been dead for months."

Simon put both hands in his hair, tugging it hard.

"I think you were talking to her ghost."

CHAPTER NINE

KETT OPENED THE BACK DOOR OF THE HOTEL AND WAS immediately embraced by a welcome hug of warm air. It did little to chase the chill from his bones, though. Simon's words had settled inside him like a gutful of ice.

I think you were talking to her ghost.

He held the door open for Savage then followed her in, happy to shut the darkening afternoon outside.

"Ghosts, sir?" she asked, one eyebrow just about hitting the ceiling.

He'd asked Simon for more information, but the kid had clammed up then bolted, claiming that he was needed elsewhere. All they had was a name.

"Niamh Bradbury," Savage said, her phone in her hands.

"Yeah."

She typed, her eyes scrolling back and forth.

"Niamh Bradbury. Twenty-two. He's right, she died late last year. Car accident."

"Let's have a look," said Kett.

Savage passed the phone over and all of the warmth of the hotel instantly evaporated.

"Holy shit," he said.

It was her, the same young woman he'd spoken to just hours ago. The photo showed Niamh standing alone against a brick wall, a large hedge beside her, her purple hair so bright it was almost glowing, the same eye shadow, the same ring through her nose. There were giant plugs in her earlobes, each bigger than a ten-pence piece and as black as coal. She wore the same black trousers and white shirt, and Kett realised that the building she was standing against had to be the building they were in right now. It was dated the 12th November.

"*Local woman killed in hit and run,*" Kett said, reading aloud. "*Tragedy struck last night as a young woman was hit and killed on the A47 near Acle. Niamh Bradbury, 22, who worked at the Topiary Lodge Spa Hotel, was last seen leaving her home on Sunday evening. Her body was found beside the notorious stretch of road early Monday morning, and it is believed that she was struck and killed whilst trying to cross it. Norfolk Police are asking anyone who was...*"

He hesitated, looking at the photo again. It was blurrier than it should have been, and that had nothing to do with the quality of the image.

"You can enlarge it, sir," said Savage.

"I don't need to."

After a second or two of squinting he passed it to her and she swiped her fingers across the screen before handing it back, the photo now much larger. He still had to push the phone away for his eyes to focus properly. He studied the woman's face, seeing past the makeup and the jewellery and the hair to the bigger cheeks, the narrower nose.

"It's not her," he said, and even though he didn't believe

in ghosts he still felt a rush of relief. "This isn't the same woman. But they are remarkably similar."

He handed the phone back to Savage and she studied it.

"Sister, maybe?" she said.

"Maybe. You remember this happening?"

"Vaguely," said Savage. "This was right in the middle of the Sweet Briar Rose case. Everything else that happened around then is just a blur. I think I saw it on the system, but it never got kicked to us."

Kett bit his lip, trying to remember exactly what the purple-haired woman had said to him earlier.

"This doesn't make sense. Simon said that Niamh Bradbury was Seb's girlfriend, right?"

"Yeah," said Savage.

"But the woman I spoke to today said the same thing. She said she was worried about her boyfriend, Seb. Surely they don't look this similar *and* have the same boyfriend?"

"Some guys have a type."

The goosebumps spread up his arms again, unpleasant and uninvited. He rubbed them away.

"I don't like this."

"Me neither," said Savage. "It's—"

The door at the end of the hall opened and Porter appeared.

"There you are. Duke's in your room, still shivering. I think we may have broken him."

"He'll be okay," said Kett. "As long as he's not in my bed. Clare anywhere?"

"Probably still having his buttocks massaged in the spa," said Porter with a shudder. "You two okay? You look weird."

"Kett saw a ghost, sir," said Savage.

Porter frowned as he walked over. Kett held up the phone.

"Have you seen her since we got here, Pete?"

"Yeah," he said, studying the screen. "She was out in the car park when we were making baskets."

He cocked his head.

"Actually, I'm not so sure. She definitely *looked* like her, though. Who is it?"

"This is Niamh Bradbury, killed by a hit and run last November."

"Shit."

"She went out with the man we found in the woods," said Savage.

"But I spoke to the other woman with purple hair this morning, who was worried about her boyfriend going missing. His name's Seb."

"Some men have a type," said Porter.

"That's what I said," said Savage.

"Either way, we need to talk to her," said Kett, handing the phone back to Savage. "But Simon, the boat guy, didn't give the impression there was another purple-haired woman working here."

Porter and Savage glanced at each other.

"What?" said Kett.

"You must really hate being on holiday, sir," said Porter, and Savage laughed.

"That's *literally* what I said."

"Great minds."

"The locals are on it," Porter said. "And if it's something more serious then Dunst can drag his wrinkly grey backside out here. Our only job for this weekend is to relax, avoid the Super, and make Duke as miserable as humanly possible."

Kett nodded, checking his watch.

"You guys know what's next on the itinerary?"

"Dinner," said Porter. "An early one. Five, I think. Then

the Boss has got some kind of surprise activity for us afterwards. He said we'd love it."

"Christ," said Kett. "You two might as well go and enjoy yourselves, then."

"What are you going to do, sir?" asked Savage.

"I'm going to hunt down our ghost."

KETT PARTED with Savage and Porter at the main staircase, waiting for them to climb up to the first floor before making his way to reception. The hotel was busier now, a queue of people waiting to speak to the flustered receptionist, the small lobby crammed with suitcases.

He walked past the breakfast room, pushing through a fire door into a quieter part of the building. A door to the right led into a small shop that boasted little more than a drinks machine, a table full of chocolate and a collection of towels, water bottles and keychains that all bore the sculpted hedge emblem of Topiary Lodge. There was nobody here, just a rather optimistic honesty box positioned by the door.

The room opposite this was locked, nothing visible through the grimy glass. So were the large double doors at the end, a keypad acting as a guardian. He knew from his earlier explorations that the kitchens were here, and sure enough, when he put his ear to the wood he heard the unmistakable chaos of working chefs.

Kett tried the door again then made his way back, cutting through the breakfast room. The outside doors were shut but he pushed the emergency escape bar and let himself into the garden. The wind found him instantly, cold fingers sliding down his sleeves, working their way into his collar. The dark clouds that had bullied the horizon had found the hotel and hung in the sky like hunting dogs.

It was too cold to walk so he broke into a run, working his way down to the deserted beach then up past the wooden huts where he'd spoken to Niamh Bradbury's doppelganger. The kitchen noises were louder here, the crash and bang of pans and the shouts of the staff. Steam billowed from the vents as he walked past the tall fencing into a small courtyard outside the kitchen door. Half a dozen large wheelie bins sat open, and a young man was struggling to heft a giant black bag into one of them. It was falling open, raining mush on his shoes.

"Fuck my life," he groaned as the bag began to turn itself inside out.

Kett took pity on him, grabbing the bin bag and helping the kid heave it over the edge. The boy looked at his clothes with an expression of profound misery, then glanced at Kett.

"Uh, thanks," he said. "You're not really, uh..."

He looked for a moment like his brain was overheating, then he turned and ran back through the door. Kett walked to the window, seeing a large commercial kitchen that was rammed with people preparing dinner. The kid scurried to the middle of the room, did a full circle, then bolted over to the sink to wash his hands. He disappeared for a minute, then came back into sight with the tall, bald man that Kett had seen earlier. The kid said something and they both turned to the window, staring at Kett.

Kett waved, then stood back, walking to the middle of the courtyard. A few seconds later the bald man walked out of the open door, bracing an elbow on the frame and taking in a deep, rattling breath. His face was wide and blunt, like underbaked dough, and his eyes were set into it like raisins.

He coughed into his hand, then pointed a yellow finger at Kett.

"I think you're lost, mate," he said in a heavy Eastern European accent, his voice thick with catarrh. He sounded like a man who'd started smoking in his crib. "Kitchen is out of bounds. Head that way and you'll find the back door."

"Actually," said Kett. "I was hoping to speak with you."

The man's eyes grew even smaller and he stepped into the courtyard. He was big, a few inches taller than Kett and wide enough to block all but a little bit of light from the kitchen. He reached into the pocket of his apron and pulled out a packet of cigarettes, a brand that Kett didn't recognise, sparking one up.

"Got nothing to say to you, or to *him*," he said. "So if you know what's good for you, fuck off."

"Is that how you speak to all your guests?" Kett said, forcing a lid onto his temper.

The man took a deep pull of the cigarette, holding it in his lungs before releasing it in a series of loose, croupy coughs. His eyes were watering so much he looked like he was crying.

"Who are you?" he asked after a moment.

Kett debated it for a moment, then pulled out his warrant card.

"DCI Robert Kett," he said. "Norfolk Constabulary."

The man's expression didn't change. He took another drag of his cigarette.

"What's *your* name?" Kett asked.

No reply, just another hacking cough.

"I'm looking for a young woman," Kett went on. "Bright purple hair, purple eye shadow, nose piercing. She was here earlier."

"No idea who you're talking about."

Kett was starting to bristle, and he had to remind himself that he wasn't on duty.

"You sure about that? I saw her talking to you."

"You sure about *that*?" the man replied. "Because I haven't seen her."

A gust of wind cut across the courtyard, hard enough to rattle the open lids of the bins and kick out a carrier bag. It jerked past Kett like it was being pulled on a string, tearing up the fence and snapping its way into the sky.

"Do you know a man called Sebastian Reilly?" Kett asked.

"I know a lot of men."

"What about Neil Enthoven?"

"Never heard of him."

"Niamh Bradbury?"

The man sucked on his cigarette again, hard enough to finish it. He crushed it beneath his black boot, grinding for far longer than he needed to. He breathed out as he looked up again, staring at Kett through the smoke.

"Like I said, I've got nothing to say to you, or to him."

"Who?" said Kett.

"If you don't know, then it's none of your business."

"You're wrong," Kett said. "I'm starting to get the impression this is definitely my business. I've asked once, I'll ask again, out of courtesy. I won't ask a third time. What's your name?"

"Call me Mantas," he said. "You want anything else, you earn it."

He turned like a tanker, one big hand grabbing the frame as if he needed to haul himself inside.

"This ain't the city, Mr Policeman. Poke your nose into things around here and somebody will cut it right off your face."

CHAPTER TEN

"Do you think we should check on him?" said Savage as she traipsed to the top of the wide, carpeted stairs. The cold had found its way into her knees, every step harder than the last.

She looked back to see that Porter wasn't listening. A number of huge paintings hung on the walls, all oiled landscapes displayed in ornate gilt frames, and he seemed lost in them.

"Why on earth would somebody want a painting that reminded them of the existence of the countryside?" he asked, catching her up. "Sorry, check on who?"

"Duke, obviously. He might have hypothermia or something."

Porter shook his head.

"It would take a polar bear to bring that guy down. He'll be fine. What are you up to now?"

Savage turned to look down the long landing, then shrugged.

"Go take a bath, read my book. Might as well enjoy the little peace and quiet we get before Clare makes us do macramé or cross-stitch or who knows what. You?"

"I have no idea," he said. "I'd go to the bar except I'm not allowed to drink."

"IVF?"

"Yeah."

"How's all that going?"

Porter waited for a man and woman to pass them along the landing. Savage could see the uncertainty in his face, the sadness that had grown a little bigger every single day in the years she'd known him.

"I don't know. Part of me thinks we shouldn't, you know? Like, if it's not meant to be, it's not meant to be."

"That's horse plop," said Savage. "The only criteria you guys need for it being meant to be is that you both want it. If you want it and Allie wants it, then it's meant to be. Everything else is just part of the process."

He smiled gently.

"You're a wise woman, Kate."

"You've only just noticed, sir?" She smiled back. "Go put your feet up and drink some fruit tea. *Without* milk. I'll see you in an hour or so."

"Sure. See you in a bit."

Savage started walking, realising that Porter was walking alongside her.

"Our rooms are in the same place," he said.

"Well, this isn't awkward at all."

They laughed, Porter holding the door open for her as they passed into the older, darker part of the hotel. They said goodbye again as Porter opened the door to his room, and Savage crossed the corridor to her own. After she'd closed the door she leant against it for a moment, breathing in that quiet, welcome unfamiliarity you always got in hotels. Other than a few distant thumps, there was no sound here at all.

If anything, it was *too* still. Against the silence, she started to see visions—Sebastian Reilly's brutally broken face, his jutting teeth, the sheer, abject terror in his eyes. It was like something from a horror film and she pushed herself away from the door to try to escape it. She walked into the bathroom and groaned aloud when she saw there was no bath. The shower head was thick with limescale and she didn't even need to turn it on to know how dreadful it would be.

Silently cursing Clare, she lay on the bed instead. The mattress appeared to be made from porridge because she sank slowly into the middle of it, the whole thing doing its best to swallow her whole. For a few seconds she stared at the badly Artexed ceiling trying to work out why her room smelled like cat sick. Then—when it started to feel a little too much like she was lying in a fabric coffin—she rolled out and walked to the chair by the window.

"Some bloody holiday this is," she said, opening her travel bag and rummaging inside until she found her book, a dog-eared Mo Hayder she'd picked up in a charity shop.

She dropped the bag to the floor and took its place on the chair, flicking through the pages until she found the corner she'd folded over. She'd barely read a paragraph when she heard a door opening—loud enough that she jumped in her seat, thinking it was her own. The sound of two people talking filtered through the wall, the conversation perfectly audible.

"Come on," said Savage, willing them to be quiet.

Her wish was granted as the conversation ended, and she'd managed another half a paragraph before she heard something else instead, just as loud and just as disturbing.

Whoever was next door was kissing.

"Come on!" Savage said.

She put the book on the floor and pushed herself out of the chair, coughing loudly to announce both her presence and the constitution of the walls. The people next door didn't notice, or care, so she grabbed the remote control and turned on the little TV, ramping the volume up.

Cursing Clare again, she turned to the window, pulling back the net curtain and staring past her reflection at the early evening. Her room was on the southern side of the hotel, and from here she could only see the edge of the car park and a partially cleared area of woodland that seemed to be a dumping ground—a swarm of bin bags surrounding two mattresses like sharks around a life raft.

The mattresses actually looked more comfortable than her own.

There was no sign of the broad from this side of the hotel, and just the smallest glimpse of the topiary hedges that patrolled the long driveway. No, the only view she had been treated to was of half a dozen cars shivering in the cold and a sickly-looking strip of woodland that stretched to the main road and—

Savage paused, using her fist to wipe away the condensation from her breath. Somebody was standing just inside the mouth of the woods, half-hidden by a tree. It was a woman, and although she was too far away to make out clearly, there was no denying the colour of her hair.

It was purple.

Savage half thought about knocking on the window and yelling for the woman to stay where she was. Something in her gut warned her not to, though. Instead, she ran for the door, scooping up her coat and pulling her phone from her pocket. She dialled Kett's number, smacking a fist on

Porter's door when she reached it. The phone rang, and rang, then went to voicemail.

"Sir," she said, hammering the door again. "It's Savage. I've just spotted the woman you spoke to before, she's out in the woods next to the car park. I'm sure it's her. Purple hair is a giveaway."

The door opened as she hung up and Porter leaned out, his phone to his ear.

"It's Kett's ghost, sir," she said. "I've just seen her."

"And...?" said Porter. "Aren't you the one who keeps telling us we're on holiday?"

Savage shrugged, bouncing impatiently on the balls of her feet. Porter rolled his eyes, speaking into the phone.

"Yeah, Allie, I've got to go. There's a ghost, apparently. I'll call you later."

They made their way back down the stairs, pushing through the dinner crowd to the deserted reception. It seemed to have dropped another ten degrees outside and the hotel's exterior lights were doing little to hold back the encroaching dark. Savage pulled her collar around her neck with trembling hands, nodding to the left of the car park.

"She was right there."

They crunched over the gravel, passing the last line of cars and a low fence to see the mattresses and the bin bags that had been left out here to rot. Beyond that was the tree-line, the space between the trunks darker than it had any right to be. Savage broke into a jog, scanning the woodland and seeing nothing.

"Check up there will you, sir?" she said to Porter, pointing towards the long drive that led to the main road. "She can't have gone far. I'll cut through the woods and meet you."

Porter grunted a reply, running up the side of the car

park. The woods were narrow, and by the looks of it they were fenced off on the other side—presumably the edge of the estate. Unless the woman had come back to the hotel, there was nowhere she could go. Still, there was no sign of her there, just that—

A flash of movement, a glimpse of a white shirt moving through the trees.

"Hey!" Savage called out, almost tripping on a bin bag as she cut past the mattresses. The ground here was overgrown, brambles hiding in the long grass, and she had to slow down as they tore at her trousers. Ahead, the woman stopped beside a tree, looking back. Savage lifted her hands like she was approaching a wild dog. "Hey, I just want to talk to you."

The feeling wasn't mutual. The woman bolted, almost turning invisible in the gloom as Savage lost sight of her bright shirt.

"Damn it," she muttered, kicking her way into the woods.

The night was already waiting here, coiled beneath the gnarled branches, under the bare, skeletal canopies. Savage stopped, holding her breath so that she could listen for the sound of footsteps, then following them. As her eyes adjusted to the dark she saw flashes of colour from the woman's hair, those bright eyes as she looked over her shoulder.

"You're not in any trouble," Savage shouted. "We just want to talk. It's about Seb."

"Leave me alone!" the woman cried back, almost a scream.

She was moving faster now, ducking beneath branches, vaulting the exposed roots. Savage struggled, tripping once and managing to halt her fall on the rough bark of a tree, then immediately tripping again and dropping hard onto her knee. The pain was unreasonably awful, filling her from her ankle to her stomach, and by the time she'd stood up again the woman had gone.

She set off gingerly, managing a limping run for a few seconds before settling for a walk. To her right she could still see the car park, and to her left the same wire fence contained the woodland. Eventually, the woman would have to come out onto the main road, and hopefully Porter would be waiting for her.

She pulled out her phone, seeing a missed call from Kett. She dialled Porter instead and he picked up straight away.

"She's coming your way, you can't miss her. Something spooked her."

"Well if I saw you running towards me at full pelt I'd probably start running too," said Porter, out of breath. "Hang on, I think she's coming. Hey!"

Savage heard his voice in the air as well as on the phone.

"Stop right there," he said.

"Don't scare her," said Savage.

"She's still moving, back towards you. Hang on."

Savage heard footsteps and readied herself, everything tense. Then Porter crashed through the trees, his phone to his ear. He looked at her and shrugged.

"Where is she?" Savage asked.

"She was right there," he replied, hanging up. "In front of me. I lost sight of her for a few seconds."

Savage circled, looking for anywhere the woman might have gone. But the trees were thin, the branches bare, and there was still enough light to pull apart any hiding place.

"She was right there," Porter said again.

"Can you check the car park, sir?" she asked.

Porter didn't reply, struggling through the undergrowth towards the cars that were visible through the thin trees. Savage went the other way, heading for the fence. It was a good eight feet tall and topped with fingers of thin wire that would be almost impossible to touch without some injury. Past it was an open meadow of short grass and muddy puddles stretching all the way to another strip of woodland. The woman couldn't have crossed it in such a short time, even if she'd managed to get over the fence.

Savage moved carefully along the length of it, heading away from the hotel. She scanned the trees, the sparse bushes, exploring the spindly canopies.

"Anything?" she shouted.

"Nothing," Porter called back.

"This doesn't make any sense," she said to herself.

She walked up a small hill, almost sliding down the other side to see the road ahead. This was fenced off too, no way through. She covered the rest of the woods as quickly as she could, past mouldering furniture and piles of discarded rubbish, before vaulting a stinking ditch into the car park. Porter stood there, shivering in his expensive overcoat and leather gloves.

"It doesn't make any sense," she said, this time to Porter. "Where the hell did she go?"

They turned to the woods together, studying them in silence for a moment.

"Maybe she really is a ghost," said Porter, his expression so serious that Savage wasn't sure if he was joking or not.

CHAPTER ELEVEN

KETT WALKED INTO THE HOTEL'S RECEPTION, RAPPING his cold knuckles on the abandoned desk. The conversation with Mantas the chef had left an unpleasant taste in his mouth and a heaviness in his gut, like something big was coiling up inside him. He knew he wasn't officially on duty here but the man's tone had been deliberately antagonistic, and the threat he'd made as he walked away was undeniable. Whoever he was, he obviously had no fear of the police.

"Hello?" he said, rapping the desk again. "Harita?"

The front door opened and a gust of freezing wind cut in, followed by Savage and then Porter. They both looked half-frozen, shivering like a pair of wind-up teeth from the joke shop.

"I got your message," said Kett. "Did you find the woman?"

Savage shook her head.

"She vanished, sir."

"Literally," said Porter, making a motion with his gloved hands like he was a magician. "Poof, gone."

"What?"

"She got away when we chased her through the woods," said Savage. "But I don't know how she did it because it's fenced off, and we pincered her. She just disappeared."

"Proper *Scooby Doo* shit," said Porter.

Kett checked his watch then knocked on the desk again, but there was no sign of life at all from the little office. The door behind him opened and a man walked in, nodding to Kett before waiting in line. He was humming a tune beneath his breath, something jaunty.

"I don't think anyone's here," Kett said to him.

"Bloody useless, aren't they?" the man replied in a heavy Welsh accent. "I think they've all buggered off on holiday themselves."

He flapped his hands like a bird then walked out again.

"Either of you seen the main office on your travels?" Kett asked. Porter and Savage shook their heads.

"Why, sir?" said Savage.

"Because I just had a run-in with a very unpleasant chef. Guy called Mantas. He was there when I saw our ghost earlier, I thought I heard them talking to each other. He denies it. I'm probably reading too much into it, but something's going on."

He rapped the desk one more time for good measure then made his way through the doors into the main corridor of the hotel.

"We've got two dead men, both poisoned by the same brand-new designer drug," he said as he walked. "Enthoven and Reilly. Reilly has two known connections to this hotel. He was dating, uh..."

He snapped his fingers, his mind suddenly blank.

"Niamh Bradbury," said Savage.

"Right, before she died. But the woman I saw this morning, the lookalike with the purple hair, said she was also dating him. I assumed she worked here but as far as we know she doesn't, and nobody seems to know who she is."

"Or wants to admit knowing her," added Savage.

Kett took the stairs two at a time, instantly regretting it. He grabbed the bannister and pulled himself up to the first floor.

"This whole thing feels off," he said.

He stopped for a moment, looking down the corridor that led to the economy rooms before walking the other way. He pushed through a fire door into a wide corridor with doors on either side. These were spaced much further apart, and each one was named rather than numbered—all after types of hedging, he noticed.

They walked along the corridor, their footsteps muffled by the thick carpet, and Kett opened the door at the far end. Beyond was another staircase, one flight returning to the ground floor with an emergency exit sign, the other heading up. A sign pointed to the executive suites and the Head Office.

"Bingo," said Kett.

"Are we allowed to be here?" Savage asked as they climbed. "I feel like a peasant who's just entered the palace."

They passed a large window that looked out over the woodland they'd just been in, the meadow beyond it bathed in twilight. A few stairs later and they walked through another door onto the top floor.

"Fancy," said Porter.

It certainly was, a crystal chandelier hanging in the wide hall, casting sparkling light on the expensive patterned wallpaper and the deep-pile carpet. One door sat to the right, three more down the corridor to their left.

"Is this where the Boss is staying?" Savage asked. "Bet his bed isn't made of wet oats and cat vomit."

"Come on," said Kett, opening the door to the right. There was a small stretch of corridor beyond, then one final door. *Office, Please Knock* was written in ornate script on the old oak. Kett knocked on it, then tried the handle. It opened slowly and noisily, as if the rusted hinges were trying to keep them out.

"Oh, hang on, wait!" came a high-pitched voice from inside. "Wait, please!"

Kett pushed the door all the way open to see a large, stark room lined with bookcases and filing cabinets. Several desks occupied the bare floor, and behind the one in the middle was a small, round man who appeared to be naked. He was doing his best to pull a buttoned shirt over his head, but in his panic he was making a pretty bad go of it, one arm through the collar and the other flailing around beneath the fabric like an irate eel.

"Wait!" he said from somewhere inside. "Oh cripes, where is the damned thing?"

He succeeded in wrenching the shirt down over his face, losing his glasses in the process.

"Sorry," he said. "I've got trousers on, look."

He stood so urgently that he cracked his knees on the desk, crashing back into his chair.

"Ow."

"Take your time," said Kett.

"You really should have knocked," said the man.

"I did," said Kett.

"Knocked and *waited*. It's just so hot in here because we're above the plant room for the spa. I end up roasting, doesn't matter what time of year it is."

The room wasn't particularly warm but the man did

seem to be excessively hot, his red cheeks damp with sweat. He was only in his early forties, but he ran a hand over hair that was maybe a month away from being called a combover, positioning his wide, gold-rimmed spectacles back onto his nose. Only then did he spread his hands over the desk and take a deep breath.

"Right," he said. "How can I help you?"

"You're Gabriel?" Kett asked, remembering what Harita in reception had told him.

"I am. Gabe Grundy, general manager. Is something wrong? Harita can help you with anything you might need, pillows or blankets, that kind of thing. She's in charge of the activities too, although I apologise that some things might have been cancelled. The parade, you know? And I think there's a storm coming. Wind's up and the water doesn't like it."

"I actually had a couple of questions," Kett said as he walked across the room. The floor groaned and creaked beneath his feet like it was ready to give way. He pulled out his warrant card and held it up. "My name is DCI Kett, Norfolk Constabulary. This is DI Pete Porter and DC Kate Savage."

Gabriel's jaw dropped so hard and so fast it almost hit the desk.

"Don't worry," Kett said, putting his warrant card away. "You're not in any trouble."

The man swallowed noisily, leaning back in his chair like he was trying to get away from them. From this angle Kett saw that he hadn't been lying, he was wearing trousers —bright green ones with a velvet sheen.

"We're actually staying here, as guests," he went on. "But it's bad timing, because there have been a couple of deaths today."

"Here?" Gabriel squeaked. "I... No, that can't be right, I would have known—"

"Not in the hotel, in the village," Kett said. "Two young men. It looks like they overdosed on a particularly nasty drug. Local police are calling it Jaw Breaker."

Gabriel folded himself forward in his chair like he was deflating, his head almost touching the desk.

"Those drugs, they're a plague. The young folk around here don't have a clue how dangerous they are." He looked up. "Who were they, the men?"

"Neil Enthoven," said Kett. Gabriel stared at him blankly. "And Sebastian Reilly."

The man flinched like somebody had slapped him.

"You knew him?" Kett asked.

"He worked here, for a little while. But that's not unusual. Most of the kids around here cut their teeth at the Topiary. Sebastian—he went by Seb, mostly—was here for a little while last year. Just a few months. Or maybe less, I'd have to check. His tenure didn't last long."

"Do you mind telling me why?"

"Hot-headed," said Gabriel. "And that's putting it mildly. He started as front of house because he was a good-looking chap, quite charismatic, if you get my drift."

Kett wasn't sure he did, but he didn't comment.

"Then there was a complaint... hang on."

Gabriel logged into the computer on his desk, his tongue poking between his small, yellow teeth like he was trying to bite it off. Kett noticed that there was another doll propped up next to the keyboard, its head made of scrunched-up paper and its body stitched from cloth. Its button eyes studied Kett.

Gabriel spun the monitor around so that everyone could

see it, navigating through a selection of files until he found the one he wanted.

Seb stared back at them, his young, handsome face untouched by the drug, his jaw unbroken. Here was a man who thought he had the whole world in front of him, Kett thought. There was nothing in his eyes except cocky, optimistic joy.

"That's it," Gabriel said, nodding. "There were a couple of complaints about him, nothing serious, just insolence, disobedience, other stuff. Thought he ran the place. So we bumped him over to the kitchens."

"Can you clarify the other stuff?" Savage asked.

"Just boy things," said Gabriel. "He tried it on with the ladies. Wasn't always happy when they said no. Never took it too far, but there were a couple of complaints of bad behaviour."

"When was this?" Savage asked, peering past Kett's shoulder.

"Early last year. He joined us in January, he'd left by March. He made the decision to leave, we didn't push him. I'd have liked to keep him on because he really was very good looking, and very charismatic, if you follow me. People like that are good to have on show. Good for morale."

"Not for the women he harassed," said Savage.

Gabriel's blush seemed to darken.

"I really must emphasise that it was just boys being boys, it was all harmless."

"And I'd like to emphasise that there's no such thing," she said.

"Do you know what he did after he left?" Kett asked.

"No idea, sorry."

"You said he worked in the kitchens for a while. Was that under your current chef, Mantas?"

Gabriel nodded.

"Can you tell me a little about Mantas?" Kett asked. "I had a run-in with him this afternoon. He's certainly *not* what you'd call charismatic."

"Yes, Mantas can be... he can get under your skin. But he's harmless. He came over from Lithuania a few years ago, used to work in the, uh, in the Kempinski in Vilnius. You've eaten here, yes?"

Kett shook his head.

"Well, you'll find out how good he is when you have dinner. I can thoroughly recommend the steak, and the oysters too, if you're into that sort of thing."

He put his fingers to his mouth for a chef's kiss.

"He's dedicated to his craft. When he first arrived here he literally brought his entire kitchen with him. I mean pots and pans, his ovens, everything but the kitchen sink, and he may even have brought that too. That's how serious a chef he is. Of course, we couldn't let him use half of it here, PAT testing regulations and all, so he ended up putting it in storage. But imagine that, carrying your own kitchen halfway around the world."

He smiled.

"Don't let him get to you, he's a bear but he's harmless. I've found many men from that region to be quite rude on the surface, but once you get to know them they're more than pleasant enough. He won't accept anything less than complete devotion to his kitchen, though. Which he sadly did not get from young Mr Reilly."

Gabriel shook his head sadly.

"Did you say Seb overdosed? I didn't even know he was into that awful poison. As much as we didn't see eye to eye, I am sorry to hear he has left us."

He made a strange motion, putting the palm of his hand

to his forehead and closing his eyes for a moment—as if trying to impersonate a mind-reader.

"Can I ask you about another member of staff?" Kett said. "Niamh Bradbury. She worked here for a little while, didn't she?"

"Oh, Niamh. You're really pulling on my heartstrings today, Detective."

He rolled his chair away from the desk and stood up. Kett was surprised to see how short he was, a good few inches below five foot tall. He walked in his stocking feet to the room's only window—a dormer in the sloping roof, and stood there for a moment, his hands clasped behind his back. His trousers were almost too bright to look at.

"She was one of my favourites," he said. "A wonderful, wonderful girl with so much going for her. She played the flute, you know? Beautifully. We offer the main room out for grade examinations and I watched her get her Grade six or seven when she was still a teenager. She was well-loved here, first in housekeeping, then front of house, and she'd just started working in the kitchen. She had a real flair for it."

He looked back.

"Why are you asking about her?"

"I know she used to date Sebastian," said Kett.

"Pft," Gabriel said. "I believe their partnership was short and inconsequential. She'd been in the hotel in one capacity or another since she was sixteen, and she was the one who asked if Seb could have a job here. I think she regretted that."

"Why?"

"Because they parted ways while they were here, and for a few weeks they had to work together. Never an easy ask. I imagine that's one of the reasons Seb decided to leave us. Niamh worked here happily for another, oh, eight or nine months I think, before that awful accident last winter."

He floated back towards the desk, his hands still behind his back.

"Did you ever catch the person who ran her over?" he asked.

"No," said Savage. "It was a hit and run, as you know."

"I hope you do."

He put his palm to his forehead again, speaking beneath his breath.

"Are you okay?" Kett asked him.

"Tired," he replied without opening his eyes. "As I'm sure you know it was the Toltham Parade last night."

"The party," said Porter, who was leaning against the wall.

"To the tourists, yes. But to the rest of us, it's Imbolc."

"You mind telling me a little more about that?" Kett said.

"What's to tell? It's the halfway point between the winter solstice and the spring equinox. It's an old pagan thing, a time of creation and hope and wonder. The plants are growing, the calves are being born. I don't know, these things used to mean something, didn't they? Before we could pop down to McDonald's for a butcher burger or whatever they're called. A quieter time, perhaps."

"What does Imbolc entail for you, Mr Grundy?"

Gabriel laughed as he climbed back into his chair.

"I'd like to say devout worship and celebration of my history and ancestors and the pagan heritage of this country. But there's not much ceremony there anymore, I must confess, just a lot of gin. I was here, if you must know. Somebody had to forego the celebrations in order to keep this place running. It's a busy night here, as you can imagine."

He nodded to the corner of the room where a little collection of bottles sat by the door.

"I was alone, before you ask."

"I'm not asking," said Kett. "Don't worry. Did anybody mention seeing Seb last night, either here or at the parade? And is there any reason he would have been in the woods north of the lake because of Imbolc?"

Gabriel shook his head.

"The whole thing takes place in town, the route runs from that god-awful new housing estate all the way up to the Church."

"Church?" asked Savage. "I haven't seen one."

"We call it our Church, but in reality it's the pub."

"One more thing, Mr Grundy, if I may?" Kett asked.

Gabriel opened his hands like a priest at the pulpit.

"Niamh Bradbury had quite a unique look. Purple hair, piercings."

"She certainly did. But we welcome individuality here."

"Is there somebody else who works here who has the same features? A young woman with purple hair, a nose ring. She's about the same age that Niamh was."

Gabriel's mouth drew in, his lips a perfectly straight line pinched between his teeth.

"Mr Grundy?" Kett said.

"I haven't seen anybody like that," the man said after a moment. "I'm sorry."

"I didn't ask you if you'd *seen* anyone, I asked you if there was somebody of that description working here?"

"No," he said. "I'm sorry. I'd had my fill of purple-haired girls after Niamh died."

He spread his hands on the desk again.

"Now do you mind terribly? I hate to ask you all to

leave, but we're very short-staffed today. It has been a nightmare."

Kett studied him for a moment, then nodded.

"Thank you for your time, Mr Grundy."

"I'll tell Mantas to look out for you all at dinner," Gabriel said. "He'll bring out something special."

"Can't wait."

Kett made his way to the door and Porter opened it for him. They walked in silence until they were back on the second-floor landing, and even then they spoke quietly.

"That wasn't just me, was it?" Kett asked.

"No, sir," said Savage. "He definitely clammed up when you mentioned Niamh's lookalike. You think he's been seeing ghosts, too?"

"Maybe," said Kett.

They fell silent when they heard the sound of footsteps climbing the stairs, then the stairwell door opened and Superintendent Clare walked out of it. He was dressed in a fluffy white dressing gown and there was an equally fluffy towel wrapped around his head. He was so busy drying his hair that he was oblivious to them as he passed.

"Sir?" Kett called out.

Clare made a noise that could only be described as a gargled scream, spinning around so fast that his dressing gown almost parted.

"Great Suffering Nora!" he roared when he'd recovered himself. "What are you three tosspots doing up here?"

"Just needed to talk to the head office, sir," Kett said. "What about you?"

"You look very relaxed, sir," said Savage.

"*Extremely* relaxed," added Porter. "Almost as if you've been to the spa."

"Well, I bloody well haven't, I'll have you know," Clare

blustered. "I... I was working outside in the cold... doing, you know, important work things and... I came back for a shower before dinner and accidentally locked myself out of my room. Ha!"

He smiled triumphantly, then pointed a long finger at them all in turn.

"Dinner's in ten minutes, so get your arses downstairs."

CHAPTER TWELVE

THE DINING HALL OF TOPIARY LODGE WAS FAR grander than it had any right to be. Located in an enormous square extension at the back of the building, it boasted a raised, circular stage in the middle of the room, decorated like a garden gazebo with fake flowers wrapped around wooden trellises. A pianist sat at a baby grand playing quietly to the two-dozen tables arranged around it. Smartly dressed diners chatted to each other, the hum of their voices strangely comforting, while staff busied themselves between the groups, trays held high. The smell of food was so intoxicating that Kett wondered if they were blowing it out through the vents.

A teenage girl greeted them as they walked inside, beaming a smile so wide it didn't look real.

"Welcome!" she said, bouncing keenly on the balls of her feet. "Have you booked with us?"

"It should be under Colin Clare," said Kett. "Table for five."

"Of course, one of your group has already arrived. This way, please."

She wove expertly around the chairs towards a table at the back. PC Duke sat there in a pinstripe suit that was obviously too small for him, his bearded face glowering. He was *still* shivering.

"Thank you," Kett said to the girl as she walked away. "Hey, Duke, how's it going?"

"I can't get warm, sir," he said, his teeth chattering. "I was in the shower for an hour and I can't get warm."

"Some food will sort you out," Porter said, sitting next to him and frowning at the suit. "Jesus, you're going to stretch it. How can it be that tight on you?"

"Because I'm not a puny weakling, sir," said Duke with the smallest of smiles.

"Puny!" Porter said, aghast.

"Put them away," said Savage as she sat down on Duke's other side. "I'm starving."

"Where's Clare?" asked Duke.

Nobody needed to answer because the Super was right there, waving away the greeter with a scowl before tramping across the room. He reached the table and eyeballed the big PC.

"Move, Duke. I can't sit with my back to the room."

"But—"

"*Now*, Constable."

Duke grumbled his way out of his chair and Clare took his place. His cheeks were still flushed, his skin almost glowing. Kett leaned in, frowning.

"There's something different about you, sir," he said. "I can't figure out what it is."

"Rubbish," said Clare, picking up the menu.

"No, Kett's right," said Savage. "You look... Oh!"

"Oh what?" said Kett. Then he saw it.

"Oh!"

"Oh *what?*" said Clare.

"Your nose, sir, they've *trimmed* it," said Savage.

"Oh yeah!" said Porter. "All the hairs have gone. I can't believe somebody was brave enough to do that."

"Those poor souls," said Savage.

"Well, it is called Topiary Lodge," said Kett. "They probably used a hedge trimmer."

Clare slammed a fist on the table hard enough to stop the hum of chatter in the room—and the piano—for a good few seconds.

"Enough!" he hissed when the diners had turned back to their food. "You will not mention my tossing nose hairs again. Is that clear?"

"They've done his ears too," said Porter, before raising his hands in surrender when Clare shot him a murderous look.

"Sorry, sir," said Savage. "You look good."

This seemed to placate him, and he turned his attention back to the menu.

"So, I hear the boat went well," he said. "Simon tells me you all put in a good amount of effort, and that you made something halfway decent."

Kett cleared his throat.

"It was mostly Duke, sir," he said.

"Good work, son," said Clare, nodding to the PC. "And good job the rest of you. Teamwork, that's what I like to see. That's what this whole trip is about."

He put down the menu and looked at Kett.

"Which is why I'm a little disappointed to hear that Dunst handed over his responsibilities to you on this double overdose. You've been out in the field?"

"Uh, well yes, sir," said Kett. "We had a little time after

the boat thing. It was literally on the other side of the lake. It seemed the right thing to do."

Clare looked like he was about to argue, then harrumphed instead.

"What did you find?"

"Another OD, sir, like you said," reported Savage. "Young man who used to work here. Seb Reilly."

"Local PC met us there, PC Sophie Jarratt. Same one we saw this morning with Wallace Marshall. She said they've been having trouble with new designer drugs out here, and this one's the worst they've seen. They've nicknamed it Jaw Breaker, although they don't know for sure what's in it. I spoke to a narcotics friend of mine and they haven't heard of it, but they think it might be heroin and coke cut with some kind of antipsychotic drug."

"Christ," said Clare.

"The other victim was Neil Enthoven, same drug. Seb showed signs of drug-induced dystonia, pretty much snapped off his own jaw."

"Horrific," said Clare. "Two men, two overdoses, in one night?"

"It's weird, sir," said Kett. "But there was the parade yesterday, the whole village was involved. Imbolc. Good chance for dealers to peddle their wares, maybe try out some new stock. Have you heard of anything like this before?"

Clare shook his head.

"But nothing surprises me," he said. "Those pricks will cut their poison with anything these days. I—"

He stopped as a teenage boy approached the table, a notepad and pen in his hands.

"Hi," he said, more of a squeak than a word. He couldn't have been older than sixteen, Kett thought, and his wide-eyed face made him look like he was being asked to feed the lions, not the customers. "Can I please take your drink order, *please*?"

"I'll have a—" Duke started, only to be cut off by Clare.

"I'd like a glass of pinot noir, please. The drier the better."

The kid wrote it down painfully slowly.

"Tea for me, please," said Kett.

"And me," said Savage.

"I guess I'll have one too," said Porter. "Something herbal. Surprise me."

"A lager for me," said Duke.

"Please," said Clare, eyeballing him.

"*Please*," echoed Duke. "*They* didn't say please."

The kid made a note of everything, which seemed to take forever.

"Are you ready for food?" he asked when he'd finished.

"Give us a few minutes," Clare said.

"*Please*," muttered Duke.

"What?" said Clare.

"What?" said Duke.

"What?" squeaked the kid, before practically running towards the kitchen.

Clare sat back in his chair, taking a deep breath.

"Dunst tells me Franklin is on her way out to look at the bodies. I'm hoping she'll come back with a conclusive ruling of accidental overdose in both cases."

"And if she doesn't?" asked Kett.

"Then—and only then—we'll take a closer look. But this isn't our case, Kett. We're working as hard as we can to shut down the dealers and the manufacturers in this part of the county. There's nothing we can do right now. So switch off your brain. Not everything you see needs to be a crime."

"Fair enough," said Kett.

He picked up the menu, his mouth watering as he took in an impressive selection of meals. By the time he'd decided what to order the kid was back at the table with a tray, the drinks clinking together in his trembling hands. Savage helped him deal them out before he dropped them.

"Mr Grundy says he's asked the kitchen to prepare our specials for you," he said, his voice an octave higher than seemed possible. "They're not on the menu, they're reserved for VIPs."

"Oh," said Clare, nodding with approval. "Very good."

"Can I have a cheeseburger?" said Duke.

"No you bloody cannot," Clare shot back. "Philistine. The specials will work fine."

Duke folded his hands over his chest with such force that some of the stitches under his arm popped.

"Duke!" Porter said. "That's a Tom Ford, you big gorilla!"

The kid's eyes widened even further, then he turned and bolted.

"So," Clare said when he'd gone. "You'll be pleased to know I want you to have a nice, relaxing evening. It can't all be work."

"Oh, good," said Savage. "I had visions of having to do—"

"There's a jigsaw competition," Clare said, interrupting her. "1,000 pieces and a prize for the winning team."

Duke threw his head back and groaned.

"Is the prize another jigsaw?" asked Porter.

"How the tossing hell would I know?" Clare said. "It's a good chance to improve your communication and organisation skills."

Duke's groan was still going.

"And I expect you to win. You're Norfolk's finest." He glanced at Duke. "Well, kind of. We mustn't let the Force down."

Kett pulled the teabag out of his cup and added milk from the jug. It wasn't the best blend in the world but it hit his stomach like a hug, chasing off the last of the chill.

"I needed that," he said.

"You're a bloody philistine too," said Clare. "Tea before dinner. It's embarrassing."

He took a delicate sip of his wine, then froze, his eyes locked on something at the front of the room. Kett followed his line of sight, taking a moment to recognise the enormous man who had just walked into the hall.

"Wallace Marshall," he said. "What's he doing here?"

The answer to that was immediately obvious as Marshall approached their table. In his hands was a large serving tray laden with food.

"Make some room," he said as he navigated the tight space like an ice breaker, forcing people to pull in their chairs. Kett cleared his cup and the menus out of the way before Wallace slammed the tray down. In the middle of it was a platter of oysters, the smell of them turning Kett's stomach. "I can see I'm dealing with a table of celebrities here. Don't see the specials come out much anymore."

"Wallace," said Clare with a polite nod.

"Colin," the man replied. "How's the holiday? Mind if I join you?"

"Actually—"

"Can you give up your seat for an old man, son?" Marshall said, putting his hands on Duke's broad shoulders.

For a second it looked like the PC was going to argue, then he huffed himself out of his chair and took the spare one next to Savage. Incredibly, even Duke looked small next to the giant ex-copper.

Marshall sat down and Kett braced himself as the sturdy wooden chair creaked beneath the sheer bulk of him.

"What are you feeding these guys?" Marshall said, looking at Duke. "This one's so big he's outgrown his suit."

"What are you doing here, Wallace?" Clare asked.

Marshall raised his hands in a show of innocence.

"What? I'm here all the time, just ask Gabriel. You met him yet? Little man in every sense of the word. But this is a nice place, the nicest place in my part of the woods."

He picked up an oyster and sucked it back in one noisy gulp, wiping his face with Kett's napkin.

"And this *is* my neck of the woods, Colin. You remember that, don't you?"

"I remember your retirement party, Wallace," Clare said, deadly serious.

Wallace's smile didn't go anywhere near his eyes. He turned to Kett, taking him in.

"Jarratt tells me you had a little wander through the trees this afternoon. A little waltz right through my crime scene."

"We were already here," said Kett. "Can't see why that would be a problem. Kid was local, you knew him?"

"Alas, yes I did. Him and Neil both. A tragic loss."

He picked up his napkin and dabbed the corners of his eyes as if there were tears there.

"I heard they were known to the police," Kett said. "Drugs."

"Oh they were harmless," Marshall said, using the napkin on his big lips before tossing it into the middle of the table. "Boys will be boys. Nothing to trouble yourself over."

"With all due respect, I'll work that out for—"

"Kett," said Clare, an unmistakable warning. "I have made it clear to my team that this is not their case. But it's not yours either, Wallace."

Wallace took another oyster, holding it in front of his face.

"I just don't want you fellas to ruin your holiday," he said. "Enjoy yourselves, enjoy the lodge, and head on home on Monday. No use getting your knickers in a twist over two unfortunate overdoses, is there?"

He tipped the oyster back, half of it dribbling down his substantial collection of chins.

"You should try them," he said after he'd tossed his shell onto the tablecloth. "Nothing beats a fresh oyster."

Nobody replied, and Marshall shrugged.

"Well, I just thought I'd pop over and say hello, see if I could be of any service. But it looks like you all got the message. Safe travels, Colin."

He pushed himself up with considerable effort, coughing wetly. Then he put his damp fingers on Kett's shoulder and squeezed hard enough for it to hurt.

"Mind how you go," he said, his loose face rising into a smile.

He squeezed again, harder still, then started back across the room. Kett watched him go, watched him stop and talk to the other diners—laughing and joking with them, clapping them on the back like an old friend, like he owned the place.

"That guy is a major creep," Savage said quietly.

"You don't know the half of it," said Clare.

Marshall reached the front of the room and Kett saw Mantas there, in his chef's clothes. The two men greeted each other with a handshake, both turning to stare at Kett's table. Mantas leaned in and whispered something, Marshall nodding. Then they walked out together.

"Do not touch the oysters," Clare said.

"Wasn't planning to," said Savage.

"What's all that about, sir?" Kett asked.

"I don't know. But it's nothing good."

The Super sighed.

"I've changed my mind. This case is officially open."

CHAPTER THIRTEEN

"It's tight on me too, you know."

Porter turned off the engine, the Mondeo rattling into the silence of the street. PC Duke sat in the passenger seat, still dressed in Porter's Tom Ford, his hands clamped between his legs in an effort to defrost them. His intense gaze was lost on something in the dark outside.

"Huh?" he said after a moment.

"I said the suit is tight on me, too. *Really* tight."

"I thought they were tailor-made?" Duke asked.

"They are," Porter said. "But that one's old and I've had major gains since then."

"Course you have," said Duke, breaking into a grin.

The PC opened his door and climbed out, the car's suspension groaning with relief.

"I bloody have," muttered Porter as he followed.

He shut the door, the sound of it echoing around the deserted street. It was the same one they'd driven up a few hours ago on their way to the lodge, lined with tired little bungalows, most of which had suffered terrible extensions over the years. *Frankenbungalows*, he thought, imagining them as victims of some terrifying experiment. Night had well and truly fallen, the sky starless.

He followed Duke to the gate of the nearest property, where Neil Enthoven's body had been found.

"Don't beat yourself up, sir," said Duke. "Gets harder when you're old."

"Old!" Porter said, almost choking. "I'm not even forty yet."

"Really?" said Duke, looking Porter up and down in surprise. "Huh."

"Huh what? I bet I could bench more than you. Is there a gym at the lodge?"

"No idea," said Duke. "But challenge accepted."

"Good," said Porter, flexing a bicep in an attempt to reassure himself. With everything that had been going on lately—the IVF, Allie's unpredictable moods, not to mention the Sweet Briar Rose case—he'd been neglecting his gym time. It was starting to show, too. The gains took years, he knew, but the losses took weeks.

"Old?" he grumbled again as he opened the front gate.

Neil Enthoven's bungalow was a lump of deeper darkness against the night. It looked like a tombstone, Porter thought as he walked down the path, the comparison more apt than he would have liked.

He waited until they'd reached the front door before pulling his torch from his pocket and clicking it on. Superintendent Clare had given them permission to be here, but he'd made it very clear they were to be discreet. He shone the light down the side of the building, and as he was turning back he heard an almighty bang from the door. Duke was there, pounding on it with his meaty fist.

"Po—" he started before Porter hushed him.

"*Discreet*," he said. "I know it's a hard concept for a man of your size and intellect to get your head around, but that means don't let the whole neighbourhood know we're here."

Duke stood back with a shrug. Porter took his place, trying the handle to find the door locked.

"We should check the back," he said.

"After you, sir," said Duke. "Age before beauty and all that."

Porter glared at him but led the way around the side of the building, one hand running along the damp pebbledash, the other shining the torch low. There was no gate but a holly tree barred the cobblestoned path with outstretched hands, almost bridging the fence and the wall. Porter squeezed past, wincing as the clawed leaves dragged themselves over his cheek.

"I hate bloody trees," he said.

Beyond the holly was another stretch of path that led past overflowing wheelie bins into a small, overgrown, dark-drenched garden. The bungalow sat quiet and still, giving away no clues as to what they might find inside it.

Porter walked to a set of patio doors and cupped his hand to the glass, but even then he was none the wiser. He tried the handle, this one locked as well. Standing back, he took a moment to consider his options, then pulled out his phone and called Dunst. Behind him, Duke sniffed wetly, the big guy still shivering.

"Pete," said Dunst when he answered the phone.

"Keith, how's it going?"

"Oh, you know, living the dream. You took a look at the OD?"

"Yeah," said Porter, studying his reflection in the dark glass and puffing out his chest. "Seb Reilly. But I'm calling about the other victim, Neil Enthoven. Did anyone work up a profile?"

"I'll check the system."

There was the sound of somebody clicking a keyboard infuriatingly slowly.

"Enthoven," said Dunst.

"Yeah."

"Neil?"

"Come on, Keith, it's bloody freezing out here."

Duke sniffed again like he was trying to drink soup through his nose.

"Enthoven's got a record, minor drug stuff. He's been in trouble since he was a teenager, went away for a little when he was nineteen, stole a couple of cars and got caught carrying weed in one. A lot of weed. Uh, seems to have kept his nose clean these last couple of years. Worked at a boat-yard over on Filby Broad. Was twenty-four as of last month."

"Known accomplices?" Porter asked.

"Two or three very small names, but nothing I'd be concerned about."

"Sebastian Reilly one of them?"

"No."

Duke sniffed again and Porter turned to him, cupping the phone.

"Can you blow your bloody nose?" he hissed.

"Me?" said Duke. "I thought that was you."

"What?"

Porter stepped past Duke, staring into the ocean of darkness that sat at the end of the garden.

Somebody sniffed.

"Fuck," said Porter, hanging up the phone. "Who's there?"

Whoever it was suddenly broke cover, a flash of shadow moving towards the fence on the right.

"Oi!" Porter yelled, no longer caring about being discreet. "Stop! Police!"

He moved fast, colliding with Duke who had also begun to run. The sniffing man was halfway over the fence now, dropping into the next garden with a thump and a groan.

"Get him," Porter yelled. "I'll go round the front."

Duke didn't so much jump over the fence as crash right through it. Porter left him to it, fighting his way past the holly bush again and bursting onto the street. He climbed into the Mondeo, starting the engine and winding down the windows. Duke was shouting from further down so he eased the car forwards, waiting for it.

He didn't have to wait long. The shadow exploded from the bushes, skidding on the path and tumbling into the road. He was up again in a heartbeat, tearing down the street with a clatter of footsteps.

Porter floored it, the Mondeo's big engine roaring. He caught up with him in seconds, braking hard to match his speed. The man glanced back, his big eyes caught in the headlights. He wasn't showing any sign of slowing down. Porter leaned out of the window.

"Go on, mate," he said. "You can do it! You can outrun a copper in a car!"

The man kept going, the sound of his breaths the loudest thing in the night.

"For fuck's sake," Porter said to himself, keeping the car at a steady six miles an hour.

Gradually the man slowed, his arms wheeling like a clockwork toy as they dropped to five miles an hour, then three until, with a roar worthy of an angry bear, Duke vaulted the bonnet of the car and took him down.

Porter cut the engine and got out, ducking onto his haunches beside the man. Duke had pinned him with one giant hand, but it didn't seem necessary. The guy looked like roadkill, his cheek on the asphalt and his tongue hanging out. His wet eyes blinked up at Porter, so bloodshot that it looked like he'd burst every single blood vessel.

"You okay?" Porter asked him.

The man opened his mouth, made a gargling noise, then vomited across the street. Porter jumped up but he was too late, sick splashing across his trousers and his shoes.

"Christ!" he said, stepping back as the man vomited again. Duke took his hand away from the man's back but left it on his shoulder, patting gently.

"Easy," said the PC. "Don't forget to breathe."

The man retched again but there couldn't have been anything left inside him. He rolled onto his back, staring at the ink-black sky. A few of the neighbours stood by their open front doors, mostly older couples, and Porter waved to them.

"It's alright," he said. "We're police."

He crouched down again, the acidic smell of sick making him feel lightheaded. The man lay in a puddle of streetlight and Porter saw that he was in his early-to-mid-twenties, his clothes crumpled and stained and his long, copper-coloured hair matted into unintentional dreads. Duke's hand was still on his shoulder, but there was nothing forceful about it. If anything, it looked like a show of compassion.

"What's your name, mate?" said Porter.

The man seemed like he was trying to rock, his body tensing and relaxing, tensing and relaxing. His hands flexed as if he was playing an invisible instrument. He stared at the sky, lost up there, sniffing wetly.

"You're not in any trouble," Porter said. "My name is

Pete. Pete Porter. I'm a policeman. I just want to make sure you're okay."

The young man angled his head around, meeting Porter's eyes for the barest fraction of a second before flitting away. His hands were working extra hard, his body still rocking.

"Can we help you up?" Porter asked. "It's cold down there."

He offered a hand. Duke did the same, and when the man didn't react they both took hold of him gently and helped him to his feet. He was obviously agitated, his head still angled up to the sky and his mouth shaping silent words. Porter's first thought was that he might be high on something, but that didn't feel quite right. He opened the back door of the Mondeo.

"Come sit in here for a minute. Is there anyone we can call for you?"

The man rocked, popping his lips the way that Kett always did. Then he reached into his pocket and pulled out a card. Duke took it from him and passed it to Porter.

"*Hi,*" he read aloud. "*My name is Joe, and I'm autistic. Please be patient with me because it can take me a while to do things.*"

He turned the card over and saw a phone number there.

"Joe, I'm going to call for some help, okay?" he said. "Take a seat, son. Duke here will turn the heat on."

He chucked the keys to Duke, who missed them completely. Then he pulled out his phone and called the number on the card. It rang three times before a woman answered, the sound of chatter so loud in the background that Porter could barely hear her.

"Hello?" he said. "Who am I talking to?"

"Val," came the answer. "Hang on, is this about Joe?"

"It is. I'm with him now. He's fine, just a little confused. My name's DI Pete Porter, Norfolk Police. You're his mum?"

There was no answer.

"Hello?" Porter said.

"I'm his gran," said Val, the sound of chatter fading. "Val Livingstone. Where is he? I'll come pick him up. I thought he was at his dad's, sorry."

"I'm on, uh..." He looked around, trying to remember. "Station Road, I think it is?"

"Oh for heaven's sake. He was at Neil's house again, wasn't he? That little... Give me five minutes. Please don't question him, he'll get upset."

The woman hung up and Porter pocketed the phone. Duke had managed to coax Joe into the back of the Mondeo, the back door open and the engine running. He was talking to him softly, and the young man was smiling. Duke looked up when he heard Porter approaching.

"He okay?" Porter asked.

"Yeah. I think so. Just a little spooked."

"To be fair, if I saw you running towards me in the dark I'd shit myself. His gran's coming to collect him."

Duke nodded, standing back to let Porter through. Porter leaned on the open door, offering Joe a smile. The young man smiled back, his eyes darting restlessly around the interior. He was drumming the tips of his fingers against each other, the sound of it like an outboard motor.

"You warming up a little?" Porter asked him, and he replied with a curt nod. "Your gran's coming. She won't be long. Can you tell me what you were doing back there in the garden?"

Joe shook his head, the speed of his fingers increasing.

"You were here to see Neil, right? Is he a friend of yours?"

Joe sniffed, then shrugged.

"No worries," said Porter.

He stood straight, looking down the road to where a pair of headlights had appeared. A little blue car accelerated with a whine, the brakes squealing as it slowed down in front of the Mondeo. It was going so fast that its bumper kissed Porter's, both cars rocking. The driver, a woman in her seventies wearing a green beanie hat and purple gloves, flapped her hands like a panicked pigeon.

"Oh! I'm so sorry!" she called from inside, reversing a little before stopping again. "I did *not* mean to do that."

"No harm done," said Porter. He walked to her door and opened it for her, taking her hand when she offered it. She was sharply dressed in a long corduroy skirt and a cardigan that matched her hat. "Val?"

"Yes. Mr Parker?"

"Porter. And it's DI."

"Oh, gosh. He's not in trouble, is he? He doesn't mean any harm, he—"

"He's fine," said Porter. "He's not in any trouble at all. We were just at the Enthoven place and he was in the garden. He bolted when he saw us, that's all. He's been sick."

"He does that when he exerts himself," Val said, looking at Porter's trousers. "I can clean them for you. Or have them dry cleaned. I can pay."

"Absolutely not," said Porter. "It's only a little bit."

He looked at the Mondeo to see Duke and Joe laughing together about something.

"While I've got you, can I just ask if you know why Joe was here?"

Val's face twisted into a look of sincere disapproval.

"It's because of Neil's Playbox or X Station or whatever the bloody things are called. Joe loves them. I won't let him have one and his dad's too broke. He comes here to play it."

"They're friends?"

"No. Neil's a... he's not a nice man, and he should know better. He..."

Val bit her lip, looking up at the same moonless sky her son was engrossed in minutes ago.

"He what?" Porter prompted.

"He makes Joe do things, as payment for the games."

"*What?*" said Porter, and Val chased her own words away with those flapping purple gloves.

"No! No, I know what you're thinking and I should have spoken more clearly. He makes Joe do *tasks* for him. Nothing sordid. At least nothing like that. Neil and the others, they're horrid little people who do horrid things, but not to my Joe. I don't want to say any more. I don't think I should."

"These things, they're not legal?" Porter asked.

"I won't say anything else. Not without a solicitor. Sorry, but I know how vulnerable Joe is, and I can't risk anything happening to him. And I know..."

She stopped, studying Porter with uncertainty.

"What's wrong?" he asked.

"I can't say, not to the police. Not to you. We have so much trouble around here."

"I can promise you, Val. I'm not after Joe. I'm not after Neil, either."

"Well you bloody should be. The man's a menace. I wish he'd..."

She stopped, her words boiling to steam in her throat,

exhaled with a fierce breath. Porter leaned in so that his words wouldn't carry.

"Val, Neil Enthoven was found dead in his house this morning."

The look of utter surprise on Val's face would have been hard to fake. Her entire body jolted as if she'd touched a live wire.

"Oh!" she said. "It wasn't... I wasn't..."

"I'm not in a position to say much, but early reports indicate that it was an accidental overdose. Do you know if Neil used any drugs, illegal or otherwise?"

Her mouth clammed up and she shook her head. Then she nodded.

"I won't say it," she said. "I won't speak ill of the dead."

"So don't say it. Just shake your head if I'm wrong. Enthoven was using drugs?"

Val didn't react.

"And he was selling them?"

Still nothing.

"And he was using Joe as a courier? An innocent face to deliver his goods?"

Val closed her eyes and bit her lips, but she didn't shake her head.

"Your grandson has done nothing wrong. I'll look after him, I promise."

"I won't say anything else, and I won't make a statement, you hear me? I won't do anything that upsets *him*."

"Upsets Joe?"

She didn't answer, letting go of a breath that seemed to last forever. There were tears in her eyes and she took off a glove to wipe them.

"This bloody village is cursed," she said, her voice shaking. "Never used to be like this. Was heaven out here when we first came. But those... those gangs out of Yarmouth, the drugs and everything else. Even the police. It's a curse. It's a cancer."

"The police?"

She looked at him again the way a mouse might study a cat. She was afraid, there was no doubt about it.

"Grammy!" said Joe from inside the Mondeo.

Val pushed past Porter and ran to the car, helping Joe climb out of it. They hugged briefly, Val's eyes never leaving Duke as if she was worried he'd scoop her up and throw her in the boot.

"Sorry," said Joe. "Sorry."

"You don't have anything to be sorry about, my darling," she said to him as she steered him to her car. "Let's get you home."

"You need anything else at all, just call," said Porter, holding out a business card that Val ignored. "And if you think of something that might help us, please get in touch. It's our job to bring them down, you know, the gangs and the bullies. It's our job to make things better."

Val spat out a laugh as she helped Joe into the car. She closed his door gently, walking around the back as if she intended to keep something between her and Porter.

"I don't believe you," she said as she clambered in. "You don't make things better at all. You make them worse."

Val put the palm of her hand to her forehead, taking a deep breath then speaking a handful of quiet words. It took her several attempts to start the engine, but even over the choking whine of it, he heard her.

"You *are* the curse. You've cursed us all."

CHAPTER FOURTEEN

NIGHT HAD FALLEN FAST, A FLICKED SWITCH. IT WAS partly to do with the clouds, Kett thought. They'd rolled in like tanks, blocking out whatever moon and starlight the evening might have offered. The road that led from the lodge to the town looked as if it had been rubbed from existence entirely, even when Kett flicked the Skoda's headlights to full beam. Toltham itself wasn't faring much better, a handful of streetlights cowering beneath the oppressive sky, looking like candles that were about to gutter out.

"Thanks, sir," Savage said, her phone to her ear. "Yeah, we'll find it."

She hung up.

"Church View. I think we just passed it."

Kett kept going until he found a side road, turning the car around and heading back. The streets were deserted, just ghostly collections of bunting and confetti dancing in the mounting wind.

"You ever heard of this Imbolc parade before?" Kett asked.

"Yeah," said Savage. "I came once, when I was a kid. Granddad brought me, he loved stuff like this. It was much smaller, from what I remember. He taught me all about the pagan traditions."

"He was a pagan?"

Savage laughed.

"No. Catholic through and through, same as Mum. But he was a copper, and he told me that religion could help people find their way, but that it also helped people *lose* their way. He said the more we understood the groundwork on which people built their lives, the better we understand why they do the things they do."

"Clever man," said Kett. "So it's a pagan festival based around the Green Man? That's a walking tree, right?"

"Not really, sir. The Green Man is a symbol of Spring, new growth and whatever. It's like Gabriel Grundy was saying, it's all about baby sheep and cows being born, spring flowers, the cycle of life."

"Imbolc's just one word for it, though? I thought I heard Harita in reception call it St Brigid's Day."

He spotted the right road and made the turn. There didn't seem to be any houses here at all, just hedges and fields.

"Kind of. Brigid was the Celtic goddess of fire and fertility. The Christians poached her, like they did all the old gods. Made her a patron saint."

"Pagan," Kett mulled. "That's all sacrifices and stuff, right? The Wicker Man? Might it be connected to our two dead guys?"

"No, sir," Savage said. "Well, I mean yes. But it's not explicitly linked to this particular festival. Imbolc literally means in the belly of the mother. It's about birth, not death."

"Your granddad taught you that too?"

Savage laughed.

"Checked Wikipedia before we left, sir, just in case anything came up. That's it, I think."

She was pointing to a low, narrow structure that sat right on the edge of the road. It might once have been a brick outbuilding or some stables, but the windows looked brand new and there was a vent for a combination boiler spewing steam into the cold air. Kett spotted a small driveway almost completely hidden by laurel hedging and he pulled the Skoda into it. There wasn't quite enough room to park behind the ancient, wheel-less caravan that blocked the gravel drive so he left his hazards on to warn anyone else who might drive past.

"Seb lived here with his mum and dad," Savage said as she opened her door, shivering in a sudden blast of cold. "Clare says they've already been told about his death. Dad ID'd the body."

Kett hesitated, wondering if he should start the engine and drive away. The Reilly family had been through enough today, hadn't they? And there was every chance that PC Jarratt or one of the local constables had already questioned them.

"Sir?"

But this case was scratching at Kett's nerves. It wasn't just the two dead men, it was everything—Wallace Marshall, the drugs, and of course their mysterious purple-haired ghost.

He got out, pulling the collar of his overcoat tight. There were no doors on the narrow side of the building, and none on the road, so he squeezed past the caravan and saw an oak porch ahead, decorated with the skeletal remains of what might once have been a wisteria. Past that was a door that glowed with welcome light. Kett walked over and gently knocked.

"Green Man," said Savage. She pointed to a wooden mask that had been fixed to the post of the porch, a face made from leaves and branches, more vegetation spewing from its mouth. Even though the carving was crude, the eyes were wild and full of a mad terror that seemed far too realistic.

"A walking tree, then?" Kett said.

A dark shape appeared in the door, hesitated for a moment, then spoke.

"Hello?"

The voice was high, and Kett wasn't sure if it belonged to a man or a woman.

"I'm sorry to bother you. My name is Detective Chief Inspector Robert Kett, from the Norfolk Constabulary. I'm with DC Kate Savage. Do you have a couple of minutes to answer some questions?"

The shape moved, sliding back at least four bolts and turning a key. The door opened and a man's face appeared in the gap. He was desperately thin, his dark hair almost gone and his eyes set so deep in his skull that he looked like a Halloween decoration. He pulled his dressing gown tight around his scrawny neck, every bone seeming to rattle in the cold. He took a moment to study Kett and Savage, then opened the door fully.

"You'd better come in, I suppose."

He stood to one side and Kett followed Savage into a small entrance hall that was absolutely packed with china dolls. There had to have been a hundred of them, stacked on the small sofa opposite the front door, crushed together on the window ledge and the shelves, even piled on the floor.

They were all shapes and sizes, wearing an infinite array of costumes, but Kett swore they were all looking right at him. The thought of it made a shudder run all the way from his stomach to his scalp.

The man closed the door and took a slow, deep breath. He wasn't tall, and he looked smaller still because he stood like a broken pole. Kett wondered if he had something wrong with his back because when he looked at them he had to twist his neck at a strange angle.

"Do you know any more?" he asked.

"Can I start by checking what you know already?" asked Kett. "You spoke to..."

"Wallace, yes," the man said. "He's not long gone, which is why I was surprised to see you two at the door."

"As you know, Wallace Marshall is retired," Kett said.

"But he's a neighbour. He's a friend. He knew Seb. He's promised me he'll find whoever did this to him."

"Whoever *did* this to him?" Savage asked. The man looked at her, a flash of anger passing over his skeletal face.

"Whoever gave him the drugs," he said. "Whoever *made* him kill himself."

"Is there somewhere more comfortable we could talk, Mr..."

The man cleared a throat that was thick with phlegm.

"Thomas Reilly. Tom."

He gestured for them to follow, leading them through a door on the right into a pokey kitchen that smelled strongly of something pungent but not unpleasant. He pulled a chair away from a dining table and folded himself painfully into it, his legs splayed out. There were more dolls in here, maybe a dozen of them. These ones were all naked, and some were in the process of being dismantled.

"Sage," Tom said, waving a hand through the air. "My wife. She burns it."

"Is she here?" asked Kett.

"Asleep. And no, I won't wake her. She's ruined. Seb was the light of her life, our only child. I don't know what she'll do now. How do you go on after this? How do you go on living after they're gone?"

"I am truly sorry for your loss," said Kett as he took a seat opposite Tom. There were dolls on the other two chairs so Savage hovered by his shoulder. "We're just following up, so I apologise if we ask you some questions you've already answered. Seb lived here with you and your wife?"

"Yes. Well, sort of. There's no room in this shithole so he slept outside in the caravan. Lived in it, really, just came in to use the toilet and the bath, to eat."

"What did he do for work?"

"Bugger all," said Tom. "Flitted from one thing to the next like he didn't have a care in the world. Which he didn't, because Gemma gives him everything he asks for."

"Gemma is your wife?" asked Savage. He sneered.

"In name only. She does piss all for me anymore. Doesn't cook, doesn't clean, and she *certainly* doesn't fulfil her marital debts. Not for years. She gives these dollies more love than she gives me, them and the Greenies."

"Greenies?"

"Her fucking Green Man club. You must have seen the mess they make. Spend the whole fucking year building up to their parade, then nobody can be arsed to sweep up all the litter."

"You weren't at the parade?"

"Fuck no."

"What about Seb?" asked Kett. "Did he go?"

Tom shrugged, his shoulders almost touching his ears.

"Probably. He weren't into the festival shit but he liked a party."

"He didn't mention who he might have gone with? Any friends?"

Tom shrugged again.

"I've seen a few pagan icons around the village, seems quite popular," Savage said.

"They're pointless, pathetic. No wonder their kind died out so long ago."

"Their kind?" Savage said.

"Fucking *Celts*."

"Was Seb part of it?" asked Kett, and Tom shook his head.

"More sense, for all the good it did him. Gabriel Grundy, up at the hotel, he tried to brainwash him or whatever it was they did, but my boy was too smart for that little prick. God knows what else he tried to make him do."

"This is when Seb worked at Topiary Lodge?"

"Yeah. Good job, even with that runt in charge. But Seb fucked that up too. A friend of his sorted out a position for him last year but he didn't have the stamina for it. Gave him the boot after a few weeks."

"That friend was Niamh Bradbury?"

Tom nodded, staring at the table.

"They dated for a while, didn't they?"

"Is that a crime?" the man asked.

"No. What about after that?"

Tom frowned, swallowing. His Adam's apple was so enormous it looked like a fist had been clenched inside his throat.

"He tried the local over Reepham way but he didn't

even last a night there before some punter tried to chin him. He always was more mouth than anything else, always giving it some. Then he went up to Filby, worked on the boats."

"Did he know a man there called Neil Enthoven?" Savage asked.

"No idea. He quit there too, but I don't think he told me if he got another job. Must have, though."

"Because he had money?" Kett said.

"Yeah. He was loaded. More than what Gemma gave him."

"Cash?"

Tom nodded, then squinted at Kett.

"Why? Wally didn't ask me any of this. What does it matter?"

"It might not," said Kett, leaning forwards. "Mr Reilly, did Wallace tell you how Seb died?"

Tom swallowed again, another flash of pain crossing his face.

"It was them drugs."

"You were aware that Seb used drugs?" Kett said.

"He was a fucking kid. Course he did. They all do around here. You can't walk down the fucking street anymore without tripping over some junkie shithead."

Tom jabbed the table with his finger.

"You see them all the time, dealers. All *European*." He spat the word out like it tasted bad. "And the kids don't know how to say no. Aren't allowed to say no. They practically have it shovelled down their throats. I thought I'd brought Seb up smarter than that, I thought I'd told him never to touch the drugs, but there's only so much you can do, isn't there? And with his soft as shit mum, he didn't stand a chance."

He poked the table again, this time without much strength.

"Giving kids drugs is akin to murdering 'em, isn't it? Somebody killed my boy, pure and simple. Wally said he'll find him, then we'll see."

His thin lips opened into one of the least pleasant smiles Kett had ever seen, as joyless as the dolls around him.

"We'll see what happens to those drug dealing pricks."

"Mr Reilly," Kett said. "Was there ever any indication that Seb might have been *dealing* drugs? Was he ever involved with any of the gangs?"

Tom fixed Kett a look that seemed to boil.

"Never."

Somebody called out from another part of the house, a feeble cry. Tom put a long-fingered hand to his face as if he was trying to hide from the world.

"You should go," he said.

"We will," Kett replied as he stood. "Can I just ask one more thing? Seb's caravan, do you mind if we take a look?"

"Can't stop you. Got no lock on the door. But Wally's already been in there. He took a bunch of stuff with him when he left. Evidence against whatever cunt did this to him."

He shoved both of his long arms out like he was trying to use telekinesis to push them out of the room. Savage went first, opening the front door for Kett. He passed Tom a card before he went.

"I know you trust Wallace. I know he's a neighbour and a friend. But if you think of anything else then you really need to call us. Okay?"

Tom looked at the card, but he didn't take it.

"Like that's ever going to happen," he said as he closed

the door. The turning key sounded like a revolver being cocked, then the bolts slid back into place like gunshots.

"Can't imagine why his wife doesn't love him anymore," said Savage as they crossed the gravel drive again. "He was delightful."

"He was. But I'd still rather be in a room with him than with all those dolls."

They shuddered together as they approached the caravan. Calling it a two-berth would be generous, it was barely longer than a car and only a few inches taller than Kett. The wheels weren't the only thing that was missing. The side window had been smashed, the opening sealed with what looked like insulating foil. It chattered in the wind like distant cymbals. When Savage tried the door it opened reluctantly, and it quickly became apparent why. It *stank* in there.

"Whoa," said Savage, one hand to her mouth. "What *is* that?"

She walked in and Kett followed, inhaling the cold, damp air. He took a couple of tentative sniffs as he switched on the torch on his phone.

"That, Kate, is what a teenage boy smells like. Old laundry, unwashed bedding and some kind of Lynx deodorant."

"It's *horrible*. And he wasn't even a teenager, he was twenty-two."

There was barely room for them both inside, partly because the caravan was so small and partly because it was packed with clutter. The small seating area at the far end was a shrine of clothes, expensive trainers scattered like mousetraps. Savage did her best to step between them but it was hopeless in the dark.

"Hang on," she said.

There was a click and the caravan filled with soft, red

light. It was a *Star Wars* lamp, Kett saw, made to look like a short lightsaber. It was the only thing in sight that belonged to a child. Everything else was cigarette packets, beer bottles and a couple of dog-eared *Playboys* next to what might have been the bed.

"I don't know a teenage boy alive who reads smutty magazines," Kett said. "Not when they own a Smart Phone."

"You think somebody else was staying here?"

He didn't answer, pulling a pen from his pocket and using it to probe the piles of paperwork that sat on the counter and in the sink. Most of it was fliers for various pizza places and cab companies—almost exclusively in Yarmouth. But there were bills and bank statements too.

"He was broke, according to this," Kett said, tapping a letter from the bank. "Overdraft maxed out, this was a couple of months ago."

"Maybe he spent it all on these," Savage said, pointing to a bowl that was full of gold. "Couple of pricey watches in here, chains, rings. Or he might have nicked them. Not sure what he'd want with a woman's bracelet."

Kett beamed his light into the open cupboards, finding a single can of beans and three packets of green Rizla papers. There were empty bottles in the space beneath the sink, all of them cheap vodka.

"I can't believe his parents let him live like this," Savage said.

"He was an adult."

"Passing eighteen does *not* make you an adult," Savage said. "I don't care what the law says. He was still a kid."

Kett peeked into a toilet that had probably never been cleaned.

"This is hopeless," he said. "If Marshall was here then

he'll have taken anything useful, and anything incriminating."

"Incriminating, sir? You don't trust him?"

"Do *you*?" Kett spluttered. "I've met some bent coppers in my time but he's got all the alarm bells ringing. I wouldn't trust him as far as I could throw him, and he's a *big* guy so I couldn't throw him far."

Savage was rummaging through the clothes on the sofa, her face screwed up with disgust.

"Don't touch the socks," said Kett. "Whatever you do, don't touch the socks."

He checked the cupboards again, just to be sure, before tripping his way over the sea of trainers and heading for the door. He hesitated before leaving, doubling back and opening the little oven. It was pristine inside, as if it had never been used, and sitting on the shelf was a large book.

"You didn't bring any gloves, did you?" he asked.

"Sorry sir, I thought we were on holiday."

It wasn't a crime scene, so he pulled out the book and set it down on the counter. It was a photo album, he saw when he opened it. The first photos showed Seb when he was much younger, hanging out with friends, all bright eyes and wide smiles. Kett recognised one of the girls immediately, even though her hair was blonde.

"That's Niamh Bradbury."

He kept going, watching Seb as he aged—sixteen, in his school uniform, seventeen next to a learner's car holding a certificate, eighteen looking as drunk as a skunk at his birthday party, then in his twenties. Niamh was in another handful of photos, two of which showed Seb with his arms around her shoulder, pulling her tight. The next photo showed Seb in his work uniform at Topiary Lodge, pretending to have sex with a hedge shaped like a chicken.

Kett kept turning the pages, seeing the gaps where a couple of photos had been removed. Towards the middle of the book the photos dried out, Seb's face darker, his smile gone. It reminded Kett of photos he'd seen of young soldiers, how different they looked when they came home.

"Anything?" Savage asked.

"No. Somebody's been through it already. You?"

"You kind of put me off when you mentioned the socks," she said, gingerly exploring the laundry pile. "There's not... Hang on, *oh God!*"

She staggered back so fast she hit the wall, slapping her hands against her legs as if to remove something toxic.

"Oh God, there's somebody in there."

"*What?*" said Kett.

"I felt them. I felt their hair."

Kett kicked the shoes out of his way, holding up the torch to get a better look at the pile of clothes. It took him a moment to see it, but Savage was right, there was definitely hair amongst the fabric.

Purple hair.

"Hang on," said Kett, leaning in. "It's shiny. I don't think it's real."

He moved the light closer, following the hair and seeing the mesh that it was connected to. Pinching it between his fingers, he gently pulled.

"It's a wig," he said, holding it up.

"Thank God," Savage said, one hand to her chest. "I honestly thought... Wait, purple?"

"Like our ghost," said Kett. "Although this isn't as dark."

"Why on earth would Seb have that?"

Kett didn't have an answer, and even if he did, he wouldn't have been able to voice it. The sound of the

Mexican Hat Dance filled the caravan and he lifted his phone, squinting at the screen.

"Boss," he said as he answered it. "I think we've still got a little while before the jigsaw competition."

"I'm not calling about that, Kett," said Clare. "Franklin's here, and she's not happy."

"Is she ever?" Kett said when he realised Clare had hung up. He turned to Savage. "Let's go."

CHAPTER FIFTEEN

Topiary Lodge's large car park had lost over half its vehicles in the time they'd been away, and the building itself seemed to have shrunk in the dark, appearing small and abandoned. When Kett walked into reception, though, he found it was busier than ever. Harita stood behind the desk, her hair almost completely shaken loose from its ponytail and her brow concertinaed with fatigue. Four people were talking to her at once, all raised voices and pointing fingers.

"Hey," Kett said in his best DCI growl.

Silence fell like a guillotine blade, everyone turning to look at him.

"One at a time, and be polite. If you can't manage that, go home."

The people funnelled themselves into a line, all of them studying the ancient carpet like they'd dropped their keys there. Harita pressed her hands together like she was praying, mouthing *Thank you* to Kett. He nodded back as he made his way into the main corridor. He caught Savage smiling at him.

"What?"

"Sometimes, sir, I really like you."

He laughed.

"You see the Superintendent anywhere?"

"No, but I can hear him."

She was right. Clare's angry voice was tramping down the corridor from somewhere to their left, rising above the general hum of hotel noise. It was coming from a large side room, and when Kett opened the door he saw the Superintendent sitting at one of a dozen tables that had been arranged in the space. He was wearing green corduroy trousers and a brown turtleneck jumper that made him look like some kind of gangly sea turtle.

Porter and Duke sat beside him, the DI checking something on his phone and the PC picking his nose. Franklin stood next to her chair, her hands braced on the tabletop. She was wearing denim dungarees over a jumper that seemed to be decorated with rainbow-coloured sloths, and her face was deadly serious.

There was no denying that they looked like an odd group of people.

"Did you get lost?" Clare barked.

"No, sir," Kett said as he walked over. "We were at Seb Reilly's house. Hi, Franklin. How's things?"

"She's annoyed because I didn't bring her on holiday," Clare said.

"You *really* don't want to be on this holiday," mumbled Porter.

"I'm not annoyed," she said. "This is *not* my annoyed face, okay? This is my *I don't like being out in the cold* face. This is my *I'd have been happy never knowing this part of Norfolk existed* face. It's my..." She licked her lips, deep in thought. "It's my *slightly freaked out* face, if you really want to know."

"Sit," said Clare, like he was talking to a dog. It took Kett a moment to realise he was talking to him, and he walked around the table and pulled out the chair next to Duke. Savage sat on Porter's other side, all of them looking at Franklin as she pushed herself up and began to pace.

"So," she said. "First things first. Local plods were not happy about me being here. I didn't think they were even going to let me see the body at first. What's that about?"

"I'm not sure yet," said Clare. "It's probably just a pissing contest because we're city police."

"Yes, from the heaving urban metropolis that is Norwich," said Franklin, as dry as always. She peered at Clare, her frown deepening. "Why do you look different, sir?"

"Nose hairs," said Kett.

"Oh, yeah. Wow."

Clare clamped a hand to his face, speaking through his fingers.

"Stop looking at me. What did you find?"

"I haven't seen the first body yet, but I made a preliminary examination of Sebastian Reilly. It's nasty, and some of what I'm about to say is pure speculation until I can take a look inside and until we get the tox screen back. I've honestly never seen anything like this before."

She reached into the breast pocket of her dungarees and pulled out a notepad.

"Sebastian Reilly, twenty-two. Fit and healthy male, no pre-existing illnesses or medical conditions that were immediately apparent. Cause of death seems to be—and I say again, I won't know for sure until I get him onto the table—a stroke caused by cerebral vascular insufficiency."

"No blood to his brain," said Savage, and Franklin nodded.

"Reilly exhibits signs of acute dystonia. It's a neurological hyperkinetic movement disorder characterised by involuntary sustained muscular contractions. At its worst it can be excruciating, it can twist your body like a wrung towel. You'll have to check and make sure he hadn't been diagnosed with it."

"He hadn't," said Clare.

"And nobody I've spoken to has mentioned him having any kind of involuntary muscle movements or spasms," Kett added.

"Then we're looking at Drug-Induced Dystonia. Reilly took something that caused him to lose control of his movements. This was, primarily, oromandibular. His jaw was fractured, with no signs at all of outward force or injury, and no damage to his teeth, which almost certainly rules out any attack from another person. His tongue was also torn at its root from continuous straining, the tip bitten off. His right shoulder is dislocated, and I'm pretty sure both his ankles are broken. At the very least, sprained. He has cuts and contusions over his body, most likely caused by contact with the ground during sustained spasms, from running through the trees, and possibly from rolling down the hill where he was found."

"Jesus," said Porter. Savage sat back in her chair, shaking her head in disbelief.

"He vacated himself entirely," Franklin went on. "A complete loss of control. And there may be more, but it will have to wait. But the cause of death seems to be a blocked or ruptured artery leading to his brain. With no sign of external force, I can only assume that one of his movements was so severe that he literally ripped a hole in it."

"There's really a drug that can do this to somebody?" Savage asked.

"I've never heard of a reaction this severe," Franklin said. "But yes, neuroleptics have been known to induce dystonia. If they were cut with cocaine, heroin and God knows what else, anything is possible."

"Tox report will be with us tomorrow," said Clare. "Time of death?"

"Between nine and eleven yesterday evening. I'm erring towards earlier rather than later because of the insect activity."

"Smack bang in the middle of the parade," said Kett.

"Pending more evidence, I would have ruled this as an accidental overdose," Franklin went on. "A catastrophic reaction to a potent mix of chemicals. It feels like it should be a freak accident. Except we know it's not."

"Because of Neil Enthoven," said Kett.

"Exactly. I haven't seen his body yet. I'm not even sure where they've sent it. But the paramedic report details an almost identical set of injuries. Two men dead from the same drug. You've either got a very lethal batch of poison out there on the streets, or—"

"Or somebody did this to them deliberately," said Kett.

Franklin nodded.

"We'll know more when we find out exactly what they took," she said. "And how they took it. Seb had residue around his nostrils but I'll have to check him for track marks and signs of ingestion too. Killing somebody like this, it's risky and it's unpredictable. Drugs have different effects on different people, which makes it extremely difficult to plan a murder this way. My guess is that somebody cut their heroin with some antipsychotics just to see what would happen, and our dead men were the unlucky guinea pigs who found out."

"Anything else?" Clare asked.

"Was that not enough for you?"

"Kett? You?"

"Uh, Savage and I checked out Seb's place. Nothing much to report except we found a wig in his caravan. Purple."

"So?" spat Clare.

"It might be nothing, sir. But Niamh Bradbury had purple hair, and so does the woman we've been chasing around the hotel all day. It's a link."

Clare's expression didn't seem to agree. He turned to Porter.

"You?"

"Duke and I tried Enthoven's place, we found a man there called Joe. He's autistic, quite severely, I think. His gran picked him up, told us—without actually telling us—that Enthoven was a dealer, and that he got Joe to do his deliveries for him in return for some *Call of Duty* time. I don't think Joe really knew what he was doing. His gran seemed to have a real distrust of the police."

"Did she mention Marshall?" said Clare.

"Not by name. But she called us a cancer."

"Nice," said Kett. "Where's Joe now?"

"Home, with his gran," said Porter. "But we have their details. If we question him, you should ask Duke to be in the room. He was good with him."

"Yeah?" said Kett.

"My kid brother's autistic," the PC said.

"Never knew that."

"You never asked," he said. "Joe's a nice guy. In the car, he told me Neil had a few other friends who used to hang out in the house. I asked him to describe them. One of them was blond, fit, could have been Seb."

"Why didn't you tell me any of this?" Porter said, lifting his hands.

"You never asked!"

"Bloody hell," said Porter. "What else did he say?"

"He said he didn't like you much because you shouted at him. He said there were four of them in the house, usually, not including him. Neil, two other guys he didn't want to name, and a girl called Catherine. All local kids."

"So it looks like Enthoven was dealing," said Porter. "And that he had a small crew. Seb Reilly might have been a part of it. We'd know more if we could get inside Neil's house."

"I don't think that will help us much," said Kett. "Marshall was in there this morning, and he raided Seb's caravan this afternoon. Took a bunch of stuff with him."

"He *what?*" said Clare. "That's not just crossing the line, that's tossing all over it. I don't care who he is, the law's the law."

"You think he's involved in some way, sir?" Savage asked.

"I won't think bad of any copper until we have proof," Clare replied. "But this is dodgy as all hell. Leave Marshall to me, there are people I can call. No luck on IDing this other woman? The one who said she was Seb's girlfriend? You think it's this Catherine?"

"I don't know," said Kett. "But according to Seb's dad, he didn't have a girlfriend. He—"

The door opened and they all turned to see Rachel Turkentine poke her head into the room. She immediately broke into a smile.

"Oh, it's you lot! Can't keep you away from the fun stuff, can we?"

She braced the door with her hip, trying to manoeuvre a trolley through the gap. Porter was out of his seat in the blink of an eye, holding the door for her.

"Thanks!" she said as she pushed the trolley inside. It was literally heaving with boxed jigsaw puzzles. "You're the first team here, so you get first pick. Team of six?"

"Five," said Franklin, putting her notepad back in her pocket.

"Six," growled Clare.

"Oh no."

"Oh yes. We need as many eyes and fingers on this as possible. Sit down, Franklin, that's an order."

She slumped in her chair and Kett gave her a sympathetic look.

"We need something with lots of contrast," Clare said as Porter studied the jigsaws. "Nothing with a limited colour scheme or repeat patterns. And no cats."

"Got it," said Porter, snatching one up. As he walked back over, the door opened again and a group of people walked in, chattering excitedly.

"Jigsaws?" one of them asked.

"Come on in!" Rachel said. "Find a table, we've got plenty of room."

Porter dropped the box on the table and Clare's eyes just about popped out of his head.

"Penguins?" he roared. "What's wrong with you, Porter?"

"You said no cats!"

"I said nothing with a limited colour scheme, you great dolt!"

"This has got plenty of... black," Porter said, studying the box. "And... white."

Clare slapped his hand to his forehead, then stood up.

"Can we swap?"

"Um, no, sorry," said Rachel with an apologetic smile. "Topiary rules."

Clare slumped back down, fuming. Duke was grinning, happy to be out of Clare's bad books for once.

"They've all got yellow beaks," Porter muttered.

"Can I interest anyone in a raffle ticket while we're waiting?" Rachel said. "Some great prizes, including a hamper."

"There is no time for raffles," Clare said, and she held up her hands defensively as if he was coming at her with a bat.

The room filled up fast, the average age of most of the teams far greater than their own.

"Okay," said Rachel when everyone had settled down. "I would explain the rules but I think everyone here knows how to do a jigsaw!"

"Apart from Porter, apparently," said Clare.

"You've all got a 1,000-piece set. First team to complete it wins a prize. Ready, steady... go!"

"Go!" echoed Clare, making everyone on the table jump.

Kett grabbed the box and worked off the lid, tearing open the bag inside and tipping the pieces onto the table.

"Edges! Corners!" Clare spat. "There's one!"

He reached for it at the same time as Duke, slapping the PC's hand away with some force.

"Ow!" said Duke.

Clare positioned the piece on the table with a triumphant smile.

"One down. 999 to go. Come on, move!"

"They all look the same," whined Porter.

"Everything okay?" Rachel asked, hovering by the table. "Remember, it's just a bit of fun, like the baskets."

"Ignore her," said Clare. "It's not fun, it's teamwork. I want us to win."

Kett found a few edges, arranging them where he thought they might go. But Porter really had made life difficult for them because there were at least a hundred different penguins in the puzzle and they all looked identical. To make it worse, he had to hold them at arm's length to make any sense of what was on them.

"Penguin?" he asked Savage, holding a piece up to her.

"Rock, sir," she said. "I definitely think you need those glasses."

"I do not." He threw the piece back in the pile. "Sir, you mentioned Marshall left the Force under a cloud. Do you know what happened?"

Clare jammed two pieces together and immediately pulled them apart.

"Tossknobs," he said. "Honestly, nobody knows what happened. He was leading a major investigation into organised crime in the county back in the early Naughties, an Albanian outfit that had moved up from London. That's upside down, Duke, even I can see that. There was supposed to be a raid on their processing plant, a huge operation, and it all went tits up. They knew we were coming. A young PC lost her life and two more were seriously injured. Duke! *Upside-tossing-down!*"

Duke was flustered, his hands too big for the tiny pieces. One pinged out from between his fingers and he bent down to pick it up, cracking his head on the table on the way back up and making all the pieces jump.

"Christ," said Clare. "It's like watching Big Foot try to tie his shoelaces."

The Super slotted another piece into place, tapping it gently. Kett did the same, Savage adding to his little line of dancing penguins.

"This was before I joined Norfolk," Clare went on. "But I was working with the NCA at the time, we knew about the gang and we were helping coordinate the raid. It was pretty clear to us that somebody on the Force was in their pocket and tipped them off. There was an enquiry which came up with toss all, but shortly after that Marshall handed in his notice. Too young to retire, too hot-headed as well. He didn't jump, he was pushed."

"To keep it quiet," said Kett.

"That's what I think. An honourable discharge in return for I don't know what. That's always the way of it. There are rumours, of course, but we'll never know the truth."

"What were the rumours?" asked Savage.

"You can guess."

"That he got a pay-out from the Albanians in return for providing police intel."

"You didn't hear that from me," said Clare. "And you do *not* repeat it."

Savage nodded, frowning at her pieces.

"There is a *lot* of snow in this puzzle."

"Fun fact," said Franklin, studying the piece in her hand. "A group of penguins on the water is called a raft, but a group of penguins on land is called a waddle."

"Not relevant," said Clare.

"I think it's pretty relevant," she shot back. "Another fun fact. Penguins poop every twenty minutes."

Clare seemed to gargle with fury.

"Can anyone see the penguin with the clown costume

on?" he said, pointing to the lid. "This one. It's the only one with any colour. If we can get this one down we can work around it."

Nobody replied. There was no sign of it anywhere.

Clare gargled again, his face turning a colour that could only be described as puce.

"Hang on," said Savage, lifting the lid. A handful of pieces were scattered there and she used the flat of her hand to scoop them into the pile. "There," she said, lifting one with a brightly dressed penguin clown. "It was hiding."

She frowned.

"Hiding," she said, looking at Porter.

"What is it?" Kett asked.

"When Porter and I were chasing the ghost, she disappeared. There was literally nowhere she could have gone."

"Not tossing relevant, Savage," said Clare, snatching the piece from her.

"Unless she was hiding."

"You checked the trees," Porter said. "The fence. Where could she have hidden?"

Savage lifted the box again.

"Underground?"

"Listen to me," said Clare. "All of you. This may be the single most important thing I've ever said to you. We will win this jigsaw competition, as a team. We will complete our puzzle before anyone else. We, the combined minds of the Norfolk Constabulary's Extreme Crime Task Force, the *crème de la crème* of this county's supreme policing outfit, will be victorious in this challenge. Because if we aren't, then you're all out of a job."

"I'm not sure you can—" Kett started, and Clare shot him down with a look.

"Try me. We cannot, and we must not, lose."

CHAPTER SIXTEEN

THEY CAME LAST.

And it wasn't even close.

A table of stout, serious women near the door finished after less than an hour, claiming their prize—the jigsaw they'd completed and a £25 voucher for the restaurant—with a quiet smugness that made Kett think they'd won this competition many times before. Superintendent Clare showed no such restraint, his curses increasing in both volume and complexity as one by one the other tables completed their puzzles.

"You can probably throw in the towel now," said Rachel when they were the only people left in the room, their jigsaw barely half-finished even though they were approaching the two-hour mark. "There's no prize for eighth place, I'm afraid."

Clare looked for a moment like he was going to swipe the entire puzzle off the table. He stood up instead, putting his hands to his drawn face as if he was planning to remove it.

"This is your fault, Porter, and I won't forget it," he said, pointing a finger at the DI. "Now toss off, you're all fired."

He marched from the room, slamming the door behind him.

"He really takes this stuff seriously, doesn't he?" Rachel said as she scooped the pieces back into the box.

"He doesn't have much else going for him," Porter said. "Poor guy. This was his one shot at accomplishing something in life. I'm gutted for him."

"Oh," Rachel said, nodding sadly. "Well, hopefully he'll have better luck next time."

She loaded the jigsaw onto the trolley.

"Sure I can't tempt anyone with a raffle ticket? The main prize is a hamper, it looks amazing."

"Sure," said Duke, pulling a Velcro wallet from his pocket and peeling it open. "I'll take one."

"Yay," Rachel said as she took his money and handed him a ticket. "So what are you lot up to for the rest of the evening? There are some great cocktails in the bar. I'd recommend the, uh, Rusty Sue, is it? Rusty *something*, anyway."

Kett checked his watch to see that it was coming up for eight. He felt knackered, and all he really wanted to do was jump in the shower, crash in front of the TV and call Billie. This was a holiday, after all.

No such luck.

"I think we've got a bit of work to do," he said, looking at Savage. She nodded.

"No rest for the wicked."

"Rachel," said Kett. "Did you know a woman called Niamh Bradbury? She worked here last year until she was killed in a hit and run."

Rachel nodded, her smile vanishing.

"She was lovely. I miss her."

"This is going to sound like a strange question, but have you seen anyone in the hotel who looks a little like her? Purple hair, nose piercings?"

She shook her head, her brow furrowing.

"Sorry," she said.

"What about Sebastian Reilly?"

"He was before my time," she said. "But I know who he is. Bit of a... a craphead, if I'm allowed to say it."

"In what way?"

Rachel winced like she was chewing something painful. She looked over her shoulder at the dark window, then closed the distance between her and Kett.

"Okay, I'll get in trouble with Harita if she hears I've said this, but I know you're police and I guess it's important. Seb worked in the kitchens and everyone said he was moving drugs through the deliveries. I don't know what drugs, I don't even know if it's true. But..."

She leaned in even closer, her voice dropping to a whisper.

"Everyone said he was working with a group of Eastern Europeans. There's a man working in the kitchen, Mantas. Big guy, really scary. He's from Lithuania. I remember it because if you want to say thank you in Lithuanian you have to sneeze. *Achoo.* That's the word for it. *Achoo.* He told me that, before I found out what he was doing."

"He told you what he was doing?"

She bounced back, unsure, one hand to her mouth.

"No, he didn't say it, not at all. I'm really sorry, I probably shouldn't have said any of that. It's just rumours, gossip."

"Do you remember where those rumours came from?" Kett asked.

"Like, *everyone*," she said as if it was the most obvious truth in the world. "Mantas and Seb and some other guys, they always used to go and smoke in the woods out front, on their breaks and whatnot. Niamh too. They'd never let anyone else go with them. Sarah Littlejohn, she's one of the cleaners, she always said they were going out there to bury bodies, but that's obviously not true."

"Out front, by the car park?" Savage asked, and Rachel nodded.

"And don't even get me started on the rumours he was a s-e-x pest. Like I said, though, it was before my time."

"Thanks," said Kett. Rachel reached out as if to touch his arm, holding back.

"Please don't tell anyone I said that. I can't lose this job."

"You have my word," Kett said. "This conversation never happened."

She smiled, but it had lost some of its magic.

Kett followed the others into the corridor, rubbing a hand over his stubbled face.

"We need to take another look in the woods," Savage said. "The more I think about it, the more I think our ghost hid out there when we were chasing her. It's the only thing that makes any sense. It must be used as a storage place for all the hotel's old furniture because it was full of junk, what if she hid under a mattress or something?"

"She's not going to be there now, is she?" Duke said.

"Obviously," said Savage. "But she might have left something."

The PC looked doubtful, but he didn't argue.

"Lead the way," said Kett.

The temperature had plummeted, a scalpel-sharp wind cutting across the broad and buffeting the hotel with some force. Past the car park, the topiary hedges were dark smudges against the darker sky, looking like prowling giants. A handful of solar lights did their best but the night was winning.

Duke fetched a slim pencil torch from his trouser pocket and Porter pulled out a giant Maglite from his overcoat, shooting him a grin.

"I'm not saying anything," Porter said.

Savage was already off, using her own torch to lead them through the scattered cars. The hotel watched them go, every light blazing. Kett scanned the windows, seeing the function rooms and the dining halls and then, in the annex on the right-hand side, the kitchen. Even though it was late it was still bustling, chef's hats moving back and forth behind the steamed-up glass.

"It was right here," Savage said as they neared the woods. "That's my room up there and I was looking out the window when I saw her. She was standing in those trees, just past the mattresses. As soon as she saw us, she bolted."

They skirted around the mouldering mattresses and pushed into the trees. Savage was right, there was stuff everywhere—dismantled beds, old dining chairs, luggage trolleys.

"It's like a hotel graveyard," said Kett. "Why would they leave all this here? Not exactly picturesque."

"I think it's because you can't really see the mess from the car park or the rooms," Savage said. "Not the nice rooms, anyway. They all look down over the broad. Just the economy ones."

"For the paupers like us," said Kett.

"That side's all fenced off," Savage went on. "Wire fence runs all the way from here to the main road, and all the way along that until the driveway. It's spiked, and I couldn't find a weak point."

"And she definitely didn't run back into the car park?" Kett said.

"Porter was there. He'd have seen her. Right, sir?"

Porter was staring into the trees, oblivious.

"Right, Porter?" said Kett.

"Right," he said, nodding. "Right what?"

"Reassuring," Kett said. "Fan out. Check the furniture, look for anywhere somebody might have hidden."

They walked slowly and in silence, navigating the overgrown brambles and the tangled, unforgiving roots. Kett lifted a mattress that reeked of smoke, seeing nothing but dead grass underneath. To his right, Porter opened a wardrobe that had been left on its back, the wood so rotten that the door came off in his hands. He reeled back, gagging.

"What is it?" Kett said.

"I think somebody's been using it as a toilet."

"Nice."

"There are a lot of cigarette butts back here," said Savage, her torch moving in slow, sweeping semicircles. "And an old sofa. Couple of beer bottles."

Kett moved towards her, his torch bringing to life the detritus that had been abandoned here: crisp packets and cereal boxes and filthy clothes and even condom wrappers. The hotel was so close that Kett could hear voices inside, the occasional bray of laughter. It didn't make any sense at all that this little piece of woodland had been left to rot.

He reached the back of the sofa, the old yellow velvet almost completely green. The back had been eaten away, or burned, revealing the wooden frame. He ducked down, shining his torch inside the cavity and seeing that it was far too small for a person.

"Cat," said Duke from a dozen yards away.

The PC was crouching next to a mangy white cat—or at

least it might have been a cat, it was really too dark to be sure. He reached out to stroke its head then recoiled with a sudden intake of breath.

"It bit me!" he said as the animal bolted, darting past Porter then jumping onto the sofa. It nervously approached Kett then pushed its face against his elbow, purring.

"What the hell?" Duke said, genuinely annoyed.

"Probably thought you were a bear," said Porter.

"Or a werewolf," added Kett. He gently ruffled the back of the cat's neck before moving on—taking two steps before he heard it.

A hollow thump beneath his boot, like somebody banging an empty oil drum.

He lifted his foot and dropped it again, hearing the same noise.

"There's something down here," he said. "Help me move the sofa."

Porter ran over, the torch tucked beneath his arm. Savage grabbed the other side and together they lifted, the cat leaping to safety with a gravelly meow. They dumped the sofa while Kett got to his knees. He aimed the torch at the ground, seeing nothing but grass—too thick, too green, too shiny.

"It's fake," he said.

He pushed his fingers into it, finding the edge and tugging. The plastic grass mat peeled away and underneath was something flat and metallic. Kett drummed his knuckles against it, hearing that same hollow boom.

He stood up, his knees cracking like shotguns. Savage took his place, tugging the artificial grass until it was clear. There was a metal box buried in the dirt, one that might once have been a utility locker or even a gun cabinet. It was a good four foot wide and six foot tall, its doors shut tight.

There was no sign of a padlock, and when Kett ran a pen through the loop of the handle and gently pulled, it opened easily.

It was empty.

"This must have been where she was hiding," said Savage. "She must have climbed in and shut the door. That fake turf would have dropped right back on top. I never even thought to look."

"Still doesn't explain why she was running in the first place," said Duke.

"She was scared," said Savage. "I could tell that much."

"Maybe because she didn't know you were police?" said Kett.

"Or maybe because she *did* know."

Savage aimed her torch into the locker.

"What's that?"

It took Kett a moment to see it, a folded square of paper tucked into the vents at the side. Savage was already on her knees, reaching in and tugging it loose. She unfolded it as she stood, struggling to hold her torch at the same time.

"Here," said Kett, and she passed her light to him. He held it up and they all crowded around to see four lines of scrawled handwriting.

Seb, where are you? I've called a hundred times. I'm scared. Do I still go through with it? I'm scared they'll hurt me if they find out. I know you'll be here so CALL ME when you read this. If you don't, I'm not going to go. Cat.

Savage turned the paper over but the back was blank. She held it up again and Kett snapped a photograph of it on his phone.

"Cat," he said. "That has to be our ghost. The name ring a bell to any of you?"

"There's that cat, sir," said Duke, pointing at the cat that had bitten his finger. It was perched on the upended sofa, watching them with unnaturally bright yellow eyes.

"Duke, I don't think this note was written by an *actual* cat," said Kett. "Cat, Catherine. Wasn't that the name Joe mentioned when you spoke to him in the car, Duke?"

"Yeah, Catherine."

"Did he give you a last name?"

Duke shook his head. Then he clicked his fingers, his face lighting up.

"Oh, but he did say she lived over the road."

CHAPTER SEVENTEEN

KETT PULLED THE SKODA TO THE SIDE OF THE ROAD and cut the engine, listening to the first few drops of rain hit the windscreen. They were on Station Road, just down from Neil Enthoven's bungalow, a plumber's van shielding the car from any of the properties further up the street. There weren't many lights down here, and the trees seemed to have positioned themselves in front of them almost deliberately, the street oil-black.

"It's a little further along," said Duke from the back.

"I know," said Kett. "But if Catherine's here I don't want to spook her."

"It's because you're embarrassed of your pink car, isn't it, sir?" said Savage. "You don't want anybody to see it."

He gave her a disapproving look as he opened his door, a gust of wind almost ripping it off its hinges. He pulled the collar of his overcoat up in an attempt to shield his neck but the cold worked its way into the gaps between every single stitch, unforgiving.

"Bit nippy, this," said Savage, her door slamming shut by itself. Porter got out too, leaving Duke alone in the back.

"Come on, Aaron," Kett said.

"I don't want to, sir," Duke protested. "I'm not even on duty."

Kett opened the door for the PC until he sullenly peeled himself out of the car. He didn't have a coat and hunkered down inside Porter's suit jacket instead.

"This is good practice for when you jump on the carousel," said Kett. Duke shook his head, water flying off his beard.

"Not for me, sir," he said. "I'm Uniform all the way."

"Fair enough."

They made their way down the street, past houses that all looked like they'd closed up shop for the winter. Only a couple of the little bungalows had their lights on, the rest as lifeless as crypts. In the minute or so it took them to walk to Enthoven's bungalow, not a single car passed by.

"It's a ghost town," said Savage. "Where is everyone?"

"Recovering from last night, maybe," Kett said. "Aaron, did Joe happen to tell you which house belonged to Catherine?"

"No," said Duke, his big arms wrapped around his stomach like he was trying to hold himself in. "But he was looking at that one."

He nodded to the property that sat directly opposite Enthoven's place. This was a bungalow too, squat and broad. The wide gravel drive was so thick with weeds that it was practically woodland. There were no lights on here either, at least none at the front. When Kett stared down the bungalow's flank he thought he could see the faintest glow from the back garden.

"I still don't understand why you didn't mention any of this earlier," said Porter.

"You never—"

"Asked. Right. How do you want to do this, sir?"

"Carefully. If Catherine is our purple-haired girl then we know she's already spooked. We don't want her to run again. You and Duke check the back. Savage and I will take the front."

Porter started to move away and Kett called to him.

"We don't know what this is, okay? So if she's home, go easy on her."

Porter nodded, jogging to catch up with Duke. Kett crunched through the weed-strewn gravel, knocking on a door that looked ready to fall right out of its frame, like a loose tooth.

"Catherine?" he called out.

He pushed his ear closer, trying to hear anything from inside. He knocked again.

"Catherine? Can you open the door? It's the police."

Kett heard the sound of a door opening, but it wasn't this one. There was a scream, then a booming shout from Porter.

"Don't move!"

"Wait here," Kett told Savage.

He ran into the back garden to see Porter and Duke pushing their way through a set of patio doors.

"I said don't move," Porter yelled again. "Put it down, now."

Kett followed Duke through the doors into a large kitchen. Porter was already moving into the narrow corridor beyond, his huge frame blocking the view. Somebody was screaming—scared, yes, but furious too.

"Get the fuck away from me!"

"Last chance," Porter said. "Put it down."

"Pete, back off," said Kett.

He pushed past the DI and came face to face with a ghost.

The woman from the hotel stood by the front door, hunched with terror, her purple wig twisted over her face so that one eye was hidden. She was still wearing her white shirt and black trousers, and in her hand she held a bread knife, sweeping it from side to side with mad, desperate motions.

"Hey," Kett said, lifting his hands to show that he wasn't a threat. "Catherine? Cat, right?"

She didn't reply, backing off a little more until she hit the front door. She glanced through the glass, groaning when she caught sight of Savage outside. Kett pulled out his warrant card, holding it up for her to see.

"You're not in any danger. My name is Robbie, DCI Robbie Kett. I'm with the police."

This had the opposite effect to the one he'd intended. Catherine stabbed the knife in his direction—too far away to hit him.

"Stay the fuck away from me," she said. "I'm serious. I haven't done anything wrong!"

"Put it down," growled Porter, and Kett rested a hand on the DI's arm to calm him.

"Cat, I promise you, you're not in any trouble. Put the knife down and we can talk."

Cat was still thrusting the blade but her movements had slowed. She turned to the door and rested her head against it, making a noise that was somewhere between a sob and a choke. She stabbed the tip of the breadknife into the wall with no real force, then let it fall from her fingers.

"Thank you," said Kett. "Come on, let's find a place to sit."

"So you can torture me?" Cat said. "So you can fucking beat it out of me? Take what's yours?"

"What? No. Why would you think that?"

Cat glared at him, her one visible eye full of anger.

"It's what you do, isn't it?"

"It's really not," said Kett. "Not us."

Cat pulled the purple wig from her head. Beneath, her curly brown hair was short and cropped into a pixie cut that wasn't too far away from the one Savage had had when Kett first met her. She seemed as if she was going to throw the wig to the floor, but it must have meant something to her because she changed her mind and clung onto it—her knuckles white as if it was a rope thrown from a boat to stop her from drowning. This close, and without the hair, she didn't look much like Niamh Bradbury at all.

She stared at Kett, then at Porter, then craned her neck to see Duke in the back room.

"Where is he?" she asked.

"Who?" said Kett.

"Marshall."

"He's not here. He doesn't work with us. Why are you asking?"

Cat frowned, licking her lips. Kett waved his own question away, using his knuckles to push open the door to his left to see a dining room. A walnut table sat in the middle of it, surrounded by an assortment of chairs. Somebody stripped half of the ancient wallpaper away, taking chunks of wall with them. It stank of damp plaster.

"Let's have a seat. Maybe Duke could put the kettle on."

"I'll do it," said Porter, and Kett pretended not to hear him.

"Duke, make some tea. And let Savage in, will you?"

"Savage?" said Cat, her eyes widening.

"In name only, don't worry." Kett smiled, gesturing to the dining room until Cat reluctantly walked through the door. She took a deep, fractured breath like she was heading to her own execution, the fear coming off her almost tangible. "Cat, is there somebody we can call for you? Your parents, or a guardian? A friend? You don't have to be alone here."

She reached the table, looking back.

"Why? Why would you do that?"

"Because whoever you think we are, we're not. And as far as I'm aware, you haven't done anything wrong. We're just here because we have some questions, that's all."

She pulled out her chair and sat down, and Kett took the seat opposite her. Porter stayed standing until Kett nodded an unspoken command, forcing the DI into the chair by the window. Duke opened the front door and Savage walked in, shaking the rain from her hair. She peeked through the door, smiling at Cat.

"Kate," said Kett. "Can you help Duke with the tea?"

She nodded, knowing full well what he was asking her to do. They walked off together, leaving the sound of the wind outside, and the short, fast breaths of the woman across the table. At this rate, she was in danger of hyperventilating.

"I have been looking for you all day," Kett said, attempting a smile.

Cat frowned, studying him for a second or two before her mouth opened.

"It's you," she said. "From the hotel, right? What are you... I thought you were on *holiday*?"

"We are," Kett said. "It's bad timing. Can I just start by asking you your name? It's Cat? Catherine?"

The woman's expression was stony, but after a little while she nodded.

"Surname?"

"Cavaney," she said.

"Thank you. Can I ask you how old you are as well?"

"Twenty-three," she said.

"Cat, when I saw you this afternoon you seemed scared. You were asking about your boyfriend, Sebastian."

Cat looked at Porter, her face motionless but her eyes giving away every ounce of confusion and fear. She put the wig on the table, kneading it between her fingers. Her hands were dry and covered in cuts where the skin had split. Billie always had the same trouble, especially in the winter.

"I shouldn't have said anything," she said. "I was..."

She buried her head in the wig for a moment, and when she sat up strands of nylon hair were stuck to her tear-damp skin. She put a hand to her nose and pulled out the ring. The way she did it made it very clear she didn't have a piercing there, it was just clipped on.

"I just need to find him because he isn't talking to me, and... And I need him."

"This is Sebastian Reilly?" Kett asked.

She nodded.

"How do you..." And she must have known what was coming because her head began to twist wildly from side to side, as if it could fan away the truth. "No. No, he isn't. Don't you dare fucking say it."

"I'm really sorry," said Kett. "We found Seb this morning in the woods by Toltham Broad. It seems like he died from an accidental overdose."

Cat's head arched back and her mouth opened as if a scream was about to tear out of it. Instead, all that emerged was a low, awful groan. She balled up a fist and slammed it on the table.

"No no no!"

Then she broke into tears, her voice lost somewhere in the breathless sobs.

"What... what am I..."

"It's okay," said Kett. "Take your time. Take a breath."

He looked through the door.

"Where's that tea, Duke?"

"Coming," the PC said. "Two minutes."

"I'm genuinely sorry for your loss," Kett said. "But we need to try to work out what happened to Seb. There could be others in danger."

"I *know* what happened to him," Cat said, her voice juddering. She pressed the heels of her hands into her eyes, still groaning. "Fuck. I know what happened to him."

She pulled her hands away, blinking hard.

"Can he still get in trouble?" she asked. "I mean, if I tell you stuff about him. Can he still, you know?"

"No," said Kett. "He can't be convicted of a crime, if that's what you mean."

"Not that it fucking matters," she said. "Except it does matter, doesn't it? For the people who know him. I don't want it coming out, what he did. It would kill his mum."

"It's just between us," said Kett. "But if Seb was doing something illegal, we need to know."

Cat sniffed.

"He wasn't my boyfriend. I'm sorry I told you that. He was a friend."

"Why did you lie?" Kett said.

"Because I didn't know who you were. I *still* don't. But... but it's not like I have a choice now, is it? He's dead, and... Fuck. He's *dead*?"

Kett could see her trying to process it.

"He never used to touch it, you know that, right?" she went on. "Seb, he never touched the gear. He always joked about the people who did, how stupid they were to let it mess them up. He always laughed at the junkies, always said how weak they were. That's why he did it, you know? That's why he..."

"He was a dealer?" Kett said when her words dried out. It took her almost a full minute to continue.

"Yeah. He was a dealer. On and off now, for over a year. More on than off these last few months. I haven't known him nearly all that long but he told me all of it."

"What sort of drugs?"

"The bad sort," she said. "I mean, weed and shit, but harder things too."

"Heroin?" asked Kett. "Cocaine?"

She nodded.

"Worse than that?"

"*Is* there anything worse than that?" she said.

"You said he never used to touch it. But he started using?"

Still nodding.

"I fucking told him not to. I told him he was a fucking idiot. That shit, once you've started you don't ever stop thinking about it. You don't ever quit, not really. Coke, maybe, but not H. I've seen what it does to people, it... it hollows them out, makes them empty, you know?"

She put two fingers to her temple like she was going to shoot herself.

"He was dead the second he took that first hit. Fucking weeks ago, but he was dead right then because I knew he wouldn't stop."

She buried her face in the wig again, her scream muted.

Beneath the thin fabric of her shirt her spine jutted out like the bones of some deep-sea creature. She was painfully thin.

"Do you know if Seb was selling a new drug? Heroin cut with prescription antipsychotics or volatile neuroleptics?"

Cat lifted her head, sniffing.

"I don't know," she said. "I wasn't involved."

"It's incredibly dangerous," said Kett.

"I don't know anything," she said. "I'd tell you if I did. I promise. I hated it."

Kett heard the sound of clinking china from the hall and a second or two later Duke walked in, holding a tray of cups and a teapot shaped like Belle from *Beauty and the Beast*. He almost tripped on the carpet, everything wobbling, then he managed to land it on the table. Kett waited for him to pour out four cups, adding the milk afterwards with all the delicacy and grace of a trained butler. To be fair, it looked like a decent cuppa.

"Sugar?" he asked Cat, and she nodded.

"All of it," she said. She watched Duke spoon in six sugars before taking the cup from him, holding it to her chest. Her entire body was trembling, the tea sloshing over her shirt.

"Cat, can I ask who Seb was working with?" Kett asked. "Who supplied the drugs?"

She shrugged, but the way she was staring into her tea made it clear she knew more than she was saying.

"Cat, he can't get in trouble. Not now. Help us, and we might be able to find the people who did this to him, and we might be able to save lives."

"And what if you don't find them?" she said.

"You're worried they'll come after you?"

"I don't know anything. I'm sorry. Seb worked with somebody else, they never told me any of their shit."

"Neil Enthoven?" said Kett, and the look she gave him confirmed it.

"You'd have to talk to Neil about that," she said. "I told you, I don't know—"

"Neil's dead. He died last night, maybe this morning. An overdose, just like Seb."

"No," she said, her chin jutting out defiantly. "No. I don't believe you."

"You didn't see the police over the road this morning? The ambulance?"

"No," she said quietly.

Kett lifted his tea and took a sip, the heat of it chasing off some of the cold. It was almost a perfect blend, steeped for just long enough to be strong, but not overdone, and with just a dash and a half of milk. He took another sip, looking at Duke.

"Did you make this?"

"Yes, sir," Duke said.

"It's great."

Duke grinned like a five-year-old who'd been told his macaroni collage was the best in the class. Kett turned back to Cat.

"Sorry. You spent time over the road at Neil's place, didn't you? You and Seb and Joe. Who else?"

"How do you know all this?" she asked. "From Joe? I mean, he's right, I used to hang out with Seb and Neil. I only met them recently, like last year. It's only been a couple of months really."

"How did you meet?"

She laughed.

"I was an elf, believe it or not. Up at the Wroxham

Barns Christmas show, helping Santa and all that. It was halfway through December, maybe? Seb saw me one night and we started talking. Wasn't romantic or anything, he was just a laugh, and he had... You know. We used to go there and play Xbox. Smoke a bit... smoke some *cigarettes* and stuff. I felt sorry for him because his friend had just died. Niamh. He was pretty cut up."

"Who else did you hang out with?"

"Pete," she said. "Pete Duggan, he's one of the gardeners at the lodge but he's freelance and he's expensive so he's hardly ever there anymore."

"So you never met Niamh Bradbury?"

She swallowed hard, her mouth a perfect upside-down smile.

"No, but all they ever did was talk about her." She studied her fingertips, her eyes filling up. "I wish I'd known her, you know? She seemed pretty sound. The way Seb talked about her..." She gritted her teeth for a moment. "She helped him with the drugs but I think she wanted out of it all. She liked the money but she wanted out, and it's not like she needed it. Her folks are loaded, own half of a village up the road from here, Somerleyton. She was in it for the thrills, I think. She just bit off more than she could chew."

"That's a lot of assumptions for somebody who didn't know her," said Kett.

"Like I said, they never stop talking about her." She gritted her teeth again, her jaw bulging. "Look, I *did* see the police today, at Neil's place. That's why I went up to the hotel, to look for Seb. I was worried they were going to arrest him. Neil, that is. And Neil would have spilled his guts, got Seb in trouble. Just wanted to see him, that's all. He didn't have his phone on but he sometimes met me at the lodge."

"You hung out in the woods at the front, didn't you?"

Kett asked. He glanced round to see that Savage had returned and was leaning against the doorframe. She shook her head—nothing to see in the house.

"Sometimes," Cat said.

"Why? I mean, you don't work there. Seb quit, and as far as I know, Neil never worked there. Why meet at the Topiary? Because of Pete?"

"Habit," she said, although it wasn't massively convincing.

"Cat, can you tell us why you were there today? Why you ran from us?"

"I wasn't," she said, her voice breaking. "I *didn't*."

"Then it wasn't you who left this note in the locker?" Savage asked, holding it up.

Cat's eyes bulged, her mouth opening silently.

"You signed it," Savage said.

"I just needed to find him. I just needed to know where he was."

"What are you talking about here?" Kett asked. "What is it you need to do?"

"Nothing."

"You still have contacts at the hotel? Friends? Maybe somebody that Seb was working with?"

"No," she said, too bluntly.

"You know the chef? Mantas?"

Cat looked at him, and there was no anger in her eyes now, just terror—the same terror he'd seen in her earlier.

"No."

"You sure about that? I could have sworn I heard you talking to him today, after we met by the lake."

"No," she said. She was still shaking but now she looked close to exploding—a motor with something jammed in its cogs.

"If Mantas was the one who was providing Neil and Seb with drugs then we need to know. It won't come back to you, Cat. But you can help us get these people off the streets, the drugs too, before anyone else ends up like Seb."

Cat's face was a mask of pure misery. She pushed and pulled at the wig like she was trying to unravel it, strands of purple hair wrapping themselves around her fingers. She opened her mouth as if she was about to answer, then the sound of a ringing phone stopped her in her tracks. It was a mobile ringtone, and it was coming from the kitchen. Cat snapped her head to the door.

"I can grab that for you," said Savage.

"Don't!" Cat said, almost a scream. She pushed her chair back but Savage was already gone. "Please don't answer it."

By the time she'd reached the door Savage was back, a little black phone in her hand. It was still ringing and Cat snatched it from her and ended the call. She clutched it to her chest.

"I need you to go," she said. "I need you to go, *right now*."

"Who was that?" Kett asked, standing up.

"You can either arrest me or get the fuck out of my house," Cat replied. "*Please!*"

"Okay," Kett said. "Okay, we can go."

The phone was ringing again and Cat was almost in tears. She ran to the front door and opened it, the wind pulling at her short hair, tugging at her shirt like it wanted to undress her. She looked wild, Kett thought. She looked like a woman on the edge of something terrible.

"We should go," he said to Porter.

"But—"

Kett shut the DI up with a look, gesturing to the door.

Porter clamped his lips together, following Duke out into the night. Savage paused by the door to give Cat's arm a gentle squeeze.

"Whatever this is, we can help," she said.

"We can," Kett echoed as he walked outside. "I promise you. We're not Wallace Marshall. We're *police*. If you trust us, we can get you out of this. We can keep you safe."

The phone cut out, then instantly started ringing again.

"You're too late," Cat said, slamming the door closed.

CHAPTER EIGHTEEN

THE WIND WAS SO LOUD THAT KETT COULD BARELY hear his boots on Catherine's gravel drive as he made his way to the road. He stopped on the pavement for a moment, looking at the bungalow and seeing the young woman's silhouette retreat from the glass panel in the door. She appeared in the dining room window, the phone still held to her chest. Then she pulled down the blind and disappeared.

"You're not going to leave her in there alone, are you, sir?" Savage asked. "Absolutely none of that felt right."

"No," said Kett. "It didn't."

He glanced across the road to the bungalow that sat opposite, the one where Neil Enthoven had lived and where this group of friends had hung out. It was almost lost behind its overgrown hedges, as if ashamed of itself.

"You heard anyone mention the name Pete Duggan before?"

"No," said Savage. Porter shook his head.

"What about you, Duke?" Kett said. "Did Joe talk about him?"

"I don't think so. He said four of them used to hang out

there with him. Catherine and Neil are the only ones he mentioned by name, but there were two other men as well. If Seb is one, Pete might be the other."

"Then we need to find him."

He started back towards the car, Savage on his heels.

"I can stay, sir? I'll just keep an eye out for her. I'm worried she's going to do something."

"Don't worry," said Kett. "We're not going anywhere."

He climbed into the car, starting the engine and dialling the heat up. The Skoda responded by throwing freezing cold dust into his face, the blowers louder than a passing jumbo jet.

"Those bloody girls," he coughed as everyone else climbed in.

"What are we doing, sir?" Porter asked from the passenger seat.

"Going back, right?" said Duke. "To the hotel? To the bar? The nice, warm bar."

"No. Not yet."

Kett put the car in gear and pulled around the plumber's van, parking again a little further up. From here he could see Cat's drive, the front of her bungalow. He switched off the engine, plunging the street into darkness.

He pulled out his phone, finding the photo he'd taken of Cat's note.

"'I've called a hundred times,'" he read aloud. "'I'm scared. Do I still go through with it?' Then she says, 'If you don't, I'm not going to go.' What's she talking about?"

"A deal?" said Savage as he put his phone away. "That was my first thought. She and Seb were doing some kind of narcotics deal. Then he died."

"And she doesn't know what to do," said Kett. "That's what I think too."

"Whoever was on that phone, she was terrified of them," Savage said.

"Who do you think it was?" asked Porter.

"I think that if we wait here, we stand a good chance of finding out." Kett tapped out a rhythm on the steering wheel, going over the conversation they'd just had. "Did you notice how she was scared of us, too? The police?"

"Yeah," said Porter. "She was worried we were going to beat her. Torture her."

"And she thought Marshall was with us," said Savage.

"Yeah," said Kett. "The longer this day goes on, the less I like that man."

"He's as bent as they come," said Porter. "Reminds me of some of the old boys we came up with in the Met. Cooper and his crowd."

Kett winced, trying not to think about the time DCI John Cooper had stuck a blade into his flank—the very same day that Billie had been taken by the Pig Man. It felt like a lifetime ago. A *thousand* lifetimes. He rubbed the phantom pain from his side, nodding.

"They were worse than all the bloody criminals," Porter went on. "Drugs, prostitution, gambling, protection. Shit, they thought they were untouchable."

"Until they weren't," said Kett.

"Arseholes," Porter said. "Marshall's got that same vibe. Smug as they come."

"Well, we saw him talking to Mantas in the lodge," Savage said. "They know each other. If Mantas is supplying drugs, Marshall would be a good person to have on side, and he's got form for it. If there was evidence at Neil's bungalow, or Seb's caravan, Marshall's already made off with it. It's gone."

"Maybe."

As dodgy as Marshall seemed, Kett didn't feel particularly comfortable with the conversation. Some serious accusations were flying around the car, the kind that carried, and the kind you couldn't always take back. He glanced in the mirror to see Duke staring out the window, one finger scratching his nose. Fortunately, he seemed oblivious.

"Right," said Savage, staring at her phone. "Pete Duggan. He's local, lives around the corner from here. New Road. No record, but I've found his Facebook page."

She held up the phone and Kett saw a young man with a short, immaculately groomed beard, one shaved eyebrow and an Adidas cap with a huge peak. He was making a gangster's salute at the camera, his angry expression instantly recognisable. Kett could almost hear the kid squeaking, *"Don't mess with me or I'll cap your ass."*

"Friends with Seb, and Neil. No sign of Cat but I haven't found her on social media yet. She may be using another name. Plenty of photos of Pete."

She flicked through a few, holding the phone up. Neil, Seb, Pete, Joe and Niamh all sat on a sofa surrounded by thick clouds of smoke. Both Pete and Niamh were holding enormous joints, and they were grinning like idiots.

"From last summer," said Savage. "That's Neil's place, you can see that tree out of the window."

She pointed to a mature monkey puzzle tree that sat in the next garden over from Cat's bungalow.

"Good spot," said Kett. "Duke, you fancy knocking on Pete's door, seeing if he's home?"

"No thank you, sir," said Duke.

"Let me reword that," said Kett. "Duke, off you trot."

The big PC moaned.

"Number 43," said Savage. "You want company?"

"That's probably not a bad idea," said Kett. "Call me when you're there."

Savage climbed out, opening Duke's door for him. They disappeared into the dark so quickly it was like the wind had snatched them away. For a moment, Kett and Porter sat in silence. The DI was lost in thought, and he didn't look happy.

"You okay, Pete?"

"Yeah," Porter said. "Well, honestly, I'm not sure."

"Here if you want to talk, mate," said Kett.

"Maybe. It's just..." He took a breath. "Back there, in Cat's house, you said Duke's tea was good."

"I said it was great, and it wasn't a lie."

"Was it... was it better than mine?"

With his big eyes, Porter looked like a puppy dog in the dark car. Kett almost felt sorry for him.

"Oh God yes, Pete. So much better. You can't even compare it. It's like asking what's better, a piece of chocolate cake or a kick to the balls."

"Oh."

"I still like you more, though," said Kett. "And—"

He fell silent as a set of headlights appeared in the rearview mirror, so bright that they blinded him.

"Incoming," he said.

A sleek black Mercedes purred past the parked Skoda, pulling up right outside Cat's driveway.

"Get down," Kett said, wiggling in his seat until he could barely see over the steering wheel. Porter ducked too, both of them holding their breath.

The Mercedes honked its horn, twice. Rain turned to fire in its taillights, framed by clouds of exhaust. Porter had his notebook out and he was scribbling down the license plate.

There was no sign of life from the bungalow.

The horn blared again. Then the driver's door opened. Somebody slid out into the night, just a silhouette. It was a man, Kett was sure of it. Big, his head almost perfectly smooth—he was either bald or he was wearing a hat. He leaned in and pressed his hand on the horn, leaving it there —five seconds, then ten, until the door of the bungalow opened.

The night fell quiet, Kett's ears ringing.

Cat walked out of the bungalow and stood on the stoop. The purple wig was back on her head and she had a huge puffer jacket wrapped around her—looking almost like a sleeping bag. She hesitated, taking small nervous steps back and forth over the threshold. The man shouted something and she called back, their words stolen by the wind.

"Should we go out there?" Porter asked.

Kett didn't answer. He wasn't sure. The man said something else and Cat flapped her arms, wrenching the door shut. She pulled the coat over her head as she ran down the drive, glancing along the street right at the Skoda. Kett froze, wondering how visible they were. But he needn't have worried because Cat opened the back door of the Mercedes and slid inside.

"Pays to have a bright pink car," Porter said. "Nobody's ever going to believe it belongs to a copper."

"It's not *bright pink*, Pete."

The Mercedes pulled away, as stealthy as a shark. Kett waited until it had vanished around the corner before starting the engine. He followed slowly, rounding the bend to see the car pick up speed. Kett eased his foot down on the accelerator, the Skoda's engine making a noise that didn't sound healthy at all. He didn't let himself get too close, the

Mercedes' taillights bright enough to be seen through the trees as it took the bends.

"You should have got one of them," Porter said. "CLS 550. It's a beast."

"Does it come in pink?"

Porter laughed quietly.

"They're turning."

Ahead, the Mercedes was pulling off the main road. Kett slowed, watching as it cut right, its headlights turning the night to day. There didn't seem to be anything up there, just hedges and trees and fields rising towards a hill.

"They're going to be onto us as soon as we make that turn," said Porter.

It was true. There were no other cars in sight. But they didn't exactly have a choice.

Kett reached the turn and steered the Skoda around the tight bend. He heard his phone ring from his pocket—he hadn't had time to set up the hands-free yet—and ignored it, keeping his eyes on the Mercedes as it gained ground. The *Mexican Hat Dance* cut off and Porter's phone immediately began to vibrate.

"Savage," he said when he answered it. "Hang on, I'll put you on speaker."

"Sir, we've found Pete Duggan's house. Nobody here but the back door's been kicked in."

"Shit," said Kett.

"What do you want us to do?"

"Hold fire. Cat's just been picked up by a mystery driver and we're following. Heading west out of the village and up the hill. Can you call Clare and let him know?"

"You want backup?"

"I don't think so. I don't really want the local police anywhere near this."

The Mercedes was a hundred yards ahead, weaving in and out of view as it approached the top of the hill. Fields sloped down on both sides of the road, and there might have been a farm up ahead because Kett thought he could see the silhouette of a huge barn against the fast-moving river of dark clouds.

"I'll call you if I need you. Just find out what happened to Duggan."

"Yes, sir."

The phone went dead.

"They're slowing down," said Porter.

The Mercedes had slowed to a crawl. There was definitely a farm up there, hiding in the night. Kett eased his foot on the brakes, watching the other car as it slipped between a couple of gate posts. There must have been a cattle grid there because Kett heard it ring out as the car crossed it. It travelled slowly for another few seconds.

Then it disappeared.

"Where did it go?" Porter said, leaning forward in his seat. "Did it pull into a building?"

"I think they switched the lights off."

"Shit."

Kett slowed to a halt, popping his lips.

"They made us," said Porter. "How do you want to do this?"

"We have no idea who they are," said Kett. He looked through the back window, no sign of any other vehicles on the road behind them. There was nothing up ahead, either, just the lightless farm at the top of the hill. He thought of Cat, her panic, her *terror*. "We can't leave her there."

"No," said Porter. "We can't."

Kett rolled the car forwards, picking up speed, its engine whining in protest as they climbed the hill. The lights picked out the edge of the steep banks that dropped away from the road, but past the tall grass, there was nothing—as if they were crossing a void.

"Stay sharp," Kett said.

They reached the cattle grid, everything shaking as Kett eased them over it. The road continued for a short stretch before reaching the barn—one of two immense corrugated iron structures that stood like the gates of an ancient citadel. There was no sign of the Mercedes in the first one, just a tractor that slept in the shadows half a dozen yards away.

"Anything?" Kett asked as they crawled forwards.

"No, but there's—"

The world suddenly lit up, as if the sun had changed its mind and clawed its way back over the horizon. Kett raised a hand to his eyes, blinded. But he heard the grunt of an engine starting clear enough.

"Go!" Porter shouted.

Kett punched the accelerator, but he wasn't quick enough. The tractor roared as it ploughed its way from the barn doors, faster than it had any right to be. It crunched into the side of the Skoda, Kett's window exploding in a hail of glass.

"Fuck!" he roared, slamming his foot down.

It was no good, two wheels already off the ground as the tractor drove relentlessly forwards. The air was full of the choking stench of diesel. Kett looked through Porter's window to see the verge, and past that the steep slope of the hill.

"Get out!" he yelled.

The tractor pushed on, the Skoda's windscreen cracking with a sound like a gunshot. They were gaining speed, the car like a toy, almost fully on its side now. There was nowhere to go, Kett's door blocked and Porter's scraping the ground. The big DI had one foot over the dash, kicking at the windscreen.

But it was too late.

"Fuck!" Kett said again, his voice drowned out by the scream of rending metal. "Hang on, Pete, we're going over!"

The car hit the verge, seemed for a second like it might stop, then it rolled neatly over the top.

Kett saw Billie. He saw Alice and Evie and Moira.

Then the ground gave out beneath them, and he saw nothing at all.

CHAPTER NINETEEN

THERE WAS NO TIME TO BRACE. NO TIME TO SCREAM. No time to do anything at all.

Porter grabbed the handle above the door, planting his other hand on the dash as the Skoda flipped onto its roof and started to roll down the hill.

It was like being under fire, the windscreen detonating in a tornado of flying glass, the other remaining windows following suit. The car slammed onto its side, metal compacting around Porter's body like they were inside a crusher. It snapped onto its wheels, then its other side, Kett's head cracking against the door with a sickening thud. Then they were rolling again, the roof punching down, the airbag detonating like a kick to the face and filling the car with a storm of white powder.

Porter fought for breath, inhaling glass and spitting blood. He didn't even know which way was up anymore, the world shaken to pieces as they rolled and rolled and rolled, as the car grew smaller and smaller until surely it was no bigger than a coffin.

Then, after what might have been forever, it came to rest on its roof.

Porter tried to speak, no air inside him. His belt was still clipped in but he was lying on the ceiling, his neck pushed at such a severe angle he thought it might be about to snap. He tried to look to the side but he couldn't, the car wrapped around him like a steel suit.

"Robbie?" he croaked.

No answer, not that he'd have been able to hear it over the ringing in his ears.

He turned the other way, to the window. There was nothing out there, no sign of the ground, no sign of the sky. The panic that ripped through him was like nothing he'd ever felt before.

I'm dead, he thought. And he saw Allie, he saw her holding a child he'd never know, a child that would never have the chance to be.

"No," he grunted, feeling for his seatbelt. "Not. Fucking. Dead."

He couldn't be dead because he could hear the distant growl of the tractor. There was something else, too. Voices. A *lot* of voices.

Getting closer.

He felt for the buckle of the seatbelt, finding the button. It was jammed, the belt stuck tight. His hand went to his pocket instead, his fingers almost too numb to feel what they were doing. They worked their way inside, finding his keys, and past that the slim metal shape of his pocketknife. He eased it out as gently as he could, his fingers slick with what might have been blood. He was going to drop it, he knew. He was going to lose it. And that would be bad. That would be *really fucking bad*. Because past the reek of spilled petrol he could smell something else.

He could smell smoke.

"Robbie?" he tried again. "You okay?"

It was a stupid question, and it didn't get an answer.

"If you can hear me, stay with me. I'm going to get us out of here."

He opened the blade, sawing at the belt. The voices were definitely getting closer, and even though he couldn't pick out any words they didn't sound friendly. Whoever had driven them off the hill was coming to finish the job.

He spat blood, feeling it drip up his nose and onto his forehead. The belt was tough but the knife was sharp. It was getting through it. He doubled his efforts, pain creeping into his hands, into his neck, into every single part of him.

The belt snapped and his body slumped onto the upturned roof. There was barely any room to move, one of his feet pinned in the crushed footwell. He tugged at it until he felt his shoe come free, then wormed his way onto his side to find Kett.

Even though it was almost pitch black, the sight of his friend almost stopped his heart dead.

Kett was motionless, his chest flat.

"Robbie?" croaked Porter. "Fuck."

He pressed the button for Kett's seatbelt and it popped free, the DCI crumpling to a heap. Still no movement, no sign of life at all. Porter would have checked for a pulse but there was no time. He worked his feet through the window, grunting as he pushed himself out of the car—his legs, his stomach, the glass grinding against his skin, his chest. The air was beautifully cold, focussing him like a slap to the face.

He peeked over the still-spinning wheel, not quite able to accept how far they'd rolled. The top of the hill was fifty yards away, and it was swarming with torchlight. Five or six people were making their way down it, all of them shouting.

They'd be here in minutes.

Porter wiggled his head back through the window, trying not to breathe in the acrid, poisonous air. There was no sign of flames yet, but they would come. You didn't have smoke without fire, after all.

"Robbie? Stay with me, mate."

He grabbed Kett under his arms, trying to get enough leverage to pull him across the ruined ceiling. He was a dead weight, his right leg trapped behind the steering wheel.

"Come on!"

Porter yanked as hard as he could until Kett's leg came free. The going was easier after that and he hauled him one inch at a time until he slid out through the window. The world tilted, veering like a wheel that had spun free of its axle, and for an awful second Porter almost slipped into unconsciousness. He put one hand on the car, biting his lip to try to keep himself awake.

Only then did he put his fingers to Kett's throat.

"Come on, Robbie. Do not Kett this up."

Nothing. Kett lay there as still as a photograph.

"Do not fucking do this," said Porter, adjusting his fingers.

Nothing. Nothing.

Thump.

He felt the pulse and the night grew instantly brighter. He left his fingers there for another few seconds, just to be sure, then he peeked past the wheel again.

The men had reached the bottom of the hill and were running this way.

Fast.

Porter looked behind him, seeing the field. It had been

ploughed, the peaks frozen stiff by the cold. Maybe thirty yards away was an old oak tree, the kind they weren't allowed to cut down anymore.

Thank God.

He stood, teetering again like he'd had too much to drink. Then he grabbed Kett beneath the arms once more and began to haul him across the dirt. It was a good thing the men had reached the bottom of the slope because now the car sat between them, shielding Porter from view. The torches cut through the night like searchlights, clustering on the car. He could hear the shouts more clearly now but he didn't recognise the language.

There was still time.

He slipped on a ridge, falling onto his backside, up again in a heartbeat. Kett was groaning, his hands grasping at the soil, his feet kicking.

"Hang on," Porter whispered, using every single thing he had to drive himself backwards over the field.

He reached the tree at the same time the men reached the car. He saw the beams of torchlight converge, then another round of furious shouts when they realised it was empty. He grabbed Kett by the lapels of his suit and hauled him over the tree's enormous roots, lowering him on the other side with as much grace as he could manage—which honestly wasn't much.

By the time he'd crouched down beside him, one hand on his chest, Kett's eyes were open.

"Hush," Porter said, his finger to the DCI's lips.

Kett blinked, putting a hand to his temple and wincing. But he kept quiet.

Porter reached for his phone but it must have fallen from his pocket during the crash. He felt Kett's pockets, finding his. Somehow, it had survived, and he unlocked it with Kett's mangled face before calling 999.

"This is DI Peter Porter," he said quietly when he was through. "Norfolk Police. I'm in need of immediate assistance. We are under attack. Uh... Toltham. There's a farm on the hill, just off the main road west of the town. Multiple assailants, one officer badly injured."

"I'm fine," croaked Kett, trying to sit up.

"Badly injured," Porter repeated. "If we don't get help soon, we're fucked."

He left the call open and threw the phone down.

"I'm fine," said Kett again.

Porter helped him up and they peeked around the tree together. The men were still clustered around the car, but they wouldn't be for long.

"I thought you were a goner," Porter said when they ducked back into hiding.

"How did we even get over here?" said Kett. "Did you drag me all that way?"

"Yeah."

"You've ruined my bloody suit, Pete," said Kett, laughing painfully.

"Well, it could have been a lot worse. Luckily this oak was here."

"I thought you hated trees."

Porter grinned.

"Not this one. This one's my friend."

He checked the car again. The men were beaming their torches everywhere, talking loudly in a language he still didn't recognise. One of them was holding something in his hand that looked like a bottle. He was using his other hand to spark a lighter.

"They're going to find us any minute," he said quietly.

"I've called for backup. They're not going to be anywhere near fast enough. Can you walk?"

"Sure," said Kett. He flexed his leg. "Probably."

"Wait here. I'm going to go find us some wheels."

He squeezed Kett's shoulder and stood up. Everything ached, but he couldn't feel the grinding agony of a broken bone. He'd been lucky.

He just hoped his luck wasn't going to run out.

"Stay out of sight, sir," he said.

"Nah," said Kett with another wincing laugh. "Thought about just getting out there, dancing a jig. Playing a little tune on the trombone."

Porter laughed quietly, took another quick look at the Skoda, then broke cover. The night was his friend, his dark suit the perfect camouflage as he ran to his left, cutting a wide circle around the men. They were arguing amongst themselves, their torches sweeping the fields. One danced in front of Porter, moving on before the light hit him.

He kept his head down, running blind. The furrowed ground did its best to trip him but he stayed upright until the slope of the hill caught his foot. There, he sprawled, getting a mouthful of wiry grass as he landed on his face.

Looking back, he saw the man with the lighter set fire to the bottle in his hand. There was a rag in it, a Molotov cocktail, and in the light of the fire Porter saw the fury on his face. The other men yelled at him but he paid them no attention, standing back and lobbing the bottle through the Skoda's window.

The car didn't stand a chance, the bottle exploding with a dull thud and setting alight the petrol that had leaked from the tank. In seconds it was an inferno, too bright to stare at. Porter could feel the heat of it from all the way over by the base of the hill.

The light reached him here too. All they'd have to do was turn around and they'd see him.

The men seemed more interested in the tree, though. The old oak seemed to dance in the firelight, its immense bare branches creaking in the wind like it was calling for their attention. Three of them were making their way over to it now, their torches laying a path of light over the stubbled field.

"Shit," Porter said.

He started up the hill, surprised at how gentle the slope actually was—it had felt like a sheer drop a moment ago when the car had been rolling down it. He broke into a run, his calves and his quads burning with lactic acid, his heart too big in his chest, thumping wetly, about to burst. He crouched as he approached the top, peeking past the grassy verge to see the tractor, its engine still running. Parked close by was the black Mercedes, its lights back on and its engine purring.

There was another man up here, leaning against the tractor and speaking into his phone. He was maybe twenty yards away, and fortunately, he was staring at the barn.

Porter couldn't see Cat anywhere.

He eased himself over the verge, the gravel crunching beneath his remaining boot, cutting into the flesh of his bare foot. Down in the field the car blazed like a sacrificial pyre, and the men were almost at the tree.

There was no time.

He had to act.

Fuck it.

Porter walked as fast as he dared, heading for the Mercedes. The man shouted into his phone, obviously arguing with somebody. All he had to do was turn around and this would be over.

But he didn't. He bunched a fist and slammed it into the side of the tractor, almost screaming into the phone now.

Porter reached the Mercedes and opened the driver's door, holding his breath as he sunk into the seat. He checked the back to make sure he was alone, then peered through the windscreen. From here he couldn't see the field past the verge, but he knew the men would have almost reached the tree by now.

If they hadn't already.

"Now or never, Pete," he said to himself, his pulse boxing the back of his throat.

He slammed the door, seeing the man with the phone spin around.

"Nu!" he yelled. "Nu!"

There was just enough time for Porter to give him the finger, then he stamped on the accelerator.

For a fraction of a second, the car didn't respond.

Then it took off, the big engine gunning hard. The wheels spun, spitting gravel, and Porter almost lost control. He eased off the pedal before punching it again, accelerating past the tractor and the screaming man—and whatever he was pulling from his jacket.

A shot ripped through the air, the unmistakable crack of a gun.

Porter ducked, the Mercedes flying over the cattle grid and down the road. He glanced right, seeing the field and the burning Skoda, seeing the men standing in confusion. He honked the horn, kept honking it, making sure he had their attention until as one they began to run towards him.

He reached the bottom of the hill in a heartbeat, but he wasn't heading for the main road. There was a gate to his right, leading into the field, and he stopped the car beside it.

It wasn't locked but it still took him longer to open it than he'd have liked.

By the time he was back in the car he could see torches strobing down the hill through the thick hedge, could hear the angry bellows of the men.

He manoeuvred the Mercedes through the gate and onto the field. It was a low car and he wasn't sure if the suspension could handle the frozen ridges, but it accelerated easily enough. Everything juddered, Porter bouncing so much in his seat that his head kept cracking against the ceiling.

He hit twenty, then thirty, and by the time the first of the men came into view he was churning across the field at almost fifty miles per hour.

He could tell they wanted to play chicken, but he was glad they didn't. The first guy hurled himself out of the way with a good few seconds to spare. The second almost didn't make it in time, the wing mirror clipping his arm. The third was trying to light another Molotov cocktail but Porter was past him before the rag caught.

Ahead was the fire, and past that the oak tree. Kett was leaning against it, waving his arm in the air. The men were all in the rearview mirror now, giving chase but shrinking fast.

Porter eased his foot off the accelerator for fear of losing the car's undercarriage. He slowed to a halt next to the tree, reaching over to open the passenger door. Kett climbed in, closing it behind him. He had his phone in his hand and he managed a smile.

"Your ride has—" Porter started.

The air was ripped in half by another gunshot, something thwacking the side of the car. Porter yelped, accelerating again. The car spun, the wheels thundering over the dirt. There was one more gunshot, lost to the wind, then Porter spotted a gap in the hedge and steered the car through it.

He found the road, threw a heartfelt thank you to the heavens, and drove.

CHAPTER TWENTY

THE UNIVERSE CHURNED, AS FAST AS A WASHING machine in full spin, and Kett rose from his dream like a man who had been hurled from a clifftop.

He sat up, pain flooding his leg and his head. Something tugged against the hairs on his chest and in his confusion he thought it was the steering wheel of the car. He grabbed it, twisting, his other arm flailing so hard that he heard something shatter.

"Easy," said a voice.

Kett tore himself from the last grip of sleep, opening his eyes to see that he wasn't in the car. He wasn't rolling down the hill, the Skoda crushing him like a metal fist.

He was in a hospital room, the lights dimmed, the door closed.

"Shit," he said, lying back down, feeling the pulse monitor on his chest. He ran his hands up his arms but there was nothing else there. No IV, no morphine. His ears were still ringing like he had microphone feedback blaring into his skull. Past that he could hear the sounds of a hospital at night, dormant bleeps and quiet voices.

And the rattle of somebody breathing.

He angled his head, pain sloshing from back to front like his skull had been filled with acid. It was too dark in the room to make out the person who sat in the corner.

"Pete?" Kett asked, his voice like gravel.

"No."

There was no kindness in the voice at all. It was as blunt as a hammer. Kett felt too vulnerable lying there so he pushed himself up as far as he could, half sitting. The pain in his right leg was localised around his knee. He felt like the cap had been scooped off, the tender flesh beneath throbbing. The man in the chair leaned forward, sniffing. There was still no light on his face but Kett recognised the sheer bulk of him.

"Wallace Marshall," he said.

"In the flesh," Marshall replied. "It's good to see you awake, son. I've been sitting here for far too long."

"Sorry to keep you waiting. Where are we?"

His memories were like shattered glass. He could see fragments of the last few hours—the interview with Catherine Cavaney, following the Mercedes, then being shunted off the hill by the tractor. What followed was less clear, the fragments harder to piece together, but he knew one thing: Porter had saved his life, and more than once.

"We're in the James Paget," said Marshall, sinking back into the shadows. "Your friend brought you here after your... *adventure* last night. Apparently, you passed out in the car on the drive over."

Kett touched his temple, wincing as the pain in his head grew worse.

"It looks bad, but it's nothing to worry about. Or so I'm told. You were lucky. Some folk slip on their bathroom floor and knock the life right out of themselves. I saw the car. The pretty pink one, although it's not pink no more, more barbeque black. I don't know how anyone climbed out of that alive."

Kett rested his head against the bed, closing his eyes for a moment. When he swallowed, his mouth was bone dry. He felt a surprising surge of remorse at the Skoda's fate. It hadn't been his car, it had belonged to the girls. It hadn't deserved to be beaten and burned.

Still, better the car than him.

"Is Porter okay?" Kett asked. He saw Marshall's head nod up and down slowly.

"He's a tank, that one. He dragged you to safety, did he tell you?"

"Yeah," said Kett as the memories continued to slot themselves into place like Tetris blocks.

"Then he stole their car from right under their noses and came to get you."

"I remember."

"There's a medal with his name on it. Of this, I'm certain."

"Who were they?" Kett asked.

Marshall sniffed again, shifting his bulk in the chair.

"Why don't you tell me, DCI Kett?"

"What do you mean?"

"I mean by the time the rest of us made it to the party, the men who attacked you had gone. Vanished into the night."

He leaned forward again, his broad face pushing into the light like some kind of sea creature looming out of the depths.

"You let them go," he said with a soft *tut*.

"Wasn't like we had much of a choice," Kett said. "One

of them was armed. Sounded like a pistol rather than a shotgun."

"Can you tell me anything else about them?" Marshall asked.

"I'm not planning on telling you anything else at all," said Kett. "You're not a copper anymore, remember?"

Marshall laughed quietly, sniffing again like he had a cold. After a few seconds of silence, he hauled himself out of the chair with considerable effort, crossing the room like an oil tanker on rough seas. He grabbed the end of Kett's bed and stood there. He looked exhausted, Kett thought, the folds of his face and chins so loose that it looked like a mask about to slip off. His eyes were bloodshot, and so yellow that it had to be a medical thing. His liver, maybe.

"You know as well as I do that once your blood is blue, it never runs red again," he said. "I'll never be anything else. Folks around here, they rely on me. I provide a service."

"Yeah?" said Kett.

"Yeah."

Marshall was an intimidating presence, and Kett tried to push himself higher up the bed. The big man's lips curled into a smile as he watched Kett strain.

"I keep things smooth," he said. "I keep things oiled. Which is why I can't have loose cannons like you running around fucking everything up."

"What things?" said Kett, his head pounding. "The drugs?"

Marshall sniffed again, then ran the back of his hand over his nose. He wiped the same hand on Kett's blanket, making a show of it. There was something about the size of him, about the shape of his face, that made Kett think of the Pig Man—Angus Schofield standing in the inferno of Bingo's flat, Alice gripped in his arms.

"I know you, Robert Kett," Marshall said. "I've seen your cases, I've watched you on the news. The truth is, I like you. I like what you stand for."

Kett didn't reply. He glanced at the door, willing Porter to come in, or Savage, or Clare. He felt like a child, dressed in nothing but hospital robes and bandages, protected by a paper-thin sheet. He felt like a child who's just watched the bogeyman crawl out from under the bed.

"You're like me. The only thing that matters is the end result. Fuck everything else. Fuck procedure. Fuck protocol and orders and consequences. Get the job done, and all is forgiven."

"That's not true," said Kett, although he could hear the hollowness of his words.

"But it is, Robbie. It is. Do you know what I would have done for a unit like yours, back in the day? Extreme Crime? I'd have given my left fucking nut for the freedom that you have. Get the job done, no matter what it takes, no matter how many blind eyes the rest of us have to turn. I weep when I think of what I could have accomplished."

"Nobody is above the law," said Kett.

"Not even you," Marshall butted in, before Kett could finish. "Not even you."

Marshall took another step towards him, holding tight to the railing to stop himself from keeling over. He sniffed again.

"I never liked the winter. But I'm still sad I don't have many left. I'm going to ask you again, Detective. What can you tell me about the men who attacked you?"

"Nothing," said Kett.

"Because you've upset the apple cart. You've blown up the fucking bridge. I don't even have a good analogy for what you've done." He paused. "Actually, I do. You *fucked* me."

"Marshall," Kett started. "You need to back—"

Marshall reached out a flabby hand and grabbed Kett's injured knee, squeezing. The pain rolled through him so hard that the room blazed white for a second, everything strobing. Kett opened his mouth and growled like an animal. He reached for Marshall's hand only for the big ex-copper to grab his wrist. He was as strong as a giant, his breaths coming in ragged, wheezing gulps.

"If you've scared those men away, then we have a serious fucking problem," he said, the words wet against Kett's ear. He squeezed his damaged knee harder and a groan spilled its way from Kett's mouth without his permission. "I have worked too long and too hard to have it all fucked up now. Stay away from me. Stay away from Toltham."

There was the sound of voices from outside and Marshall let go, standing back.

"Remember, son," he said. "I know where you live."

The door opened and Porter's face appeared, instantly breaking into a grin.

"You're awake," he said.

Kett nodded, the pain ebbing its way from the rest of his body back into his knee. He drove his fists into the thin mattress and pushed himself up the bed so that he was sitting, the effort leaving him breathless. Porter's smile vanished as he looked at Marshall.

"What's going on?" he said. "What are you doing here?"

"I'm just leaving," Marshall said, lifting a wide-brimmed Panama hat from the back of the chair. "I just came in to tell your friend how thankful I am that he's still with us. You too, Detective. I'm amazed, to be honest. Those were some bad men."

Porter stood to one side as Marshall walked to the door.

"I can say with some authority that your escape tonight was a fluke. I don't think you'll be so lucky next time."

"Yeah?" Porter said, spluttering. "Well..."

He shrugged his shoulders, but Marshall was gone.

"Where's a good comeback when you need one?" he said, walking to the bed. "You okay, sir? You're whiter than those sheets."

"I'm fine," said Kett, the chaos of his thoughts starting to settle. "But I think we did a good job of pissing him off last night."

"That's the only reason I did it. I thought, shall I have a good night's rest and put my feet up, or get into a car chase and firefight just to annoy Wallace Marshall?"

Kett laughed, then clamped his mouth shut around it to stop the pain from spreading.

"Seriously, sir, are you okay?"

"Got a munter of a headache," he said. "But it will pass."

"Good news is nothing's broken," said Porter. "They x-rayed you when you were out, checked you for concussion too. Knee's a bit twisted but other than that, you ain't broke."

"Ain't broke," said Kett, relieved. "That's a professional medical diagnosis if I ever heard one. Are you okay?"

"I ache like a bastard," said Porter. "But by some miracle, yeah, I am. That Skoda was tougher than it looked. Saved both our lives."

"To the legend that was the Mermaid Adventure Castle," said Kett, lifting his hand in an imaginary toast. "Does Billie know?"

"That you almost died? No. We thought we'd wait for the doc to report back, and when he gave you the all-clear we figured we wouldn't worry her."

"Good," said Kett. "Thanks. What *was* that last night?"

Porter sighed, but before he could answer there was a knock at the open door and Savage walked in.

"Good to see you awake, sir," she said, taking a seat on the chair that Marshall had just vacated. "For a little while there..."

She shook her head, the words better left unsaid.

"Timeline is this," Porter said. "We got out of the farm at 9:37. We—"

"Thanks, by the way," Kett said. "Thanks for pulling me out. And thanks for coming back for me."

Porter looked genuinely embarrassed. He nodded to Kett.

"I was just imagining what your girls would have done to me if I hadn't brought you home," he said after a moment. "But yeah, we got out of there at 9:37. I didn't wait for backup because you were out like a light again as soon as we hit the road. Came straight to the closest A&E."

"Helicopter reached the farm about fifteen minutes after you'd left," Savage said. "It was deserted. They scoured the countryside with the infrareds but no sign of anyone."

"I don't know how they got away so fast," said Porter. "Because the only vehicle they had left was the tractor, and that was still there when Uniforms arrived."

"Any sign of Cat?" asked Kett. Porter shook his head.

"We have no idea what happened to her. I'm pretty sure she went with the men, although I can't say if she went voluntarily or not."

"That's got to be our priority," Kett said. "Find her.

They might think she's responsible for what happened, and that would not be good."

"The farm's a dead end," said Savage. "It's been empty for years. They're still searching it but they haven't found anything."

She glanced at Porter.

"But there is some good news. You want to, sir, or shall I?"

Porter gestured for her to carry on.

"The Mercedes you stole, the one they picked Cat up in, had a boot full of drugs."

"Really?" said Kett.

"Really. I'm talking a serious haul. We found six kilos of cocaine, two of heroin, and a suitcase full of methamphetamines."

"Holy shit," said Kett.

"We crashed a deal," said Porter.

"Jaw Breaker?" Kett asked.

"I don't know. The chemists are working out exactly what we're looking at, but that's a lot of poison off the streets."

For the first time since he'd woken, Kett let himself relax. He closed his eyes again, the pain an actual physical pressure against his skull.

"We can talk about this in the morning, sir," said Savage.

"I'm okay," he replied. "So it was a deal. Cat was part of it, right? You were right, that's what she was talking about in her note. She was scared because Seb was supposed to be there too. But why the wig? I still don't get it."

"I think I do, sir," said Savage. "I was thinking about it, about that little gang of them. We know Seb was dealing, Neil too and probably Pete. Cat was tied up with all this somehow, and before she arrived on the scene Niamh was helping them."

"Cat told us that, didn't she?" Kett asked, opening his eyes. Fireworks raced across the dark but he suspected they were more to do with his exhaustion than anything else.

"Yeah. She said that Niamh was dealing alongside Neil, Seb and Pete. Maybe she built a reputation as somebody to trust, a go-between for the gangs. Then she died in the hit and run last year, which is a problem because maybe the dealers don't trust anyone else. But the dealers don't know Niamh died, and Seb spots Cat at Christmas in her elf costume or whatever and he realises the two of them look alike. He befriends her, lets her in on their activity, asks for her help."

"Gives her the wig," said Kett.

"Right. We found another one in Seb's caravan, the wrong shade. He gives her the *right* wig, a fake nose piercing. The other dealers show up to collect their drugs and there's the same girl there with purple hair and piercings. In the dark, from a distance, they assume it's Niamh. Nobody is going to be looking too closely. The deal goes through, everyone goes home."

"That makes a lot of sense," Kett said. "Good thinking."

Savage grinned.

"So Cat was picked up last night by whoever worked with Seb and Neil and the others," Kett said, thinking out loud. "They drive to the farm with a carload of drugs. There were too many of those men to have fit in the Mercedes, so either they were heavies who were already at the farm, or they were the buyers. They were foreign, weren't they?"

"Yeah," said Porter. "I remembered a few words, gave them to Clare. He thinks they sounded Eastern European."

"Lithuanian?" said Kett. "Like Mantas. I thought the guy at Cat's house, the one driving the Merc, was bald."

"Hard to say, sir," said Porter. "Most of them were wearing hats, and it was dark."

"The pieces fit, though," Kett said. "Rachel said the gossip at the hotel was that they were working with a European outfit."

"Europe's a big place, sir."

"Fair point. What does Clare make of it all?"

"Well, he wasn't happy to be dragged out of the spa," Porter said.

"He was *back* in the spa?"

"Foot massage," Savage said, and the three of them shuddered.

"But he agrees there's something big going on. We were in the right place at the right time." Porter laughed, but there was no humour there. "Well, depending on how you look at it. He's bringing out some more people to try to find these arseholes."

"Good," said Kett. The conversation was making him feel sick, the room starting to spin. "As soon as I'm out of here I'll..."

He had to stop, because the words were simply too painful.

"We'll leave you," said Porter. "Get some rest. Tomorrow's going to be a busy day."

"And not for the reason you think," Savage said. "The boss has signed us up for a communication through mime workshop."

"Oh no," Kett said, sliding back down into the bed and letting his eyes close. "I think I'd rather have the concussion."

CHAPTER TWENTY-ONE

Sunday

DURING THE DARK TIMES, AND THERE HAD BEEN MANY over the years, Billie often told Kett that sleep was the best medicine.

And she was right.

Kett slept so deeply that he didn't dream, the night a pocket of darkness as quiet and as peaceful as the grave. When he next woke he saw the sun streaming through the window, heard the birds singing outside.

He sat up carefully, waiting for the agony to return to his skull, for the fire to start burning in his knee. His leg still ached, but his head felt like it had been flushed with ice water. Apart from a slight tenderness in his temple, he felt fine. It was like the entire evening had been a dream.

He sat up, finding his phone to see that it was dead. Shards of porcelain lay on the floor and he remembered knocking a cup off the table last night when he'd woken in a panic. There was no clock in his room so he swung himself off the bed—trying not to look at the ugly purple bruise that circled his kneecap—and tested his legs. There was a second of dizziness, then the world settled.

You're a lucky bastard, he told himself, hunting the room for his suit. There was no sign of it but somebody had left a bundle of clothes folded neatly on the chair. He hesitated before picking them up, thinking about his visit from Wallace Marshall. He didn't doubt that the old ex-copper was corrupt, but that wasn't the extent of what bothered him. Marshall had made him feel like a child last night, and Kett hated him for it.

He picked up a pair of Adidas jogging bottoms and eased them on, discarding the robe before picking up a hooded sweatshirt. There was an illustrated picture of the Yarmouth seafront on it, with the words '*I'm your Beach*' written in glittery rainbow letters.

"Classy."

He pulled it on, flexing his neck to try to work out some of the knots of discomfort. In the safety of the day, the events of yesterday were coming back to him. He had to brace a hand on the wall as he remembered rolling down the hill, the car shrinking like it had been in a compactor. After that, there was nothing until he'd woken in the shelter of that oak tree, Porter's hand over his mouth.

He couldn't believe he was still alive, that *either* of them had survived.

His boots were where he'd left them, caked in dirt, and he sat on the chair to pull them on. He had to stay sitting for a moment, breathing hard, before pushing himself back up again. His wallet was next to his phone and he grabbed both, looking for his keys before remembering they'd been lost to the fire. Knowing that he'd never get the little keychain back, the one Evie had made for him in nursery with two smiling stick figures, hit him harder than anything else.

The hospital was busy, the nurses on duty too tired to argue with him when he asked to be discharged.

"Hey, what time is it?" he enquired as he was walking out the door.

"Just after ten."

There were taxis outside and he jumped into one, asking to be taken to the lodge. It was a shorter journey than he'd expected, just over ten minutes before he found himself on the long, winding drive lined with topiary animals.

"Cheers mate," he said, tapping his card to the reader.

"No worries, pal," the man replied. "Take a card, we're out this way all the time if you want to do any sightseeing."

Kett nodded his thanks, taking a business card from the box and exiting into the brisk morning air. A handful of people stood outside the main doors, chatting to each other and drowning in cigarette smoke. They barely even glanced at Kett as he walked in, and most of their attention was taken up by his jumper. The empty reception was dark, the lights and computers off. When Kett walked into the main corridor he saw that the lights were off in here, too. Staff scurried back and forth in a mad panic.

"What's going on?" he asked a young woman as she passed him.

"I don't know," she called back. "Somebody's cut the electrics."

That wasn't good.

Kett doubled back into reception, checking the office behind the desk to see that it was empty. He made his way past the dining hall and the breakfast room, heading for the main office, but stopped when he passed the little room where they'd made the baskets yesterday. He could hear Porter's voice from inside, and sure enough when he peeked through the door he saw the big DI standing by the window, scratching his head. There were a dozen other people in the room, all of them sitting around tables laden with tea-making equipment. Rachel Turkentine stood next to Porter, examining the electrical sockets in the wall.

"I just don't understand it," she said. "This has never happened before."

"It wasn't me," Porter said. "Was it?"

"Everything okay in here?" Kett asked, and everybody turned to look at him.

"Welcome back, sir," said Porter with a smile that didn't last.

"What's up?" Kett asked.

"I'm not sure," said Rachel. "Everything was swell, and then it wasn't."

"My kettle isn't working," said Porter, gesturing at the little kettle plugged into the wall by his table.

"I think the electrics are out," Kett said. "Nothing is working."

"Um, yeah," said Rachel. "Everything *was* working. We managed to get every other kettle working."

The other people in the room nodded.

"Until Peter plugged his in," Rachel said. "Then it all went dark."

Kett couldn't stop the smile from landing on his lips.

"Are you telling me that Pete tried to make a cup of tea and managed to short the entire hotel?"

"No," said Porter. "That's not what happened."

"I think that's exactly what happened," Rachel said. "I don't understand it."

"He's cursed," Kett said. "That's the only explanation.

Don't let him touch the tea bags or planes will start falling from the sky. Come on, Pete. I need you anyway."

"Sorry, Rachel," Porter said. "Sorry, everyone."

He followed Kett into the corridor, shaking his head. There were a few small bruises around his eyes, and a nasty cut on his chin, but other than that—and the fact he was wearing bright white trainers with his suit—there was no indication at all he'd been in a car accident the night before.

"Cursed," Kett said again as they started walking. "Where is everyone?"

"Clare's out coordinating the search up at the farm. Savage is with him. I have no idea where Duke is. How're you feeling, sir?"

"Good," said Kett, climbing the stairs. "Amazingly. I need to pop to my room and get cleaned up. Was this thing your doing?"

He gestured to the jumper and Porter barked out a laugh.

"Kate's, believe it or not. There's not many places open in Yarmouth at that time of night, she got it from the garage."

"She get your shoes from there too?"

"No," said Porter with a pout. "These are Nike Metcons. Brought them myself in case there was a gym."

"Fair enough. I thought you'd have woken me up, day's half gone already."

"Boss said to let you rest."

Porter held open the door to the economy rooms and Kett walked through.

"Still no sign of the men who attacked us," he said "No hits on any NPRs, no CCTV footage. They vanished. The plate on the back of the Merc was a dud, stolen from another vehicle."

"They're organised," said Kett. "They'll know the area, they'll know how to avoid being seen. What about Cat?"

"Nothing," said Porter. "It looks more and more likely that they took her with them."

"Not good."

Kett reached his room, realising that he didn't have the key card. He pounded on the door instead.

"Duke? You in there?"

"No," groaned a reply.

"Open the door."

Another groan, and the sound of somebody clomping across the floor. The door opened to reveal PC Duke in nothing but his pants. With his beard, his six-pack and an enormous Celtic cross tattooed over the ridges of his chest, he looked like a cross between a Viking and an underwear model.

"It is way too early to see that," Kett said. "Put some bloody clothes on, Duke."

"Why are you still in bed?" Porter exclaimed. "It's half-past ten you great sloth."

"It was a late night, sir," Duke said, retreating into the room. "And nobody woke me. And I'm on holiday."

"Unbelievable," said Porter. "I'll wait here. Smells like somebody's been collecting dog farts in that room."

He wasn't wrong, and the first thing Kett did was open the curtains and crack the window. He turned to the small room, frowning.

"Duke, did you sleep in my bed?"

"You weren't using it, sir," he said.

Kett glanced into the bathroom, seeing the open Colgate packaging in the bin.

"Tell me you didn't use my toothbrush."

"I'm not going to lie, sir."

"Great. Get dressed."

Duke grumbled beneath his breath but proceeded to pull on his tiny shorts, which had been drying on the radiator.

"Not them, Duke," Kett said. "The *suit.*"

Kett plugged in his phone then pulled his spare clothes out of the wardrobe, walking into the microscopic bathroom and closing the door behind him. He could see Duke almost perfectly through the barely frosted glass as the big PC buttoned his shirt.

"What happened at Pete Duggan's house last night?" he asked as he pulled off his trousers and underwear, easing the jumper over his head. He turned on the shower, which let loose a shuddering moan and a trickle of water.

"Back door was open," said Duke. "We made entry, the place had been trashed."

"Trashed as in untidy, or ransacked?"

"Ransacked, definitely. Furniture overturned, couple of windows smashed. We had time to knock on a couple of doors. One bloke said he heard yelling on Friday night, crashing, but he said Pete always had unsavoury people round, parties, that kind of stuff, so he didn't even bother checking."

Kett stepped into the shower, feeling like he was standing beneath a leaky gutter. The water was cold and it felt almost *greasy*. He pumped some shower gel from the container and washed himself, aware that Duke was still talking.

"Hang on," he yelled. "I can't hear you."

To his horror, he heard the bathroom door open.

"I said his neighbour told us he saw Pete leave his house after all the racket, maybe ten o'clock on Friday evening. He looked in a state, but he put it down to, and I quote, 'Whatever toxic shit that little druggie prick had snorted that night.'"

Kett rinsed himself off then peeked around the shower curtain.

"Do you mind?" he said.

"Oh, sure," Duke replied, stepping out of the room and leaving the door wide open. Kett had one foot out of the cubical when the PC returned, a towel in his hand. "Neighbour couldn't tell us where he was going, just that he was heading into town."

He proffered the towel and Kett took it, shaking his head in disbelief. Duke carried on, oblivious.

"We didn't have time to ask any more questions because the call came in about you and Porter and we scrambled. Is it true they were shooting at you?"

"Yeah," said Kett.

"Scary."

"Not as scary as it's going to be in a minute when I step out of here stark bollock naked."

Duke nodded, frowned, then nodded again.

"No problem, sir."

He vanished, leaving the door wide open again.

"For fuck's sake," muttered Kett.

He got out, his knee almost giving way beneath him as he lunged for the door and slammed it shut. It took him longer to dry himself than he'd have liked because the room was so small, but after a few minutes he was dressed. He brushed his teeth and ran his hand over his stubble, wishing he'd remembered to bring a razor. Then he grabbed his jacket from the back of the door and walked out.

Duke was sitting on the bed lacing up his boots, and Kett had to squeeze past him to reach his phone. It was still charging, but it was back on. Seven texts were waiting for him, two from Savage, one from Clare and the rest from Billie—each one more concerned than the last.

Sorry, phone died. Everything's fine, he wrote to his wife. *Hope you're all okay. Miss you.*

He called Clare, the Super picking up after two rings.

"Kett. How're you doing?"

"Better, sir. Knee hurts like a bastard but everything else is fine. What's going on?"

"I'm still at the farm," Clare said. "Get over here ASAP, and see if you can find Duke on your way."

"Be there in five," Kett said.

He looked at Duke, who was *still* trying to tie his laces.

"Better make that ten."

IT DIDN'T LOOK like the same place.

Porter steered the Mondeo off the main road, its engine booming as they climbed the steep hill that led to the farm. Kett saw the skid marks on the road from when Porter had been driving the Mercedes, then the sculpture of tortured steel that sat halfway between the verge and the lonely oak tree. He felt another pang of guilt that the Skoda had met such a terrible end, and a deep sense of gratitude that the car had kept them alive.

A handful of coppers in white forensic suits were dotted across the field like seagulls, pecking at the furrowed dirt. They all looked up at the sound of Porter's car, none of them waving.

"They found anything?" Kett asked.

"Not as far as I know," Porter said, steering them carefully over the cattle grid. "But those men scattered like tenpins when I was coming to get you. There's no way they didn't drop something."

The twin barns loomed into view, one on either side of the road. Sitting beneath them like the corpse of some medieval monster was the tractor that had shunted them over the verge. There wasn't even a scratch on it. Clare stood beside it, speaking on his phone, and he turned to them as Porter stopped the car behind an IRV.

"Come on then!" he yelled as they were opening their doors. "I'm not getting any younger."

Last night's storm had done a good job of clearing the air, the exhausted wind now barely more than a breeze. The sun was low but Kett could feel the warmth of it as he made his way over to the Superintendent. In the light of day, he saw the farmhouse that sat in the shadow of the second barn, most of its roof missing. It was swarming with Uniforms, and Kett could see Savage in the middle of them, dressed in civilian clothes—black jeans and a black hoodie.

"Sir," said Kett with a nod.

"Good to see you up and about," Clare said, putting his phone into his pocket.

"You should have woken me."

"I wasn't even sure we'd get you back today. I still don't know how you two are alive. That's a heck of a hill."

It was. From here Kett couldn't even see the wreck, just the topmost branches of the tree that had sheltered him.

"Luck of the Devil," said Clare. "Toss all here. We can't even find any shell casings from the gun, they must have collected them. Somebody's been squatting in the farmhouse but they don't seem to have been there for a while. One of the wrappers we found was for a Marathon Bar."

"A what, sir?" said Duke as he and Porter caught up.

"Exactly. There's a fresh set of tyre tracks coming from

the south, past the farmhouse. A van. I think that's how they got away. You remember much about them?"

"They were European," said Kett. "I remember one word. *Grabitiva*, or something like it. They were yelling it at each other when Porter stole the car."

Porter had his phone out and Kett frowned.

"Thought you lost that last night."

"CSI folk found it on the field," Porter said. "Must have fallen through the window. It's cracked but it still works. A bit like me. You said *Grabitiva*?"

Kett nodded.

"First hit is Romanian. Means 'hurry up.'"

"Makes sense," said Kett. "That's all I remember. They were in dark coats, beanies. Two or three were wearing balaclavas."

"I could probably identify the man who was on his phone," said Porter. "The one with the gun. He was older, short grey hair. Mean face."

"That could describe most of the old men in the village," said Clare. "But it's something. Porter tell you we got the drugs?"

"Yeah," said Kett, breaking into a painful smile. "That's got to sting."

"Indeed, but they'll be angry." Clare looked at the sky, the breeze toying with his hair. He looked a good ten years younger without his nose foliage. "I'm going to pack the village with coppers just in case they try to retaliate."

"Does this mean we're not on holiday anymore?" Porter said.

"I'm afraid so."

"Yes!" the DI said with a fist pump. "Thank God for that."

"No sign of Catherine Cavaney yet?" Kett asked.

"No."

"And anything else on our two dead guys?"

"Tox report is back in, I haven't had a chance to check it in any detail yet but both young men had heroin, cocaine and what looks like quetiapine in their systems. That's an antipsychotic, a powerful one, and they were loaded with it. Franklin says there were needle marks in the arms of both men, but more than one so she doesn't know how fresh they are, and if they're related to what happened to them on Friday night. There is narcotic residue in their noses and in their stomachs, which means they were snorting and ingesting as well. She confirmed that there was no immediate sign of force or violence."

"You don't think it was intentional, do you, sir?" Kett asked.

"Suicide? No. It's highly doubtful. No letters, no reports of either of the men being in a suicidal state of mind. Seb had put down cash on a new car he was due to collect next week, and Neil had arranged to go visit his sister and his niece in King's Lynn. It's more likely to be a bad batch, and almost certainly linked to what we found in the boot of that Mercedes."

"What about Pete Duggan? Anything new on him?"

"Other than the fact he didn't show up for work this morning, and hasn't been seen since Friday night, no. We've got all eyes looking for him."

There was a shout from the direction of the farmhouse and Kett looked to see Savage running their way. She was holding something in her hand, a plastic bag that caught the light and seemed to glow like burning phosphorous.

"Morning, sir," she said to Kett.

"Savage."

She held up the bag and they all craned in to see what

looked like a crude child's toy—a doll made of twigs and wrapped in a dress stitched from strands of blue fabric and red ribbon. Leaves jutted out of the sleeves, and where its head should be was a ball of silver foil, two buttons glued there for eyes.

"What in the name of toss is that horrible thing?" Clare said.

"A doll," said Savage. "We found it in the farmhouse, in a basket."

"So?"

"The basket was lined with newspaper. Last week's. It was filled with white flowers."

Clare jutted his jaw out, then shrugged his bony shoulders.

"I was doing some reading," Savage went on. "This whole Imbolc thing the village was celebrating, St Brigid. Back in Celtic times, people would make dolls like this. Bit weird, isn't it? That we find one all the way out here?"

"I've seen these before," said Kett. "In the hotel reception and the office. And back when we went to look at Seb's body, by the lake. There was an archery range and it was lying by the fence. I'm sure of it. I didn't think anything of it at the time."

Clare turned to Savage.

"Find it."

"Seb's mum was into dolls as well," said Kett. "She had hundreds of them. Not like this but might be worth a trip."

"Savage, I need you on the cult," said Clare.

"It's hardly a cult, sir."

"Well, whatever they are, the Greenies. Knock on some doors, see if they're hiding anything."

"They hang out in the pub, don't they?" Savage said. "I'll start there."

"What about Mantas, sir?" Kett asked. "Should we question him?"

Clare considered it for a moment, then shook his head.

"I need you to focus on Wallace Marshall. I don't know what that man is doing, but I know in my gut that it's something to do with the drugs and the dead men. He came to your room last night, didn't he?"

"Yes, sir. Gave me a lot of shit about messing things up, getting in his way. He told me that if I'd scared those dealers away then I was in trouble."

"You think he's in on the action?" Savage said. "He still has enough clout with the locals around here to impede an investigation or give the dealers a warning when we're coming. He's obviously not poor, I saw him leaving the hospital car park in a Rolls, a *new* one."

"That was *his*?" asked Kett, remembering the car he'd seen outside Enthoven's place.

"And he has form for tipping off the bad guys," Clare said. "I've got a CI in Yarmouth, a guy called Noddy. I've worked with him for years and he's got his finger in just about everything. If anyone knows what Marshall's up to, it's him. I'll give you the address, I need you to go speak to him. He's a slippery bastard, so watch out."

"Yes, sir."

Clare shook his head, something on his mind.

"I have a confession," the Super said after a moment. "This whole holiday thing, I wanted to give you all a break, that part was true. You earned it after the Sweet Briar Rose case. But that wasn't the only reason I wanted to get us out here. We've been hearing talk about Toltham and about the lodge for months now, rumours about it being part of the east coast narcotics ring. About Wallace Marshall too. I just figured this was a good chance to take a closer look. I had no idea any of this was going to happen."

"I thought this whole trip was about teamwork, sir," said Porter.

Clare managed a grim smile.

"It is, Pete. It's all about teamwork. Because this is the Extreme Crime Task Force, and we're going to take these tossers down together."

CHAPTER TWENTY-TWO

Savage pulled the IRV into the small car park of Toltham's only pub, laughing when she saw the name.

"Pretty sure we're in the right place," she said to Duke. "The Green Man."

It was an old brick building that looked like it had always been a coach house of one kind or another. It was well-tended, the path from the car park to the front door lined with pots that boasted trees and bushes of all shapes and sizes. There were flowers, too, bluebells and snowdrops in hanging baskets and plenty more that Savage didn't recognise. Songbirds chased each other between the bird feeders that seemed to hang from every branch, the sound of them instantly soothing. With the sun coating the pub in golden light, the place was idyllic.

"Looks a bit shit," Duke said, cracking his knuckles.

Savage ignored him, leaving the car in the shade of an enormous willow tree and cutting the engine. The wind was picking up again, but with none of the strength of the previous night. She held her hair to stop the breeze from messing it up, but it was a lost cause.

It wasn't quite eleven yet and the door was locked, so Savage thumped on it. It was solid oak, probably a good couple of hundred years old, but it rattled in its frame like it wanted to jump out and run away.

"Hello?" she shouted. "Can you open up, please? It's the police."

She was aware she didn't really *look* like police in her jeans and hoodie, but there wasn't much she could do about that right now. Duke was wandering down the side of the building and she watched as he cupped his hand to the glass.

"People in there," he said. "A lot of them."

Savage hammered the door again and this time she heard somebody approaching. A bolt was pulled back and it creaked open like something from a horror movie. A tall, slim woman stood there wearing a pair of orange glasses and a matching dress. She was somewhere around sixty, her grey hair tied back in one of the most severe ponytails Savage had ever seen, one that pulled almost every single wrinkle out of her forehead. She peered at Savage over the top of her glasses, looking like a librarian about to reprimand a child for stealing a book.

Savage pulled out her warrant card and the woman's fierce eyes took in every detail.

"Hi. My name's DC Kate Savage, I work for the Norfolk Constabulary. This..."

She turned to introduce Duke only to find that he'd disappeared.

"Uh... never mind. May I come in?"

"It's really not a good time," said the woman, subtle shades of Irish in her haughty voice.

"Is there ever a good time?" Savage said. "It won't take long."

The woman huffed quietly, opening the door all the way. Savage wasn't exactly tall, but she still had to duck beneath the low lintel. The ceiling inside wasn't much higher, lined with dark beams that made it feel like a prison cell. Straight ahead was a small bar, draped with a veritable jungle of plants. The pub opened out to the right where nine people sat in a circle on the carpeted floor. They all had the palm of their right hand pressed to their forehead, rocking gently back and forth and making a low, droning noise that sounded almost like a Tibetan prayer. None of them looked up, but she recognised Gabriel Grundy from the lodge and the woman whose dog had discovered Sebastian's body, Mavis Kane.

"Like I said, this isn't a good time."

The woman closed the door behind Savage, locking it. She stood there looking just about as inconvenienced as anyone Savage had ever seen. She was making little tutting noises and shaking her head, her hands clasping the air by her sides.

"I can see I've interrupted something," said Savage, loud enough for everyone to hear. "I won't take up much of your time, I promise. Can I ask your name?"

"Amanda Walsh," she said.

"You're the landlady here?"

She nodded curtly, staring past Savage to where the group continued whatever it was they were doing.

"This is for Imbolc?" Savage asked, and the woman's eyebrows rose in surprise.

"Yes," she said. "Yes, it is. You're familiar with the tradition?"

"Brigid," Savage said. "The Celtic goddess of fire and fertility, right?"

"Indeed."

"You're Pagans?"

"Of a kind," Amanda said. "A hybrid faith, we're not keen on labels. My great-grandfolks brought it with them when they came to Norfolk. We're just humans, part of a vast and unbreakable chain of life and warmth and growth. Imbolc is only one of our traditions. What you see here is something slightly different. Imbolc has passed, and now we continue to give thanks."

"They're praying?" Savage asked.

"In a sense."

The sound of their throaty warbles was getting louder, the speed of their movements quickening.

"I really should get back to them," said Amanda, champing at the bit.

"I'm not sure if you're aware," said Savage. "Two men have died in the village."

"I am aware. And I know the two men. Neither will be missed."

"That doesn't seem particularly in tune with a vast and unbreakable chain of life and warmth and growth, Ms Walsh."

"They made their choice. Turn against nature and you'll soon find your own nature will turn against you."

"You mind telling me if you had something to do with their deaths?" Savage asked, growing tired of the cryptic answers. Amanda spat out a breath, one hand feeling her ponytail for loose hairs.

"Yes, I did."

Savage's heart thumped, a bolt of adrenaline making the dark pub bright. Amanda smiled, and there was nothing nice about it.

"I prayed for it."

"You *prayed* for it? For them to die?"

"When there is famine, you pray for rain. When there is disease, you pray for a cure. When there is blight, you pray for it to be purged. Those young men were a plague, and yes, I asked for the plague to be eradicated."

Savage's mouth fell open. She wasn't sure what to say.

"You're a police officer," said Amanda. "Can you honestly tell me you've never done the same? You've never wished for somebody's rack and ruin?"

"I, uh... *No*. Because it doesn't work like that. Even if it was real, even if it was possible, that's not what we do."

And she had to look away because she knew the lie was written on her face. She had wished for it, of course. Maybe not in the same way, maybe not to the same gods, but those prayers had entered her head more than once.

Why can't they just die?

"Can I ask you where you were on Friday night?" Savage said.

"You can. I was in the village along with everybody else. We were at the head of the parade, and after that, we came here. The pub was full, we were all celebrating Imbolc. Ask anyone and they'll tell you I was here, and if you don't believe them, there's always that."

She pointed a long, perfectly manicured fingernail at a security camera mounted above the bar.

"We keep the files for a week. Help yourself."

"Was anybody notable missing?" Savage asked. "Anyone conspicuously absent?"

"No. Not on Imbolc. I would have noticed."

"Were Neil or Seb here on Friday night?"

Amanda scoffed.

"They were not. They would not have been welcome."

"What about a young man called Pete Duggan, do you know him?"

"Another locust. They stay well clear of this place."

"Joe Livingstone?"

Amanda's eyes moved immediately to a member of the circle, an older woman who was just as well dressed as she was.

"Joe was here, yes. That's his grandmother, Val Livingstone, but Joe's surname is actually Nix, after his father. He has troubles with his mind. A spectre. He stayed here most of the evening, but when we left for the procession he went upstairs. He doesn't like crowds. There's a flat above the pub, we keep a few games there, books."

"CCTV up there as well?"

"No. But there's no other way out of the building so if he'd left the camera would have caught it."

"What about Catherine Cavaney?"

Amanda shook her head.

"A newcomer to the village. I would have welcomed her, but she made her choices, just like the men she hung out with."

"Neil and Seb and Pete?"

Amanda nodded.

"Do you know what they were doing, these men?"

"Everyone did. They never tried to hide it. Selling that *poison*."

She spat the last word so loud that the group seemed to lose its focus. A few of the members looked up, frowning at Savage like they hadn't noticed her walk in. She lifted a hand to them.

"Sorry," she said. "But I could do with any help that anyone here has to offer. Neil Enthoven and Seb Reilly, Pete Duggan as well. Do any of you know who they were working with? Who supplied them with drugs?"

Silence, apart from the hum of the two or three Greenies who were still lost in their reverie. Savage felt the first flicker of anger ignite in her.

"Last night, two police officers were driven off the road in the village," she said. "They were *shot at*. The farm just west of Toltham, on the hill. Does anyone know anything about that?"

"We heard it," said the woman Amanda had identified as Val. "We heard the whole thing. The helicopter too."

A few of the others nodded.

"So, *speak*."

But nobody did.

"You've got about thirty seconds to tell me something useful," Savage said, her pulse almost drowning out the sound of her own voice. "Because we found something at the farm where the attack took place, and the only people I can see it belonging to are the people in this room."

For the first time, Amanda's steely exterior seemed to collapse.

"What?" she asked.

Savage pulled out her phone, finding the photo she'd taken of the doll. She showed it to Amanda, who turned to the group and glanced at Gabriel—only for a fraction of a second, then she looked up again.

"It's a doll," she said quietly. "Our Goddess Brigid. Was it found in a basket of white flowers? Or shredded paper?"

Savage nodded.

"We make them every year in honour of her, and in honour of the spring."

"Who made this one?"

"I... I have no idea. They're all the same, and they've been made that way for centuries. This could be from years ago."

"It isn't," said Savage. "Who made it?"

Amanda shook her head, and there were blank stares from the rest of the group.

"We found another one close to Seb's body," said Savage.

"You'll find them *everywhere*," Amanda said, leaning against the bar like she was running out of charge. There are scores of them at this time of year. I've got about a dozen upstairs as we speak, leftover from Friday night."

Savage could have screamed with frustration.

"Anything else? This is a village, you all live in each other's pockets. You must know something."

"All I know is that these things have a way of sorting themselves out," said Amanda, the smallest of smiles dancing on her lips. "The goddess provides, and if you turn your back on her then she'll fuck you up."

"*What?*" said Savage.

The rest of the group were slowly getting to their feet, all of them staring at her. There were four men and five women, none of them particularly young, but she still took a step back, suddenly aware of how alone she was here, the locked door.

Where the hell was Duke?

She reached instinctively for the baton she hadn't carried for months now, not even sure why she felt she needed it. Then she reached for her wallet in order to pull out a business card, but stopped, because for some reason she didn't want to leave these people with a record of her name.

"If you think of anything else, come find us," she said, still retreating.

Amanda was walking towards her, the others too, that same ghostly smile on every face. Savage hit a bar stool, knocking it over, and the shock of it almost shattered her heart like hammer-struck glass. She forced herself to stop, to stand tall.

"Who are you people?" she asked. "None of you even thought to ask how they were, the police who were attacked. What's wrong with you? I thought you were supposed to worship nature? Goodness? Kindness?"

"There's nothing kind about nature," said Amanda. "Have you never looked outside? Nature will eat you alive and grow flowers in the rotting remains of your corpse. That's what nature is. No kindness at all, just order."

Savage reached the door and pulled back the bolt. The group was so close now she wasn't sure she'd have room to open it, but she managed, squeezing herself back into the day.

"We don't need you," Amanda said from the shadows. "Nature will take care of all of us. And if you're not careful, it will take care of you, too."

The door slammed shut so hard that Savage had to stagger back to avoid it. She put one hand to her chest, disappointed at how hard her heart was beating. She felt spooked, and it had been a long time since anyone had left her shaken like that. She walked towards the car, searching the car park for any sign of Duke, calling his name when she couldn't see him.

"Where the hell are you?"

She heard footsteps behind her, expecting to see the PC but seeing Val instead, ducking through the door. The woman broke into a trot, holding up a hand asking Savage to wait.

"I'm sorry," she said, breathless from the short run. "Sorry about all that. Ignore Amanda, she's full of drama. Full of it. She doesn't speak for all of us."

"Good," said Savage. "Val, isn't it?"

"Valerie Livingstone," she said, glancing back at the pub. "I shouldn't really be out here, not in the middle of a service, but I wanted to check with you. I heard Joe's name mentioned. He's not in any trouble, is he?"

"Not as far as I'm aware," Savage said. "My colleagues spoke to him earlier, didn't they? At Neil Enthoven's place."

Val nodded.

"He keeps trying to go back, even now he knows what's happened. Joe doesn't really get death. I mean he understands it, but he doesn't quite grasp what it means for him."

"In what way?" Savage asked, squinting against the sun that had just started to push over the roof of the pub.

"In the sense that he thinks it's still fine for him to hang out at Neil's house, play on his computer, that sort of thing. He doesn't understand that that's all over now. But he's not a bad man. He wouldn't ever do anything wrong, not knowingly."

"I think Joe's fine," Savage said. "Unless there's something you haven't told us, I wouldn't worry."

Val chewed her lip in a way that made it very clear there *was* something she hadn't mentioned. Savage knew better than to push, waiting for it to come out by itself.

"It's probably nothing," Val said. "Probably just me making a big deal out of thin air. But Joe was with Neil on Friday, before we all assembled for the parade."

"At Neil's bungalow?"

"Yes. I didn't approve of it, not at all. I didn't like Neil one little bit, and I knew he was using poor Joe. But it's so hard when your child—or grandchild, in this case, but he's no different to me than a child because I've raised him for so long, since he was yay tall." She held a hand to her hip, laughing nervously. "It's so hard when they can't find good friends. That's all Joe wanted, all he ever wanted. His tribe.

All his life he's struggled, and who am I to deny him a friendship, even if he doesn't grasp that it's not entirely genuine?"

She sucked in air, breathless. Savage waited.

"What I'm saying is that Joe was there on Friday, at Neil's bungalow, and Seb and Cat as well. But Joe came home in tears because... And I didn't tell the other policeman this, I'm afraid, because I didn't want to get Joe in trouble. But that was before I knew about last night, about the shootings. And it's gone too far, hasn't it? I don't want to be responsible for any more death."

"What is it?" Savage asked, willing her to get to the point.

The pub door opened, two faces peering out from inside. One was Amanda, her orange glasses glinting. Savage thought the other one might have been Gabriel Grundy. Val looked at them and her face fell.

"Oh dear," she said. "Dear oh dear oh dear."

"Tell me what you know," said Savage. "Not everyone deserves to be eaten alive. Joe doesn't, does he? Neither did Seb or Neil. Not like that."

Val nodded, turning her face to the ground.

"On Friday, Joe came home with a letter," she said. "A note, really. On a scrap of paper. He didn't want to show it to me at first but I knew something was up. He can't tell a lie, my dear grandson, even if he wants to. He showed it to me."

"You still have it?"

Val shook her head.

"Sorry. I didn't want it in my house. It was a tainted thing. I burned it. But I remember what it said. It said that Joe needed to come to the north side of the broad, at midnight. It said he had to come or something bad would happen."

"This was on Friday?" Savage said. "The day of the Imbolc?"

"Yes."

"And that's what it said *exactly*?"

"More or less. But the gist was clear. Joe had to go to the broad at midnight, and he had to be alone."

"Who sent it?"

"It didn't say, but I know who it was. It was signed WM. Wallace Marshall. He wanted to get my boy alone."

A gate to the side of the pub opened and Duke walked out, scratching his beard. He saw Savage and nodded to her.

"Why would he want to get Joe alone?" Savage said.

"Because he knew what those men were doing and he wanted to be part of it. He wanted to know who they were getting the drugs from. Not Joe, because he never did anything like that, not willingly anyway. But Neil and Pete and Sebastian. Marshall wanted to know who they were working for. He's been trying to find out for forever."

"Because it's competition?" Savage said. "Because he's working with the gangs as well? Helping them?"

Val shrugged.

"Maybe. Probably. Anyway, Joe gave me the note and I burned it. But that's not all."

She turned to the pub again, speaking her last few words as if she was addressing the people who watched from the door, who stared back through the dark windows.

"It wasn't just Joe who got a note. It wasn't just Joe that Marshall wanted to get alone in the woods. It was *all* of them."

"How do you know this, Val?"

"Because Joe told me he saw Seb with a note too. He said it looked exactly the same as his."

She glanced up at the willow tree, lost in its frenzied branches.

"The only difference is that Seb went. And he didn't come back."

CHAPTER TWENTY-THREE

"Thanks for the update, Kate. Be safe, and if you see any sign of Marshall let me know."

"I will, sir," said Savage, her voice buzzing from the phone's speaker as Porter drove. "Nobody seems to know where he is, he hasn't been home."

"We'll find him."

Kett ended the call, leaving his phone on his lap.

"Sounds more and more like Marshall's neck-deep in this," he said.

"No shit," Porter replied.

The DI eased the Mondeo up the shallow hill that led from the Acle Straight into Yarmouth, the traffic a nightmare. He seemed on edge, his foot drumming the floor like he was beating out a tune. He kept looking out the window to his right, and Kett knew what he was searching for.

A set of headlights, the roar of an engine, a tractor lunging at them from the night.

Kett knew because he was thinking the same thing himself.

He grabbed the strap over the door as a sudden panic

squeezed his heart—almost too much to bear until he closed his eyes and fought it off. He cleared his throat, taking a breath, opening his eyes again.

"This fucking job," he said quietly.

Porter breathed a laugh through his nose, pulling onto the roundabout. Yarmouth opened up in front of them, bathed in morning light. Kett was surprised at how weird it felt to be back here. He'd come all the time when he was a kid, with his mum and dad—and then just his mum. They'd spent hours walking the seafront, feeding chips to the seagulls on the pier and playing hide and seek in the dunes and losing small fortunes to the 2p machines.

Happy times, he thought.

Then they crossed another roundabout, turning away from the seafront into the middle of the town, and Kett remembered why they'd stopped coming. A gang of young men stood outside Iceland, beer cans in their hands, jeering at each other. One of them looked like he was taking a piss up the shop window.

"Fancy a quick stop?" Porter asked, glaring at them.

Kett would be lying if he said he wasn't tempted, but he could already hear a siren in the air and the day was busy enough as it was. He motioned for Porter to keep driving and they made their way through the cavernous Market Gates underpass, zigzagging down the narrow side roads until they reached King Street. It was packed with shoppers, even though half the windows down here were boarded up.

"Clare said Noddy's gaff is above a vape shop," Kett said, and they drove for another minute or so before he saw it. "*The Great Escvape?* That is a truly awful name."

"Why on earth wouldn't they go with the *Vape Escape?*" Porter said as he bumped the car onto the kerb.

They got out together, the air a good few degrees colder

here than it was inland. More men stood in the doorways of the shops, all of them smoking. A couple of younger boys rode up and down on their bikes, their tracksuits filthy. Every single line of sight was directed at Kett and Porter, and there wasn't an ounce of welcome anywhere.

"Bizzie," yelled one of the kids, his bike clattering as he wheeled it around and sped off. "Bizzie."

"Are we that obvious?" Kett said.

"You should have kept your *I'm Your Beach* sweatshirt on," Porter replied.

The shop was shut up tight, a pile of mail visible through the glass door. There was an alleyway down the side of the building, though, barely wide enough for Kett to squeeze down. It widened up after a few steps and he spotted the door to the flat above.

"Christ, it reeks down here," Porter said, holding his nose.

It did. Piss, and worse.

"Watch your feet," he said as he stepped over a giant turd that had been left in the middle of the alleyway.

"That must have been one big dog," Porter said.

"If it *was* a dog."

He shuddered, knocking on the door with his fist. There was no window in the peeling red paint, just a peephole, and when Kett heard feet on the other side he lifted his hand in a wave.

"I'm not here," said a muffled voice.

"Neither am I," Kett said. "So open the door."

There was grumbling on the other side, then a key turned in the lock and the door opened a crack—the security chain snapping taut. The face that looked out might have belonged to a man or to some kind of animal, it was so hairy Kett couldn't be sure.

"Who the fuck are you?" it asked.

"You want me to get my warrant card out here, or inside?" Kett said.

"For fuck's sake, not out there."

The door shut, the chain slid free, and then it opened again. It *was* a man standing there, but Kett honestly couldn't remember ever seeing anyone with more hair. It spilled down over his shoulders in long, unbrushed clumps, almost reaching his chest. His beard covered his cheeks, bushy enough to hide a sparrow's nest. Even his eyebrows were a solid line of fur. He waved them in.

"Come on, come on, gonna get me battered standing out there like that."

The door opened immediately into the stairwell and Kett made his way up, assaulted by a combination of smells that made his toes curl. There was a low, serious bark as he got to the top and he flinched as a dog galloped down the corridor towards him. It was a bloodhound, an old one, and it only got halfway before it needed to stop for breath. Kett stuck out his hand and let it sniff his fingers, then he rubbed the back of its neck.

"Don't mind her, silly old bag," the man said as he followed them up. "She's twatted."

Kett didn't ask him what he meant by that. The man walked into the living room and Kett saw another guy sitting on a sofa, almost completely buried in blankets and duvets. His eyes were red and puffy, and it took him so long to turn his head that it looked like he was moving in slow motion. There was a nasty scar on the side of his head where his left ear had been.

The first man picked up a joint from an ashtray on the coffee table and sparked it up, taking fast, dainty puffs like he was dining with the Queen.

"Noddy?" Kett asked, and he nodded. "Why'd they call you that, then?"

Noddy put the joint back with exaggerated finesse, then cocked his thumb at the man on the sofa.

"Because he's Big Ears."

"He doesn't have *any* ears," Kett said.

"Yeah, but he used to, and they were big. So everyone called 'im Big Ears and I was just Noddy."

"How'd you lose your ears?" Porter asked, and Big Ears lifted a hand to his head like he hadn't noticed they were missing. He spoke, but his words were so slurred Kett couldn't make any sense of it.

"Right," said Kett. "Noddy, I need intel. I heard you're the man to ask."

"Might be," said Noddy, shuffling back and forth from one leg to the other like he really needed the toilet. "Depends who's asking. Depends *how* they ask, n'all."

"You know a place called Toltham?"

"Course," Noddy said. "Full of cunts."

"You know an ex-copper called Wallace Marshall?"

Kett wasn't sure, but there might have been a smile under all that facial hair. Noddy turned to Big Ears.

"He wants Marshall," he said with a high-pitched giggle. Big Ears laughed too, low and slow. Noddy turned back to Kett. "Big fish, copper. I ain't going anywhere near that fat fuck, not even with your pole."

"He's bent?"

"Benter than Big Ears' cock, in't that right, Biggie?"

Big Ears nodded.

"And he's mean. Looks like a fat old prick but he's dangerous."

"I need to know where to find him," said Kett.

"So find him, he's one of you, *in't* he? Knock on his fucking door."

"I need to know where to *find* him," Kett said again, taking a step towards Noddy. "Like you said, he's clever, he's not at home and even if he was he wouldn't have anything there that would incriminate him. There was a deal last night, in Toltham. It went wrong. I think he was involved. I need to know where he operates from."

Noddy licked his lips, moving to the sofa and sitting down so close to Big Ears that he was almost on his lap. There was a clatter of feet as the bloodhound trotted in, the old girl making a leap for the cushions next to Noddy, missing, and rolling onto her side on the floor. Noddy reached down and scooped her up, holding her to his chest.

"Dog food these days costs a fucking fortune," he said, scratching her back. "You ever noticed that? Not to mention vet bills. Fuck me, I'll have to sell a kidney soon."

Kett sighed, pulling out his wallet to see a lone fiver and a lot of lint. He glanced back at Porter, who opened his and pulled out a twenty.

"Got another one in the back," Noddy said. "She's even older."

Porter muttered something beneath his breath, pulling out a second twenty-pound note. He passed them to Kett, who held onto them.

"Not until you talk."

"Word is," he said, sneezing into the dog's fur. "Word is that Marshall's been after a gang that works out of Dene Street. I don't know where. They're all foreign, Russian or some shit."

"Romanian? Or Lithuanian, maybe?"

"Fuck knows. They ain't even been here that long, but

they ain't afraid of carving their way. I know a couple of lads been skewered by them."

"Heroin? Cocaine?"

"All the good stuff," said Noddy with another childish laugh. "They move it on the boats like every other fucker around here."

"What's the connection to Toltham?" Kett asked.

"Now that, I don't know for sure," he replied. "But I heard there's somebody there who takes the gear and splits it, makes sure it gets to where it's going."

"You know if they work in the lodge?"

"I don't know shittery doo-dah about that. But Marshall's been asking around about these guys and he's seriously pissed off with them. Rumours always were that he was indebted to the Albanians, some deal he made with them years ago. So they've probably got him chasing the new crew, take them down before they get too big."

"You got any proof of this?" Porter asked.

"Oh, yeah, sure. Hang on." Noddy reached under the dog and Kett heard him unzip his fly. "It's right here, I hide it under me ball bag."

He burst out laughing, pulling his hands free and elbowing Big Ears.

"Of course I don't have proof, you twat. But it's what everyone says, right? People tell me things, they talk to me, and now I'm talking to you."

He reached out, snapping his fingers.

"You haven't given me a location," Kett said.

"Oh, daft twat I am. So, listen, I can't promise nothing, because these fucks move around all the time, never sit still. Like fleas, they are, bouncing here there and shitting every-where. But I always got told if you needed Marshall, if you had stuff for him, take it to the Landed Pike."

"The Landed Pike?"

"Yeah, the Pike. It's a holiday park about ten minutes out of town, fishing place. Been empty for years. I don't know if it's his or if he just uses the place, but he's there more often than not."

"Thanks," said Kett.

Noddy reached for the money and Kett handed it to him, but he didn't let go.

"If you're wrong, I'm coming back for this."

"Course you are." Noddy gently pushed the dog off his lap and groaned his way to his feet. "I'll see you out."

"You ever hear of a drug called Jaw Breaker, by the way?" Kett asked as they were going down the stairs. Noddy shook his head. "Might go by another name. Heroin, cocaine and prescription antipsychotics."

"Oh, right," said Noddy. "Nasty shit. They say that's what you take when you've tried everything else. When nothing hits the spot no more. I won't do it, though. No fucking way. That stuff'll fuck you."

"Anyone round here deal it?"

"Nah. Shit's too expensive to make, all the prescription shit that goes in it, nobody's gonna pay those prices."

Kett slid back the bolt and opened the door, stepping down into the stinking alleyway. Porter followed, losing his footing and almost ending up in the giant turd that lay there. Noddy leaned out the door.

"Anyone see you come up 'ere?"

"Couple of lads on bikes," said Kett.

"I told you," Noddy shouted, his voice echoing off the bricks. "I ain't saying nothing, so fuck off!"

He leant in, whispering again.

"Can you hit me?"

"Huh?"

"Hit me, makes it look like, you know, I didn't tell you nothing."

"I'm not hitting you, Noddy."

"You?" he asked Porter.

"Uh, as much as I'd love to, no."

"Fat lot of fucking good you two are." He swung a fist into his own face, reeling onto the stairs. "Argh, bastard coppers, always hitting me when I won't talk! Why won't you leave me alone?"

He grinned toothlessly through the door, then kicked it shut. Kett could hear him howling on the other side.

"You've broken my nose! Bastard cop, and just because I keep my mouth shut and don't tell anyone anything because I'm not a grass!"

"That's bloody Shakespeare, that is," Porter said. Kett laughed.

"Come on, let's go fishing."

CHAPTER TWENTY-FOUR

It was more like thirty minutes later that Porter spotted a handmade wooden arrow strapped to a road sign, the words LANDED PIKE FISHING LETS written in black paint. He slowed the Mondeo, taking the next turn onto what was little more than a dirt track surrounded on both sides by towering walls of rushes. They bumped along it, rounding a corner to see a low, wooden cabin fifty yards ahead.

"Stop here," said Kett. "If he's in there, I don't want to give him any warning."

Porter did as he was asked, switching off the engine and letting in the complete and utter silence of the countryside. Kett grabbed his phone, calling Clare. It went to his voicemail.

"Sir, we're at a place called the Landed Pike, a fishing let just outside of Hopton. Your CI claims Marshall uses it. I'll report back."

"You want backup?" Porter asked as they got out of the car. "I've seen enough of Marshall to know that if he *is* here, he won't make this easy."

"As soon as we call it in, word will reach him. We'll take a look. If we see anything we don't like, we'll back off."

"Says Robert Kett, who's famous for backing off from dangerous situations."

"You can stay in the car if you like, Pete. I'll crack a window, leave the radio on."

"After you, sir," said Porter.

The rushes here had to be eight or nine feet tall, swaying gently in the wind and whispering quiet secrets. Kett's boots crunched in the dirt, the loudest sound in the world. They passed a large, faded sign of a grinning cartoon fish, its flipper raised like a thumbs up and the words *Open For Business* written on its chest. Just past that was a wide metal gate that was locked with a chain. The car park on the other side was deserted. The smell of stagnant water hung in the air.

"Do you think Noddy might have been talking out of his hairy backside?" said Porter.

Kett wasn't sure. He grabbed the top of the gate and boosted himself up, almost crying out as the pain tore through his injured knee.

"You want a foot-up, sir?" asked Porter. "Step-ladder? Stannah Stair Lift?"

"No," he wheezed, lowering himself gently on the other side.

Porter leaped over the gate in one go, smiling smugly as he landed like a gymnast. The wooden cabin was close enough now that they could see its windows were shuttered, the door sealed with a padlock as big as Kett's hand. Reeds grew everywhere, crowding the little building like a besieging army. Kett held his breath for a moment, listening, hearing absolutely nothing.

"He thinks I won't go back for that forty quid," he said. "But I bloody am."

He walked on, reaching the cabin. It was thirty foot long, made entirely of logs, and it looked like it had been recently creosoted. The gravel car park was weed-free, too. The place wasn't as abandoned as it looked. They walked on, reaching the end of the cabin and stopping abruptly.

"Oh shit," said Porter. "I did not expect to see one of those."

A police IRV was parked just behind the cabin, tucked away so that it would be invisible from the road. It was empty. Beside it was the silver Rolls Royce that Savage had seen Wallace Marshall driving. Kett pulled out his phone, calling Control.

"Hey, this is DCI Kett. Can you run a plate for me?"

He read out the Rolls Royce's registration plate, waiting for a moment.

"That's registered to Wallace Andrew Marshall. No outstanding warrants."

"Thanks," he said. "One more thing. Have you had any response calls for a place called the Landed Pike, just off Hall Road in Hopton?"

"Nothing I can see," said the operator. "You need one?"

"No, thanks," he said, and hung up. "I don't like this. One bent copper is bad enough, but if there's an IRV here too then something else is going on."

"It'll be that PC," said Porter. "Jarratt. She seemed well dodgy too."

Past the two cars were three more cabins, all the same size as the one they'd just walked by. Two were shut tight, but the door of the next one along was open, the chain hanging unsecured. Now that they were clear of the wind, Kett thought he could hear voices raised in anger.

"How do you want to do this?" Porter asked.

"Carefully," Kett said. "Wallace is a bear."

He took a step, then retreated. The conversation he'd had with the giant ex-copper in his hospital room last night was all too fresh in his mind. As was the way that Wallace had made him feel like a child, the way he'd crushed Kett's injured knee in his fist just to make a point. He pulled out his phone and called Clare again. This time, the Super answered.

"Speak."

"Sir, we've found Marshall's bolt hole. His car is here, and there's a police IRV too, parked up. I don't know what's going on but I think you should send out a couple of units, just in case."

"Okay," Clare said.

"But send them yourself, and use people you trust. If something's going down I don't want Marshall to know you're coming. Place called the Landed Pike, Hopton."

"I'll do it now. Stand down, Kett, until they get to you. You two almost left us last night, permanently. I don't want you taking any chances."

"Yes, sir," he said. "We'll stay out of sight."

He hung up, pocketing his phone, ready to retreat into cover. Before he could, though, somebody stepped out of the wooden cabin right ahead of them. It was the same sergeant they'd met in the woods yesterday, Fred Patch, his jacket off and his sleeves rolled up. He'd put a cigarette in his mouth and lit it before he realised he wasn't alone. His eyes landed on Kett, almost bugging right out of his skull.

"Shit!" he said, the cigarette flying.

"Shit is right," Kett replied.

The sergeant turned so clumsily that he slammed his

shoulder into the door, disappearing back into the building. Kett glanced at Porter and Porter looked back.

"Fuck it," said the DI, breaking into a run.

Kett limped after him, Porter already through the door by the time he'd reached it. He ran into the cabin, blinded by the sun that streamed through the windows opposite.

"He's still going," Porter said, powering through another door that led back outside.

There was a lake ahead, much smaller than Toltham. On its banks was a wide, squat building that looked like a boat shed or an equipment store. The sergeant had almost reached it, yelling his head off.

"Hang on, Pete," Kett called, but there was no stopping Porter. He was charging towards the doors like a train, closing in fast. Past his grunting breaths and the sergeant's cries was another voice, one that was almost a scream.

Kett put his head down, trying to ignore the agony in his knee as he navigated the uneven terrain. The sergeant was trying to close the door of the equipment shed but Porter crunched into it, splintering the wood and knocking the other man back.

"Police!" the DI roared.

Kett reached the door, shunting his way through and coming to a halt next to Porter.

And even though he knew Wallace Marshall wasn't a good man, even after everything that had happened to him and Porter last night, even after the horror of the dead man he'd found in the woods, he still wasn't prepared for the sight that greeted him.

The building was unexpectedly big, its back wall open to the lake that lay beyond and a small mooring quay where boats could be worked on. The sergeant was running across the largely empty floor to a group of people who were clustered by the water, all of whom were looking up in shock.

Marshall was there, stripped to his underwear and his vest, his folds of flesh slick with sweat and streaked with blood. Next to him was PC Sophie Jarratt, still in full uniform, her face warped into a grimace of anger and fear.

Three men were hogtied on the concrete floor, their legs secured to their wrists behind their back with coils of thick rope. They were all gagged, and they all looked like they'd been beaten half to death.

A fourth man sat on a kitchen chair on the lip of the quay, completely naked except for a suit of blood and vomit that covered his face and torso and the ropes that bound him. He was alive, but only just, his head hanging limply and his leg twitching like it was trying to escape without the rest of him.

For a moment, nobody moved—except for the sergeant, who scuttled behind Jarratt like a kid hiding behind his mum and stood there shaking.

"What the hell is going on?" Kett said, his voice echoing around the cavernous space. The men on the ground were grunting into their gags, their mad eyes roving as they tried to call to him.

Marshall flexed a giant fist and Kett saw the blood that stained it. He picked something small and white from between his swollen knuckles, flicking it to the floor. It looked almost like a tooth, Kett thought, his stomach contracting.

"How the fuck did you find me?" Marshall said, his face dark with anger. He glanced at the sergeant, who shook his head, then turned to Kett again. His face broke into a ghastly smile and he held his arms out to his sides. "And maybe a better question would be what are you going to do about it?"

"I'm going to ask again," said Kett, hearing the tremor in his voice. "What's going on?"

"Just a cosy little get-together with some Romanian friends of mine," Marshall said, his confidence returning. "None of your fucking business, to be honest."

"These are the guys from last night," said Porter. He pointed to one of the hogtied men, a lean older guy with neat grey hair. "He was the one with the gun, the one on the phone."

Marshall's grin grew wider and he looked down at the man.

"This one, you're sure?" he asked. "Well thank you, DI Porter, you've saved me another round of heartbreak. Get him up."

PC Jarratt hesitated, one hand on her holstered baton. She looked from Kett to Marshall and then back again.

"Do it," Marshall barked. He walked back to the chair and picked up a knife from the floor, sawing through the ropes of the man who sat there.

"Stop," said Kett, pointing a finger at Marshall. "Stop fucking moving. I'm not going to tell you again."

"You got lucky, DCI Kett," Marshall said, showing no sign at all of doing what he'd been told. "The men you chased off last night, we found them. The idiots were hiding in Gorleston. Obviously, nobody told them this was my little corner of the world. Nothing happens here I don't know about."

The ropes pinged loose and Marshall gave the man a mighty shove. He collapsed to the floor like a ragdoll, no sign of life there anymore.

"What have you done to him?" Kett asked.

Marshall ran the back of his arm over his face, struggling for breath. He pointed the knife at Kett, then at the man by his feet.

"This piece of human excrement? I just gave him what he was after. Gave him a whole gut load of heaven, made him high as a kite so he'd talk to us." He looked at Jarratt again, his voice like gravel. "Get the other one up here."

"Don't fucking move, Constable," Kett said, glaring at her. "Marshall, this ends now. We've got units on the way, you're finished."

"That true?" he asked Jarratt.

She put a hand to her radio almost instinctively, then shook her head. Marshall's grin almost split his face, and he turned the knife towards Kett again.

"I knew it wouldn't be. Because I know *you*, Robert. I said it to you last night, and I'll say it to you again now, I like you. I like what you stand for. Because we're not so different, you and I."

"Yeah, we are," Kett said. "I don't sell drugs, for one. I don't help out the dealers, the bad guys."

Marshall's grin wavered.

"You think that's what's going on here, son? You think I'm *bent*?"

"You're telling me you're not?" Kett said, gesturing to the men on the floor. "I know that's why you got kicked out of the Force, for helping those Albanians, tipping them off about the raid. And I know you're still working for them. They've asked you to take out these guys for them, right? Get rid of the competition."

"You know exactly Jack shit," Marshall said, angry again now. "And you'd better be careful what comes out your mouth or you won't be able to use it for much longer. Hard to speak with no teeth. Fred, get that prick in the chair."

The sergeant cleared his throat, nodding.

"Leave him alone," said Kett, taking a step towards them. Porter moved with him, unbuttoning his jacket. The atmosphere in the building felt explosive. It felt *dangerous*. But Fred knew who his master was because he got down on his knees, undoing the ropes that secured the man's legs to his wrists.

"I thought you were smarter than this, Kett," said Marshall. "I thought you were police."

"What are you talking about?"

"The end justifies the means," he went on. "Always. Whatever it takes to keep these monsters off our streets."

The man who had been sitting on the chair had broken into a fit, vomit spaying from his mouth and his nose.

"He needs help," Kett said.

"No, he doesn't."

"Last chance, Marshall," Kett said, taking another step. Porter was moving out to the side, his fists bunched. PC Jarratt stepped forward, pulling her extendible baton from its pouch and flicking it to its full length. Her face was carved from stone, no sign of fear there. Kett looked at her. "Stand down, Constable. That's an order."

"You really want to do this, Kett?" Marshall said. "You really want to let them win?"

"You do this and *nobody* wins."

"You're wrong, Kett. You're wrong about everything. You think I'm bent?" Marshall roared out a laugh. "Christ, I'm *you*, you prick. I'm police. Blood doesn't run any bluer than this. You know why I left the Force? Because it was crippling me. It cripples all of us. What do you do? Arrest someone for drugs, for rape, for murder, wait for the CPS to wake the fuck up, for a jury to sit on their arses? Then what? If you're lucky they're in a nice prison cell for a few years, but most of the time they're back on the streets in days. You know how fucking demoralising that shit is? How fucking soul-destroying?"

He took a step, the knife still pointing.

"So I left, and I've been doing it my way ever since. Old school, you know? Somebody's selling drugs on your street corner, I'll break his face. Somebody exposes themselves to your kid in the park, I'll fucking castrate him. And it works, you know? After a while, you don't even need to do it because people are so scared of what will happen to them that they toe the line. That's how it should be, and I know you agree with me."

"No," said Kett. "Not like this."

"No?" said Marshall. "Not like Schofield? Not like Raymond Figg? They're not in prison, are they? They're not walking the streets."

"Don't listen to him, sir," said Porter. "He's full of shit."

Marshall scoffed.

"Yeah? I don't see either of you on your phones calling for backup. You want to know what I think? I think you want in on this."

His knife turned towards the men on the ground.

"These pricks almost killed you last night, didn't they? They saw you coming and rammed your car off the road, then set fire to it. You think they wouldn't have set fire to it with you inside? They would have, they'd have burned you to ash without a scrap of guilt. These cunts were there to buy a shitload of heroin and cocaine from a bunch of kids who live in my village. And you know why those kids were out there selling drugs in the first place?"

Kett didn't respond, but he took another step.

"Because the gang that owns those drugs thinks it's better to pay some kids a couple of quid to carry them than it is to do it themselves. That way, when the guns come out and the knives start stabbing, it's just a few local boys and girls who die. No big fucking deal."

The anger rose in Marshall almost visibly, the muscles tensing beneath his layers of fat. He kicked the man on the floor in the head so hard that the spray of blood from his mouth hit Jarratt's boots ten feet away.

"Hey!" yelled Kett. "That's enough."

"They don't give a shit about anything that isn't money. And I don't give a shit about them. No arrest warrants here, my friend. No reading of rights. No custody sergeant and a cup of tea and a blanket. Just blood and guts. The way it should be. That prick didn't tell me what I wanted to hear, not after the beatings, not after the drugs I made him eat, not even when he knew he was dying. But there's three more, and now I know which one's going to tell me what I want to hear. So how about it, *copper*? You really want to make a difference? You want to do something good? Have at him."

For a terrible moment—for a fraction of a second, no more—Kett almost fell for it. A lifetime of frustrations, of fighting with dealers on the streets of London, arresting them only to see them laughing their way out of the nick the next day; of giving evidence in court just for the case to collapse because of a technicality; of pulling a dead boy's body from a flat in Elephant and Castle because nobody knew how to keep him safe from his father. He thought about how it had felt when he'd sunk the hammer into the back of the Pig Man's head. How awful it had been.

How *good* it had been.

Because it meant it was over. It meant Billie was safe, it meant the girls were safe.

You can escape a prison cell. You can't escape a coffin.

"No," he said, his voice hoarse. "Not like this. You can't be police, jury and executioner, Marshall. You can't go around killing guys like this, like Seb Reilly and Neil Enthoven."

Marshall shook his head.

"You're wrong," he said. "I—"

Jarratt's radio chirruped, a voice filtering through.

"Delta Patrol, anyone out there for an instant response? Units requested for a possible incident on Hall Road in Hopton."

Marshall's wet lips pulled back to reveal small, yellow teeth.

"So that's that, then," he said. "I told you before, Kett. I won't let you get in the way of this. Fred, Sophie."

"We shouldn't—" Jarratt started, but Marshall pointed the knife at her and she sucked the rest of the sentence back in. She took a couple of steps their way, her baton out. Sergeant Patch was close behind her.

"Back up, Pete," Kett said, retreating to the door. "Get out."

Then he stopped, because Marshall had his hands around the neck of the man who'd been in the chair. With a Herculean effort, he slid him across the concrete floor and then rolled him over the edge of the dock. There was a splash as he landed in the water.

"Fuck," said Kett.

If the man wasn't already dead, he would be in seconds.

Kett broke to the side, keeping a safe distance from Jarratt as she moved towards Porter. She changed her course to intercept, looking back and forth between them. With every step she seemed less certain.

"I don't want to do this," she said. "They're police."

"Drop the baton, Constable," Porter said.

Jarratt was slowing down, the sergeant walking past her, one hand reaching for something in his pocket.

"Take them out," said Marshall. "Or we're all going down for this. What did I teach you, Sophie? Trust me."

"I do, Dad," she said. "But..."

"Pull yourself together, Jarratt," grunted the sergeant. "That's an order."

Patch was moving towards Porter, murder written into the lines of his face. He wasn't a big man but he looked like he was no stranger to violence, and when he pulled his hand out of his pocket he was holding a long, brutal hunting knife.

"Pete, watch yourself," Kett said. "Jarratt, it's not too late to do the right thing."

She looked at Marshall, desperate now.

"This is wrong," she said. "Sarge, put it down."

Patch was oblivious, ten yards from Porter now and picking up speed. Porter was hunched, ready, but there was fear in his eyes.

Marshall was on the move too, heading right for Kett.

"You're police, Constable," Kett said, backing away. "So are we. *Police.*"

Something in Jarratt's face changed, everything tightening. She moved fast, running for Porter, the baton raised. Fred was already there, the knife pulled back like a scorpion's tail. Porter raised his hands in defence, stepping back and almost stumbling.

"Pete!" roared Kett.

Jarratt brought the baton down hard on the back of the sergeant's head, the sound of it like a cracked egg. Momentum carried the man forward but Porter was ready, grabbing him under the arms then hurling him to the floor. The knife slipped from his fingers, clattering out of reach. It wouldn't have mattered, because Patch hit the floor face-first, utterly still.

"Fuck!" Jarratt shouted, her hands in her hair. "Fuck!"

Marshall was furious, charging like a wild boar. He was faster than he looked, his giant strides bringing him to Kett in an instant. It was like being hit by an avalanche of flesh, the sheer size of him bowling Kett backwards.

His knee gave way and he landed hard, Marshall falling on top of him, squirming there, too much skin for Kett to be able to open his mouth. He screamed into him, biting at whatever he could find, his lungs empty.

Then Marshall rolled away, Porter's hands around his face, fingers digging into his eyes.

"Get the fuck off him!" he shouted.

Marshall swung the knife upwards at Porter but Kett caught his wrist, struggling with the insane strength of him.

"Dad! Just give it up!" Jarratt was shouting. "Don't hurt him!"

Kett twisted Marshall's wrist and the man screamed, dropping the knife. He rolled out from beneath the suffocating bulk of him, clawing in air, trying to push himself onto his knees.

Marshall had gripped Porter's jacket and was trying to stand up, making a noise like a broken jumbo jet. Porter did his best to push him off but Jarratt had her arms wrapped around the DI. The baton was nowhere in sight and Kett had no idea if she was trying to fight him or help him.

With a howl of defiance, Marshall pushed himself forward and all three of them collapsed, Jarratt at the bottom and Porter sandwiched between them. Kett ran over, using handfuls of Marshall's back to pull himself onto the pile. There was no oxygen in the room anymore, flashes of light shotgunning across his vision.

"That's..." he started. "Enough."

He grabbed Marshall's shoulder and hit the ex-copper in the face. It was a solid strike, just not enough. Marshall threw an elbow back but the angle was wrong and it glanced off Kett's hip.

"Fuck you," the big man grunted. "Fuck all of you."

Marshall lurched to his feet, the sheer strength of him lifting Kett off the ground. Kett clung onto his back, bunching his fist and punching Marshall square in the side of his head—his jaw making a sound like a cracked nut.

He fell off, staggering back, readying himself for another attack.

But there wasn't going to be one.

Marshall took a single step before crumpling to his knees and rolling onto his stomach.

"Cuffs," Kett panted. "Pete, cuff him."

There was no time. Kett crawled to the edge of the quay, ready to climb into the water to help the guy Marshall had thrown in. When he got there, though, he found that he couldn't. He couldn't do anything other than kneel on the cold concrete and stare.

The dead men stared back.

Four of them, almost invisible in the billowing reeds, their eyes wide, their mouths open in silent screams.

A sob ripped its way out of Kett before he could contain it. He put his hands to his face, rocking back. PC Jarratt sat in the middle of the room, her head pushed into her knees, her screams loud enough to tear off the roof. Porter sat on her dad, snapping the handcuffs around his wrists.

"Wallace Marshall, you're under arrest for the murder of Neil Enthoven, Seb Reilly, and whoever the hell that was. You do not have to say anything, but it may harm your defence if you don't mention when questioned anything you later rely on in court. Anything you do say may be given in evidence."

The DI leaned back, exhausted, and met Kett's eye— equal amounts of horror and relief written in his face. Kett nodded to him, and he nodded back. But nobody spoke.

There just weren't the words.

CHAPTER TWENTY-FIVE

KETT LEANED AGAINST THE SIDE OF ONE OF THE
Landed Pike's locked cabins, watching as the world turned
yellow and blue.

The place was crawling with police, a dozen uniformed
constables searching what had to be five acres of holiday
accommodation, storage units and waterways. Two ambulances sat next to the long line of IRVs and Marshall's Rolls
Royce, the paramedics already inside the boathouse where
they'd found Marshall. More were on the way, and they
were needed.

Kett was soaked through, Porter too. Between them,
they'd pulled all four men from the water, and even though
they'd tried CPR on the one who'd fallen in last there hadn't
been a hope in hell of saving him. The chances were he'd
been dead before Marshall had even pushed him over the
edge. The three men who'd been hogtied were in a bad state
too, but they'd live.

PC Sophie Jarratt sat against the wall beside them, her
legs pulled up and her head buried between her knees. She
was soaked through too because she'd jumped in to help

pull out the dealers, but Kett didn't think the tremors that rocked her body had anything to do with the cold. Every now and again, when she surfaced, her face was a ruin of emotion. Kett hadn't cuffed her. He didn't see the point. She was a prisoner of something far worse than chains.

There was a rattle from the open door of the cabin and one of the paramedics appeared, trying to steer the stretcher through the narrow opening. Her eyes were red and puffy, like she'd been crying.

"You need a hand with that?" Porter called to her, and she shook her head. The stretcher shifted, another paramedic pushing from the other side. He nodded gravely towards the little group of coppers. Kett saw that it was Sergeant Fred Patch lying on the stretcher, an oxygen mask strapped to his face and a collar around his neck.

"He's still out cold," the man said. "Definite skull fracture but I think he'll make it."

Nobody replied, and the paramedic frowned.

"He's one of yours, isn't he?"

"No," said Kett. "He's not."

They wheeled the stretcher over the rough ground of the car park towards one of the ambulances. Jarratt lifted her head, watching her old boss go with wide, frightened eyes.

"He's going to be okay?" she asked in a voice made of dust.

"Yeah," said Kett. "Looks that way."

Jarratt sobbed, wiping her nose on her trousers.

"What's going to happen to me?"

Kett glared at her.

"What the hell were you thinking? This isn't what we do. Marshall was your *dad*?"

Jarratt nodded.

"Stepdad, yeah. But I never knew my real one. He's always just been Dad."

"How long has this been going on? How long was he going rogue?"

"Forever," she said, taking a long, shuddering breath. "He got me into this job. He told me I could make a difference. And I did. *We* did."

"He was bent," said Porter, and a flash of anger crossed Jarratt's face.

"No, he wasn't. He wasn't bent, not like that. All he wanted was to make things better, to clean up all the shit. He spent his life doing that for you lot, in the job."

"Until he got the can for helping some Albanian drug lord," Porter said.

"No, you've got it all wrong. He had nothing to do with that. You want to know what he did that was so awful? The thing that cost him his job? He beat some scumbag dealer within an inch of his life to find out where that gang was storing their gear. And he uncovered some massive deal that was going down. But the gang caught wind of what had happened to their man and they pulled out. Everyone thought Dad had warned them but he hadn't. He wouldn't. But he had fucked up. So they let him go, quietly."

She thrust her legs out, her fists bunched in frustration.

"You'd do the same thing. You probably have already. We all would."

Kett was too tired to argue, too tired to answer.

"You do the greatest good for the people who deserve it," Jarratt went on. "That's what he always said."

"You helped him kill those men," Kett said. "No arrest, no trial, no chance for them to clear their name. It can't be like that."

And again he thought of the Pig Man, and heard the hollow sound of his own words.

"They were guilty," Jarratt said. "After you messed up the deal last night we tracked them to a warehouse up Gorleston way. They're an outfit we've been aware of for a while now, mainly Romanian. Most of them were asleep, bagged them easy enough. We found all sorts of shit there, including the money for the deal. Guns, too. They were scum, the world won't miss them."

"You and your Dad and that Sergeant, Fred Patch, right?" Kett said.

"Couple of others. But you won't get their names out of me. Not ever. They're good people. Good police."

Kett swore beneath his breath, staring at the flawless sky for a moment until it became too bright. Jarratt was hammering the back of her boot into the dirt like she was trying to dig herself a hole.

"What about the girl who was with them last night? Catherine Cavaney? Is she here too?"

Jarratt shook her head, although Kett wasn't sure if she'd processed the question.

"He was getting worse, Dad," she said. "He was losing it. I've seen him use force before, a lot of force, but... But what he did to those men..."

She made a sound in her throat like she was going to be sick.

"And he's never gone after coppers before. We don't do that to each other, we're a fucking family, right? We never turn on each other, not good police."

She looked at the stretcher that was now inside the ambulance, Patch still unconscious. Then she held up her hands, staring at them like they didn't belong to her.

"What have I done?"

"The right thing," said Kett. "In the end, you did the right thing."

She spat out a bitter laugh.

"How do you know what that is? In this fucking job, how do any of us know?"

Kett didn't have an answer.

He looked up at the sound of an engine, seeing a handful of constables scatter. Superintendent Clare's hulking Mercedes pushed through the crowd, parking across three empty spaces. Savage was the first one out, then Duke, both of them halfway across the car park before Clare had managed to unfold his gangly frame from inside.

"You okay, sirs?" Savage called. "What happened?"

"I don't even know where to start," said Kett.

"What the tossing hell is going on here?" Clare said as he caught up. "There's dead men in there?"

"Four of them," said Kett. "Beaten and tortured to death by Wallace Marshall."

"Jesus Christ. He came at you, too?"

"Yeah. He did. Him and that sergeant over there." He glanced at Jarratt, at the tears that rolled down her cheeks, at the sheer, abject misery there. There wasn't much he could do to help her, but he could at least give her a fighting chance. "He might have got us, too. PC Jarratt here took down the sergeant. She's Marshall's stepdaughter."

"You *what*?" Clare said. "You knew about this, Constable? You were a part of this?"

"She helped us," Kett said, and Clare silenced him with a look.

"Constable?"

"I knew," she said, her teeth chattering. "I knew. I've known for a long time. You'll find more of them here. In the water, and buried too. More bodies. I don't know how many."

"Christ," said Kett.

"They're bad men, all of them. That's the reason the world hasn't come looking for them, isn't it? You take out the bad ones and the good ones stand a better chance. That's... that's what we do."

It was like Marshall was speaking through her.

"Cuff her," said Clare. "There's nothing good here. You should be ashamed of yourself, Constable Jarratt. You are now under arrest for kidnap, torture and murder. You do not have to say anything, but it may harm your defence if you don't mention when questioned anything you later rely on in court. Anything you do say may be given in evidence, and you've just said it all."

Jarratt groaned.

"Get her out of here."

Clare stormed off, heading for the boathouse where the men had died. Porter walked after him.

"I'll get some cuffs," he said.

"What a mess," said Savage. "I can't believe this. So Marshall wasn't working for the gangs?"

"He was a vigilante," Kett said. "What he was doing in there was evil."

"He's not evil," said Jarratt. "He's not."

"Killing people is evil," Savage said. "Doesn't matter who they are. Killing men like this is one thing. But killing kids is another."

Jarratt frowned, looking up.

"Kids?" she said, shaking her head. "No, never. He only ever went after the gangs, the bigger players. I've seen him cut loose the younger ones. He cut them loose and told them this was their one chance to sort themselves out."

"But he didn't do that with Neil, did he? With Seb?"

"He didn't touch them," Jarratt said. "He wouldn't have, not in a million years."

"They were dealing," Kett said. "Why wouldn't he go after them?"

"Because they were local kids, he's watched them grow up here. He wasn't after them, he was trying to find out who they worked for. He wanted to *help* them."

"I saw him in there," said Kett. "He fed that poor arse-hole heroin and God knows what else, he said he was giving him a gutful of heaven. You're telling me he didn't force Neil and Seb to take Jaw Breaker?"

"No," she said, and there wasn't a hint of a lie in her face. "He loved those kids. And yeah, he punished them sometimes."

Her eyes closed, her head twitching left and right like she was in denial.

"What is it?" Kett asked.

"This is going to look bad, but it isn't what you think it is. Dad has this place he takes people, a place for them to sweat. He uses it for punishment but he never hurts them."

"Who's *them*?"

"Anyone," she said. "But he takes the local kids there to scare them straight. There's somebody in it right now."

"It's Catherine, isn't it," Savage said. Jarratt nodded.

"We found her out in the village last night, after the deal went bad. We thought the Romanians had taken her but she was trying to hike her way to safety. Dad took her up the hill, grilled her about who she was working with. It's how we found the gang. She's still there."

"This case is getting worse by the second," Kett said. "Savage, get her in the car. And *you*, tell me where she is."

CHAPTER TWENTY-SIX

Savage drove, the IRV's siren wailing as they sped down the country roads. Kett gripped the strap above the door with both hands, closing his eyes every time they went around a bend, then opening them again because in the dark all he could see was his Skoda rolling down a hill, the windows exploding, the roof compacting.

"It's not far," said PC Jarratt from the back seat. Her hands were secured behind her back, and every time they hit a bend she almost toppled. "There's a turn in about half a mile, you'll miss it if you don't slow down."

"Slowing down is definitely a good idea," said Kett, and Savage tapped the brake.

"Is Cat going to be okay?" she asked.

"I think so," Jarratt said. "She'll have plenty of air."

"Air?" said Kett. "How come nobody's mentioned this place? We've spoken to half the village. How come nobody's told us the truth about Marshall?"

In the mirror, Jarratt tongued her lip.

"Because everybody knew he was doing what was best.

Nobody liked it, nobody liked him, but he kept the gangs out, he kept the kids safe. He was necessary."

Savage actually laughed.

"Are you listening to yourself?" she said. "The kids in Toltham were dealing drugs for the gangs. The village was crawling with crime. Your dad didn't make it better, he didn't do anything but make it worse."

Jarratt sniffed, staring out the window.

"So, Catherine Cavaney, she's dealing too?" Kett asked.

"Yeah," said Jarratt. "I think Seb and Neil were using her as a go-between."

"Because she looked like Niamh Bradbury, right?" said Savage.

"Yeah. Niamh was heavily into this shit. She, Seb, Neil and Pete Duggan were making a small fortune moving drugs from an outfit in South London and selling them to the European gangs. From what I've been told, the gangs hated the lads but they were happy enough to work with Niamh."

"Were the gangs involved with her death?" asked Kett. "The hit and run."

"No, they weren't, because they didn't even know she'd died. It was clear from the chatter we listened to they thought she was still alive, they thought they were still dealing with her. But they weren't."

"They were dealing with Cat," said Savage. "In a purple wig."

"They don't even look alike," Jarratt said. "But on a dark night, who's going to notice? When Dad found Cat walking the streets last night he took her up the hill for her own good. Place to think about all the wrong choices she'd made, but he also knew the gangs would never find her there. Like

I said, he never wanted to hurt those kids, he wanted to keep them safe. There it is."

She nodded to her right and Kett saw the turn, almost hidden in the tall verge. Savage braked hard, the IRV skidding on some loose gravel, then steered them through the gap. The ground here rose steeply towards a wooded hill.

"So what the hell happened to Seb and Neil, then?" Kett said.

"I don't know," Jarratt replied. "I honestly don't. But ask me, they took some gear from the stash they were supposed to sell, and it was a bad batch. I think they were just unlucky."

"This doesn't feel like bad luck," Kett said. "Did any of those men you tortured and murdered have anything to say about it?"

"No," said Jarratt. "They didn't know squat about the kids. And believe me, Dad would have got it out of them."

She closed her eyes, her brow furrowing like she was trying to push out the memories.

"It's right at the top," she said. "You'll see it clear enough."

Savage switched off the siren, the lights dancing on the trees as they bumped their way up the hill. After a couple of minutes they reached the summit and Kett saw the concrete pillbox drowning in a sea of brambles.

"There," he said, and Savage stopped the car.

Kett climbed out, pointing a finger at Jarratt.

"Do not move."

Savage was already running to the pillbox, calling Catherine's name. A sheet of plywood covered the opening, braced there with two lengths of two-by-four which had been staked into the dirt. Savage grabbed one and Kett pulled the other, tugging hard.

"Cat?" said Savage. "It's the police. Stay away from the door, we're coming in."

A scream from inside answered them, somebody pounding on the wood. There were screws in it, but only a couple.

"Grab that end, sir," Savage said, and Kett took hold of the heavy panel. "Now."

They pulled together, the wood resisting for a moment before the screws gave up. A scalpel of pain drove its way into Kett's knee and he fell back with a cry, the wood landing on top of his leg. Then Cat threw herself out of the darkness with a guttural, animal cry of desperation. She fell on the plywood, causing another fist of agony to crush Kett's knee.

She crawled away, staying on all fours until she'd reached the car where she curled herself into a ball and looked back with big, frightened eyes. She didn't have the wig on, her dark hair clogged with dirt, her hands filthy. She looked feral, and Kett didn't blame her. The inside of the pillbox was tiny and dark, and the smell of human waste was suffocating even from out here.

"You okay, sir?" Savage asked, offering Kett a hand.

"I'm good," he said, sliding the plywood away. "Go get her."

"Cat," said Savage, her hands up. "Nobody is going to hurt you. You're safe. We're police."

"*He* was fucking police!" the young woman screamed. She looked around, a mouse hunting for a hawk. "Where is he? Where is he?"

"Marshall has been arrested," Kett said, back on his feet. "He can't touch you."

Cat put her filthy fingers to her mouth, shaking her head.

"He can. He can fucking get you from anywhere, him or that bitch."

"Sophie Jarratt?" Savage asked. "You don't have to worry about her, either. She's in the car, but—"

Cat actually screamed, moving away from the car like it was on fire.

"No! Get her away!"

"She's in cuffs," said Savage, moving to intercept the girl. "She can't hurt you. I promise."

Savage squatted beside Cat, holding her hands out like she was dealing with a wild dog.

"I promise. You're safe."

Cat sobbed into the wet dirt.

"I thought I was going to die in there. I thought I was going to die in there."

Savage looked at Kett and he read her unspoken request. Pulling his phone out, he called Clare.

"Sir, we've found Catherine Cavaney. Marshall had locked her in an old pillbox. She's okay, but she needs an ambulance. Anyone free over there?"

"I'll check," said Clare. "Text me the address."

Kett hung up, texting the name of the road.

"Ambulance on the way," he said as he walked over. Savage had her hand on Cat's shoulder, stroking gently. "We could drive her, but there's no way I'm putting her in the back of the car with Jarratt."

Jarratt was banging on the window with her head, her words too muffled to make sense of. It sounded like she was yelling 'sorry'. Cat's cries had died out and she sat up, cross-legged, like she was five years old. She looked like a poor imitation of a person, Kett thought. An empty husk. He started to pull off his jacket then realised it was knackered from the fight with Marshall. He walked to the IRV instead and opened the boot, finding a yellow coat.

"Here," he said, draping it over her shoulders. "Stay warm."

She didn't say a word, the jacket so big she was almost lost in it.

"Cat," said Savage. "I have to double-check, did Marshall put you in there?"

She nodded, her words shaken to pieces by her trembling lips.

"Last night, after the deal went wrong..."

She looked up.

"Was it you lot that followed us? I didn't know, the pink car, all I saw was the tractor push it down the hill. Are they okay?"

"We're fine," said Kett. "Can you tell us what happened?"

"I..." her mouth gaped.

"Cat, we know about the drugs, we know about the deal you were doing last night. The more you lie, the worse this gets. Start by telling us what was supposed to happen."

"Can't this wait, sir?" Savage said. "She's exhausted."

She really was. She seemed to be shrinking into the dirt.

"Yeah," he said. "Yeah, it can wait. There's an ambulance on its way, kid. It won't be long."

Cat sniffed.

"I didn't want to do it," she said. "I don't know if it means anything, if it matters, but I didn't want to do it. Seb said I didn't have to do it either, but they didn't have anyone else who looked like her, did they? Like Niamh. And they'd only come if she was there. I didn't want to, but I knew Seb would be in trouble if I didn't. I knew they'd come after him. He promised me he was going to stop after this one."

She looked up, squinting into the sun that sat over Kett's head.

"And by the time he was dead, it was too late. I didn't know how to stop it. They came to get me, right after you left. But you saw that, didn't you? You saw I didn't have a choice."

Kett didn't answer. He didn't know what to say.

"Then when it all went to shit, when you lot arrived at the farm, I tried to run. The men were all chasing you, shooting at you, whatever. I wasn't going to hang around. Just wanted to get the fuck out of the village but that twat Marshall found me first, stuck me up here."

"It's okay," Savage said.

"The man who picked you up yesterday, in the Mercedes," asked Kett. "Who was it?"

She shook her head, her lips shut tight around the answer.

"This is important, Cat. Whoever it was, they might have had something to do with the deaths of your friends."

Cat glared at him, her face full of rage.

"I won't say it," she said. "You don't know that Peckham lot. They'll kill me."

"Not if we arrest them," said Savage, and Cat scoffed.

"You have no idea who these people are, how many of them there are, what they're capable of. I won't say anything. Never have, never will. And you can tell *her* that too."

She screamed the last sentence at the car, where Jarratt had fallen silent.

"Okay," said Kett. "Okay."

"One more thing," Savage said. "I spoke to Joe's mum. Gran, even. Val. She said Joe got a note from Marshall on Friday, asking him to go out into the woods. To meet him there. She thought you all might have got one. You and Neil and Seb and Pete. Is that true?"

Cat nodded. She reached into her pocket with her filthy hands, pulling out a piece of white, crumpled notepaper which she passed to Savage. Kett leaned over as Savage opened it, seeing four lines of small, neat capital letters.

Catherine, I know what you've been doing.

You've got one shot of surviving your crimes.

Meet me on the Northside of the broad, tonight. Just past the range. 10. WM.

"You didn't go?" Kett asked.

"Hell no. That fat prick would have killed me or something."

"You saw him deliver the note?"

"No, came through my door on Friday morning. He was always doing stuff like this, creepy shit. Thought he was... I don't know. Thought he was God, you know? The little God-man of Toltham."

"And the others got one of these too?" Kett asked.

"Yeah. All different, mind. Different times. Like he was lining us up for a job interview or something. Seb's was nine-thirty, although he wouldn't let me see it. Joe's was midnight. I don't know about the others, I never saw them. But I didn't think they'd actually do it. And they didn't, did they?"

"Neil was found at home," said Savage. "But we discovered Seb's body in the woods, not far from where the note says."

"Stupid," she said quietly. "If he was dumb enough to go then he deserved what he got."

"You think Marshall killed him?" Kett asked.

She considered it for a moment, everything shaking.

"I think Marshall is a man with a temper, and Seb was an arrogant arsehole. I don't know if he did this to himself or if somebody else did it to him. I don't care, anymore. I just want to get out of here. Out of this fucking village. Worst mistake of my life was coming here."

Kett heard an engine and he walked along the track to see an ambulance climbing the slope. He waved to it, waiting as it lumbered to the top of the hill then guiding it to a halt behind the IRV.

"You again?" said the paramedic as she hopped down from the cab.

"Sorry," Kett said. "Busy day."

"Honestly, if it gets me away from that fishing place then you're doing me a favour. Closest thing I've seen to hell. How are you doing, missy?"

The paramedic crouched next to Cat, beaming a great big smile at her. Savage stood up and walked to Kett's side, both of them watching.

"Marshall sends the notes," she said. "Gets Seb into the woods, wants to teach him a lesson."

"Yeah," said Kett. "We've seen his MO already. He feeds Seb what he thinks is heroin, maybe a speedball, but it's a bad batch laced with antipsychotics—it's Jaw Breaker —and he ODs."

"Then, when Neil doesn't show, Marshall goes to his house? Does the same thing to him?"

"And maybe Pete Duggan too. Neighbours said they saw Pete leave his house at ten, what if he was heading into the woods to meet Marshall?"

"That feels... it feels right, doesn't it?" Savage said, but there was more than a little uncertainty in her voice. "It feels like it should be case closed."

"Yeah," Kett said. "It does."

He looked at the pillbox, then at the IRV—Jarratt's face peering back at them through the glass.

"So why am I feeling like everything is still wide open?"

CHAPTER TWENTY-SEVEN

THEY WAITED FOR THE AMBULANCE TO PULL AWAY, Catherine in the back, then climbed into the IRV. Even though the sun was out, Kett's bones ached from the cold like they'd been wrapped in frozen wire. He glanced at Jarratt to make sure she was still secure, the PC lost somewhere in the nightmare of her thoughts. Savage started the engine, tapping the wheel.

"Where now, sir?" she asked. "The nick?"

"Yeah," said Kett. "Let's get her processed."

Savage turned the car around, everything bumping as they made their way down the track. They'd just reached the road when Kett's phone started to ring, and his heart seemed to lift when he saw Billie's name on the screen.

"Hey," he said. "How's it going?"

"Hey," she said, a sudden gust of wind tearing the word away. "We're good. We're out your way, actually. Yarmouth."

"Yeah?" he said. "How come?"

"The sun was out, the kids were chewing the furniture. Just fancied it so we got the train. Wasn't sure what your plans were but I figured if we came out this way you might be able to sneak away for an ice cream."

She shivered.

"Make that a doughnut. A hot one. No pressure, though, I know you're busy doing holiday stuff. How's it going?"

"You wouldn't believe me if I told you." He turned to Savage. "You okay getting her back yourself?"

"Sure, sir. Where are you going?"

"To the beach. Billie's out with the kids, thought I'd pop by and say hello."

"Sounds good. We're done here, right?"

"Right," he said.

With Wallace, Jarratt and Fred Patch in custody, Catherine safe and the forensic team on their way out to the fishing lets, there wasn't much more he could do.

So why was it that the jigsaw pieces still felt loose inside his head? Why did it feel like he was missing something?

"I'll drop you," she said. "We're going that way anyway."

She took the beach road past the open greens and mini-golf courses, the car parks and Victorian hotels and skeletal roller coasters. Despite the time of year, the promenade was packed, kids and dogs weaving their way chaotically between the crowds of older people. To the right, the choppy sea gnashed toothlessly at the wide, sandy beach. On the other side of the road, the arcades flashed their wares with faded showmanship, the sound of them making Kett feel like a little boy again—in a welcome way, this time, not like when Marshall had paid him a visit.

"That's them," said Savage, pointing towards the beach.

Kett followed her finger, seeing Billie, seeing his girls, feeling like he'd just slid into a warm bath. Savage blipped the siren and Billie turned, a flash of worry creasing her face before she saw them.

"Thanks, Kate," Kett said as they came to a stop. "I won't be long. Call me if you need me."

He looked into the back, Jarratt still quiet and calm and utterly beaten.

"You're sure you'll be okay with her?"

"I'm sure," she said.

He climbed out, checking the road before crossing it. All three of his daughters had spotted him, their shouts loud enough to turn every head in sight. Alice and Evie were already on the run, Billie holding Moira by the hood of her coat until Kett was clear of the road, then letting her go like an unleashed hound. He got down onto his good knee and opened his arms, the force of their hugs almost knocking him over. He laughed into them, the world just that little bit warmer.

"Dad! What are you doing here?" Alice asked, squeezing his head so hard it hurt, then bouncing back. "We tried to win a teddy but Mum couldn't do it and Evie messed it up."

"No I didn't," said Evie.

"She dropped a pound under the machine."

"I didn't!" Evie said, her cheeks crimson.

"It was our last pound."

"Hey, stop arguing." He looked at Billie. "I can't stay long, it's all gone a bit wrong."

"I'll say," she said, staring at his suit. "What on earth has Colin got you doing over there?"

She studied his face, seeing the bruise.

"Are you okay?"

"I am," he said. "But it hasn't been much of a holiday. I'll tell you everything, but not now."

"You can't get away from it, can you?"

"It's the job," he said with an apologetic shrug. "Come on, let's have a walk on the beach."

The girls took off, chasing seagulls into the air as they charged over the plaza and onto the seafront. Kett offered his hand to Billie but his fingers were filthy. She slid her arm through his instead, squeezing tight.

"You're sure you're okay?"

"I'm not," he said, the wind tugging at his words like it wanted to keep him quiet. "But I think it's over. How're you?"

She laughed.

"Oh, you know, it's like trying to herd a group of rabid badgers, as always. But we're having fun. Sorry, I know you wanted to get away from us."

"From you? Never. I didn't want to come out here at all."

He dropped from the promenade onto the sand, helping Billie down next to him. The girls were fighting each other, arguing about something that Moira was holding.

"How's the new car?" Billie asked as they walked.

"I'm not sure it's going to work out," he replied.

"Too pink?"

"Something like that. Hey, Alice, that's not nice."

Alice was trying to pull something out of Moira's hand, the youngest Kett fighting her off with some force.

"It's mine!" Alice said.

"Mine!"

Alice lost her temper, giving her sister a mighty shove that sent her sprawling over the sand.

"Hey!" Kett yelled. "Enough!"

Evie threw herself into the melee, her fists pounding Alice's back.

"I know karate, mister!" Evie was shouting.

"I said that's enough," Kett growled over Alice's screams. "Pack it in. I've had enough fighting today without you lot joining in."

Evie turned and ran, Alice starting to give chase before Kett managed to wrap her in his arms. She was stronger than ever, his injured knee almost giving way from the sheer weight of her.

"Calm down," he said. "You're okay."

He held onto her for a moment more, until he felt the tension drain from her wiry limbs, then he let go.

"Evie hit me," she said.

"She was just defending her sister," Kett replied. "Remember, we talked about this. If you do something unkind to somebody, you're asking for an unkindness back."

The wind pulled his words away, but not before they'd sparked something—an itch at the base of his skull. He reached for it, only for Evie to shout something at her big sister that sounded an awful lot like an insult. Then Alice was off again, charging across the sand. Evie bolted, shrieking, Moira doing her best to follow before faceplanting.

"Rabid badgers," said Billie, scooping Moira up. "What are we going to do with them?"

"Put them in the bin," he said. "There's one right there. They can all go in and we can go get a drink."

"That sounds perfect," she said, smiling.

Kett winced his way onto his knees, calling out to his girls.

"Who wants to build a sandcastle?"

This seemed to cheer them up. They bounded over in a storm of sand.

"I'll go get a bucket from the shop," Billie said. "Doughnuts?"

"Never say no to a doughnut," Kett said.

She smiled, walking away towards the little shops that sat on the promenade. Kett scooped some wet sand into a pile, trying to shape it into a mound.

"I'll get stones, for the walls!" Alice said, delighted. She ran towards the water, Evie chasing her, both of them collecting the pieces of stone and flint that had gathered there. Moira was too busy dismantling the mound that Kett had made, pulling it to pieces then using the sand to make her own shapes.

"That can be the gatehouse," Kett said to her.

"No. Toilet."

"Good thinking. Every castle needs a toilet."

Alice and Evie were running back, their arms full of stones. They dropped them by Kett's leg then started arranging them into a perimeter wall. Moira joined in, and Kett took a moment to appreciate how nice it was when they all stopped shouting at each other. It wouldn't last, it never did, but right now it was heaven.

"Here we go," Billie said as she made her way across the sand. "Three little buckets, three little spades. No doughnuts, I'm afraid."

"I'll live," said Kett. "Listen, here's an idea. Why don't we see if we can find a hotel for tonight, maybe finish this holiday just the five of us?"

He was answered by his phone, and he half thought about ignoring it. He pulled it from his pocket, seeing Porter's name there.

"Sorry," he said to Billie as he answered it. "Pete?"

"Thought you should know, sir, we found the *other* Pete, Pete Duggan."

"Alive or dead?" Kett asked, seeing Billie's face fall.

"Dead," said Pete. "I'm on the way there now. I'll text you the address."

The DI hung up and Kett turned his face to the sky. The clouds were gathering again, preparing for a second assault.

"Some holiday," said Billie.

"Sorry," he said again. "It won't take long. See you back at the house?"

"Aren't you supposed to be staying until tomorrow?"

"Not going to happen," he said. "And I mean it, let's go away. A proper holiday. Not tonight, but soon."

"I'd like that," she said.

The moment of harmony had passed, as he always knew it would. Evie and Alice were in a pile, sand flying as they fought. Kett opened his wallet and pulled out the lone fiver, handing it to Moira.

"For the teddy," he said, ruffling her wind-mussed hair. "Love you, Moo-moo. And you too."

Billie kissed his cheek.

"Be safe," she said.

He made his way across the beach, climbing the stairs onto the promenade and taking one last look back. They looked so small out there, his family, alone on the freezing sand. They looked so vulnerable. He almost couldn't bring himself to go.

But he did. Of course he did.

What choice did he have?

———

"BLOODY NORA, MATE," said the cab driver as he pulled up behind the second of two police cars parked by the side of the road, their lights flashing. "You sure this is the right place? Looks like trouble."

"Trouble everywhere," Kett said as he tapped his card on the reader. "Thanks."

He got out, watching the taxi do a clumsy seven-point turn before rattling back up the narrow road. There was nobody else in sight but Kett could hear voices from the woodland to his right—although woodland seemed too grand a term for the overgrown scrub that grew there. Straight ahead was a gate that led to a surprisingly long railway platform, deserted of everyone except a family of crows.

He followed the sounds down a dirt path, forcing his way through gorse bushes and brambles. The world opened up to his left into an enormous field where a sailboat seemed to carve its path across the scrubby land, the sight of it unnervingly impossible until Kett realised there was a canal hidden there. He pushed on into a copse of taller trees, seeing the yellow uniforms just ahead and hearing Porter's booming voice.

After another couple of steps, he saw the dead man.

Kett had seen Pete Duggan before, of course. The young man's grinning, bright-eyed face had been in several of the photos they'd discovered in Seb's caravan.

He barely recognised him now.

Pete's face was so tortured that it looked like it had been crushed. His mouth was a ruin, his dislocated jaw bulging and his tongue a slab of blue and purple meat that seemed far too big to be real. He lay on his back on a shallow slope so that the blood from his nose ran down his forehead and into his hair, coating eyes that were wide open and still wild with panic, even in death. The ants had found him, the way they always seemed to find the dead, colonising the cave of his broken jaw.

"Jesus," said Kett.

He looked at Porter, then nodded a welcome to the Uniforms who stood by the DI's side. Porter had a wallet in his gloved hands and he opened it up so that Kett could see the driving license in its clear plastic sleeve.

"Peter Robert Duggan," he said. "I've called Franklin, and Cara Hay is on her way. Looks like he's been dead for well over a day."

Kett nodded. Pete's corpse had that almost sweet butcher's shop smell about it, not old enough to rot but still old enough to make Kett's stomach churn.

"You found anything else?" he asked.

"Yeah. Sports bag just over the rise there. Haven't had a proper look but it's full of clothes, toothbrush, iPad. Looks like he was running somewhere. There's a doll back there too, button eyes and everything. Too close not to be related. And we got this."

He pulled a clear plastic evidence bag from his pocket and Kett saw the note inside. It was a scrap of paper with one rough edge, as if it had been torn from a notebook—just like Catherine's had been. Kett held out a hand and Porter passed it over.

"'*Peter,*'" Kett read aloud. "'*You are guilty of a terrible crime. But redemption is possible if you obey me. It's not too late. Meet me tonight, 11pm, by Somerleyton Station. Come alone. WM.*'"

Kett glanced back through the trees.

"That's Somerleyton, right? Why have I heard that name before?"

"That's it, yeah," said Porter. "No idea, sir. I should probably tell you, though, this is technically Suffolk."

"Really? Whoops." Kett glanced over his shoulder. "Well, what Suffolk Constabulary don't know won't hurt them."

"He came, with his bag," Porter said. "What do you think that's all about?"

Kett popped his lips, staring into the swaying branches.

"Maybe he was going to make a deal with Wallace Marshall," he said after a moment. "Maybe he was going to get out of town in exchange for Marshall leaving him alone?"

"Makes sense," said Porter. "Jarratt said her dad loved the local kids, but she'd stand up for him, wouldn't she? Anyone who's angry enough and violent enough to beat a man to death then chuck him in the lake wouldn't think twice about killing a young man like Pete Duggan. Those Romanians weren't much older than this. Just kids, really."

Kett scratched his head, then rubbed his face. He felt exhausted, the events of the previous night and the lack of sleep catching up with him fast.

"I honestly don't know," he said.

The note had been damaged in the rain, the paper covered in wet blotches that made the ink blossom.

"Where was it?" he asked. "The note. Where did you find it?"

"In his pocket," said Porter. "Fell out when I grabbed his wallet, sorry."

"Was it wet?"

"A little. Body's wet through, but his wallet was dry. Coat kept him out of the worst of it."

"Paper looks soaked," Kett said.

He turned it over, seeing the same stain on the back. There was a yellowish tinge to it.

"What is that?" he said. "Pete, you got any gloves?"

Porter handed some over and Kett fumbled his way into them. He opened the envelope and pulled out the note as carefully as he could, holding it up. The stain was definitely yellow, the paper oily where it had been damaged. He sniffed it, then held it out for Porter to do the same.

"What does that remind you of?" Kett asked.

"Not sure. But it's making me hungry."

"It's oil," said Kett. "Cooking oil."

He thought back to the lodge, to the visit they'd had at dinner from Wallace Marshall. He'd stopped to talk to somebody on his way out, somebody he obviously knew well.

Somebody he could easily have worked with.

"Mantas," said Porter.

"Mantas," Kett echoed. "I knew it. Let's go."

CHAPTER TWENTY-EIGHT

KETT CALLED CLARE AS PORTER DROVE.

"Speak," barked the Super. "Savage tells me you found the girl?"

"We did, sir. Marshall had locked Catherine in a pill-box. Jarratt said he's done it before with other young people from the village, trying to scare them straight. She's okay, I think. We found Pete Duggan dead, he had the same note as Cat and the others."

"From Marshall?"

"Yeah," said Kett. He frowned. "Well, I think it was from Marshall. It's signed WM. Pete's note is covered in what looks like cooking oil. Smells like a kitchen. I'm thinking it could be the chef at the Topiary, Mantas. Maybe that's what the M stands for? Maybe it's Wallace *and* Mantas? WM?"

"That's a pretty giant leap, Kett," said Clare.

"It would be, if I didn't already think he was dodgy as hell. When I first saw Cat at the hotel yesterday she seemed scared, and I swore I heard Mantas talking to her. There's definitely a connection between them. She seemed frightened when I mentioned him to her last night as well. We saw Marshall speak to Mantas at dinner, and he pretty much told me to keep my nose out of his business or risk losing it."

"Mantas said that?"

"Yeah. What do we know about him, sir?"

"I'm not sure," said Clare. "Let me check. I'll call you back. You heading to the hotel?"

"Yeah. Can you send somebody to meet us there?"

"I'll send a car. And Kett, go easy. One smudge of cooking oil isn't exactly conclusive evidence. We've got Marshall and everything points to him being behind this. I asked around and he was in the village on Friday, riding about in Jarratt's car. She's his only real witness, and any credibility she had has flown out the window."

"When have you ever known me *not* to go easy, sir?"

He hung up before Clare could answer, surprised to see that they were already at the lodge. The county seemed to be shrinking around them, like a draining pond. Porter took the bush-lined drive at thirty, the Mondeo's suspension soaking up the bumps. He didn't bother with the car park, he just pulled up in front of the main door, skidding on the gravel. A couple of women smoking cigarillos staggered back, both cursing Porter as he opened his door.

"Sorry," he said, offering a wave.

"Round the back," said Kett, jogging across the grass, past the big windows, towards the area of waste woodland where they'd found Cat's hiding place beneath the sofa. His phone rang as he went, Dunst's name on the screen.

"Keith?" he said.

"Doesn't sound like much of a break," Dunst replied

with a wheeze. "Only you could end up in the middle of something like this on holiday."

He laughed at his own joke, then cleared his throat.

"Boss asked me to call, about Mantas Markunas?"

"Yeah." Kett slowed as he reached the end of the hotel. The big windows here looked into the kitchens, and although they were too high up for him to see through he could hear voices inside. "What did you find on him?"

"Not much," Dunst said. "He's forty-three. Same age as you, right? Born and raised in Vilnius. Married, two kids, both girls and both teenagers, then he got divorced. They're still over there, I think. Came here in '09, been working at the lodge for three years."

"Any links to the drug community?"

"None. He's been collared once for using his phone in the car. Paid the fine, never got in trouble again. He's got a great rep as a chef, nothing but good feedback from the lodge. I couldn't find anything on him."

"There must be something," said Kett. "Keep looking."

"Yes, sir."

Kett slid his phone into his pocket as he cut down the side of the hotel.

"He's not on Interpol's most wanted, then?" asked Porter.

"Maybe he's just careful. Maybe he's just never been caught."

The broad opened up in front of them, its arms full of sunlight. Kett turned onto the lawn at the back of the building, heading for the fenced-off area where he'd spoken to Mantas before. The smell of food greeted him, making his stomach contract. He hadn't eaten since he'd left the hotel—since dinner *last night*, in fact, the cheeseburger he'd ordered when they'd finally taken the oysters away—and it felt like his guts were chewing themselves to pieces. The sound of people shouting was louder now, as was the clatter of saucepans and plates and cutlery.

Kett rounded the corner into the area with the bins, the back door open as it had been before. And he hesitated, suddenly doubting himself. Clare was right, Marshall was almost certainly responsible for the deaths, aided by Jarratt and Patch. They could close the case right now if they wanted to.

Then he remembered Mantas standing right there, a cigarette in his fingers.

This ain't the city, cop. Poke your nose into things around here and somebody'll cut it right off your face.

Who said that unless they were hiding something?

Unless they were *guilty*?

"We're just going to talk to him," said Kett. "But stay sharp, he's a big guy."

"Aren't they all?" Porter said.

Kett stepped through the door into the bustling kitchen, the change in temperature making him feel light-headed. The kid he'd spoken to yesterday, the one who'd been trying to get the bag into the bin, was washing up in the sink, and he did a perfect double-take when he saw the two coppers. He looked like a mouse that had been caught nibbling cheese on the kitchen counter.

"Oh," he squeaked. "Sorry, you can't be here."

"I'm police," Kett reminded him, pulling out his warrant card. "I need to speak with Mantas. Where is he?"

"Mantas?" said a woman who had stepped out from behind a shelving unit. She took off her chef's hat and ran a hand through her short hair. Her skin was drenched in sweat.

"Yeah, where is he?"

"You tell me. He buggered off a little while ago, left me right in it. Got to make Sunday roast for a hundred people and I can't do it on my own."

"When was this, exactly?"

"Twelve, maybe?"

"You know where he went?"

"No," she said. "I'm not his secretary."

Kett rubbed his face, the heat of the kitchen almost unbearable.

"Is this normal for him?" he asked. "Leaving in the middle of a shift?"

"Never," she said. "Solid as a rock, usually. That's why I'm so pissed off."

She pulled on her hat and walked away.

"Got to run. If you find him, tell him I'm going to kill him."

"Anyone else know where Mantas has gone?" Kett called out to the room.

It took him a moment to notice that the kid by the sink had his hand up like he was answering a question in class.

"Yeah?" Kett said.

"He, uh, he had a phone call," he said. "He was outside and so was I, and I heard him."

"When?"

"Just before he left. About twelve, like Megan said. He spoke on the phone just before then."

"What was he saying?"

The kid swallowed like he was working down a whole apple.

"I didn't hear much. I was doing the bins. But he seemed angry. He seemed like he didn't like the person he was talking to. I don't know, angry or sad or something. I don't really know what he's thinking, Mantas. He's always a *bit* angry."

"Did you hear anything specific?" Kett said. "Anything that could help us find him?"

The boy shrugged.

"Uh, I think I remember him saying something like, 'it's over,'" he said.

"It's over?"

"No, it was more like 'it's finished.' Or..." He looked like his brain was about to overheat, his eyes staring at the ceiling. "No, I remember. He said it was 'time to finish it.' That's it. That's what he said. 'It's time to finish it, once and for all.'"

———

PORTER SLAMMED on the brakes a little too late, the Mondeo bumping onto the kerb. Kett was out before the car was fully at a standstill, pain radiating from his knee. He hopped, skipped and jumped his way to the row of terraced houses on Trafalgar Street, in the middle of Yarmouth, searching them for any sign of a number.

"There," said Porter. "The grey one."

Kett stepped over the low wall and knocked on the door.

"Mantas?" he called out. "Open up. It's the police."

He knocked again, standing back. There was no hint of noise from inside, no curtains twitching.

"Go round the back, Pete," he said.

Porter bolted and Kett knocked again, opening the letterbox and peering into the dark, still hallway.

"Mantas, we really need to talk to you."

He heard the sound of a key in a lock, standing back to

see the door of the next house over open. A young woman peered through the gap left by the security chain, her eyes dark and her lips chapped.

"Keep it down, will you?" she said quietly. "Just got the fucking baby to sleep."

"Sorry," said Kett, holding up his warrant card. "I'm looking for the man who lives here. Mantas Markunas. You seen him today?"

"He went out," she said. "His car's gone."

"When?"

"Like, a little while ago," she said, ready to close the door.

"Do you know him?" Kett asked. The woman shrugged.

"No. Not really. He's nice enough. Helped me move all my stuff in, and... Yeah. No. Sorry."

She tried to close the door again, and this time Kett leaned over the low wall and braced his hand against it.

"Please," he said. "This is important. If you know something about him, tell me."

The woman swallowed, resting her head on the door frame.

"It won't get him in any trouble?"

Kett didn't answer, but eventually she nodded.

"Fella who had this place before me was a right creep. Kept the keys. Tried to come in one night, before I had Bella. I was pregnant and he still tried it on. Mantas heard me screaming because he came through the door like a battering ram, took him on. Never saw the little prick again."

"Mantas attacked the man?"

"Didn't really need to, he's scary enough. Chased him off."

"You file a report with the police?" Kett asked, and the woman scoffed.

"What would you lot have done? Sometimes you have to take care of yourself, yeah?"

"I've been hearing that a lot today," Kett said. He passed a card through the door and she read it.

"Never met a Detective Chief Inspector before," she said. "La-di-dah."

Kett smiled, and she smiled back.

"He's a good man, I think. Mantas. Don't hurt him, will you?"

"Can you remember what kind of car he drives?"

"Little white thing. A Fiat or something. He looks ridiculous in it."

"Thanks."

Kett pulled his arm back and she closed the door. A second or two later, Mantas' front door opened and Porter stood there.

"How'd you do that?" Kett asked.

"Back door was open. Thought I heard somebody talking. Was inside before I realised it was you."

He stood to one side to let Kett through. The front door opened straight into a small living room, the walls covered in textured, patterned paper, the carpet so thick that Kett was worried he might sink into it. A TV sat in the corner by the window, a brown leather sofa opposite. There were framed photos everywhere, mostly of two girls—babies, toddlers, then older, both in glasses with their hair done in French braids, then as teenagers. Mantas was in some of them, but not all.

"Mantas?" Kett called out. "You here?"

Nothing, and the house sat still around them. Even the dust seemed calm, caught in the light from the window.

Kett walked past a steep staircase into the kitchen, the back door still open. It was a neat and tidy room, a stack of clean dishes on the drainer, a pile of folded laundry on the table. There were more photos here, Mantas and the same girls.

And there, above the microwave, Mantas with a *different* girl.

"That's Niamh Bradbury," said Kett, pointing. The photo looked like it had been taken at the lodge, Mantas in his chef's outfit, Niamh standing next to him. Both of them held cigarettes in one hand and were flipping the bird at the camera with the other. They seemed happy.

"That one too," said Porter, nodding to a framed photograph by the back door. Sure enough there they were again, the two of them, this time against the backdrop of arcades on the Yarmouth seafront.

"What the hell is going on?" Kett said.

"You think they were *dating*?"

"I don't know."

"Looks like he had his life in order," Porter replied, picking through a pile of paperwork that had been carefully filed in a letter holder on the counter. "This house was his, mortgaged, no arrears. Has a bit of money in his bank but not loads. Looks like he sends most of his paycheque home every month. He doesn't give the impression of being a dealer."

"But the connection with Niamh, the European gangs, how does it all add up?"

Kett took the stairs, finding two bedrooms and a small bathroom. There was nothing but clothes in the wardrobes, and the walls were covered with more framed photographs. He made his way downstairs again, pinching the bridge of his nose to try to stop the ache that was spreading there.

Then he pulled out his phone and called Savage. There was no answer.

"Sir, look at this."

Porter had removed a handwritten letter from the rack and he held it out, the words indecipherable. He pointed to Mantas' name at the bottom.

"It's nothing like our notes, sir," he said. "Look at it. The writing couldn't be more different."

"Shit," said Kett.

He pulled out the bagged note they'd found with Pete Duggan, placing it on the table. The letters were big and blocky, almost like a child's. Mantas' letter was written in Lithuanian but the script was small and painfully neat. Even if he'd made a deliberate attempt to mask his writing, there would be some similarities.

Kett's knee was throbbing, so he pulled out a chair and sat down. Nothing was fitting together the way it should have been, and the more he tried to force the pieces, the more his head ached.

"We've got five kids dealing drugs for some County Lines outfit down in Peckham," he said. "Selling to a Romanian gang. Seb, Neil, Niamh, Pete and Cat."

"Six," Porter said.

"Six?"

"Yeah. Joe was part of that group too, remember? He used to hang out at the house all the time. I know he was only there for the Xbox, but they used him to courier the drugs. Willingly or not, he was a part of the operation."

Kett nodded.

"Six kids. Four of them are dead. Niamh died last year in a hit and run which nobody thinks is connected to the drugs. Seb, Neil and Pete all died this weekend after over-dosing on a bad batch of a brutal drug, gear that they probably stole from the people they were dealing for. They were supposed to do a deal last night, with the Romanian gang that Marshall butchered. The boys were already dead so Cat did it, along with whoever was there from the Peckham crew, but it went wrong because we showed up."

"Right," said Porter, leaning on the counter. "Jarratt seemed pretty sure the Romanians didn't kill Seb and the others, and it doesn't make sense that the County Lines folk would, unless they knew they were skimming some product off the top. And even then, it would have to have been more than they were taking, surely, to risk losing this whole operation."

Kett nodded, rubbing his stubbled face.

"But there's no way three young men happened to overdose on the same quantity of the same drug on the same night. It just doesn't happen, even if it's a bad batch. They were either forced to take it or spiked. Either way, it's murder."

"So it was Marshall, then?"

They'd seen the ex-copper beat a man to death. They'd seen the corpses of his other victims and heard from his own daughter that he was a murderer. But Kett still found himself shaking his head.

"Marshall was a monster, no doubt. We know he bullied the kids, locked them away in that pillbox. We know he did his best to scare the crap out of them. But kill them? Young folk from his own village? That doesn't fit."

He studied the framed photos on the wall, Mantas' daughters back in Lithuania. There was no mistaking how much he loved them, and how much they meant to him.

His daughters, and Niamh.

That same familiar itch returned to the nape of his neck, his skull tingling.

"What if we're way off track?" Kett said. "What if this has nothing to do with the drugs at all?"

"Sir?"

"Everything we know about Mantas indicates he's a good guy. Divorced, but he still dotes on his daughters. I spoke to the woman next door and she said Mantas had helped her when she was attacked, he came running."

Kett groaned his way out of his seat, lifting the photo of Mantas and Niamh at the beach from the wall.

"Mantas starts working at the lodge, meets Niamh. Maybe he takes her under his wing. Gabriel said she worked in the kitchen for a while, right? They spent time together. He looked out for her. Not romantically. More like, I don't know, more like father and daughter."

"Then she dies," Porter said. "She's killed."

"What if he knows something we don't?" Kett said. "What if he knows who killed her?"

"Then he'd go to the police."

"Go to Marshall? No, I don't think so. Mantas lived in the village long enough to know not to kick that particular wasp's nest. But he knew what Marshall was doing. He knew what *he* had to do."

"Revenge?" said Porter.

"Yeah. No police. He wanted to take out Niamh's killers himself."

"That's stretching it," said Porter. "And by that logic, you're saying it was Seb and the others who killed Niamh?"

"Niamh wanted to leave," Kett said. "We've heard it from more than one person. They fell out. Maybe Seb and the others didn't want her to go, pressured her into staying."

"You think Seb and the others killed her? Savage looked it up, there was no hint of anything like that in the report.

All of the men had alibis, they weren't anywhere near Niamh when she was killed."

"What if one of Marshall's cronies was in charge of the case?" said Kett. "What if he altered the report, let it slide? Seb and the others killed her, but... what is it we keep hearing? Kids will be kids?"

"No, boys will be boys," said Porter.

"Right. Boys will be boys. And these were *his* boys, right? Local kids. Niamh was an outsider, different village."

"Christ," said Porter. "So Mantas finds all this out. He writes the notes—or gets somebody to write them for him—pretending to be Wallace Marshall. Asks the lads to come into the woods."

"And they go, because they know that even though Marshall's a psycho, he won't actually hurt them."

"They think he'll lock them in his pillbox for a while, scare them straight. They've all done it before, they know it isn't too bad. They'll be out the next day. Pete Duggan even brought his suitcase."

"Only it's not Marshall they find out there. It's Mantas."

Porter was still shaking his head.

"There's no link between Mantas and the gangs, right? If he killed Seb and the others, where did he get the drugs he used to poison them?"

"Small village, a lot of activity," Kett said. "Wouldn't be hard to make some Jaw Breaker, if you know who to ask."

"This feels too much of a stretch," said Porter.

It did, but there was no doubt the pieces were clicking together a lot more neatly than they had five minutes ago.

"If I'm right about any of this," Kett said. "If this is Mantas going after the people he thinks are responsible for Niamh's death, then we've got a problem."

"Let's finish this, once and for all," said Porter, his eyes widening. "He's not done yet. But who's left to... Oh, shit."

Kett dropped the photo and moved as fast as his injured leg would let him, heading for the open front door.

"Joe was given same note as the others," he said.

"So was Catherine."

"He's going after both of them," Kett said, running for the car and pulling out his phone. "He's going to finish what he started."

CHAPTER TWENTY-NINE

"Thanks, Sarge," said Savage as she walked through the reception of Great Yarmouth Police Station. "Sorry again. Last thing any of us want to see is a copper behind bars."

The desk sergeant nodded sadly, looking over her shoulder to the corridor that led to the cells. There had been a profound sense of shock when Savage had walked PC Jarratt through the door in cuffs, and the entire building seemed to have arrived to watch her be processed. It was a rare thing to see a police officer on the other side of the cell door, and it left a bad feeling. But more than one constable had quietly spoken to Savage of their relief. Even though nobody had dared to say it, they'd all known the truth about Wallace Marshall and his daughter—not to mention Sergeant Fred Patch.

"Any word about Marshall?" Savage asked the sergeant as she reached the door.

"In hospital, under guard," she replied. "He isn't talking, mainly because somebody broke his jaw. That you?"

"No," said Savage, smiling at the irony.

Jaw breaker.

He'd got exactly what he deserved.

She walked outside, heading down the steps. The sun was blinding, but it didn't carry much warmth. It felt almost like an imposter. She called the hospital as she went, asking for A&E.

"Hi, I'm DC Kate Savage, just checking in on a patient that came to you a little while ago. Paramedics would have brought her in. Catherine Cavaney."

"Hang on," said the woman on the other end of the phone.

Savage walked to the car, shivering as the wind tried to force its way down the collar of her hoodie. She could hear the familiar chatter of the hospital in the background, the bleeps and the tannoy and the never-ending patter of footsteps. She unlocked the IRV and climbed inside, starting the engine just so she could ramp up the heater.

What next? she thought. It was just past two, and she knew there would be mountains of paperwork to get through.

But *technically* she was still on holiday.

It was a short drive to Hemsby from here, to her Gran's house. She hadn't seen her for weeks, mainly because of the Sweet Briar Rose case and all the fallout that had come from it. She felt terrible, because it wasn't easy for her Gran to leave her little chalet—the diabetic ulcers on her legs seemed to be worse every week—and she didn't exactly have an amazing social life. Savage owed her a visit, and if she was lucky there would be some fresh baked bread and homemade marmalade waiting for her in the kitchen.

She could even swing by the kennel and pick up Colin the dog a day early, pack a bag, stay at her Gran's for the night. A *proper* break.

"Hello?" said the woman on the phone. "You still there?"

"Yeah, hi."

"I can't find her, sorry. Cavaney, you said?"

"Right, Catherine."

"Paramedics say they brought her in the ambo but they gave her a clean bill of health. Never made it inside the building."

"She walked?"

"She walked."

Savage thanked her and hung up. She drummed the wheel, wondering what to do. Catherine hadn't been injured when they'd found her—not physically, anyway—but there was no way she hadn't been traumatised, and probably in shock. Wherever she was, she shouldn't be alone.

She threw the phone onto the passenger seat and pulled the car out of the car park, heading for the bridge out of town. It was only a ten-minute drive back to Toltham. She'd swing by Cat's place just to check on her, let her know there was support there if she needed it. Marshall was in custody in the hospital, Fred too. Jarratt was behind bars. Cat was safe from everyone, but not necessarily from herself—because Savage knew how dangerous the mind could be, she knew the tricks it would play.

She still had dreams about women wrapped in thorns.

Toltham was a ghost town, no sign at all that it had been the site of a major drug bust less than twenty-four hours ago. There would still be a police presence up at the farm, she knew, but most of the coppers there had been called over to the Landed Pike to help with the search for bodies.

They'd be there a long time.

"Monster," she said.

She passed the entrance to the lodge, casting a glance down the drive at the topiary animals who stood there. Marshall *was* a monster, there was no doubt about it. Porter had given her the debrief. He'd said that Marshall had compared himself to Kett when he'd claimed that the end was greater than the means. But there was no similarity to be found between the two men. She'd worked with Kett long enough to know he didn't always follow the rules, to know that sometimes the bad guys got hurt.

Sometimes they got *killed*.

But there was no denying the goodness she saw in Kett. It was hard to put into words, but he was a good man, a kind man. It showed in everything he did, even in the violence, and especially in the toll it took on him, the price he paid. All he wanted to do was help. Marshall, though, was rotten. It seeped out of every pore, hung heavy in his eyes, sat on those fat lips. The worst kind of monsters saw themselves as heroes, and that didn't get any more obvious than with him.

She slowed down as she reached the junction that led onto Station Road, letting an Amazon Prime van pull out before she made the turn. It seemed like days since they'd been here, when in fact it had just been the previous night. There was a car parked on the street across Cat's drive so she pulled past it, parking a little way down. A young couple were walking by with a baby in a stroller and they glanced nervously at the police car. She waved, waiting for them to pass before opening her door.

"Hi," she said as she climbed out.

They looked back together, no smiles.

"Lovely day," Savage tried, only for them to face forward and double their speed.

"Charming," she muttered, looking at herself in the dark window of the IRV and seeing the stains on her hoodie, the mud that streaked her sleeves from where Cat had grasped at her after they'd freed her from Marshall's prison.

"Not good," she said, wondering whether she should have stopped at the hotel first to get changed.

She locked the car, walking up the street. Neil Enthoven's bungalow came into view first, the gardens looking even more overgrown than they had yesterday, as if the bushes were doing their best to hide what had happened inside. Somebody had strung up lines of police tape over the gate, like yellow bunting, and the wind was doing its best to tug it free.

Cat's place sat on the other side of the road, and it looked deserted. The car that straddled the drive was small and white, so clean that the reflected sun in its trim made Savage's eyes hurt. She stopped to look through the window —copper's instinct—to see nothing at all, then crunched her way across the gravel.

She knocked gently, partly because the door looked ready to give up and partly because she didn't want to startle Cat if she was home.

"Cat?" she called out. "Catherine? It's DC Kate Savage, from earlier."

She wouldn't blame the young woman at all if she didn't open the door. Cat's experience of Norfolk Constabulary hadn't exactly been joyous so far, and she had no reason at all to trust Savage. Still, she knocked again, walking to the dining room window and cupping her hand to the glass—not that it did any good, because the blind was down.

"I just wanted to check in with you, Cat. You don't have to open the door, just let me know you're okay, yeah?"

Still nothing. There was every chance that she wasn't even here. She might have gone home or stayed with a friend or relative. Savage reached for her phone before remembering she'd left it in the car.

"Cat?" she said, returning to the front door and knocking again. "I know you didn't go into the hospital. You're not in any trouble, I promise. I just want to make sure you're okay."

Nothing.

Savage's stomach gurgled loud enough to be heard over the wind. She rubbed it, trying not to think about her Gran's bread, fresh out of the oven, about melted butter and jars of orange and lemon marmalade, about pots of strong, hot tea. The image was just too good and she stepped away from the door, pulling a card from her pocket and writing her mobile number on the back of it.

"If you're in there, and you can hear me, I want you to know you can call me anytime, okay? This is my number, if you need to talk."

She pushed open the flap and dropped the card through.

And heard somebody crying.

Ducking down, she looked through the letterbox into the bungalow's dark interior. It was hard to see much because the doors were all shut.

"Cat?" she called. "You okay?"

The wind rattled the house, but past the roar of it Savage heard another sob.

She moved down the side of the bungalow towards the rear garden. The gate opened and closed by itself, clattering in its rotting frame. The garden was deserted, but the patio door was open.

"Cat?" Savage said as she approached. "It's DC Savage, I'm going to come in."

But she hesitated by the door, looking into the gloomy

kitchen—the curtains drawn and the lights off. Stepping inside felt like the absolute last thing she wanted to do. She patted her pocket again, hoping the phone might have magically turned up.

"You're an idiot, Kate," she said quietly.

Another sob floated up from deeper in the house, desperately sad. It broke Savage's heart to think of the young woman alone in there.

She stepped into the kitchen, fumbling along the wall for the light and finding it. There was a landline next to it and she pulled the receiver from its cradle, using it to dial Kett's number. It rang for too long before he answered.

"DCI Robert Kett," he said. "Who is this, please?"

"It's me, sir. Savage. I'm inside Cat's bungalow. Came to check on her and—"

"Catherine's place?" said Kett. She heard the growl of an engine. "Where's your phone? I just tried to call you."

"Left it in the car, sir, sorry. I—"

"Get out of there, Kate," Kett said, and she felt a lance of adrenaline spear her heart. "It's Mantas. We think he killed Seb and the others and he might be after Catherine. We're on our way. Do not engage, Savage. That's an order."

"I think he's already here, sir," she whispered, backing up, the cord of the phone growing taut. "I think—"

And the room suddenly grew darker, a breath on the back of her neck from the open door. Savage snapped her head around to see a hulking shape, a bald head, a clenched fist.

"He's—"

Then Mantas punched her in the side of the head with a boxer's hook, and she fell right out of the world.

CHAPTER THIRTY

"Step on it, Pete."

Kett kept the phone to his ear, trying to make sense of what he was listening to. Savage had broken off mid-sentence and he'd heard something hit the floor. It could have been anything, of course—a dropped phone, a line caught in the wind, a slamming door—but he knew it wasn't.

This was something *bad*.

"Kate? You okay?"

He heard what might have been a breath, then a woman's voice rising towards a scream.

Then the phone went dead.

"Fuck! Move it, Pete, she's in trouble."

Porter took them around a corner so fast the tyres whistled. The Mondeo hit a pocket of gravel and Kett felt the back start to slide before Porter grappled with the wheel and straightened them out. They were on the main road into Toltham now and there were blue lights up ahead, an IRV in front of them. Porter punched the accelerator, catching up in a heartbeat.

"Bloody plods," he said. "Come on, *drive*!"

Kett cleared the line, calling Superintendent Clare.

"Speak," the Super barked. "Where the tossing hell is everyone?"

"It wasn't Marshall," Kett said, bracing his hand on the dash as they turned another corner at breakneck speed. "Mantas killed our three men."

"Christ, you're sure?"

"He's going after Cat, sir. I think he's at her place now and I think he's just attacked Savage."

"What?" roared Clare. "Is she there alone?"

"Not for long," Kett said. "We need the village sealed off. Every road, just in case he makes a break for it. He must know we're coming for him. Mantas drives a white Fiat Punto. It won't be hard to spot."

"On it," said Clare. "Go get our girl."

Kett hung up. They were almost there, the turning in sight. The IRV's brake lights blazed and it made the turn painfully slowly, Porter almost ramming it onto the pavement as he followed. They accelerated up the road, parked cars thumping past the window until Cat's bungalow appeared. The IRV pulled across the empty driveway and Porter slammed on the brakes so he wouldn't hit it.

"We're looking for a big, bald guy," Kett yelled to the coppers who climbed out of the IRV. "He's dangerous, so don't engage unless you have to. There's one of ours in there, DC Savage. Might be a young woman too, so watch your step."

The constables both flicked out their batons, making for the front door. Porter was halfway to the garden but Kett hung back, scanning the street.

There was no sign of Mantas' car.

That was bad news.

The PCs were pounding on the door, yelling over each other.

"Move," Kett ordered, stepping in between them and driving his boot into the wood. His knee screamed, and he almost did too, but the old lock splintered out of the frame. He charged it with his shoulder and it gave way without a fight. "Police!" he roared. "Mantas, do not move."

He opened the door to the dining room at the front of the house, seeing the same table they'd sat at the night before. By the time he'd made it to the kitchen, Porter was there, the big DI shrugging.

"Empty," he said. "But there's blood."

He stood to the side so that Kett could walk past. He was right, there was a spatter of blood on the tiles next to the phone, which drooped on its cord like a hangman's rope.

"Check the garden, Pete," he said, the panic rising in his voice. "They were just here, they can't have gone far."

Porter vanished outside.

"Guv?" came a shout from the front of the building. Kett followed it into the hall, looking through a door on the right to see a small bedroom. One of the PCs stood by the wardrobe, a coil of rope by his feet and a bread knife on the duvet.

"Tear this place apart," he told him. "Find them."

But he knew they wouldn't. The house was empty, they weren't here.

"Garden's clear," Porter said. "Fenced all around, there's no way Mantas got over it with two hostages."

Kett ran through the kitchen and out into the garden, doubling back down the drive. Another IRV was pulling up, Clare's Mercedes bullying past it then coming to a halt in the middle of the road. Duke was out of the passenger seat in a flash, his face deadly serious. Clare followed, looking like a man who had woken from his grave.

"She there?" he yelled.

"We're too late. Mantas has gone and he's taken Kate with him. I think he knocked her out."

Clare visibly paled.

"I think Mantas has Catherine too," Kett said. "He must have left right before we got here. If we're quick, we can catch him."

Clare nodded, climbing back into the car.

"I'll take the Beccles Road south," he yelled. "You go north. I've got units heading over from Yarmouth, they know what they're looking for. We'll find her."

"We'd better," Kett said.

He climbed into the Mondeo, Porter starting the engine.

"How the hell did he get two women into his car and disappear before we got here?" the DI asked.

"He's a big guy. Strong. If he knocked them out he wouldn't have had any trouble. Go, Pete!"

Porter waited for Clare's car to accelerate up the street then he swept the Mondeo in a tight circle, almost taking out Enthoven's hedge. They roared back the way they'd come, taking a right. Kett sat forward in his seat, scanning the road ahead.

"Come on," he said, more to himself than to Porter. "Come on, where the fuck are you?"

Porter took the corners as fast as he dared, oncoming drivers swerving out of his way or leaning on their horns. He slowed as he approached the track that led up to the farm, seeing an IRV making its way down the hill towards them. Porter lowered his window as they both pulled up to the junction.

"Seen a white Fiat Punto anywhere up there?" he said.

"No," said the PC at the wheel. "Just heard the shout on the radio. Where do you want us, sir?"

"Back in the village. If he's not on the street, start knocking on doors."

Porter didn't wait for a reply, stamping on the accelerator, the big engine roaring. Kett's stomach rolled and he grabbed the strap, resisting the urge to tell Porter to slow down. He pulled out his phone, calling Dunst.

"I just heard," the old DI said. "What do you need, sir?"

"Did you find any properties connected to Mantas?" Kett said. "Anything at all to tell us where he might have gone?"

"Just his house in Yarmouth," Dunst said. "And the lodge."

"The lodge," said Kett, turning to Porter. "Hang on, didn't Gabriel say Mantas brought a load of stuff with him when he came to Toltham? He brought his own kitchen. There was no room at the hotel so he put it into storage?"

"I think so," said Porter. "You think that's where he's going?"

"Keith," Kett said into the phone. "Can you check to see if there are any storage units around here?"

He heard Dunst typing something into his computer, coughing wetly.

"Closest one's over in Belton, just off the Beccles Road. I'll call them."

"Keep going," Kett told Porter once he'd hung up. "There should be a turning up ahead for Belton. It's not far."

Porter sped up along a straight stretch of road, his knuckles white around the steering wheel. He was going so fast Kett almost missed the sign, and when Porter slammed on the brakes the car juddered hard. He steered them left, bushes and trees crowding over the road like they were jeering at them, cutting out the sun. There was nothing down here, just fields, until the road suddenly split.

"There, Pete," Kett said, pointing to his left.

Porter jerked the wheel and they flew onto a gravel track, everything bumping, gravel spraying out behind them. It was deserted down here too, and Kett thought he'd made a mistake until they passed a sign for a plastic wholesaler and a self-storage unit.

Then they took the next turn and almost collided with the car that was hurtling towards them.

"Fuck!" said Porter as the little white Fiat buzzed past them, so close that their wing mirrors clipped. Mantas sat behind the wheel, his eyes wide with panic. Something dark lay across the back seat, motionless.

"That's him!" Kett yelled, spinning in his seat as the Fiat raced back towards the main road. "Turn around."

Porter was trying, but the track was narrow and the car was too long. Kett had his phone to his ear, calling Clare.

"He's just south of Belton," he said before the Super could say anything. "Heading for the Beccles Road. We're in pursuit."

"Have you got eyes on Savage?" Clare asked.

"No, but he was moving fast. We need cars on the A143, block the road."

"Already done. We'll get him."

Porter spun the wheel, pulling them back onto the track. The engine boomed, the DI's face a mask of concentration as he took the corners.

"Careful, Pete," said Kett. "You don't want to go into the back of him."

Porter didn't reply, reaching the main road. Kett looked

right, then left—a flash of brake lights as somebody took the corner.

"Left, left, left," he said, but Porter had seen it too, pulling out and gunning it.

Mantas had a head start but the Fiat was no match for the Mondeo. They caught up to him in seconds, Porter touching the brake to stop his bumper from connecting with the little car's boot. The DI slammed his hand on the horn in frustration.

"Pull over!" he roared.

But Mantas was speeding up, the car hitting the verge so hard it almost tipped. It was doing sixty—way too fast for the sharp turns.

"Slow down, Pete," said Kett. "We're not going to save her if that car comes off the road."

Any minute now they'd hit Clare's roadblock and Mantas would have to stop.

Unless he didn't, of course.

Right now, he was a man with nothing to lose.

Mantas' rear lights flared and Porter had to slam on his own brakes as the little car broke off the main road, heading down a track into the woods.

"Shitting hell," said Porter, wrestling with the wheel as he tried to go after him. He took the turn too wide, needing to reverse and then try again. By the time they were on the track, the Fiat had vanished.

"Do *not* lose him," said Kett, calling Clare again.

"He's trying to shake us in the woods, sir," he told the Super. "We're..."

He looked out of the window, something about this place familiar. He could see a clearing up ahead, a half-finished climbing frame.

"We're on the north side of Toltham Broad, sir. Off

Miller's Lane. Not far from where we found Seb Reilly. There's nowhere for him to go."

"I'm on my way."

Porter bumped them down the track, then steered them around a corner.

Mantas' car was right there, the driver's door open. The chef was running into the woods, his arms out as he tried to stop himself from falling. Kett opened his door, running for all of three seconds before his knee gave out. He tried to ignore the pain, limping to the Fiat.

"Get Mantas!" he yelled to Porter, the DI already giving chase. "Kate?"

He bent down to look through the open door.

It was empty.

"Shit," he said, fumbling with the front seat, tipping it forward.

A black coat lay across the back. Mantas' coat. Nothing underneath it.

He clambered onto the seat and looked in the boot, but it was empty too.

"Savage?" he shouted, climbing out of the car. "Kate?"

Had Mantas dropped her in the woods somewhere? Stopped the car and kicked her out? He wouldn't have had time, they'd only lost sight of him for a few seconds.

Kett swore again, jogging over the uneven ground. There was no sign of Porter or Mantas but he could hear them shouting.

"Pete?"

The track curved past the climbing frame, and there Kett saw Porter standing in the fenced-off clearing.

He had his hands in the air.

Never a good sign.

"Pete?" Kett said again.

He reached the gate and Mantas came into view, yelling in his own language. He had a wooden bow in his hands, the string pulled back and the arrow gleaming. It was a training bow, taken from the equipment shed that stood open behind him, but there was no denying how lethal it would be at this range. He spotted Kett and swung the bow around, his shouts dying out in his mouth.

"Mantas?" Kett said. "Put down the weapon. Right now."

"No," the man said, his voice like distant thunder. "What did I tell you, cop? You poke your nose into things around here, you get it cut right off."

"Put it down," Kett said again. "Then we'll talk."

"Talking now," Mantas said.

Porter took a step towards him and Mantas swung the bow back around. His fingers were clenched around the arrow, his arms starting to shake with the effort of holding the string taut. Sooner or later it was going to fire whether he wanted it to or not.

"It's over," said Kett, hearing the faintest of sirens. "Hear that? There's nowhere to go. Things are bad enough already, Mantas. You don't want the death of a copper on your hands as well as the murders of three young men. Where is she? Where's the police officer you attacked?"

"Who cares?" he said. Beads of sweat rolled down his face, the tremors growing. "One less corrupt policeman? One dead policewoman? That's no bad thing."

"Wallace Marshall is in custody," said Porter. "Jarratt too."

This brought a thin smile to Mantas' face, but it didn't last long.

"Good," he said.

"So where is she?"

"I do not know."

He pulled the string tighter, his face slick with sweat, his eyes blinking wildly.

"Why did you do it?" Kett asked, trying a different tack. "Why kill Seb and Neil and Pete?"

Mantas licked his lips.

"They were arseholes," he said. "They deserved it."

"Because of what happened to Niamh?"

Mantas nodded. He swung the bow back towards Kett, every muscle in Kett's body seeming to contract in anticipation.

"Put it down," Kett said. "Think about your girls. Your daughters. Killing bad men is one thing, but killing police is another. You want them to know you shot a copper? You want them to know you shot another *dad*?"

"You're a father?" Mantas asked.

"Three girls," said Kett. "They're still little. Please, put it down."

Mantas sighed, staring into the trees for a moment. The birds were singing, the sound of them barely audible over the wet thump of Kett's pulse.

"You arrest me, I confess to everything," he said.

"Sounds good," Kett replied.

Mantas pulled the string even tauter, aimed the arrow at the dirt, then let it fly. The arrow thumped home with surprising force, burying itself almost to the first feather. Porter started moving towards him but Mantas pointed a finger at the DI.

"No hero shit," he said. "I will come gently."

He thrust out his wrists. Porter shrugged, looking at Kett.

"I haven't got any cuffs," he said.

"Me neither," Kett replied. He nodded to the ground.

"Sit down, Mantas. Don't move, and we don't have to get physical."

The chef nodded, collapsing onto his backside like an old bear. He folded his legs as best he could, one hand in his lap, the other in the dirt behind him to support himself.

"I'm going to ask you again," Kett said. "Where is the police officer you found in the house, the young woman? And where's Catherine Cavaney? Are they okay?"

"I don't know," Mantas said. "Cop was out like light. I dropped them at my storage unit."

"You okay with him?" Kett asked. Porter nodded, tugging the arrow from the dirt and tossing it into the trees. Kett pulled out his phone and called Clare, feeling the tremor in his arms, the ache of the fading adrenaline rush. "Sir? We've got Mantas but we could do with some backup as soon as possible."

"Thank toss," said Clare. "Savage?"

"He says he dropped them off at the storage unit in Belton. Get an ambulance there, he knocked her out."

"On it," Clare said, hanging up.

Mantas was lying on the dirt now, his hands laced behind his head like he was enjoying a bit of sun at the beach. Kett walked over to Porter, the DI shaking his head. There was something in his face and Kett could read it as easily as if he was a book.

"This feels too easy," Kett said, and Porter nodded.

Easy wasn't the right word, though. It hadn't been easy.

But it didn't feel *right*.

"You were friends with Niamh, weren't you?" he asked the man on the ground. Mantas grunted. "Or was it more than friends?"

At this, the chef threw Kett a glare.

"Friends," he said. "I'm not a pervert. I was like a father to her. Like family."

"Right," said Kett. "I think you're a good man."

The sirens were louder now and Kett could hear an engine too. He looked over his shoulder to see the trees shimmering with blue light.

"I think you wanted to help Niamh, somehow. I think you wanted to put things right because of the way she died."

Mantas shrugged, staring into the swaying branches above him.

"You wrote the notes, you lured those young men into the woods, and you fed them enough drugs to kill them. All for what? Revenge?"

Mantas frowned.

"Yes," he said after a second or two. "All true. I confess."

But his expression was as easy to read as Porter's had been.

"You're lying," said Kett.

He turned away, feeling that itch at the back of his neck, feeling like there was something there he just wasn't seeing.

Like family, Mantas had said.

Kett remembered his girls on the beach, the way Alice had pushed Moira into the sand, the way Evie had come after her, the way she'd defended her.

Or *avenged* her.

"I know karate, mister," he said, feeling the pieces in his head suddenly shift, seeing the picture that emerged.

"What's that, sir?" Porter asked.

"We got it wrong."

An IRV pulled around the corner, two PCs out in a heartbeat.

"We got what wrong?" Porter asked.

"I'm so stupid. It's not Mantas. He didn't kill those men."

"I did," Mantas said, looking up. "It was me. All of it. I confess."

And he looked like he was about to stand up and start fighting except the first constable reached him. He pinned a knee on Mantas' leg, the other PC snapping the cuffs around his wrists. Together, they rolled him over onto his stomach, his face pushed into the mulch.

"You read him his rights?" asked one.

"You do it," Kett said. "Not murder, just assaulting a police officer."

"Seriously?" said Porter. "If it wasn't him then who the hell killed Seb and Neil and Pete?"

"You got any of those notes, Pete? The ones telling the men to go to the woods?"

"Got Pete's in the car," he said. "Hang on."

He ran off to get it. Kett pulled out his phone, scrolling through the photos he'd taken on the case, knowing he didn't need to.

There it was, the first note they'd found. Not any of the ones signed WM, but the one left in the buried locker next to Toltham Lodge.

Seb, where are you? I've called a hundred times. I'm scared. Do I still go through with it? I'm scared they'll hurt me if they find out. I know you'll be here so CALL ME when you read this. If you don't, I'm not going to go. Cat.

"Here," said Porter, handing over the bagged note. Kett studied it, seeing the same rounded letters, the same slanted I's—not identical, because there had been some attempt to mask the writing, but close enough to confirm what he already knew.

Family.

Mantas had been like a father to Niamh.

But she'd had a sister too. A sister she hadn't known, a sister she'd never met, a sister not by blood, but by circumstance.

Sisters would fight for each other.

Sisters would *kill* for each other.

"It's Catherine," said Kett, looking at Porter. "It's Cat. It was her all along."

CHAPTER THIRTY-ONE

SOMEBODY WAS PUNCHING SAVAGE IN THE HEAD.

Not hard, but repeatedly.

Smack, smack, smack.

She tried to open her eyes and for a moment she found that she couldn't. The panic washed through her like burning fuel, and past the shock of it she could feel the agony in her skull as somebody hit her again, and again, and...

She screamed silently, lifting her head, managing to open her eyes. Bright light screwed its way into her head, an explosion. She tried to speak but all that came out of her mouth was a low, animalistic groan.

"Easy," said a voice. "He really did a number on you."

The light was fading, the world taking shape around her. She was in the back seat of a car, she realised, her hands bound together and strapped to the door handle. When she tried to pull her legs up she realised that her feet had been tied as well. The car was moving, the tops of trees racing past the windows. Every time they went over a bump in the road her head hit the door.

Smack, smack, smack.

From here, Savage couldn't see the driver.

But she knew the voice.

"Catherine?" she said, the word painful to speak. Her jaw felt swollen, and she could taste blood.

"I wondered if you'd guess," said the voice from the front. "I'm amazed you didn't realise it was me, to be honest."

"What?"

"Seb and the others. I thought you'd crack it, like, straight away. The notes were a dead giveaway. I tried to change my handwriting but there's only so much you can do."

The car hit a bump and Savage's head slammed into the door.

Smack.

She lifted it as best she could, the pain almost liquid as it moved from the back of her skull to her temple. She tried to remember how she'd got here but the last thing in her memories was leaving the hospital. She'd been looking for Cat.

She'd found her.

"You hit me?" she asked, realising it wasn't quite right but saying it anyway.

"No," said Cat. "That was Mantas. He's gentle most of the time, and it's not like him to hit a woman. I imagine he hates that he had to do it. But there was no choice, not if we wanted to finish this."

The pain was growing worse by the second. It was a frightening pain because she'd never felt anything like it before.

"Cat, where are you taking me?"

"We're almost done," she said. "Almost done. I'm not

going to hurt you, don't worry. Just as long as you stay where you are."

"Can you pull over?" Savage asked. "Can we talk? There are police everywhere, they're looking for you."

"They're not," Cat said, her tone jovial and light. "They're looking for Mantas. He promised me he'd take the rap for all this, at least until it's over. Then he'll go free."

The car was slowing, and Savage heard the gentle click of the indicator.

"You killed them?" she said. "You killed Seb and the others because of Niamh, right?"

"So you *were* close," Cat said. "You almost had it figured out."

There was a flash of purple as Cat strained over the back of her seat, her wig so bright it was almost glowing. The smile on her face seemed utterly genuine, but there was a glint in her eye that bordered on madness. She vanished again.

"I'm relieved, to be honest," she said. "I was getting worried that you lot weren't actually very good at your job. Oh, incoming, hang on."

Savage heard a siren, the relief flowing through her like cool water until she felt the thump of the passing IRV. The siren dulled, faded, then was lost behind the sound of Cat's laughter.

"Phew," she said. "I'm glad I wore the wig."

Savage tried to pull her legs up again but the ropes were tight—so tight she couldn't feel her toes. She lifted her head to study her wrists, wondering if she could bite through her restraints. The terror was almost overwhelming, it seemed to make her blind and deaf until she fought to suck in a breath, and then another.

"What are you doing back there?" Cat asked. "Don't

bother trying to get out, Mantas tied you up before he left. He's good with knots. He was in the Navy for a while, back in Lithuania. It's where he learned to box."

"Please, Catherine," Savage said. "This has to stop."

"Why?" she replied. "Why do I have to stop when they didn't?"

It really did feel like her head was on fire, the flames spreading. She tried to see past the agony, tried to make sense of what Cat was saying.

"You think they killed Niamh? Seb and the others? That's why you went after them."

"No," said Cat. "I know who killed Niamh. She took her own life."

"What? It was a hit and run, it—"

"She walked into traffic. She knew what she was doing. She took a shit-load of heroin, trekked all the way to the A47 in the middle of the night, and she stepped right out in front of the first lorry she saw."

"How do you know that?"

"Because she wrote it all down. She left a note. Seb had it. He kept it like some kind of trophy. She said she was going to kill herself because of what they'd done to her."

Savage heard the indicator again, the car slowing down then turning.

"Cat, you told me you never knew Niamh. You never met her. How do you know what happened?"

"It's weird that you'd ask me that question instead of the important one," said Cat. "It's weird that your first question wouldn't be 'What did they do to her?' Makes me realise I'm doing the right thing. You didn't care about her. Nobody did, except Mantas maybe. And no, I didn't know her. Not to start with. But this..."

Savage saw another flash of purple as Cat lifted a strand of her wig, letting it fall again.

"There's something weird about pretending to be somebody, isn't there? Not at first. At first it's just a job, but then you start to imitate them, you start to learn about them, you start to... I don't know, you start to *feel* like them, too. And people start treating you the way they treated them. I think they forget. All those times I had to sit in Neil's shitty bungalow with those shitty drunk men waiting to be told where to take the drugs, where to pick up the cash. They made me keep the wig on, you know? Even when I didn't need it, even when nobody else was there, they made me keep it on."

The lightness had gone from her voice.

"And they called me Niamh as a joke. They called me Niamh, and when they were pissed and high they used to do the same things to me that they did to her."

"No," said Savage, closing her eyes.

"Oh yes. They tried to, I should say. But I was older than she was when they first started on her. I said no. And when that didn't work, I said no in a way that they would listen to. Hurt somebody enough and they'll learn to leave you the fuck alone. And they needed me, so they dropped it. But Niamh, she never knew how to fight them. I think she gave up even trying."

"They abused her?" Savage said.

"Over and over and over. They told me so themselves. Didn't call it what it was, of course. But the way they spoke about it? If you'd heard them, you'd have done the same thing I did."

"Why didn't you talk to us?" Savage said. "We could have helped. We could have locked them up."

Cat spat out a laugh.

"Yeah? You'd have helped, would you? I *did* tell the fucking police. I wrote an anonymous letter, left it on Wallace Marshall's car with Niamh's suicide note, because everyone knows Marshall's a fucking psycho. I thought once he knew what had happened to Niamh, what they'd driven her to, he'd kill them. You know what he did? You know what that fat fucking arsehole did?"

"Locked them in his pillbox," said Savage.

"Yeah, one night apiece and a promise never to touch another girl again without her permission. One night in the box to make up for all her suffering, all her pain, and her death. And it didn't even work, because the next time I saw them they hadn't changed at all. They were laughing about it. They told me Marshall had been laughing too. 'Boys will be boys,' he said. You hear that? Boys will be boys."

"He wasn't police," Savage said. "I'm so sorry, Cat. Marshall was a monster. You could have come to us."

"Too late," she said, sniffing. "Too late now. Marshall destroyed the note the way he destroyed all the evidence, to keep those lads safe. You find anything in Neil Enthoven's house? Seb's caravan? No, course you didn't. Boys will be boys, that's the way it's always been. But you know what? Girls will be girls, too. Girls will be girls, and we're really fucking angry."

Savage tried to free her hands again, the rope burning through the top layer of skin, the agony of it almost as bad as the inferno in her skull.

"I hear you, Cat," she said. "I feel your anger, your pain. But it's done. Seb is dead. Neil and Pete are dead. It's over."

"No, it isn't," she said, the car slowing. "There were four boys in that group. Four of them."

"Joe?" Savage said. "But he didn't touch her, did he? His gran said he just went there to play on the Xbox. He wouldn't have hurt her."

"He didn't," said Cat. "I know he didn't do what the others did. But you know what else he didn't do? He didn't tell anyone. He didn't help. From what I hear, he sat there playing that fucking computer day after day while Niamh was getting raped in the next room."

"He's autistic, Cat. He didn't know what was happening. He didn't know about the drugs he was delivering, they were just using him."

The car came to a stop, gravel crunching beneath the tyres.

"Cat, listen to me," said Savage, trying to crane her head up to see the driver. "Don't do this. Let us deal with Joe. If he's guilty of something, he'll be punished."

The horn blared, making Savage jump. Then Cat leaned past her seat, holding up a slim, lethal-looking knife.

"If you say anything before he gets in, I'm going to kill him right here," she said. That spark of madness was back, no sense at all that she was lying. "And I'll kill you too."

Cat leaned on the horn again and Savage heard a door closing, footsteps running this way.

"Joe!" Savage called out, tugging at her ropes hard enough to make the car rock. "Joe, stay away!"

Cat turned on the radio, ramping it up to full volume—loud enough to make Savage's ears feel like they were bleeding.

"Joe! Run!"

It was hopeless. The passenger door opened and Joe climbed in with a big smile on his face. He'd closed the door and was buckling his seat belt before he noticed Savage in the back. His brow furrowed, his mouth opening, his words lost to the deafening music.

"Cat, please!" Savage screamed, one last attempt at reason.

But it was too late. The doors locked, and the car pulled away.

CHAPTER THIRTY-TWO

BACK IN THE CAR. BACK ON THE MOVE.

But Kett knew they weren't going fast enough.

Porter overtook a delivery lorry, cutting back in to avoid the tractor that was steaming towards them. He sped up, hitting sixty on the long stretch of country road, barely slowing for the bend.

Still not fast enough.

Please let us find her, Kett said silently. *Let her be okay*.

If he was right, then Catherine Cavaney had proved herself more than capable of murder, but that was against three men who she felt had wronged her—her or Niamh Bradbury.

Would she hurt a police officer? One that had been trying to *help* her?

Would she kill Savage?

His phone rang, Superintendent Clare.

"Kett, I'm at the lock-up. There's no sign of Savage or Catherine."

"Shit," said Kett, punching the dash in frustration. "Nothing?"

"We've cut every unit open and we've searched the site. There are cameras but I think they're duds, and even if they aren't there's no sign of the owner. We can't access them."

"Slow down, Pete," Kett said. "Sir, where is she?"

"There's woodland all around here," Clare said. "Cat might have made a run for it, Savage might be in pursuit. But it's unlikely. I think they must have had another car."

"Mantas dropped them off then split, knowing we'd chase him," said Kett. "Knowing he'd pull us off the scent."

"Why?" said Clare. "What's he getting out of this? What's it got to do with the drugs and the gangs?"

"Nothing, sir. This is about revenge. I don't know what happened, not really, but I think Seb and Neil and Pete were involved in the death of Niamh Bradbury. Catherine found out and decided to go after them. Mantas is covering for her, trying to take the blame. I still don't know why, but he knew Niamh. There are photos of them together in his house, they were good friends. I think it has something to do with his girls at home, his daughters. He's doing what he thinks is the right thing."

"Tossing hell," said Clare. "But they're all dead. Seb and the others. It's done, it's finished."

"It's not," said Kett. "There's one more person. Joe. He got a note on Friday too, but he didn't get a chance to follow the instructions because his gran took it off him. Burned it."

Kett looked up, seeing the woods of Toltham ahead.

"Cat's going after Joe, I'm sure of it."

"Then make sure she doesn't reach him," Clare said. "You know where you're going?"

"He stays with his gran during the week," Kett said. "He's probably with his dad now. Dunst's looking for his address. Can you call his gran? Val Livingstone. See if she remembers what was on the note. Is Duke still with you?"

"Like a boil on my arse."

"Ask him if Joe told him where his dad lives. They were talking."

Clare grunted, then hung up.

"Where we going, boss?" Porter said.

"Head into the village. He's probably local."

Porter nodded, slowing down as they reached the Toltham sign. It seemed utterly impossible that they'd driven out this way just a day ago. The village was deserted, the bunting gone—torn away by last night's storm. The houses sat with dark windows and closed doors, as if they had shut their eyes and mouths to the horror of this place.

Which is exactly what had happened.

Everyone had known about Marshall. Everyone had probably known about Niamh, too. But nobody looked, nobody listened and nobody spoke.

His phone rang again and he was ready for it. It was Clare's number, but Duke was the one who was speaking.

"He's not with his gran," he said. "His dad's over on the east side of the village. His name's Ian Nix. They've built some new houses there and he's in one of those. Orchard Street, number 14."

"Thanks, Duke," said Kett. "Pete, keep going, it's those new builds on the other side of town."

"Boss says Val doesn't remember what was on the note."

"Okay. Thanks, Duke."

"Sir, Joe gave the impression he hated his dad," Duke said. "I think he was probably violent. Watch yourself."

"I'm not the one who'll need to watch himself."

Kett hung up, champing at the bit as the Mondeo roared up the main street, the spacious bungalows giving way to smaller ones before the estate came into view. They were still building here, barricades of stacked bricks, the polythene wrapping snapping like gunfire. The houses to the right were all unfinished but a handful of matchbox-small red-brick semis occupied the endless mud further in, hiding behind the immaculate show home.

"There," said Kett, pointing to a road sign. "Orchard."

Porter pulled up in front of number 14, using the Mondeo to block the road in case any of the cars parked further down belonged to Catherine. They ran for the door together and Kett knocked hard.

"Mr Nix? It's the police. Open up."

Too slow, they were losing too much time. He knocked again.

"Hang on," came a voice from inside. The door opened to reveal a short, skinny man dressed in jogging bottoms and a vest. He was holding a can of Foster's and the first thing he did was belch into his hand. He had the same bright copper hair as his son, but the similarity ended there—Mr Nix's face seemed to have been shaped by a lifetime of misplaced smug superiority. "What?" he said in a way that made it clear this wasn't his first drink of the day.

"Is your son home, Mr Nix?" Kett asked, holding up his warrant card. "It's urgent that we speak to him."

"Well you're too late," Nix said. "He's gone."

"Gone where?"

"Fuck should I know? He's not a kid, he's a grown man. Comes and goes as he pleases."

"When did he leave?"

Nix stood there, swaying. It seemed to take him an age to remember how to shrug. Kett swore beneath his breath, walking through the door and pushing past him.

"Hey," said Nix. "You can't just..."

"Living room," growled Porter as he walked in behind Kett. "Sit down."

There was no way the man was going to argue with Porter. He staggered through the door, almost falling. He made it to the sofa and perched there.

"Tell Marshall I haven't done nothing," he said. "Tell him I haven't done nothing, I swear."

Kett took the stairs, heading for Joe's room. It wasn't hard to see which one was his, the door propped open with a hoarder's trove of belongings. Kett leaned in, looking for something—*anything*—that might help. Most of the walls were covered in posters for various movies, the shelves overflowing with toys and books and games.

On Joe's bedside table were three framed photos. One showed him in Neil's living room with Seb and Niamh and the other two men. All of them were grinning, apart from Niamh, who sat back in the shadows, her purple hair bright but her expression dark. In the next were two men, Joe and somebody too similar not to be an older brother.

The last photo was newer, taken by the broad, by the look of it. Six people stood by an improvised raft, all in wetsuits. Joe was there, beaming.

So was Cat.

Kett left the room, returning downstairs. Porter was in the kitchen.

"What are we looking for?" the DI asked.

Kett ignored him, walking into the living room to see Nix still on the sofa, his phone in his hand.

"Put that down," Kett said. "I need you to think, real hard. Your son's life could depend on it."

"He's fine," said Nix, his voice slurred.

He took another sip of his drink and Kett snatched it off him, slamming it onto the coffee table so hard that beer slopped out of it.

"You can't do that!" Nix protested. "Joe's fine. Probably

with his nan. Little runt disappears there whenever he can because she gives him food and shit."

"Because she looks after him?" Kett said, trying to reign in his anger.

"He's a grown fucking man," Nix repeated. "Fuck do I still want with him? I'm glad he's gone. Hope he never comes back."

Kett realised his fist was clenched.

"Your son knows a woman called Catherine Cavaney, doesn't he? Cat?"

Nix shrugged.

"Didn't think he knew any girls," he said. "Didn't think he had it in him. Other than that Bradbury girl, of course."

There was nothing nice about the smile that spread over his face. Nothing good.

"What does that mean?" said Kett, stepping closer.

"Nothing," Nix said, still grinning.

"There's a photo of the two of them in Joe's room. Him and Catherine. He knew her. Have you seen her today? Has she been to the house?"

Nix sniffed, lacing his hands behind his neck and sitting back, deliberately nonplussed.

"She drive a red car?" Nix asked.

"I don't know."

"Joe walked out of here about fifteen minutes ago. Thought I saw him get into a red car. No idea who was driving it."

"You have any idea where they might be going?"

Nix leaned forward, staring at Kett with eyes that were so blotchy they looked diseased.

"I don't fucking care. What am I supposed to do with a son like him, eh? Both of them, Joe and his brother."

"His brother?" Kett said.

"Yeah, Paul. He's fucking broken *n'all*. Both of them. Their fucking mother's fault."

"Joe isn't broken," said Kett. "You're the one who's broken. You—"

"You think Joe's bad, wait till you see Paul. Fucking schizo, isn't he."

"Schizophrenic?"

"Yeah. Batshit."

"Is he on medication? Antipsychotics?"

"Fuck do I care? Haven't seen him in forever. Joe goes to visit him, with his nan. I'm happier without both of them, wish I'd never had the little cunts. Wish they'd never been born."

Kett's anger was a physical thing, it was overwhelming. He felt like he could have killed Ian Nix right here, right now.

Then he thought of Marshall, of the man who'd been tied to the chair and beaten, hurled into the water and left to drown. His stomach turned and twisted.

"I'm not done with you," he said, pointing a finger at Nix.

He made for the door, out into the brutal cold.

"Think that's where Cat got the quetiapine?" Porter said as he followed him out. "You think she asked Joe to get it? They could be working together."

"Makes sense," Kett said. "She had access to the cocaine and the heroin already, nobody would miss the amounts she borrowed to kill the men. She's friends with Joe—or at least pretending to be—she asks him to get the drugs from his brother. He trusts her, he has no idea what she's doing, what she's planning. But they're not working together. She was just using him until she was ready to kill him."

"He trusts her," Porter said, nodding. "That's why he got in her car today. But where are they going?"

Kett stared past the unfinished houses, towards the woods of Toltham.

"Are we missing something?" he said. "The dead men. Cat wrote them notes asking them to meet her. But the notes were different. She asked Seb to meet her in the woods behind the broad, the archery range. Pete was told to come to the train station in Somerleyton. We thought Neil might have ignored his note, stayed at home. But what if his note told him to wait there? The house, the lodge, the station. What if they mean something?"

"If this is all about Niamh," said Porter. "If this is Cat's way of avenging her death, then maybe they were all places that meant something to Niamh. Didn't she come from Somerleyton?"

"Yeah," said Kett. "You're right. Her family is from there, she was probably born there. She worked at the lodge, and Neil's place is where she met the others, where she met the men who might have killed her."

"So that only leaves one more place to look, right?" Porter said.

Kett nodded, running for the car.

"She's taking Joe to the place where Niamh died."

CHAPTER THIRTY-THREE

IT FELT LIKE A CAR RIDE TO HELL.

Savage lay in the back, her wrists bleeding, her feet numb, her head still cracking against the door every time they turned a corner or hit a pothole. The music was deafening, loud enough to be painful, the songs bad enough but the DJs worse, every word a needle in her ears. Cat sang along, her voice as quiet as a ghost's even though she was screaming. Joe rocked back and forth in the passenger seat, his hands over his ears, howling.

Savage had long given up calling Cat's name. The woman was lost. She worked on the ropes around her wrists instead, biting into them until her injured jaw burned, until her teeth bled. The thick rope had been tied well, but Mantas had been in a hurry. It wasn't as secure as she'd first thought. She'd felt the stubborn knot give a little once already. She just needed to keep working on it. She just needed time.

She wasn't going to get it.

The car suddenly slowed, Savage almost sliding off the seat until the ropes halted her. Cat steered them left, the road much bumpier, and only here did she turn the radio down, the relief of it enough to make Savage want to cry until another sound took its place. Joe was sobbing, his distress visible in every single cry, every single motion.

"Oh hush it, Joe," said Cat, her voice still jaunty, as if she was taking him for a sightseeing tour in the countryside. But there was hysteria there too, a cyclone of sharks beneath the calm surface. "It's not that bad."

Joe's cries grew even louder, his head connecting with the dash every time he rocked forwards.

"Joe, can you hear me?" Savage said. "It's going to be okay, it's going to be okay."

"It's going to be okay," said Cat with a laugh. "Oh thank goodness for that!"

Joe showed no sign of hearing either of them. Savage turned her attention back to her restraints, spitting blood before biting into the rope, tugging at it. Her teeth felt loose, the agony in her jaw unbearable.

But it was working, the rope giving in millimetre by millimetre.

The car went over a particularly large bump before turning again, moving up what felt like a hill.

"Here we are," said Cat, and Savage heard the way her voice shook, as if she'd only just remembered what she was supposed to be doing.

"It's not too late," Savage said.

"Isn't it? You mean you can bring Niamh back to life? Because that's the only thing that will stop this, the only thing that will make it fair. Can you do that?"

"No," said Savage. "But if you do this, your life is over too."

Cat laughed, a sound full of sadness.

"It's already over."

The car ground to a stop and Cat switched off the engine. Joe stopped rocking, stopped groaning, and the silence that fell around them was almost worse than the noise.

Except it wasn't silence, not really.

Savage could hear a softer noise, a rushing whisper like waves on a stony shore.

Or like fast-moving traffic.

"Me and you, Joe, we haven't really spoken much," Cat said. "You always had your nose in a video game at Neil's place, but I always liked you when we bumped into each other at the lodge. You remember the time we went out on the boats?"

He didn't reply.

"It was fun, even when we started to sink," said Cat, more serious now. "I know life hasn't been easy for you, Joe. I do understand that."

Cat sniffed again, and Savage realised she was crying. Joe listened to her, his eyes on the floor, his hands performing complex manoeuvres in front of his chest.

"It hasn't been easy for me, either. And it certainly wasn't for Niamh."

Joe's head dropped, his hands returning to his ears.

"I didn't hurt her," he said. "I didn't hurt her."

"I know," Cat said, sobbing now. She pulled his hands away from his head, holding them. "But you didn't *help* her, Joe. And she needed your help. She needed you to do the right thing."

"I didn't," said Joe, shaking his head wildly. "I didn't hurt her."

Cat opened her door, the sound of traffic growing in volume. It was the dual carriageway, Savage realised. The A47.

It was where Niamh had killed herself.

"Cat, *please!*" she said. "He didn't do anything!"

"Exactly," said Cat, getting out.

Savage twisted her head up, seeing the young woman pause outside the window. In the glaring sunlight, with her purple wig, it could have been Niamh standing right there. Then she turned and met Savage's eye and it was Cat again—so full of rage, so full of sadness, so full of resignation.

"Somebody will come and help you soon," she said with another sob. "I'm sorry. You won't have to see me again."

"Catherine?" Savage shouted. Cat closed the door, walking around the car.

"Joe, you need to run," Savage said. "As soon as you're out, run."

The passenger door opened.

"Come on, mate," Cat said, offering her hand. "Not much longer."

She took Joe's arm, gently helping him out. There was no sign of the knife. She held his hand as they walked into the trees, like old friends or young lovers.

"Joe, run!" Savage yelled. "Jesus Christ."

She bit into the ropes, chewing them, blood pouring down her throat, dripping onto the seat. The pain in her jaw was so bad she felt the shadows crowd into her skull, trying to drag her down into the quiet, into the dark, but she screamed into her restraints, she screamed until the light came back, she screamed and she bit and she wrenched at the knot.

The rope released a little more with each desperate tug of her head until she managed to rip her right hand free.

A guttural growl of triumph escaped her. Her fingers were so numb she couldn't feel the rope to pull out her other hand. She kept trying, her bones glass, her wrists limp, until the ropes fell to the floor.

Her legs were still bound but she sat up, digging her fingers into the knot around her ankles. The rope was as tough as concrete, as stone.

"Fuck!" she cried, turning to the front, seeing it there.

Cat's knife.

Sobbing as she lunged between the front seats, the gear stick digging into her ribs. It was almost too far away to reach but she grabbed for it, enough sensation in her tingling fingertips now to know she had it. She sat up, her stomach fluttering, threatening to cramp as she sawed at the rope.

The knot gave way and she pulled her legs out. She was exhausted, nothing left in the tank. But somehow she managed to open the door, climb out of the car. She tried to walk but her feet were dead, her legs giving out beneath her. She crawled instead, following the dirt track that rose into the trees.

"Joe!" she shouted. "Run!"

She crawled until the pins and needles burned in her feet, then she struggled up, breaking into a clumsy jog. The trees helped her, close enough to grab. She hauled herself up the steep embankment, the rush of traffic almost straight ahead—voices, too.

"Joe! Don't listen to her."

Joe called out, his voice coming from somewhere to the left. Savage followed it, climbing until she reached the top of the slope, gripping the metal barrier.

The A47 was right there, cars and lorries barrelling past just feet away, spraying freezing drizzle. Savage looked to her left, through the trees, seeing Cat already over the barrier. She was holding Joe's hands, talking calmly to him as she guided him over. He was scared, he was *terrified*, but he didn't run, he didn't fight. He knew her, he trusted her.

"Joe!" Savage yelled.

He looked up and so did Cat, her face falling—not with anger, but with panic.

"Joe, you have to run, you have to get away from the road!"

The passing traffic stole her voice, ripping the words out of her throat.

Savage started towards them, the treacherous ground falling away to her left, the road on the right. A truck horn blared as it roared by at seventy miles per hour, the sound of the world ending.

Joe and Cat were twenty yards away, his hands over his ears, hers guiding him past the barrier onto the side of the road. There was no hard shoulder here, just three feet of kerb and then death.

As carefully as she could, Savage stepped over the barrier. Another truck growled past so fast she almost dropped to her knees and screamed. Then another, its klaxon horn blowing a hole in her skull. She broke into a run, so close to Cat and Joe that she could almost reach out and touch them.

Cat looked at her, her eyes wet with tears, her body racked with sobs. She offered Savage a sad smile.

Then she grabbed Joe's T-shirt and pulled him into the road.

"No!" Savage screamed.

A lorry thumped past Savage, its air brakes hissing, its horn blaring. The driver managed to steer the vehicle wide, missing Cat by less than a metre before hitting the central divide in a shower of sparks. Two cars flew by, their tyres smoking as they tried to stop. Savage glanced right, seeing more cars—too fast, too close.

She ran, reaching Joe just as the first car scraped down the side of the lorry, spinning out. There was no time to think, she just rammed her shoulder into Cat's chest sending her flying back.

A car squealed between them, still doing well over fifty, the concussive blast of air making Savage think she'd been hit. She dragged Joe away, not even sure which direction led to safety anymore, just hauling him back, back until her leg caught the metal railing and she toppled over it.

Another blast of a horn, the shuddering sound of brakes, then the unmistakable sound of metal hitting flesh.

Joe fell on top of her, punching the last of the air from her lungs. He lay still and Savage screamed his name, rolling him away, seeing his wide eyes, his clenching hands. She ran a hand over his body, no blood, no injuries.

"You're okay," she said, her voice a whisper lost behind the softer sound of engines, the clatter of doors opening and people calling.

He was okay. She reached for him but he got to his hands and knees, scrabbling back until he hit the railing.

"Calm down, Joe," she said, holding up her hands, worried he was going to run into traffic again. "You're safe. Nobody's going to touch you, I promise."

He pushed his head into his knees, wrapped his hands over the top, hiding himself.

On the road, the traffic had almost come to a halt. But it was chaos out there. There was a line of lorries backed up as far as she could see. Most had escaped unharmed, but some had crumpled into each other, their windscreens shattered—a line of destruction that stretched almost a quarter of a mile to a distant flyover. Cars lay dotted between them like scattered dominoes, some of the drivers already out. Traffic had come to a halt further down the road, a dozen hazard lights blinking in the drizzle.

There was no sign of Cat.

Savage could hear sirens, thank God, an ocean of them.

"Wait here," she said to Joe. But when she started to step over the barrier he grabbed her hand, placing it on top of his head.

"Please," he said. "Please."

She stayed with him. She owed him that.

"Hey," she called out to a driver. "I'm police. Can you see a young woman anywhere? Purple hair?"

The man shook his head, but a lorry driver was running back this way, his cap in his hand.

"She got hit!" he called out. "One of the trucks hit her."

The sirens were louder now, two IRVs weaving through the parked cars. Savage saw Porter's Mondeo as well, feeling a rush of relief that was almost euphoric.

"Where is she?" Kate asked the trucker as he clattered to a stop. "Where's the girl?"

"She's gone," the man said. "She was hurt bad, she's bleeding. But she ran."

The IRVs stopped as close as they could, Porter muscling his car past them. The passenger door opened and Kett climbed out. It took him a moment to find her in the bushes, but when he did his entire face seemed to open.

"Kate?" he said as he limped over. "You're okay?"

"Yeah. So's Joe. We're okay. She tried to get him to walk into traffic. But we're okay."

Joe rocked beneath her, still holding her hand to the top of his head. He was speaking quietly in a long, unbroken sentence that she could make no sense of.

"Where's Cat?" Porter asked, running up.

"She got hit," Savage said. "Bad, I think. But she's running."

"How does she think she's going to get away from all this?" Porter said. "She must know she doesn't stand a hope in hell of escaping."

Savage closed her eyes, saw Cat's smile—sad, and full of a terrible, inevitable acceptance.

"She doesn't want to get away," she said, looking up the dual carriageway again. Traffic on this side of the road had stopped, but cars still tore down the northbound stretch. "She wants it all to end. She's heading for the flyover."

CHAPTER THIRTY-FOUR

She's heading for the flyover.

Kett stared down the dual carriageway, looking in between the tangle of lorries, over the roofs of the cars, seeing it two hundred yards away.

Savage tried to get up but Joe was holding onto her like she was the only thing stopping him from drowning. She gave Kett a look of such sadness, such urgency, it almost broke his heart.

"Cat's not a bad person," she said. "She's doing this because she thinks it's the right thing to do. She doesn't think she has a choice anymore. *Please*, sir, don't let her die."

"I won't," Kett said.

There was no way they were getting a car past the wrecked trucks, and even if they could have crossed the central divide, traffic still moved on the northbound side of the road—slower, now, because of all the rubberneckers.

"Come on, Pete," he said, forcing the shell of his body to break into a painful run. He called out to the constables behind him as he went. "Stop the traffic. Whatever it takes."

Porter took the lead, his feet drumming the asphalt.

People watched them go from outside their cars, a little huddle of truck drivers standing next to the barrier. One, a younger guy with tears in his eyes, called out to them.

"I didn't mean to hit her, mate. I swear. She just ran out."

"You see where she went?" Kett called back, and all of them pointed down the road.

The flyover was further away than it looked, the long, wide carriageway seeming to go on forever. After a minute of running, Kett was exhausted, his knee burning. He was slowing, Porter slowing with him.

"Go," Kett said. "Just stop her from getting up there."

Porter charged away, his arms and legs like pistons. Kett heard sirens from up ahead, seeing an ambulance speeding up the other side of the road. He waved his arms to get the attention of the driver, yelling as hard as he could when they slowed down.

"I need you back that way. We've got an injured girl, she might jump."

It was impossible for them to turn, but there was nothing Kett could do about it. He ran as fast as his knee would let him, never taking his eyes off the flyover as it grew nearer and taller.

He was thirty yards away when he saw Catherine stagger into sight overhead.

She was badly injured, he could see that from here. She ran with a limp, one arm cradled across her chest and held there with her other hand. She wasn't wearing the wig, her dark hair caught in the wind and her face spattered with blood. Somebody must have stopped the traffic further down the A47 because the road was impossibly still and quiet. All Kett could hear was the slap of his own boots and Cat's gasping, desperate breaths.

"Catherine?" he called to her. "Just wait there, please."

If she heard him, she showed no sign of it. She lurched along the road overhead, her hip skimming the barrier. Porter jogged into sight behind her, slowing to a stop. Cat jerked her head back, snarling at him like an animal.

"Leave me alone," she said, the wind pulling her words to pieces. "Just leave me the fuck alone."

There was thick woodland to the side of the road and Kett pushed into it, fighting his way up a steep hill— breathing so hard the world flashed white. He had to stop, sucking in air, using the spindly trunks to haul himself to the road above.

Please let her still be there, he thought. *Don't let her have jumped.*

He jogged along the road, rounding a corner to see the young woman standing right in the middle of the flyover, holding onto the railing with her good hand. Porter had taken a few steps towards her but he stopped again when she screamed at him.

"I'll do it, so fuck off! Just leave me alone!"

"We can't do that, Cat," said Kett, his hands up as he approached.

She whirled around to face him, momentum almost pulling her over the railing. Kett glanced at the road below, deserted other than the ambulance which sat in the fast lane, its lights rolling. They were high up here, maybe thirty feet above the dual carriageway. High enough to kill, maybe. Certainly high enough to injure. The wind pushed and snatched at them, a cat toying with its prey.

"Please, just listen to me for a moment," Kett said, taking another step so he wouldn't have to shout so loud. "Nobody is going to touch you, I promise."

Cat was panicking, using her good hand to smudge the

blood from her face as she looked from Kett to Porter and back again. She braced one foot on the railing, looking like she might just hurl herself over and be done with it.

"Whoa, it's okay. Cat, it's okay. We're backing off."

He took a step back.

"Pete, no closer."

Porter paused, but he didn't move away. He had one hand on the railing too, his knuckles white, his body as tense as a sprinter on the starting block. He was a good twenty yards away from the young woman. He'd never reach her in time.

"No closer, mate," Kett said, shaking his head. "Cat, are you hurt? There's an ambulance right there, can we at least take a look at you?"

Cat spat out a bitter laugh.

"That's a joke, isn't it?" she said. "Are you stupid? Do you not know what's about to happen?"

"It doesn't have to happen," said Kett.

Another laugh, this one full of sadness.

"It does. Of course it does."

She looked up.

"Is Joe okay?"

Kett nodded.

"He's in shock, but he's not hurt."

Cat stared at the road below, swallowing.

"I'm glad," she said, so quietly he could barely hear her. "I know you don't believe me, but I'm glad he's okay. I tried. That's the main thing. I didn't give him the drugs because I knew it would kill him. But I wanted him to feel the way she did. I wanted him to be scared. I needed to do it for Niamh."

"I believe you," said Kett. "I know why you did it."

She turned to him again, her body shaking so hard she

could barely stand. Blood was dripping from the sleeve of her injured arm, a *lot* of blood.

"You believe me?"

Kett still didn't know the whole truth, but he knew enough.

"Niamh died because of them, didn't she? You wanted to make it right for your friend."

"She wasn't even my friend," Cat said. "I never met her. But all this..." She reached for her head as if she was still wearing the wig. "I think maybe she was acting *through* me, you know? Like she's a ghost or something. I think we were doing it together. Seb made me dress like her, made me act like her, made me talk like her. Somewhere in all of that..."

She shrugged her one good shoulder.

"I think she's in me now, her spirit."

"If that's true, Cat, she wouldn't want this for you. She wouldn't want you to get hurt, she certainly wouldn't want you to die. Niamh was a good woman. You are too."

"But she's lonely. She's so lonely down there." She let out a choked sob. "And I'm not good. You saw that. I killed them, all of them. I killed Sebastian, and Pete, and that arsehole Neil. He was the worst of them, you know?"

The sadness was going, eroded by a sudden, ferocious anger.

"He was the one who started it with Niamh, who made her life so awful. He got the others to join in. I killed him first. He was high anyway, he was always high. I just gave him a little more, mixed in some of my own shit."

"The drugs Joe got for you, from his brother?"

"Yeah. Crushed it, mixed it with Neil's gear. A whole fucking month's worth of pills. You should have seen him. It was like..."

Her face turned to the sky, a terrifying madness in her eyes.

"It was like she was there with me, because he couldn't stop moving. It was like he was a puppet, like she was controlling him, throwing him around, crushing him. She was there, and it was... it was glorious."

She broke into another sob, one that doubled her up. Porter met Kett's eye, asking a silent question, but Kett shook his head again. Even though neither of them moved, Cat pushed herself up, delirious with panic. She leaned over the railing, panting so hard she was close to hyperventilating.

"Cat, please," said Kett.

"They deserved it," she said. "They deserved it, they deserved it."

"They *did* deserve it," Kett said. "They were bad men, Cat. Not Joe, but the other three. Bad men. They deserved it."

She turned to look at him, still halfway over the barrier.

"There are so many bad men out there, Cat," he said. "I'm sorry, but there are. Bad people. They're everywhere. They're in every village, in every town, in every street. I wish I could tell you different but I've seen it for myself. Bad people, doing terrible things."

Cat sobbed, worming her way further over the railing.

"But there are good people, too," Kett said. "And you know something, Cat, the good people outnumber the bad. There are so many of them. Pete Porter there, he's one of them. And Kate, the woman you had in your car, she's a good person. A kind person. And..."

He hesitated, because he honestly wasn't sure if what he was about to say next was true.

"I think I'm a good person too, Cat. I try so hard to be a

good person. But I've done bad things too. I've done terrible things. I've hurt people, *bad* people."

She looked at him, the tears rolling down her face. Her expression had gone slack, like her body was slowly shutting down. The railing seemed like it was the only thing holding her up.

"I've killed people too, Cat," he said. "Bad men. I didn't think I had a choice. I did it because I thought I had to. And I have to live with that every day, I see them every single day."

He had to close his eyes, because there they were—Angus Schofield with a hammer in his head, Figg and Percival falling into a lake of shit, Ocean Everett sinking into the wet, unforgiving sand of the Norfolk coast.

His dead.

"I always will," he said, quieter now. "That's the price we pay for what we do."

He heard an engine and glanced down to see Clare's Mercedes approaching slowly from the south, dragging a tail of IRVs behind it.

"Doing a bad thing doesn't always make you a bad person," he said when he turned to Cat again. "It certainly doesn't mean you can never be a good person again. And we need good people. Christ, we need them more than ever, because the bad ones are getting worse. They're getting stronger, they're getting braver. We need all the good people we can get, Cat. We need *you*."

She sobbed again, her good hand going to her mouth.

"Let us fix this," Kett said. "Let me help you."

She was fading fast, but there was enough left in the young woman for her to nod.

"I'm sorry," she said, stepping away from the drop. "I'm so sorry, I don't want to..."

Her eyes rolled up in their sockets, her body folding over the railing.

"Pete!" Kett yelled, already on the move.

Cat's top half flopped down the other side of the barrier, her legs wheeling up. Kett reached for her, too far away, seeing her fall.

Then Porter was there, his big hands wrapped around her ankle, her weight almost pulling the DI over too.

Kett slammed into them, grabbing Porter around the waist until his feet were back on the ground, snatching at Cat's clothes, grabbing anything he could get hold of. Together, they heaved her over the railing, falling on top of each other.

Kett gathered the young woman into his arms, hugging her as her body spasmed, as the sobs ripped out of her.

"It's okay," he said. "You're okay. You're okay, I promise you."

He heard the clatter of feet, looked up to see Clare running along the flyover, Duke beside him and the paramedics close behind.

"It's going to be okay," Kett said quietly, clinging onto Cat like *he* was the one who was sinking now and she was the only thing holding him up. "It's going to be okay."

Porter sat beside them, his back to the railing. He met Kett's eyes and Kett saw the truth there, unspoken but undeniable.

It wasn't okay at all.

None of this would ever be okay again.

CHAPTER THIRTY-FIVE

PORTER PULLED THE MONDEO OFF THE MAIN ROAD, following Clare's Mercedes along the long, winding driveway that led to Topiary Lodge. Kett sat in the passenger seat, staring at the giant hedges as they peeled themselves from the overcast sky.

He didn't speak. He wasn't sure he even remembered how.

They'd waited on the A47 until Catherine had been examined by the paramedics, and watched as she had been carried into the ambulance. She hadn't spoken either, her eyes as glassy as a doll's. The injury to her arm had been more severe than Kett had feared.

But she was alive. For now, that was all they could have hoped for.

The car park was largely empty. The police presence—not to mention the reporters who had been rolling into town in droves since Marshall's arrest, filling the local news with talk of murder and vengeance and torture and corruption—had driven most of the hotel's occupants away. Toltham would never be the same, Kett knew. It would always be known for what had happened in the last few days, and what had happened to a young woman in the months before.

Porter pulled up next to the Mercedes and cut the engine, scrubbing his face with his hands. The rain drummed the windscreen like it was trying to wash them all away, trying to erase everything that had happened.

"You okay?" the DI asked after a moment.

Kett breathed a laugh through his nose.

"No. Not really."

The passenger door of Clare's Mercedes opened, clunking into the side of the Mondeo. Porter rapped on the window as Duke loomed into view.

"Watch the paintwork, you big baboon," he said.

"Well why did you park so close, sir?" Duke replied. "There's a whole bloody car park."

"He's got a point," said Kett. "Come on."

He opened his own door, only to pull it shut again as an IRV slid in beside the Mondeo. Savage was in the driver's seat, and she threw him a tired smile. Kett opened his door again, squeezing out as best he could. His knee twisted, the agony of it taking his breath away.

"You didn't leave me a lot of room, Kate," he said as he closed the door. Savage opened hers, climbing out.

"Oh, sorry, sir."

They looked around, the three cars almost shoulder to shoulder in the vast, empty space. Porter was trying to get out of his seat, Clare yelling at *him* to watch the paintwork.

"Maybe we just don't want to be on our own right now," Savage said.

"True enough," said Kett. "How're you doing?"

She shook her head, wincing. The paramedics had taken a look at her head and given her the all-clear on the proviso she'd go straight to A&E at any sign of drowsiness or dizziness. Right now, she looked drowsier and dizzier than Kett had ever seen her.

"I'm honestly not sure, sir," she said.

"Come on, you tossers," Clare shouted as he stomped towards the lodge. "It's bloody raining."

"Yes, sir," Kett muttered, following the Superintendent through the hotel's main doors into the reception. Harita sat behind the desk, Gabriel visible in the little office further back. Both looked up when they heard them.

"Good evening," Harita said. She looked like she'd been crying, her mascara smudged over her cheeks. "I wasn't sure if you'd be coming back tonight."

"We saw it on the news," Gabriel said, stepping out of the room. "Is Joe alright? Val was beside herself."

"He's doing okay," said Clare. "Catherine too."

"And Marshall's really been arrested?" Gabriel said. "You got him?"

"We got him," said Clare.

"We'd have got him a long time ago if somebody had told us what was going on," said Kett.

Gabriel started to reply, but Kett shut him up with a glare.

"You knew. You all knew. Maybe not the whole truth, but enough. Everything that happened here in the village, it was as much your fault as anyone's."

Harita looked like she'd been slapped but Gabriel lowered his head, nodding sadly.

"It's the way of things, isn't it?" he said. "It's how nature works. If you trust it, it looks after you."

"Bullsh—"

"Detective, that's enough," said Clare. "Is the bar open?"

Harita nodded and Clare ushered Kett through the door before he could say another word. They walked down the empty main corridor into the cosy bar, Clare pointing to a round table beside the roaring fire.

"Sit down and shut up," he said. "All of you. I'll get them in."

Kett limped to the table, Savage pulling a chair out for him.

"Need a hand, sir?" she asked.

"No, I bloody do not, Kate." He flexed his knee, feeling how swollen it was. "Okay, fine, help me down."

She took his hand and he groaned his way into the chair like an old man, noticing that it wasn't just his knee that ached, it was *everything*. It was like somebody had filleted his bones and replaced them with drawing pins. He took a breath, enjoying the warmth of the fire.

"Get you a blanket, sir?" Porter grinned, sitting opposite.

"There's a rocking chair over there," added Duke. Kett was about to reprimand him when he noticed the PC was right. A rocking chair sat by the window, and to be fair it *did* look very comfortable. "Bet they could grab you a pair of slippers, sir."

"Hey, Duke, show a little respect for your superiors," Porter said, frowning at the constable.

"Oh, right. Sorry, sir."

"Savage and I are the only ones allowed to take the Mickey out of the old man."

"I'm not bloody old."

Duke sat next to Porter, and Savage took the last chair next to Kett.

"I don't know about you lot," she said. "But I am ready to go home."

"Well tough," said Clare as he stormed over, a tray of pint glasses in his hairy hands. He lowered it gently to the table. "Because I paid for two nights and it's too late to ask for my money back."

Duke looked at the ceiling and groaned. Clare glared at him, glared at all of them, the anger bubbling just beneath the surface.

"I'll get my own tossing chair then, shall I?" he roared, stomping to the next table and dragging a chair back with him. Duke shuffled up but Clare made a show of moving to the other side of the table, squeezing in between Kett and Savage. He gestured to the beers. "Go on."

"Thanks, sir," said Porter. "I'm driving."

"No you're not, you're staying another night. Kate?"

"I don't drink beer, sir," she said.

Clare growled at Kett.

"Honestly, sir, I could just do with a cup of tea."

"Well that's just fantastic," Clare said. Duke was halfway through his first pint, swallowing noisily. He stopped for breath, gurning.

"What is this?"

"Ale," said Clare. "Yorkshire ale. The best you can get."

"I'm going to get myself a lager," said Duke, pushing himself out of his chair.

"Un-tossing-believable," Clare said, sitting back. He took another sip, staring at the table but lost somewhere else. When he spoke again, his voice was much softer. "I am sorry. I had no idea any of this would happen."

"It's not your fault, sir," Savage started, but he waved her down.

"It is. I knew something was going on out here. I knew about the drugs, and I knew about Marshall—or I thought I knew about him. I thought he was bent, I thought he was working with the gangs. I had no idea what he was really doing."

He lifted his glass to his mouth but hesitated.

"I think PC Jarratt is going to testify against him. Spalding has her in the interview room as we speak and from the sounds of it, she seems happy to cooperate. I don't think she liked what her father was doing, but family is hard."

"What will happen to her?" Savage asked.

"Depends on what she confesses to. They've found nearly a dozen bodies at that Pike place and they're only just getting started. No IDs yet, but all young men. I'd bet they're dealers, manufacturers, money men. Marshall was trying to take out the gangs all by himself."

There was no hint of respect in Clare's voice, no sign of admiration. Only disgust.

"He's set us back years," he said. "Decades. I hope he rots. But you know the ironic thing? He's got cancer. Jarratt told us. It's in his liver, and it's advanced. He's got months left. That's no punishment at all."

Duke came back to the table with a pint of lager and a packet of salt and vinegar crisps. He put them down so that he could adjust his chair, and Kett snatched the crisps before he could object.

"Thanks, Duke," he said, opening them up. "I haven't eaten a thing all day."

Duke huffed his way back to the bar and Kett munched on the crisps, the taste of them almost divine. His stomach grumbled almost painfully.

"And Marshall was just one of the vigilantes who crawled out of the woodwork this weekend," said Clare. "Who can tell me what the hell was going on with Catherine Cavaney?"

Savage sat forward, her elbows on the table.

"Cat killed Seb Reilly, Neil Enthoven and Pete Duggan because of what they did to Niamh Bradbury," she said.

"Because they killed Niamh?" asked Clare. "The hit and run?"

"It's worse than that, sir. Neil and the others were abusing Niamh. I don't know how, exactly, but Cat said it was sexual. Niamh was young when she met them, I think Neil groomed her. It probably started with the drugs, they used her as a courier and a dealer. But it got a lot worse than that. Eventually, it drove her to take her own life."

"Christ," said Clare, putting his beer back on the table.

"Seb recruited Cat to do the same work. She looked similar, and she was happy to make some extra money posing as Niamh and running point for the deals. It worked for a while, she oversaw the meets, kept the gangs happy. The men tried to abuse her too but she didn't let them."

She shook her head, frowning.

"The more she found out about the woman she was pretending to be, the angrier she got. She told me Seb had Niamh's suicide note, that he had kept it as some kind of trophy. Cat took it to Marshall hoping he'd punish them— hoping he'd *properly* punish them, the way he did with the gangs."

"But he didn't," said Kett. "Because they were local lads, right?"

"Right," said Savage. "It was all a bit of harmless fun. Boys will be boys."

Clare was holding his glass so firmly Kett thought it might shatter.

"I'll make sure Marshall goes down for that as well as for the murders," he said. "For all the good it will do. The world will remember."

"Cat didn't think she had any choice," said Savage. "I believe that. She was so... so consumed by her anger that she didn't feel she could do anything else. But she hated herself for it. That's why she wanted to end it all herself."

Savage wiped away a tear.

"They're evil, those men. I'm glad..."

And she managed to close her mouth around the end of the sentence, but there was nobody sitting at the table who disagreed with her.

"Sorry," she said. Clare put his hand on top of hers for a moment, squeezing gently.

"It will all be taken into account when she goes to trial," he said. "All of it."

It wouldn't help her, Kett knew. Even though Catherine hadn't jumped, her life was over. There was no coming back from that.

"Be careful," Clare said, deadly serious. "Be careful what you say, and how you look at things. In all likelihood those three men were monsters. Dealers, rapists, God knows what else. There will be no trial for them, though, no chance to tell their side of the story, whatever that might have been. What you're feeling right now, Kate, is how it starts. That anger, that sense of righteous indignation. That's how people like Wallace Marshall stray from the path. How vigilantes are born."

Savage looked like she was going to be sick.

"I..." she started, and Clare waved her down.

"I know, Kate," he said. "I know."

He took a sip of ale, wiping the foam off his lips.

"We've managed a cursory interview with Mantas. He won't say much, but it's clear you were right. He was helping Catherine. He's sticking to his story that he killed the men, although it's clear he didn't."

"He thought he was doing the right thing too," said Kett. "He lost his own daughters, in a way, so he was protecting Cat. Niamh too. He's doing what all fathers would do."

"He aided and abetted her," said Clare. "He was the one who got the dolls that we found near Seb's body and with Pete Duggan. They were using them to try to pull any attention away from what they were doing, trying to link it to the Greenies. He delivered the notes, too. Can anyone tell me where the drugs used in the murder came from?"

"Cat used Joe's brother's prescription antipsychotics," Kett said. "Paul is a diagnosed schizophrenic, in and out of Hellesdon. He doesn't always take his meds, and Joe knew where to find them. Cat mixed the quetiapine with the heroin and the cocaine, threw another few choice ingredients in as well. She couldn't have known what affect it would have, but she knew what the end result would be."

"And they trusted her enough to let her drug them?" Clare asked.

"It was Friday night, the parade," said Savage. "They were high as kites anyway. They might not even have known what was happening."

Kett saw Seb's bulging eyes, his twisted jaw, the way his nails had been stripped off their fingers.

"They knew," he said.

Duke walked back to the table, his hands full of crisp packets. He dropped them all, a couple spilling to the floor.

"That should be enough for everyone," he said.

"I don't see a single pack of pickled onion Monster Munch in that pile, Constable," Clare said.

Duke groaned again, making his way back to the bar.

"How was Joe?" asked Kett.

"Not good," Savage replied. "But not hurt, if that's what you mean. I'm not sure what he makes of it all."

"Maybe it went over his head?" Porter suggested.

"It didn't," said Kett.

"No, it didn't." Savage wiped her face, her fingers trembling. "He won't get charged, will he? For everything that happened to Niamh?"

"We'll have to wait and see," Clare replied. "But from everything I know so far, I can't see us going after him. He seems as much a victim of those men as Niamh was."

"I think so too," said Savage.

There was a moment of quiet contemplation around the table, a moment of silence for those who had been lost, and those who had lost everything.

And for those who had lost their way.

Then Duke appeared, throwing a giant bag of Monster Munch onto the pile of crisps on the table and slouching in his seat. Clare picked up the bag and ripped it open with such force half of the crisps went flying, eyeballing Duke like he was imagining doing the same to the PC's head. He popped a couple into his mouth, chewing noisily, then he reached into his pocket and pulled out a Bounty. Kett watched in horror as he shoved half of it into his gob along with the crisps.

"Oh, God, *no* sir," said Kett.

"What?" Clare sprayed.

"Coconut and pickle?" said Savage. "Are you *pregnant*, sir?"

Porter laughed like a cannon going off, and even Duke managed a smile.

"No, Savage, I'm not pregnant," the Super said. "I'm stressed. Which is why I'm keen to leave all this alone for a moment and talk about how we should be spending the last few hours of our holiday."

The door of the bar opened and Harita walked in, escorting a couple of guests to their table.

"Speaking of which," Clare said, clicking his fingers at the woman as she walked back across the room. "Harita, are all the scheduled activities still taking place this evening?"

"The candlelit cruise is cancelled, I'm afraid," she said, redoing her ponytail. "Wind is up again. Most of the other stuff is still going ahead. You're booked into the pottery, aren't you?"

"We are, yes," Clare said. "I thought we could work as a team to craft some bowls for the office."

Nobody said a word, everyone at the table giving Clare a look he would have been able to feel from the other side of a thick wall.

"If you're too tired for that, then there's another jigsaw competition," Harita went on, a faint smile on her lips. "Just 500 pieces this time, maybe more your speed."

"Please no," said Porter.

"And if you're really feeling adventurous, we've got an evening talk with one of our topiary artists in the conservatory. I believe she'll be demonstrating her craft and letting you all have a go as well."

Clare lit up.

"That sounds—"

"Awful," interrupted Kett. "So awful."

"Well, whatever you choose, I'm happy to say we're upgrading you to our premier rooms. Gabriel insisted. For all of you. We've got an executive suite free as well, if anyone would like to join Mr Clare on the top floor."

They were saved from having to answer when the bar door opened again and Rachel Turkentine walked in—at least Kett thought it was Rachel, because she was holding an enormous hamper of gifts in front of her face. She struggled through the door, peeking over the top of the hamper and spotting their table.

"Oh, gosh," she said as she arrived. Porter cleared a space amongst the crisps and she dropped the hamper, leaning on it with one hand while she collected her breath. "That's heavier than it looks."

"What is it?" Clare said, peering through the shrink-wrap.

"The raffle. This is the main prize. Which one of you is Aaron Duke, again?"

Duke's hand shot up, a wide grin appearing beneath his beard.

"You have got to be kidding me," said Clare, pouting. "There are truffles in there."

"Congratulations, Aaron," said Rachel. "This is all yours."

"Thanks," grunted Duke. He started to pull the hamper towards him but Clare grabbed the handle.

"Teamwork, Duke," the Super growled. "I think you'll find this belongs to all of us."

"I don't think so, sir," said Duke, tugging. "It was *my* ticket."

"It's *my* holiday, Constable. I'm the only reason you're here. Do you even like sugar-coated almonds? I bet you wouldn't know Manuka honey if you tossed in it."

"Nope," said Kett, shaking his head. "Just nope."

"Give it to me, Duke, we won this as a *team*."

"I won this as a *me*," the PC protested.

The two men grunted quietly as they fought over the hamper, looking absolutely ridiculous. Kett turned to Porter.

"Right, on that note, I'm off. Can I grab a lift back to the city?"

"With pleasure," said Porter, pushing himself out of his chair. "Kate?"

"Yes please, sir. Just got to grab my things."

"Meet me in the car park in five," Porter said.

They walked out of the bar together, Kett turning back to see Clare hurling bags of crisps at Duke to try to make him let go of his prize.

"This was some holiday," he said. "Remind me to never leave home again."

He let the bar door close behind him, but not quickly enough to stop Clare's booming reply.

"I bloody heard that!"

CHAPTER THIRTY-SIX

IT FELT LIKE THE MIDDLE OF THE NIGHT BY THE TIME they made it into Norwich, but impossibly it was only just past six. Nobody spoke, Kett and Savage staring through the window at the arriving night and both doing their best to tune out the awful noises that were coming through the speakers, thanks to Porter's *Best of Smooth Jazz* CD. It was only when they were on the inner ring road that Kett broke the silence.

"Pete, can you drop me off here?"

"The showroom?" said Porter. "It'll be closed. Sunday."

"Worth a shot."

Porter pulled into the car park, driving right up to the doors. There were still lights on inside, a couple of people visible through the glass.

"Here to replace the Mermaid Adventure Castle?" he asked. Kett nodded. "Then do what I said, get yourself a Merc. Lovely motors."

"Yeah," Kett said.

He opened his door and hesitated, looking back. He wasn't sure what he wanted to say, his mind too exhausted to really make sense of what he was feeling. In the end, he settled for a tired smile.

Porter and Savage smiled back.

That said it all.

He closed the door, grabbed his bag from the boot, and watched the Mondeo pull away. Then he turned to the showroom door and knocked. One of the guys sitting at his desk tapped his watch and shook his head, but the other was the young man who'd sold Kett the Skoda yesterday morning, Josh. He grinned, getting up from his seat and opening the door.

"Well, if it isn't..." He stopped, looking at Kett's dirty suit, his exhausted face, the bag by his feet. "You okay, mate?"

"I'm fine," said Kett. "But I need a car."

"We're closed. Sorry. If you come back in the morning I'll find you something great. I'll be here from eight."

Kett pulled out his warrant card, holding it up.

"Make an exception, will you?" he said. "I won't need long."

Josh looked into the showroom, unsure. Then he nodded.

"Come on, then. What happened to the Skoda?"

"Got rolled down a hill by a drug dealer in a tractor," Kett said. "Then somebody set it on fire."

Josh's mouth opened like he was trying to catch invisible flies.

"Seriously? Is that, like, an Extreme..."

"An Extreme Crime thing, yeah. You got any Mercedes here?"

"Of course," said Josh, leading Kett across the showroom to a fleet of smart, black cars, all with matching price tags. Two looked exactly like the one Porter had saved his life with, the one owned by the dealers. "Probably the best drive you'll ever have, unless you're upgrading to a Bentley or something. This 550 is a beast, great car for a bobby."

"It's ready to go?"

"It is, if you are," said Josh. "You want to take it for a spin? It's a little late, but—"

"No," said Kett.

"I'll get the paperwork," Josh said, obviously delighted. "This works a lot better without your kids running all over the place, right?"

He jogged into the office and Kett looked at the car. It was nice. Smart. Safe. A good car for a copper. Josh was right about that.

But he was wrong about the girls.

They'd picked the Skoda for a reason. They'd picked it because they loved it. He thought of them now, of Moira, of Evie, of Alice, and the idea of them not being here with him made him feel like a man who was being held underwater.

"Here we go," said Josh. "You need finance for this? That might take a little—"

"Hold up," said Kett, searching the showroom, managing the smallest of smiles. "Forget the Mercedes. Have you got anything else in pink?"

HE PULLED into his street forty minutes later, parking the Volvo V6o in the closest space he could find. It wasn't pink, it was orange. *Bright* orange. It wasn't particularly fast, and it definitely wasn't the best car for a copper, but the girls would love it.

The rain was coming down hard now, gurgling in the gutters. Kett grabbed his bag from the back seat and ran for the house. The street was packed with cars, most of them empty, but there was a clunky black Peugeot 407 right outside his house, its interior lights on. A young man sat at the wheel, staring at Kett as he walked past.

Kett ignored him, pulling his keys from his pocket, dropping them, trying again. A blast of warmth escaped the house and he almost fell into it, closing the door behind him before taking a deep, glorious breath of home.

Home. It seemed to get better every time he came back.

He waited for the screams of his girls, for the cries of "Daddy!" to find him—or for the arguments to start, which was infinitely more likely. All he could hear, though, was the sound of the TV. He dropped his bag and poked his head around the living room door, seeing Billie and Alice under a blanket on the sofa. They both looked up and smiled.

"Hey," Billie said. "You okay?"

He'd called her before he'd left Toltham, but he hadn't told her much. He would, of course. He told her everything now.

But he needed a cup of tea first.

"Yeah," he said. "Where are the other two?"

"Fast asleep in Evie's bed. The beach knackered them out."

"I know the feeling."

"Clare let you go, then?" Billie asked.

"Yeah. A little while ago, but I had to stop by the showroom. There was a problem with the Skoda."

"The Mermaid Adventure Castle?" Alice said, sitting up. "Is she okay?"

"She was too awesome," Kett said, throwing up another silent prayer of gratitude for the sturdy pink car. "She was so awesome that the Queen called and asked if she could have it. I couldn't say no, sorry. She's the Queen."

Alice frowned, thought about it for a moment, then nodded.

"Cool!"

Her hands flexed in front of her chest, making invisible patterns the same way Joe's had on the side of the road. Kett felt such a sudden, overwhelming love for her that it almost broke him, and he opened his arms.

"Hug for your old man?"

"Yeah," Alice said, extracting herself from the blanket, tripping, almost falling into him. He caught her, holding her as tight as he dared. Alice hugged him, just for a second, then turned herself around so that her back was to him. She held his arms against her chest so hard he thought his bones might snap. "I love you so much, Dad."

"I love you too, Alice. And I know I don't tell you this enough, I don't tell you anywhere near as much as I need to, but you're amazing. You're an incredible, kind, beautiful, wonderful girl and you've got so much to look forward to. Your life is going to be so good. *So* good. And I'm going to be here for you, okay? Always."

Alice pulled herself free, throwing her gangly body back on the sofa.

"Okay," she said, engrossed in the TV again.

"Ten minutes," said Billie, pushing herself up. "Then bed, yeah?"

Alice didn't reply. Billie walked to Kett and kissed him on the cheek, then she looked at his suit.

"Another one ruined?" she said.

"Two, actually," said Kett. "Sorry."

"But you got them? You got whoever you were chasing?"

"Yeah," said Kett. "We did."

She kissed him again and walked out of the room, pausing by the slim window next to the front door.

"Go shower," she said. "I'll make the tea."

But she didn't move from where she stood, chewing her lip as she stared through the glass.

"What's up?" he asked.

"Probably nothing, Robbie. I'm probably just..." There was no probably there, he knew. She was scared. "It's just everything that's happened. I'm paranoid, you know?"

"What is it?" said Kett as he walked to her side.

"The man in that car, he was there when we got back from the beach. Did you see him?"

"In the Peugeot?" said Kett. "Yeah."

He looked through the window, past the steam of Billie's breath. The man was still sitting there in the glow of the interior lights. He was looking right at the house.

And he was grinning.

The chill that ran through Kett was so sudden and so powerful that he couldn't hide it. Billie put a hand in her hair, her face drawn with worry.

"You know him?" she asked.

"No," said Kett. "I don't."

He grabbed the door handle, but Billie pulled his arm away.

"Don't," she said. "What if it's *them*?"

She didn't say their name. She never did. But it hung in the air, unspoken and deafening.

Hollenbeck.

"Stand back," Kett said, and she did.

Kett opened the door, instantly ambushed by the rain and the wind. He stepped onto the path, walking to the car, the man still looking at him—his smile as sharp as cut glass.

"Hey," Kett yelled.

The man started the car, never taking his eyes away. He waited until Kett had almost reached him—until he'd thumped a hand on the Peugeot's roof—before pulling out onto the road, the engine gunning as he took off into the night.

"Fucker," Kett growled, his heart trying to punch its way out of his chest and take off after him.

He walked back to the house on legs made of glass.

"Who was that?" Billie said, her voice shaking.

"Nobody," said Kett, locking the door. "He's gone now."

But he wasn't gone, not really.

They won't stop coming. They'll never let you go.

"Come on," he said, forcing a smile. "I'll put the kettle on."

Billie nodded, but there was nothing in her face except misery.

"I'll put Alice to bed," she said after a moment. "But Robbie, I've been thinking. Maybe it's time for us to move. Not out of the city or anything, just a new house. Our own house. Somewhere safer."

"Yeah," he said. "I've been thinking it too."

He waited for her to collect Alice from the living room, waited for them both to climb the stairs. Then he checked the lock, lacing the feeble security chain through its hook. He rested his head against the glass for a moment, listening to the sound of his own breathing.

There are so many bad men out there, he'd told Cat on the flyover. *I'm sorry, but there are. Bad people. They're everywhere. They're in every village, in every town, in every street. I wish I could tell you different, but I've seen it for myself. Bad people, doing terrible things.*

And now they were here. Right outside his front door.

"But there are good men," he said quietly.

He checked the lock a third time and made his way to the kitchen. He filled the kettle, putting teabags into two mugs, getting the milk out of the fridge. As he waited for the water to boil he made a note of the Peugeot's license plate. Then he walked to the cupboard at the back of the room, finding his tool chest.

"And good men can do terrible things too," he said as he opened the lid.

As he pulled out his hammer.

DON'T ANSWER THE DOOR

KNOCK KNOCK

A DCI ROBERT KETT NOVEL

not final cover not final cover not final cover not

ALEX SMITH

THE INTERNATIONALLY BESTSELLING SERIES

KNOCK KNOCK

THE TENTH DCI ROBERT KETT NOVEL

**Whatever you do,
don't answer the door…**

When a severed foot is delivered to the unsuspecting residents of a student house in Norwich, DCI Kett's Extreme Crime Task Force begins one of the most gruesome investigations of its career.

And it's not just a foot. Several more packages appear at random on people's doorsteps, all of them containing body parts that have been surgically removed and meticulously wrapped.

Kett, Porter and Savage find themselves in a race against the clock to identify the victims and their killer, who shows no sign of stopping.

And it quickly becomes clear that this monster isn't just delivering corpses, he's delivering a message.

A message that will change everything.

Relentless action, compulsive mystery and dark humour abound in the internationally bestselling series that Thrilling Fiction calls "Heart-stoppingly gripping!" from the million-selling author that James Patterson describes as "fresh and ferocious!"

ABOUT THE AUTHOR

Alex Smith wrote his first book when he was six. It wasn't particularly good, but it did have some supernatural monsters in it. His latest books, the DCI Robert Kett thrillers, have monsters in them too, although these monsters are very human, and all the more terrifying for it. In between, he has published thirteen novels for children and teenagers under his full name, Alexander Gordon Smith—including the number one bestselling series Escape From Furnace, which is loved by millions of readers worldwide and which is soon to become a motion picture. He lives in Norwich with his wife and three young daughters.

Find out more at alexsmithbooks.com

Printed in Great Britain
by Amazon

78898672R00233